REHEARSAL FOR THE MAIN EVENT

Duckworth turned around. "Hey, man, what it is?"

"LeRoy Duckworth?"

"Might be. Who's askin'?"

Tony took a long stride toward the desk. "I have a message from your daughter."

Something sparked behind the black man's eyes. "Celia?"

Tony frowned, his fingers tightening around the bolo knife. "Mai Linh."

The ebony face went blank.

"Your daughter sends you greetings from Saigon."

Duckworth raised an open palm to take the blow, recoiling as he lost three fingers.

The wounded man retreated. Tony's prey was cornered now. The bolo whispered as it fell, and Duckworth suddenly went limp.

CHILD
OF
BLOOD
MICHAEL
NEWTON

BANTAM BOOKS
TORONTO • NEW YORK • LONDON • SYDNEY • AUCKLAND

CHILD OF BLOOD
A Bantam Book / May 1988

ISBN 0-553-27162-8

Published simultaneously in the United States and Canada

Bantam Books are published by Bantam Books, a division of Bantam Doubleday
Dell Publishing Group, Inc. Its trademark, consisting of the words "Bantam
Books" and the portrayal of a rooster, is Registered in U.S. Patent and
Trademark Office and in other countries. Marca Registrada. Bantam Books,
666 Fifth Avenue, New York, New York 10103.

PRINTED IN THE UNITED STATES OF AMERICA

KR 0 9 8 7 6 5 4 3 2 1

With grateful thanks to Judy for the idea, to Mark Howell and Russ Galen for aid and encouragement, and to R C for turning it down.

Prologue

SAIGON, FEBRUARY 1968

It was the first time in eleven days that Lin Doan Kieu had seen the sky. The fighting had moved on, beyond the Cholon district on Saigon's east side, and urgent warnings from her parents could not keep the teenaged girl inside a moment longer. The smell of sulfur burned in her nostrils and she could taste it like acid in the back of her throat. The smoke made her eyes sting.

Without a destination, moving aimlessly, she followed the Kinh Ban canal, alert to any sign of danger. Black smoke was rising on the eastern skyline, small-arms fire still audible from the direction of the presidential palace and the U.S. embassy, downtown. To the north, more fighting in the shadow of the Cong Ho stadium, and four miles beyond the city limits, rockets and mortars were pounding American troops at the Tan Son Nhut airbase. Lin Kieu felt as if she were in the eye of a storm, surrounded by the pain and suffering of war, but privately immune to its effects.

It was the child that made her feel that way. The miracle occurring in her body made Lin Kieu feel powerful and weak, invincible and vulnerable, all at once. At times, Lin felt that she might stop the world by force of will alone; at others, she was certain that the earth would turn and crush her in her sleep.

Her family did not know that she was pregnant. Her belly was not swollen, and her parents paid no real attention to her recent morning illness. The war stole everyone's awareness of anything, except the war. She could not conceal the truth from them forever—but none of that would matter once she broke the news to Tony. He would carry her away, across the water to America and bright tomorrows, free of hunger, free of fear.

Lin's parents would not miss her. They had seven other children still at home to occupy their time. And if her father in his fury should delete her name from the *Ho Kau*, she would survive.

Her meeting with the tall American had been a fluke . . . or was it destiny? She had been working as a cocktail waitress in a topless bar on Chu Lai Street, enduring her father's silent anger (though he cashed her paychecks all the same), refusing offers of a raise if she would only shed her clothes and join the other dancers up onstage. Lin knew of the "arrangements" that her fellow workers sometimes made with servicemen, the extra money they earned on their backs. Still, she fended off the drunken soldiers with their furtive, groping hands. She had remained aloof, until the night Tony came into the bar alone and asked if she would drink with him.

Lin still did not know why she had agreed. He was handsome enough, with his sergeant's stripes and green beret, but there were better-looking Americans. It had been something in his young-old face, the battle-weary eyes. Or had she known, instinctively, that Fate had chosen him to be the father of her child?

In any case she had agreed to sit with him, despite her father's warnings, and despite her knowledge of the favors that Americans expected in return for a meal and a glass of cheap rice wine. He waited for her after work and bought her dinner, walked her home. Outside her door, he kissed her gently as he said good-night, no probing hands or propositions. The sadness in his eyes made her slip her arms around him, pull him close, and whisper to him that she hoped she might see him again. For a girl of sixteen to speak such thoughts was audacious, but he had not reprimanded her, nor had he pressed his advantage in the moment of her weakness. He had seemed pleased, and that was all.

He had returned the next evening, and the next. Lin felt him watching her, ignoring the display of naked flesh onstage. Each night he took her to a restaurant and walked her home, a perfect gentleman. The fourth night, when he bashfully suggested that they find a hotel room instead of dinner, Lin had not refused. Inside the room, when Tony's hands slipped underneath her dress, she made no protest, welcoming his touch.

He was her first and seemed to know it. Afterward he held her close and whispered words of caring while she clung to his chest. She came to understand that it was more to him than just a casual encounter. When he did not offer money, Lin believed in him, and she was in love.

They were together every evening for the next two weeks, her passion mounting, matching his, until she could not get enough of him. He had released an unimagined fire within her, tending it with care, preventing it from consuming both of them alive. When he was ordered north to fight along the DMZ in early January, Lin thought her heart would break. He left her with a photograph and a promise.

Lin's monthly time of bleeding passed, without result, ten days after she and Tony first made love. She had dismissed it as a side effect of losing her virginity, a mark of womanhood. In January, when she again failed to bleed, Lin knew she was in trouble. Hoarding money from her tips, she visited a clinic patronized by other girls from work. She was humiliated by the close proximity of prostitutes, afraid of the diseases they might carry, as she waited for the aging doctor to examine her. His tests confirmed what Lin already knew. The doctor had reminded her abortion was illegal—and of course a mortal sin—but for a price . . .

She put him off, pretending she needed to think. The child within her was a part of Tony, created out of love, and she would not be a party to the destruction of a gift from God. Tony had been reassigned before Lin knew that she was pregnant, but she was convinced that when he heard the news he would share her excitement.

She could not trust her secret to a letter—and did not even know where Tony was. She preferred to tell him personally, just as soon as he returned. She wanted to share her joy, but only with him.

On January 30, the Viet Cong and North Vietnamese had launched their Tet offensive. Saigon was hardest hit, but from her father's radio, Lin knew fighting was also heavy in the provincial capitals. Throughout the countryside guerrillas and the northern regulars were mounting a ferocious drive against the ARVN forces and Americans. Lin had no interest in politics or "liberation," knowing only that her lover was endangered. Each night throughout the siege, while heavy weapons rocked the city, she had prayed to God and Buddha for Tony's safe return.

A splash of color on her right drew Lin's attention to the canal. Hesitating on its muddy bank, she peered down to find a bloated corpse entangled in the reeds, arms fanning gently with the current. An American—the patches on his uniform familiar from the bar. Half his face was gone, and as Lin felt her meager breakfast rising in her throat, the shattered face suddenly changed, and she was staring down at Tony in the murky water, trapped among the reeds.

She bolted, choking on her sudden fear for Tony, for their child. For all she knew he might already be dead. The thought of bringing up their child alone terrified her. Lin Kieu ran from images of death and desperation, panicked by the thought of losing Tony, certain that she would not wish to live without his warmth, his touch.

Not knowing how long she ran, how many empty blocks she covered, Lin found herself surrounded by the hulls of burned-out stores. From a blackened jeep, capsized in the middle of the street, still smoldering, came the stench of burning rubber. Automatic weapons fired closer now, their rattle punctuated by the detonation of grenades.

A shout alerted Lin to danger closing from behind. The voice had been Vietnamese, but that meant nothing in itself. Both sides were shooting first and might ask questions later. Alone, exposed, she was just another moving target in a city that had, overnight, become a free-fire zone.

Ducking through the doorway of a blasted shop, Lin curled herself into a corner. Survival, the protection of the precious, growing life inside, was her first priority.

After another shout, much closer now, Lin Kieu risked a

peek through an empty window frame. A rifle squad of ARVN regulars trooped past at double time, sweat streaming down their faces, helmets banging on their necks. When the cadence of their footsteps receded, she emerged from the shadows of her hiding place, moving toward the center of the floor.

The place had been a chemist's shop, she realized. Grenades and fire had scoured the room, but Lin could read the merchant's trade from the debris. Some of the glass beneath her feet had come from broken windows, but most was from shattered jars, repositories of a healer's herbs and potions. Spices, arcane roots and mushrooms, desiccated eels, ginseng and powdered rhinoceros horn for virility. Beneath the acrid stench of burning, she could almost pick out the aroma of the shop.

But there was something else as well.

Lin drifted slowly, cautiously, toward the rear of the shop, following her nose. The ripe-meat smell, familiar in a haunting way, made Lin Kieu wonder if the family's dinner had been left to sit when they evacuated. Tattered curtains screened the chemist's living quarters from the store, all blackened now by smoke and torn by shrapnel. Gingerly she nudged the curtains back, stepped through the doorway—and recoiled immediately from the charnel house inside.

Four bodies? Five? She could not tell, the flaccid arms and legs all intertwined, blood spattered over walls in abstract patterns where the automatic fire had cut them down. One was a woman, one a child, and that was all Lin knew before she turned away, surrendering to sudden nausea.

After several moments the room stopped spinning and her fear returned full force. Tony, who would have shielded her from this, was gone. His promise to return and keep her safe would be as dust if he should fall in a faraway battle. If only he had known about their child before. . . .

A sudden pang of doubt chilled Lin Kieu to her soul. What would she do if Tony heard the news and turned away? If he grew angry and accused her of deceiving him? Lin knew of other girls who had been left alone with children to support, rejected by their families, deserted by the men in uniform who had used them without a thought for anything beyond the moment. What if Tony hated her, despised their child?

Lin stopped herself before the morbid train of thought could gain momentum. Tony loved her. He would love their child. He would come for her when the fighting stopped in the north.

In the meantime, Lin Kieu was in hostile territory. It was death to step outside, and only Providence had carried her this far, providing her sanctuary in the midst of the killing ground. She had been taught that God took care of fools and children. Scarcely more than child herself, with another child inside her, Lin felt doubly protected, but she dared not tempt her fate. She would be forced to wait for nightfall, trusting darkness to conceal her then.

Moving, Lin found a corner comfortably distant from the back-room slaughterhouse. She forced the twisted corpses from her mind, breathing through her mouth to mask the smell of death, concentrating on the miracle of life. Alone, she settled down to wait. For darkness. For her lover's safe return.

1

SAN FRANCISCO, 1986

By eight o'clock the fog was closing in, a chill, damp blanket
smothering the stars. It had already swallowed up the San
Francisco–Oakland Bay Bridge, but it was not yet thick enough
to bury traffic flowing past on the Embarcadero. Further inland,
Telegraph Hill stood out in stark relief against a velvet sky.

The *Corazón de Oro* nestled in her berth along Pier 23, the
city's foreign trade zone. She was a tramp of Filipino registry,
her rusty hull in need of paint, encrusted heavily with barnacles.
She carried rubber, coffee, sugar . . . and a smattering of contraband. Despite her name, the tramp did not possess a "heart of
gold."

From the starboard railing, Tony Kieu studied the dazzling
city lights. They mesmerized him, almost driving out the chill of
damp and fog that cut through cheap blue jeans and a denim
jacket like a knife through butter. Unaware that he was trembling,
Tony clutched his bundle underneath one arm and concentrated
on the lights, imagining the city from a distance. He had studied
picture books in preparation for this moment, but reality was
something else. It took his breath away.

At six feet, Tony Kieu was tall for his seventeen years. He

would be tall for *any* age in Vietnam, his homeland, but in the United States he thought that he might pass without attracting undue notice. Tony's height was a legacy from his father, like the high cheekbones, the finely chiseled nose, the almond eyes that only hinted at his Asian blood. From Tony's mother and her people, he inherited his slender build and straight, dark hair, coupled with endurance, the ability to suffer silently. A part of Asia and America, he belonged to neither one.

He broke the skyline's sensuous, hypnotic grip and dropped his eyes to scan the pier below him. Seven members of the *Corazón de Oro*'s nine-man crew had gone ashore already. Tony might have joined them, would have gladly put the tramp behind him, but he was not finished with her yet. He still had work to do on board.

Leaving the railing, he headed aft, along the open deck. Climbing a rusty ladder to the upper deck, he continued past general quarters for the crew, then along a narrow, dim-lit corridor, until he stood outside the captain's cabin. Esquivel was topside, preoccupied with business on the bridge. Tony should not be disturbed.

The ancient lock resisted briefly, quickly surrendering to Tony's screwdriver. Slipping inside, he closed the heavy metal door behind him, struck, as always, by the squalor of the cabin. The room reflected its occupant. Charts and ledgers littered the captain's tiny desk. Wrinkled clothing was draped over furniture, while the bunk—a snarl of rumpled, musty sheets—had not been changed in days. The cabin smelled of sweat.

Tony knew the room by heart. His passage had been paid for in the captain's bunk, his flesh the only currency available. Ten thousand miles, from Bangkok to the States, with stops at Singapore, Manila, Honolulu, half a dozen smaller ports of call. The trip had taken seven weeks all told, and Esquivel had called upon him often for his services as "cabin boy," relieving the monotony of open water with the captain's favorite pastime. Tony had endured humiliation from the other members of the freighter's crew, ignoring their remarks and smirking laughter.

He had known about the captain's predilections from the moment of their interview in Bangkok. After two weeks of scavenging the docks and living off the street, he had come to Esquivel desperate, and when the captain placed a calloused hand upon his thigh, expressing the desire to find a nice, cooperative cabin boy to share the lonely hours of the night watch, Tony forced a smile and said he understood.

No nautical experience was necessary. Tony's duties were limited to waiting hand and foot—or hand and mouth—on Esquivel. He brought the captain's coffee, served his meals, and turned his bunk down on the rare occasions when the skipper ordered up fresh linen from the laundry. Once, when he had tried to tidy up the cabin, Esquivel accused him of misplacing vital charts and knocked him to the floor. Immediately penitent, the captain then had carried Tony to his bunk and ministered to him in ways that did not ease the swelling of his jaw.

When Esquivel was drinking, he was more likely to be cruel, but alcohol reduced his stamina and kept the drunken sessions brief. When sober—say four nights a week—the captain showed more interest in endurance, sampling a wider range of pleasures with his most cooperative cabin boy. On more than one occasion, Tony Kieu had staggered to his bunk exhausted, sickened, in the first gray light of dawn.

But Esquivel had served his purpose. Were it not for him, Tony might still be in Bangkok, living hand-to-mouth with countless other human skeletons along the Chao Phraya waterfront. The pig had done his job, and now, in parting, Esquivel would serve his cabin boy in yet another way.

The young man dropped his bundle on the desk and moved to a chest of drawers in one corner of the cabin. Stooping to the bottom drawer, he pulled it open, rummaging through discolored underwear and mismatched socks until he found the strongbox. Bringing it to the desk, Tony set it down beside his bundle, studying the box that he had seen a hundred times, but which, until this moment, he had never touched.

How many times had Tony watched the captain count his money? Sitting at his desk in dirty boxer shorts, he had resembled a demented Midas, shuffling the currency and muttering to himself. He must have paid the crewmen as they disembarked, and still the box was fairly heavy, promising some recompense for Tony's stoicism of the past two months.

The lock was new and solid, but the hasp was loose and showing signs of wear. Working the blade of his screwdriver under the strap, Tony twisted, applying brute force to the hinge.

And again. On the third try he felt the joint yielding. Encouraged, he put his full weight on the tool—and collapsed as the hasp came away with a sharp squeal of protest. Tony froze, frightened that the sound might have carried to Esquivel's ears on the bridge. With a smile at his own foolish caution, he threw back the lid of the strongbox, revealing the pig's private stash.

The *Corazón de Oro* had been paying off for Esquivel. Inside the box were pesos from the Philippines, ringgits from Malaysia, rupiahs from Indonesia, together with a smattering of kinas from New Guinea. There was other currency as well, which Tony did not recognize, but he was focused on the American dollars.

He knew the rest could be traded for proper U.S. currency, but that meant dealing with officials, answering their questions, and it was not worth the risk. He pocketed $650 and threw the rest aside, then sifted through the coins that lined the bottom of the strongbox. So engaged, he nearly missed the creak of rusty hinges as the cabin door swung open, framing Esquivel in the dim light from the corridor outside.

The captain towered over Tony by a full six inches, black eyes narrowed with perpetual suspicion in a meaty face that could not quite support his straggly beard. Still powerful, his muscles had been overlaid with fat in middle age, his stomach swollen with the ale he consumed in epic quantities. His rumpled uniform appeared to have been slept in, which was very likely true, and pastry crumbs were caught in his mustache.

For all of that, it was the eyes that bothered Tony Kieu. They skittered over him like insects, lingering on the currency that lay around his feet. Without a word the captain stepped inside and closed the cabin door behind him, leaning against it with his shoulders, looking Tony up and down.

"Ungrateful pup," he said in pidgin French. "Is this how you repay my kindness?"

Concentrating on the only exit from the cabin, blocked by Esquivel, Tony did not answer.

"Your passage to America is not enough, I see." The captain glowered, taking time to scratch himself. "You must be paid for little favors, eh?"

If Tony bolted, he could reach the bathroom, lock himself inside—and then what? He could never wriggle through the tiny

porthole that provided ventilation. Esquivel could smoke him out
or have the bathroom flooded with the fire hose that was kept on
deck. He could sit back and wait while Tony starved. And what
would happen once their business was completed? Would the
Corazón de Oro sail again, with Tony locked inside the metal
coffin?

He knew that Esquivel was capable of such a thing, and in
that knowledge, Tony found the resolution necessary for survival.
Leaning back against the captain's littered desk, he found the
screwdriver by touch and closed his fingers around the fluted
handle.

Esquivel straightened to his full height, pushing off the bulkhead, and spread his massive hands. He smiled, all sweet accom-
modation now. "Don't worry, boy," he purred. "I pay you
gladly. But I must have something for my money, yes?"

As he spoke, the captain was unbuttoning his jacket, shrug-
ging out of it. The dress shirt underneath was dingy gray, the
cuffs and collar frayed. He draped the jacket on a chair and
moved toward Tony.

"You make me feel good, Tony, maybe I forget you try to
rob me, eh? If you are good enough, I may not call police. I
might even give you some dollars to spend in America."

Esquivel was close now, his rancid breath washing over
Tony Kieu and making Tony's stomach churn. The captain
brushed his cheek with dirty fingertips and slipped his hand
around to cup the back of Tony's head, the grip immediately
tightening.

"You will do well in the United States. Your skills will take
you far, I think." The captain's voice was growing husky.
"Make me feel good, now."

His free hand groped for Tony's crotch, but Tony scarcely
felt the stroking fingers. In a single fluid motion, he brought the
screwdriver around and slipped the blade home beneath Esquivel's
ribs, twisting when it grated on bone. He felt hot blood against
his knuckles, on his wrist, as the captain's eyes widened in
shock and pain.

Esquivel lurched backward, glancing down at the handle of
the tool protruding from his abdomen, the dark stain spreading
on his shirt. He bellowed out his rage. He swung one giant paw
and batted Tony Kieu aside like a dummy filled with straw.

Tony struck the metal bulkhead painfully, rebounding, sliding to the floor. Snarling like a wounded animal, Esquivel clutched the screwdriver in one hand and tugged it free, releasing a spout of crimson that spattered the front of his slacks. Disgustedly, he flung the bloody tool aside. Tony heard it clatter on the floor before the captain lumbered after him, intent on killing him bare-handed.

Scrambling to his feet, he sidestepped as Esquivel reached for him, big hands leaving bloody palm prints on the bulkhead. Bellowing and cursing, Esquivel pursued him on a circuit of the cabin, fresh blood soaking through his shirtfront, glistening darkly on his pants from waist to knees. The man was dying, but he did not know it yet.

The second time around, his fingers snagged the collar of Tony's jacket, hauling sharply backward. Tony turned on him with lightning speed, fingers clawing at the captain's eyes, and shook the jacket off before he could be dragged into a death embrace. Reeling back against the desk, he grabbed the strongbox and swung it, spraying coins of every size in all directions as the box made solid contact with Esquivel's skull.

The captain staggered, blinking, fresh blood streaming from a gash along his hairline. Tony lunged at him, swinging the cash box onto Esquivel's forehead, rocking him back on his heels. Esquivel was reeling, dazed, as Tony gripped the twisted box in both hands, putting all his weight behind the blow, and slammed him full across the face.

The captain toppled, and Tony leapt to take advantage of the moment, raining blows upon the lacerated face and scalp until Esquivel was stretched out, still and silent, on the floor. When he was certain that his enemy would not rise again, Tony stood, the battered strongbox slipping from his fingers onto Esquivel's motionless chest.

Still breathing hard, Tony scanned the shambles of their battlefield. The blood was everywhere: on walls and floor, on Tony's face, his hands, his clothing. Before he left the pig's sty, he would have to wash himself and change his clothes.

Wedging Esquivel's favorite chair against the door to keep out any other unexpected visitors, he stripped down for the last time in that cabin. He took special care with the precious oilcloth packet, setting it beside his bundle on the desk before he padded naked into the adjacent bathroom.

Tony turned the shower up as hot as he could bear and stood beneath the steaming spray, head down, rinsing Esquivel's blood from his skin. He felt no guilt or triumph at the captain's fate; in place of the expected feelings, there was only satisfaction with the knowledge that he had survived.

When every trace of Esquivel had been sluiced down the drain and into San Francisco Bay, he soaped himself all over, twice, compulsively washing away the captain's touch along with his blood. Stepping out of the shower, Tony snared a towel from the rack and scrubbed himself dry, his skin tingling.

Back in the cabin, scattered currency adhering to the damp soles of his feet, he saw that Esquivel still lay where he had fallen. He had fantasized the captain's death a thousand times, but now, confronted with the grim reality, he was amazed by the complete and utter absence of emotion. Esquivel had not been on his list, but once again the pig had served his purpose. He had proved that Tony Kieu could do his job.

Crossing to the desk, Tony untied his bundle, extracting a clean shirt and jeans. He pulled the pants on first, tucking the oilcloth packet into his waistband, against the small of his back. A simple cotton shirt went over all, and Tony stepped into his sneakers, wishing that his feet were large enough to fit the captain's boots.

His other shirt was ruined, streaked with blood, and Tony left it on the floor. He could not leave the jeans, his only other pair. He transferred stolen money from one set of pockets to another, rolled the first pair up with bloodstains innermost, and tucked them inside his bundle. Scooping up his denim jacket, Tony was surprised to find it neither torn nor stained. He slipped it on against the creeping chill and moved to scrutinize the contents of the captain's closet.

Esquivel's favorite pea coat hung beside two other uniforms, each as wrinkled as the one in which he died. Tony pulled the pea coat out and tried it on for size. The hem hung almost to his knees, and he was nearly lost inside the heavy garment. Worse, it smelled of Esquivel, but that would pass, and it would help keep him warm while he searched for a place to sleep.

So much to do before he could begin the hunt. He would

need lodging, food, and documents to satisfy authorities if he was stopped for any reason. Once settled, he would have to find his quarry. It would be no easy task, he knew, but Tony was prepared to wait and search as long as necessary.

His bundle tucked beneath one arm, he left the cabin, pulling the door shut behind him. Retracing his steps along the corridor, he cleared the hatch and breathed fresh air again, thankful for the salt-spray aroma after Esquivel's musty cabin. He scrambled down the ladder, walking forward to the boarding ramp where Inouye, the Japanese mate, was on night watch.

Inouye was slouched against the rail, his cigarette a red eye winking in the darkness. Tony felt the sailor's mocking smile before he saw it, knew the mate could not resist a parting insult.

"You leave us, Tony? Thass too bad." Inouye's smile was crooked, hateful. "Captain gonna miss you, boy. No more hot chocolate."

Tony brushed on past him, down the ramp. The mate was nothing to him now.

"You gonna love this town," the mate called after him. "Your kind of people here. They gonna eat you up."

Inouye's laughter followed Tony down the ramp and into misty darkness. Walking rapidly, he waited for the chill and damp to cool his burning cheeks, resisting an urge to double back and teach the mate a proper measure of respect. It was enough to be away from Esquivel, the *Corazón de Oro*. Later, when the captain's body was discovered, Inouye would realize how close his brush with death had been.

You gonna love this town. Your kind of people here.

He doubted that, but there was one at least who shared a common bond. Somewhere beyond the highway with its rushing traffic, hidden in the city's darkness, was the first of several men whom Tony Kien had traveled halfway around the world to kill.

2

Crossing the Embarcadero was a challenge in itself. The traffic showed no sign of letting up or slowing for pedestrians, and after fifteen minutes, Tony Kieu decided he would have to cross as best he could. The highway might be bustling with traffic all night long for all he knew, and he could not afford to stand and wait for someone on the *Corazón de Oro* to discover Esquivel and summon the police.

He waited for a break, and saw it coming as a giant semi rumbled toward him, northbound, in the outer lane. The truck was moving slower than surrounding vehicles, and Tony knew that he could beat it to the median. No sooner had he left the curb, however, than the driver started laying on his horn, accelerating, headlamps looming over Tony like a pair of glowing dragon's eyes. He cleared the semi's lane in time to meet a low-slung sports car passing on the left, its bleat of warning shrill, defiant. Tony made it to the median with nothing left to spare, the sportster's tailwind whipping angrily around his legs.

The southbound lanes were easier, the traffic slower. Tony made the crossing without futher incident and paused a moment on the far side, staring back in the direction of the waterfront, already lost in fog. The mist would overtake him soon if he stood still.

He struck off to the south, on Front Street, simply to be moving. He could feel the city's size, its weight, though the heart of it still lay miles away. He knew from reading everything available that San Francisco was a midget in comparison with Bangkok or Saigon; it sheltered 700,000 people, as compared to millions in the teeming Asian anthills, but it still felt safe.

Before the thought had time to form, he realized that safety was a mere illusion. Tony was a stranger here, completely vulnerable. Hurrying to keep ahead of the pursuing fog, he felt as if the city might roll over in its sleep and crush him like an insect, ignorant of his existence and uncaring. He was cold, despite the pea coat and his denim jacket underneath. He wondered how much farther he would have to walk before he found a place to sleep.

He had begun to ponder Front Street and its implications— would there be a Back Street somewhere on the other side of town? A police car turned the corner two blocks down and headed north in his direction. As it passed, the driver stared at Tony, scowling from the safety of his heated cruiser, and the young man forced himself to slow his pace, act casual, when every nerve was screaming out at him to run. *Escape!*

When Tony dared to risk a backward glance, the squad car was already disappearing down a side street, cruising like a hungry white shark in the creeping sea of fog.

Another short block brought him underneath the elevated freeway ramps that run east-west from Battery to the Embarcadero. It was dark beneath the overpass, and Tony Kieu walked down the middle of the street, instinctively avoiding deeper shadows off to either side. The shadows were alive, it seemed, with shifting, rustling movement, and he wished for his screwdriver, anything at all that might serve as a weapon. No more than a hundred feet away, the lights of Front Street now seemed hopelessly beyond his reach.

On Tony's right a pallid face thrust forward from the darkness, linked by a grimy sleeve to a reaching hand. As Tony recoiled, another human scarecrow materialized on his left, immediately followed by a third. "A dollar, couldja?" croaked the first one. "Any change at all?"

Before the others could speak, he hurried past them, broke into a trot that brought him to the lights. No stranger to poverty himself, he was unnerved by the encounter all the same. Somehow, he had imagined that the residents of San Francisco would be uniformly wealthy, or at least secure within what the Americans referred to as their "middle class."

He reached another intersection, thankful for the lights of many colors that surrounded him. Some of them, Tony understood, controlled the flow of traffic, red and green and yellow, flashing in the night by turns. A different set of lights instructed those on foot to WALK or DON'T WALK. Aside from traffic lights, he was surrounded by the glow of street lamps, neon messages emblazoned on the tall facades of shops, the incandescence spilling out through giant picture windows. Glancing upward at the street signs, Tony found that he had reached the point where Front Street crosses Broadway.

It was not the *real* Broadway, of course. That famous street was in New York, much farther east than Tony planned to travel . . . but then, who could say? When he was finished, all his work behind him, he might wish to see America. It was his homeland as much as Vietnam had ever been. But that would have to wait. For now he had his duty for the others and for himself.

Where Front Street had been sparsely populated, Broadway was alive and bustling, a feast for Tony's senses. And before he had traversed a single block, he understood that reading about a city in the picture books could not prepare a stranger for encounters with the people of the streets.

In all his reading, all the photographs that he had studied, he had seen no such Americans as these. Young men and women, dressed in leather or in rags, with spiky, multicolored hair that stood out from their heads at crazy angles, some of them bedecked in chains or wearing cartridge belts. One girl had shaved her head with the exception of a bristling crest, dyed purple, and he saw with horror that she wore a safety pin through her nose. The eyes she turned on Tony Kieu were blank, sedated, lifeless. Here, against the curb, a line of motorcycles sat with bearded riders dressed in denim cut-off jackets. From time to time, the scruffy nomads kicked their engines into life and opened up their throttles, never budging from the sidewalk, drawing sustenance from all that throbbing power between their legs.

On either side the street was lined with bars and "niteclubs," jostling for space with strip joints, tattoo parlors, pornographic theaters and bookstores, pawn shops, "health clubs" promising unique massages. The amusements catered to a wide variety of clienteles, and Tony Kieu was startled by the frank displays of homosexuality outside a number of the clubs. Here, men were holding hands, embracing, kissing one another on the mouth; there, women sauntered, arm in arm, caressing with a passion that appeared grotesque beneath the garish neon lights. In Bangkok, where the flesh trade did a thriving business and the coupling of animals with women was a staple of the tourist trade, such obvious behavior on a public street would have resulted in reprisals by police.

Inouye's words came back at him again—*Your kind of people here*—and Tony wished that he had killed the mate while there had been an opportunity. No matter. It was all behind him now, and Tony felt no shame for anything that he had done to come this far.

A slender woman wearing fur and leather blocked his path. "You wanna party, sailor?"

She might have been fifteen or thirty-five beneath the layers of makeup. Tony could not tell and did not care. "No, thank you," he said.

"Huh? No *thank* you? Listen, man, for thirty-five I'll take ya roun' the world."

He shook his head and waited for the woman to retreat, but she stood firm. "You get off on a little French? I gotta special on tonight. Fifteen an' you're in business, whatcha say?"

"Not interested." He tried to step around her, but she caught him by the sleeve.

"Hey, what's the story, man? You don't like girls?" Before he grasped the meaning of her words, the prostitute turned, still clinging to his arm, and hailed a tall brunette who stood beside the curb observing traffic with a practiced eye. "Felice, get over here. I gotta live one for ya."

As the brunette turned to face him, Tony glimpsed a trace of stubble, dark beneath the pale cosmetic mask. Felice responded in a raspy baritone, "Well, hello, lover. You look good enough to eat."

He shook off his tormentor, stalked away from her with anger burning in his cheeks. Behind him, dwindling with distance, he could hear the woman's mocking laughter. "Where ya goin', lover? Runnin' home to Mama?"

He sensed that every other person on the street was staring at him with contempt or curiosity. A furtive, sidelong glance in each direction proved him wrong, but Tony covered two more blocks before he dared to slow his pace and lift his head. With relief, he saw that no one seemed to take the slightest notice of him now, devoted as they were to the pursuit of private pleasure. When a young black boy approached him, offering to sell him "ups or downs, whatever," Tony shook his head and kept on walking. He had learned the folly of extending courtesy to strangers on the street.

His stomach had begun to growl, and Tony started searching for food. He passed two restaurants with menus posted in their windows, but he judged them both to be beyond his means. He had $650, out of which he must expect to pay for lodgings, vital documents, and extra clothing, in addition to food.

He reached another intersection, scanned the cross street, and was drawn by curiosity in the direction of a squarish, red-roofed structure halfway down the block. A market of some kind, it seemed to have no name, its address—"7-Eleven"—emblazoned on a tall sign in the parking lot. A crowd of noisy youths were gathered out in front. Tony, eyes downcast, made his way inside.

Before the door had closed behind him, Tony was aware of being watched. A burly black man stood behind the counter, larger even than the late captain of the *Corazón de Oro*, glowering at Tony Kieu as if he thought the young man intended to rob him blind. Behind him, on a shelf, a compact television set broadcast a static picture of the store in black and white, and Tony was amazed to see himself at center screen. He searched and found the camera, mounted in a neutral corner so that it could cover both the door and register at once.

Crammed with goods in cans and cartons, the shop bore some resemblance to a warehouse with its narrow aisles. Along the back wall refrigerators with doors of glass stood side by side.

Without an inkling of where to start, he chose the nearest aisle and stepped around a rack of comic books. He had progressed from sanitary napkins to the pet food section when the black man hailed him from his place behind the register.

"You need some help?"

The suspicion in the voice made Tony wonder why his presence made this giant of a man afraid.

"I'm hungry. I need food."

"And you came *here*?" The giant shook his head and muttered something to himself, then said, "Forget it, man. Bad joke. Why doancha try the coolers?"

Tony passed the candy, chips, and other "snack" food, homing on the shelves of sandwiches and precooked foods, all vacuum-packed in cellophane. The prices still seemed high, but they were better than in the restaurants that he had passed.

"Which is the best?" he asked.

"The best?" His question seemed to puzzle the proprietor. "There ain't no *best*. Watch out for tuna salad, anything with may-o-naise, you dig? Those babies wasn't born yesterday."

"What do you like?"

"It ain't on sale round here. But if I had to choose, I'd go with French-bread pizzas. Middle shelf there, on your right. They haven't killed nobody yet."

He chose a package that contained a sort of roll, split down the middle, with the halves laid side by side and topped with cheese. Beneath a layer of frost, he picked out wedge-shaped pieces of a meat he did not recognize. The label on the package told him it was pepperoni and assured him that the pizza he had chosen was "deluxe."

He took his purchase to the checkout counter, picking up a quart of chocolate milk en route. "I see you're a gore-may," the black man said. "You want that heated?"

Tony frowned. "Is there an extra cost?"

"No charge for microwaves, my man."

His pizza disappeared inside a box resembling a television with the screen on hinges. When the black man punched a button, the device began to hum, reminding Tony of the small space heaters that were popular on ship with the night watch. Interrupted by a buzzer after several moments, the machine shut down, and Tony's pizza was returned to him, the package limp and steaming now. The black man handed back his change and said, "Enjoy."

Tony was about to leave when he had a sudden inspiration. Turning back to the proprietor, he asked, "How may I get to Chinatown?"

The black man raised one eyebrow like a hairy question mark, then said, "Get back on Broadway there and keep on west until you get to Stockton. Hang a left—that puts you facin' south—and walk another five, six blocks, until you smell the egg rolls. Got it?"

"Got it."

Once outside he found a corner of the sidewalk for himself, away from the assembled youths. One of them had produced a radio resembling metallic luggage, and the screaming, indecipherable lyrics of a rock band blasted at him while he ate his pizza. One slice was cold, the other hot enough to sear his tongue, and both possessed the general consistency of cardboard, but he wolfed them down and chased them with chocolate milk. In Tony's mind, the combination tasted like America.

Back among the lights and sights of Broadway, Tony headed west. Halfway to his intersection, Tony Kieu almost collided with a young man dressed unseasonably in a tank top and a pair of skintight jeans. Two older men, dressed all in leather, were pursuing him with grim determination. Tony stepped aside to let them pass, lost contact as the leader ducked into an alleyway, his angry shadows close behind. The sound of scuffling from the alley was abruptly terminated by a squeal that scarcely sounded human.

Moving south on Stockton, Tony was relieved to find the bars—and people—thinning out. He still passed theaters which catered to ADULTS ONLY, some of them OPEN ALL NITE, but they were getting rarer as he put more space between himself and Broadway. Here, the shops were more conventional: dry cleaners, haberdashers and boutiques, a florist, cut-rate tax consultants. Tony walked six blocks before the changing faces and aromas told him that he had discovered Chinatown.

And it was true: he *could* smell egg rolls. Also dim sum, tea, fried vegetables and rice, the varied fragrances of Canton, Hunan, and Szechwan. He passed restaurants and groceries—the latter with their peppers, squid, and stringy chickens hanging in the windows—storefront temples, gift shops offering an infinite variety of paper dragons for the tourists, pharmacies where ginseng and powdered shark's fin would be sold along with Anacin and Bufferin. The signs of many shops, printed in Chinese, were illegible to Tony, although he could manage certain rudimentary phrases if he had to.

Moving among the residents of Chinatown and Anglo visitors, Tony passed Hangah and Pagoda streets, reaching the Chinese playground. Groups of teenaged boys collected here, and Tony watched them from a distance, recognizing them for what they were. He had seen their kind in Thailand, predators who harassed local merchants with petty thefts and amateur extortion schemes. No girls were in evidence—tradition would forbid their being out of doors at night without a chaperon—and many of the boys affected trappings of the martial arts to symbolize their status as the members of a fighting gang. Most of them practiced their karate or kung fu, adept enough to terrorize the elderly and sundry round-eyed tourists, but he wondered how they might stand up against the ragged, unwashed warriors of a Bangkok street tribe.

Turning away, he left them to their posturing, exploring side streets as he sought a place to spend the night. He found no rooming houses or hotels, as such, though several homes displayed signs announcing ROOM FOR RENT. The windows, all darkened now, told Tony it would be too late to rouse the landlords. Better to approach them in the morning.

Aware that San Francisco's chief hotels were miles away and far beyond his means, he wandered aimlessly until he had a sudden inspiration. Getting his bearings, Tony made his way to Stockton Street and started hiking north again toward Broadway, searching for the theaters that advertised OPEN ALL NITE. The first one he encountered specialized in films with all-male casts, and Tony moved past without a second glance. The next was smaller, but its marquee promised a "Sexational Triple Feature" with showings around the clock. The box office was closed, but Tony followed the instructions of a crudely lettered sign and pushed his way through twin glass doors that had been painted over on the inside, entering a tiny lobby.

Sampling the fragrances of perspiration, popcorn, and perfume, he discovered he was not alone. A thin, anemic-looking woman in her forties perched behind the snack bar on a stool. Scarcely glancing up from her supermarket tabloid, she launched into her spiel. "Five-fifty for the ticket, popcorn costs a buck, the same for drinks, an' candy's fifty cents."

Grimacing at the ticket price, he handed her ten dollars, turning down the popcorn while he waited for his change. The theater was larger than the lobby had suggested, seating some two hundred people, but he counted barely half a dozen when his eyes adjusted to the darkness. On the screen, nude giants grappled on a sofa. The cameras zoomed in for close-up shots of breasts or thrusting genitals and then retreated, angling for a long view of the lovers, coupling mechanically.

He found a seat in back and watched for several moments, till the setting changed. It was a different couple now, the man black, the woman younger, with a whitish scar inside one thigh. Initially, they showed more ardor than their predecessors, but as time and camera angles slipped away, they fell into the same lackluster movements, hammering at one another like a pair of tired machines.

Six rows in front of Tony Kieu, a young man and his date were all attention, studying the screen as if it might impart some special secret, teach them something vital. Tony scanned the other patrons, all of them middle-aged, solitary men in shabby dress, two of them sound asleep and snoring louder than the scratchy sound track.

Tony yawned. Twisting in his seat, he wedged his bundle in beside him, making one last check of the oilcloth packet tucked inside the waistband of his jeans. Sleep took him in a moment, while the giants struggled endlessly on screen, their breathless voices weaving through his troubled dreams.

3

He was awakened, moments later it seemed, by the insistent prodding of a dwarfish janitor. "I gotta sweep here, man. Cudjoo sit somewheres else?"

"What time is it?"

The munchkin checked his wrist, which bore no watch. "Two freckles past a hair," he said. "How the hell should I know?"

Tony tucked his bundle underneath one arm, got stiffly to his feet. He ran a surreptitious hand beneath his pea coat, checking on the packet tucked inside his jeans, and squeezed out past the janitor, who made no move to step aside. On screen, the same black man was going through the same tired calisthenics with his partner, as if Tony had not slept at all.

A man was perched behind the snack bar in the lobby, now. The tabloid scandal sheet had given way to *Penthouse* magazine, which the man held upside-down, studying the centerfold with something close to reverence.

Tony interrupted him. "What is the time?"

"Six twenty-five. You in or out?"

"I'm out."

Outside the sky was gray, with clouds obscuring the newly risen sun. Hunger followed Tony south, toward Chinatown, where he searched out a sidewalk vendor selling rice and dim sum. As he ate, he watched the district come alive, shops opening to catch the early tourists, merchants sweeping off the sidewalks, fragrant odors wafting from the omnipresent restaurants. He moved slowly through the streets, relieved that no one seemed to give him a second glance.

When Tony estimated that an hour had elapsed, he resumed his search for lodgings. Two of the houses advertising rooms for rent appeared too rich for Tony's blood in daylight, while a third was teeming with unruly children. He approached an old, two-story house on Mason, near the Chinese Recreation Center, punched the bell, then knocked. Several moments passed before an ancient, wizened woman dressed like Mao Tse-tung opened the door. She stared at Tony through two wary slits.

"You have a room for rent?" Tony inclined his head in the direction of the sign.

"You not Chinee."

"Vietnamese. *Half* Vietnamese."

"I want no trubber here."

"No trouble," he assured her. "May I see the room?"

She led him up a creaking flight of stairs and showed him to a tiny back room that overlooked the alleyway. The view was dismal and the quarters cramped, but he would have a bed, a toilet, and a shower of his own.

"How much?"

"Seventy-five dollars for the week. One week in advance."

Tony counted out the first week's rent and passed it over, waiting while the woman squinted closely at his money. Finally satisfied, she stuffed the bills inside a pocket of her high-necked jacket.

"You got things to move?"

He shook his head and held the bundle up for her inspection. "This is it."

"You sailor?"

"Used to be. I'm looking for a job."

She fished around inside another pocket, finally handed him a key. "Find job, work hard. Pay rent on time. I want no trubber here."

Alone, he locked the door and lay down on the lumpy mattress, his bundle tucked beneath his head as a pillow. He'd acquired a base of operations much more easily than he had dared to hope. With cash on hand, allowing for the bare necessities, he could maintain the room for perhaps six weeks. He estimated that if all went well he should be finished with his work and on his way in half that time.

Before beginning, however, Tony decided to familiarize himself with San Francisco. After showering, he donned the same clothes he had worn on disembarking from the *Corazón de Oro,* made a mental note to buy replacements, and set off to study his immediate surroundings.

Chinatown was bounded roughly by Pacific on the north, by Kearny on the east, by California on the south, and Mason on the west. Within that quadrant, Asian immigrants had done their best to recreate the homeland their fathers had left behind. As with the residents of any ghetto, they had not been left alone. The Anglo influence was evident in clothing styles, bilingual signs, the slang young people spoke to one another on the streets, the music emanating from their radios and tape decks.

Most recently, the residents of Chinatown had been unsettled by infusions of Vietnamese. Despite the ancient enmity between their peoples, refugees from Vietnam had perceived Chinatown as their least offensive option. At present, several hundred families had collected in the southeast corner of the Asian neighborhood, between Kearny and Grant streets, adjacent to St. Mary's Square. There had been incidents between the new arrivals and their grudging hosts, sporadic war between the youthful Chinese gangs and troops conscripted by the Vietnamese in self-defense. But Tony was unaware of all this.

Tony Kieu felt no affinity for any of the Vietnamese refugees he met that morning. His Asian roots were severed, and his adopted homeland seemed a cold, forbidding place to strangers. He might never truly feel at home here, but it scarcely mattered while he had his hate to keep him warm.

As morning waned, he left Little Saigon, spending the afternoon studying the streets of Chinatown. Before he broke for supper, he had memorized the major avenues, together with an overview of the alleyways and side streets, parks and playgrounds. He could find his way about the Asian neighborhood by day or night. Returning to his room at dusk, he stopped at a local "thrift shop," purchasing two more shirts, an extra pair of jeans, a pair of combat boots, an army-surplus jacket, and a duffel bag, to hold his recent acquisitions. As he was leaving, he passed a bin of tools and saw a bolo knife, its heavy blade secure inside a leather sheath. A pocket on the sheath contained a whetstone. Backtracking to the register, Tony peeled off ten dollars for the knife, slipping it down inside his duffel bag.

The second morning of his stay in San Francisco, with a street map in hand, Tony caught a cable car on California Street and rode it to the terminus at Bay and Taylor. Disembarking with the other passengers, he walked the final quarter of a mile to Fisherman's Wharf, purchasing clam chowder on the pier. He spent the afternoon around Aquatic Park, then caught a south-bound cable car at Beach and Hyde, returning homeward by a different route and disembarking near the Chinese Recreation Center. Tony dined in Chinatown that night, a modest celebra-tion of his first two days as an American, then locked himself inside his room and spent three hours with his map, preparing for the next day's expedition.

In the morning, Tony rode the cable car due east to Main and the Embarcadero Station of the rapid transit system. Moving with the crush of businessmen and women, bound for office jobs downtown, he passed below the surface of the street and through the turnstile, waiting on the platform for a southbound train. When it arrived, the sides emblazoned with graffiti that reminded him of temple art in Bangkok, Tony stepped aboard and found himself a window seat. Having memorized his map, as the train sped southward, Tony marked the stations in his mind: Mont-gomery Street, Powell, then Civic Center, which would be his stop tomorrow. He had business there, but for the moment he was simply riding. Many of his fellow passengers had disem-barked at Civic Center, but the young man kept his seat. Past Sixteenth and Twenty-fourth street stations, Glen Park and Bal-boa Park. He rode in silent awe through the man-made caverns, disembarking only at the southern terminus in Daly City.

At a single stroke he had bisected San Francisco. From the crush of Chinatown he had progressed into a neighborhood of country clubs and palatial homes on tree-lined streets with names like Westlawn, Castlemont, and Forest Grove. Tony moved along those streets, smiling fiercely at the Oriental and Hispanic gardeners who mowed expansive lawns and sculpted hedges, pausing at their work to study him with frank suspicion. Tony hated them because they had a place in all of this, a role that was eternally denied him by an accident of birth.

So lost was he in private thoughts that Tony did not see the squad car coming. Only when the driver made his siren moan in warning did he realize that danger was approaching on his flank. He froze, his mind racing, knowing he was vulnerable without documents. If he was carted off to jail, they might discover his illegal status. Would they lock him up in prison, or deport him? Either way, it would mean the end of everything that he had worked for over thirteen months.

The officer remained inside his cruiser, rolling down the window, beckoning to Tony with one black-gloved hand. "You live around here, sport?"

As he plainly knew the answer before he asked the question, there seemed no point in lying.

"No, sir."

"Work around here, maybe?"

"No, sir." Thinking fast, he added, "I was visiting my uncle. He works there."

The officer ignored his offhand gesture toward the northern end of Parkwood Drive. "I'll needta see your driver's license."

"I don't have one," Tony answered truthfully. "I rode the train."

"The *train*?"

"BART."

"Mmm. Some other kinda ID, then, let's go."

"My wallet is at home." He had no wallet, but it did not seem to matter now.

"Where's home?"

"I live on Mason Street."

"In Chinatown? You lost, or what?"

"I came to see my uncle," he repeated. "He works there."

"Yeah, yeah, I heard that. Has your uncle got a name?"

"Yes, sir."

"I'm waiting boy."

"His name is Anh Nguyen."

"Vietnamese?"

"Yes, sir."

"Must be a Yankee in the woodpile, huh? And you are?"

"His nephew."

"Your *name*."

"Tony Giap."

"Tony Jap?" The cop grinned maliciously. "I thought you were Vietnamese."

"Yes, sir."

The grin went sour, fading. "What say we go back and have a powwow with your uncle, shall we? See if he remembers having any nephews."

Tony bluffed. "Yes, sir. Please."

The officer looked bored. "You're lucky that I got another call an' don't have time to run you in. I'll let you have some free advice, though. Neighborhood like this, you make the people nervous, understand? You got no business here, an' everybody knows it. Makes 'em wonder if you might not have a little criminal activity in mind."

"Yes, sir." He understood too well.

"Now, my advice to you is, turn your ass around, get on the train, an' choo-choo back to Mason Street, where you belong. You follow that advice, we'll all be happy."

"Yes, sir. Thank you, sir."

"Well, move it!"

Tony moved it, walking back in the direction he had come from, fearful that the officer might change his mind and arrest him on suspicion. It was too early for relief; he would not let himself relax until he climbed aboard the rapid-transit train at Daly City Station and the doors hissed shut behind him. Riding back to Chinatown, he cursed himself for taking such a foolish chance and jeopardizing his mission. He would have to be more cautious in the future.

Locked inside his room, he paced the threadbare carpet, pondering the various mistakes that he had made. Foremost among them was his failure to acquire the necessary identification documents. In Tony's mind, acquiring those documents assumed a new priority. He would postpone his visit to the Civic Center and devote the next day to finding documents that would confirm him as a U.S. citizen. Sitting on his bed, Tony worked on the bolo with his whetstone. By the time he felt relaxed enough to sleep, the weapon had a wicked razor's edge.

Next morning, Tony loitered at the Chinese Playground, waiting for the street toughs to appear. Some of them obviously went to school, but others had begun to straggle in by noon, self-conscious in their satin jackets and their martial arts apparel. Striking poses like Bruce Lee, they shadowboxed with one another, grimacing theatrically. He watched them from the side-lines with amusement, finally picking out the one he would approach when it was time.

A small cafe across the street was headquarters for the gang. He watched them come and go with drinks, food, and noticed that they never seemed to pay for anything. He recognized the system; the proprietor had purchased an insurance policy of sorts, extending "credit" to the gang and thereby gaining "protection" from other roving bands. It was a system Tony had observed in Bangkok, in Saigon, Manila—anywhere the street gangs operated.

He crossed the street and sat down on the curb outside the restaurant. Gang members came and went, some of them glancing at him with disdain, the others passing by as if he had no substance whatsoever. Tony waited for the youth that he had chosen, certain he must cross the street at some point, doggedly resigned to waiting all day if necessary.

His target left the playground fifteen minutes later, moving toward the restaurant and shadow sparring all the way. Tony watched the cafe doors swing shut behind his mark, then rose and waited. The youth reemerged, paper cup in hand.

"Excuse me."

"Excuse yourself, man."

Tony's smile was infinitely patient. "I have business to discuss with you."

"What kinda business, man? I don't use any kinda shit, you know? It kills your body."

Tony masked his incomprehension with a simple nod. "I have been watching you, and I believe you may be able to assist me with a problem . . . for the proper price." He slipped one hand inside a pocket of his army-surplus jacket, certain that he had the young man's full attention now.

"I'm listening."

"I am a stranger. I do not have the documents that I need to carry out my business here. I hope that you, or one of your companions, may be able to suggest a source."

The young man licked his lips and glanced across the street where his friends where throwing snap-kicks at the shrubbery, at air.

"Forget about those guys. You need ID, I'm pretty sure I can fix you up. I know this guy . . . but you gotta pay up front."

Uncertain of his meaning, Tony played it safe and nodded in agreement. His companion shifted restlessly and cocked a thumb in the direction of the playground and his friends. "I gotta tell 'em I'll be gone awhile. Wait here a minute."

Tony nodded again and watched his benefactor cross the street. The young man huddled with a pair of his companions, and the others glanced at Tony surreptitiously while he explained his mission. That the others knew of his quest for documents didn't concern Tony; the very knowledge made them all accomplices, and there would be no profit for them in betraying him to the police.

The huddle broke, all three young men extending and slapping palms before his guide returned to Tony. "We're all set," the young man said. "By the way, the introduction's gonna cost you twenty."

Tony handed him a twenty-dollar bill and walked beside him, east on Sacramento, turning north on Grant, continuing to a tea room sandwiched between a laundry and a barber shop. Inside, they took a table near the window, ordered tea, and waited for the waitress to retreat.

"I've gotta go an' tell the man you're waiting for him. Shouldn't be too long, okay? He'll fix you up with what you need."

A quarter of an hour passed before a slender man of middle years came in and walked directly toward Tony Kieu. He smiled and said, "May I sit down?"

"Are you the man?"

"I am a man. Were you expecting someone?"

"Yes."

"Then, here I am."

He sat and ordered tea with rice cakes, waiting for the order

to be served before doing business. Tony noticed that his hands
shook as he raised his cup.

"What is it you need?"

"ID."

"You are in the United States illegally?" When Tony Kieu
made no reply, he waved off the question. "You wish a driver's
license?"

Tony shook his head.

"A wise decision. They are difficult to counterfeit, requiring
photographs. A birth certificate, perhaps? Social Security? With
these, you may obtain a legal driver's license from the state."

"How much?"

"Three hundred dollars for the two."

Though it would deplete his cash by more than half, Tony
knew the documents were vital. He could not survive for long in
the United States without the paper trappings of legitimacy.

"Very well."

"You were informed that payment would be in advance?"

He nodded, finally understanding what it meant to pay *up
front*. Reluctantly he pulled the roll out of his pocket, counting
out three hundred dollars in his lap and sliding it across the table,
where it quickly disappeared.

"How long?"

"An hour, more or less." The man drank his tea and dropped
his hand below the table to hide its trembling. "You will wait
for my return."

An hour passed, then ninety minutes. Tony drank more tea
and ordered rice cakes, growing nervous when the waitress asked
him if his friend was coming back. He had not asked the man his
name, had no idea of his address or place of business. As the
second hour slipped away, he settled up his bill and stepped
outside to wait. By four o'clock he knew he had been cheated,
and he walked back to the playground, finding it empty save for
two young mothers and their children.

Tony walked back to his room, disgusted with himself. He
had been foolish, trusting strangers in this city where he was,
himself, an alien. He knew that he might never find the man
again, and if he did, revenge would not replace his money or
provide him with the documents he sought. He would be forced

to try again, next time with greater caution. Next time, Tony would not pay up front.

But locating another source might take him days, and in the meantime preparations had to be made. With care, and a little luck, he might be able to proceed without ID. Somewhere among the 700,000 residents of San Francisco, Tony's target awaited, spinning out his life on borrowed time.

The young man did not plan to keep him waiting long.

4

On Friday morning Tony rode the BART to Civic Center Station, disembarking there and walking north on Hyde, then west on Fulton to the San Francisco Public Library. Surrounded by the looming glass and stone of city, state, and federal offices, he was conscious of the fact that he was perfectly invisible, an ant maneuvering between the feet of giants.

Mounting marble steps, he pushed through tall glass doors and found himself inside a bustling lobby with vaulted ceilings. He spied the information booth, where chic young women fielded questions from a dozen patrons simultaneously, and a smiling blonde directed Tony to the reference section on the second floor. He shared an elevator with two Arabs and a black man dressed in a dashiki, stepping out beneath a poster that reminded him that silence was golden.

The reference department was a warehouse of encyclopedias and indexes, directories and ancient magazines bound up in volumes. Tony stood in awe of endless titles, filling endless shelves that stretched from floor to ceiling. He had no idea of where to start and finally turned to a librarian whose silver hair belied her youthful eyes. Tony explained to her that he was looking for an old friend who had come to town. She led him to a corner of the room where telephone directories from every state and nation were shelved alphabetically. She walked him through the section, explaining the system and how he could best go about locating his friend. Then she left him settled in a carrel with the San Francisco White Pages and a street directory.

The phone book, a long shot, was his only hope. He had a name to work with, nothing more, and he believed that everyone—or nearly everyone—in the United States possessed a phone.

Riffling through the phone directory until he found the letter *D*, he kept going past the Disselkamps and Doningers, beyond the Doughertys and Driscolls. There were sixty-seven Duckworths, nine whose first names started with *L*. Two names were prefaced by the first initial only, and he scanned the other seven, from Lamont to Louis, finding none remotely close to LeRoy.

With a pencil stub and index card from his carrel, Tony copied down the addresses and numbers for the two "L. Duckworth" listings, then pushed the phone book to one side and focused on the street directory. Unlike the White Pages, this volume listed *street* names alphabetically, from A Street to Zoo Road, with a separate section listing numbered streets, from First to Forty-eighth. Beneath each name or number, individual addresses were arranged in their numerical progression, with the names of tenants listed. Tony was gratified to find that residents of individual apartments were also included.

One of Tony's possibles lived on Portola Drive, the other on Shotwell, in the 700 block. Working alphabetically, he found Portola Drive and ran an index finger down the list of numbers, suffering a pang of disappointment as his first choice was revealed to be Duckworth, Luann. She had no husband and apparently no others shared the address.

Thumbing to Shotwell, Tony held his breath. Finally he had it: 720 A. He scanned across the column, eyes devouring the tiny print, suddenly releasing his pent-up breath. The tenant was Duckworth, LeRoy G.

The second address he sought was more difficult. There were at least three dozen telephone directories for Indiana, but the small town he sought had no phone book of its own. At

length he found it in a slender volume with listings for no
fewer than seven rural towns. From that point it was child's
play to locate the name . . . or, rather, names, for there were
two. He wrote both on his index card and wondered idly if the
second signified a male or female. It would make no difference
in the end, but Tony knew that it was always best to be prepared.

The listing offered no specific address. Tony copied down the
street's name, confident that he would find his quarry when the
time came, even if he had to scour the countryside on foot. But
that would be later, after he had finished his business here and in
the other cities on his list.

Passing through the lobby, Tony detoured to the men's room,
locked himself inside an empty stall, and sat down on the toilet.
From an inside pocket of his jacket, he removed the oilcloth
packet, carefully unfolded it, and sorted through the faded,
too-familiar photographs that it contained. Selecting two of the
eight, he put the others back in their protective wrapping, folded
it, and returned it to the safety of his pocket. Only when finished
with the ritual did he pause to scrutinize the snapshots.

One revealed a black man, smiling at the camera from beneath a heavy military helmet. A stenciled name tag on the
breast of his fatigue shirt branded him as DUCKWORTH. In the
second photograph was another smile, this one more tentative,
with a disarming trace of innocence. An Asian woman, beautiful
beyond enduring, had been captured by the lens before a life of
grim privation turned her soft face hard and cynical. As always,
Tony felt the tight knot forming in his stomach, and he tucked
the pictures out of sight inside a pocket of his shirt before the
rage could take control.

Outside, the day was clear and cool. It was a three-block
walk from the library to the post office, and Tony took his time,
enjoying the sunshine despite the fact that it afforded little
warmth. Pedestrians who passed him on the street ignored him,
but he did not take offense at their indifference. It meant that he
was one of them.

The post office was smaller than the library, but no less
crowded. Patrons seeking service were lined up from the cages
to the entryway, and Tony shied away from them, avoiding the

uniformed officials ranged behind the counter stamping envelopes, accepting cash, dispensing postage. One of them might see through his anonymity, and he could not afford the risk.

Feeding eight quarters into a machine, he was rewarded with a pack of prestamped envelopes. Extracting one, he stashed the others in a pocket and proceeded to a solitary table where a dozen ballpoint pens lay tethered. The third pen he tried had ink. Carefully he addressed the envelope in square, block letters. No return address.

A banner sign above the mail slots cautioned him to "Use the Proper ZIP Code." Although Tony had no previous experience with codes, he could not permit his envelope to be rejected— possibly examined—on the basis of a clumsy oversight. A second poster, mounted under glass beside the scowling visages of men and women WANTED BY THE FBI, informed him that a number, called the zip code, helped move mail efficiently. A sample envelope reproduced below showed random digits following the address and a cartoon postman beaming as he whisked the letter on its way.

He thought there must be several thousand zip codes covering the vast United States. No citizen could possibly remember them all, which meant they must be written down. But where? Scanning the lobby, he searched for another poster, afraid that asking might betray him.

Near the entrance two old men were hunched together at a table, poring over a directory no less than twice the thickness of the San Francisco White Pages. Joining them, Tony stood off to one side, feigning interest in a stack of printed cards that invited him to voice "Complaints? Criticism? *Compliments?*" Watching the old men from the corner of his eye, he observed the envelope beside his closest neighbor, devoid of zip code.

They scanned endless columns, flipping pages, muttering to one another. Waiting patiently, Tony pretended to fill out one of the customer response cards, watching as the old men found their zip code, scrawled it on the envelope, and tottered off. Going to the book, Tony easily found the code for Calvary in Forrest County, Indiana. Unlike larger cities, Calvary had but a single zip code, covering the town and its immediate surroundings. Writing it down on his envelope, Tony carefully made the numbers legible.

Satisfied that it would serve, Tony took the snapshot of the smiling woman from his pocket, stared at her for several moments, and finally sealed her up inside. Though it was his only picture of the woman, he did not need it now, her face being burned forever in his memory. Poking the envelope inside a slot marked "Out of Town," he watched it disappear.

He found a bench outside and sat down, facing City Hall. Behind him stood the Veterans' War Memorial. His own war had begun in earnest now, and while it was a modest start, he felt a kind of grim elation at the progress he had made. His first and final targets were identified and more or less located. Much remained to be done, of course, and other targets had to be found, but it was a start, and Tony felt a twinge of pride.

His mother would appreciate what he was doing. And his friends . . . if only there was some way to communicate his feelings to them, let them know that they were not forgotten. Soon they would have justice, and it would have suited Tony Kieu to let them know the risks that he had taken, all that he had dared and done in their behalf.

Only Charley Nhu had understood the mission. He might have been with Tony, helping him, if he had not been killed in Saigon. Tony tried to conjure up an image of his friend, and was disturbed to find that he could not clearly remember Charley's face. His voice was clear enough, the laughter that had always echoed with a trace of mockery, but Charley had become a ghost, devoid of features that would give him personality, substance.

Touched by sudden panic, Tony focused on the smiling woman in the photograph, relieved to find her image crystal clear, without significant distortion. Charley Nhu might fade away, but as long he had the woman, Tony still had strength to carry on. Though dead three years, she was with him still. As she had never failed him during life, so Tony would not fail her now. Pursuit of justice was the duty of a murdered woman's only son.

Tony rose, turning his back on City Hall, examining the veteran's memorial. How proud were these Americans, his people, of their sacrifice in foreign lands. They loved their wars and should not mind another small one, fought upon their own soil. *His* soil. In Saigon, there had been no hope of finding justice for his mother; in America, whatever justice Tony found he would be forced to carry out himself.

That night, alone inside his small apartment, Tony dreamed of Vietnam and dreaming, wept.

5

SAIGON

From the day of his birth he was *different*. His early impressions of life in Saigon were composed of sensations that hinged on that sense of separation—of isolation. Mirrors told him that he bore small resemblance to the other children of his neighborhood, and Tony did not mind, at first. He *was* concerned and puzzled by the lack of seeming family resemblance to his mother, but at three years old he did not know the proper questions, would have been afraid to ask in any case. Instinctively he knew that any mention of the *difference* might cause his mother pain.

He was different, also, in the absence of his father. Other children in the Cholon neighborhood had fathers in the military or in jail, but Tony's case was . . . *different*. The others all knew who their fathers were and where they were, in spite of the embarrassment that knowledge might entail. When Tony asked his mother to explain, she told him bluntly that his father was an American soldier who had abandoned them. The three-year-old, not grasping the concept, experienced a feeling of rejection that would follow him throughout his life.

Without an extended family, as his playmates had, Tony and his mother were alone. He vaguely understood that there had been a rift between his mother and her parents, sometime in the past, and while he was not privy to the cause, he sensed that trouble had arisen from the fact that he was *different*. As for his father's family, Tony was confronted with a yawning void.

Hazy childhood memories revolved around the tiny single room where he resided with his mother in Cholon. All around them were saloons, and his mother worked in one by night. While she was working, Tony stayed with neighbors. Above all else, he waited for his mother to return and take him home, unconsciously afraid that she might change her mind some evening and desert him. In their tiny flat a blanket hung on rope divided Tony's sleeping pallet from the bed his mother sometimes shared with servicemen. The men were always gone by morning, and he seldom saw the same one twice. He did not understand why they should seek out his mother when they had quarters of their own in which to sleep.

One night he was awakened by voices whispering and moaning in the darkness. Curious, alarmed, he stepped around the blanket-curtain to discover what was happening. In the light from neon signs spilling in through flimsy curtains, he saw his mother, naked, straddling a man stretched out nude beneath her on his back. As Tony watched, she leaned forward, stretching catlike, while the man began to lick and bite her nipples. She moaned, and Tony realized it was her voice that had awakened him.

The child began to cry. Lin Doan Kieu came to him, still naked, and steered him back to bed. She loomed above him as she tucked him in, her round breasts swaying inches from his face, and Tony reached our for her, driven by an urge to suckle, to draw sustenance and safety from the primal source. Impatiently she pushed his hands away and tucked the blanket up around his chin, commanding him to sleep. She drew the makeshift curtain closed, rejoined her pale companion on the bed, and soon Tony heard the sound of creaky bed springs, voices whispering and moaning in the dark. By slow degrees he came to understand that his elusive father was a man like the Americans who came to see his mother.

Tony Kieu was four years old and still too young to understand when "peace with honor" was declared in Washington and 50,000 combat troops were summoned home in early 1973.

He *was* aware that the Americans appeared less often now. His mother had less money now, less food, and Tony drew a mental link between the disappearance of the white men and his own descent into poverty. Sometimes he lay awake and listened to his mother with her guests; sometimes he watched them surreptitiously, confused and frightened by the early stirrings of his sexuality. He had his first erection as he watched his mother move beneath a tall American, and he was frightened by the sudden swelling, terrified that he might burst and watch his life run out around his feet. With trembling fingers Tony clutched his swollen penis, squeezed it tightly, startled by the pleasant jolt from his touch. Experimentally he had begun to masturbate, still watching as his mother serviced the American, and as he reached his immature approximation of a climax, he was overcome by guilt and shame. Returning to his pallet, Tony lay awake and wept until the first gray light of dawn.

Deprived of military and financial aid from the Americans, the South Vietnamese resistance finally collapsed in April 1975. On April 29, Lin Kieu led Tony by the hand through milling crowds to the U.S. embassy on Thong Nhut Street. Marines and diplomatic personnel inside the embassy had been expecting one hundred evacuees, but now three thousand people jammed the compound, other untold thousands pressing close against the gates. Some of the would-be refugees threw money at the guards, but it was hopeless in the crush. Some others threw their babies, but the walls were eight feet tall and topped with double strands of wicked concertina wire. In the intervening years, he would remember images of babies screaming, hanging on the wire.

Next day the northern infantry and armored columns entered Saigon without opposition. Indoctrinated to believe that people in the south were poorer than their brothers to the north, the conquerors were stunned to find themselves inside a thriving city, filled with healthy, well-fed citizens. Confusion yielded gradually to anger, jealousy. Reprisals were inevitable as the Lao Dong—Workers' Party—undertook to unify the formerly divided nation. Religion was suppressed and rigid censorship imposed upon the media; the right to open trial was swept away, and thousands were committed to "reeducation camps." Saigon was renamed to honor Ho Chi Minh.

Where ethnic prejudice had once been thinly veiled, it now

erupted overtly. Lao Dong commissars were pledged to punish all "collaborators" who had offered aid and comfort to the enemy. Among their targets, none stood out so obviously as the women who had borne the children of American combatants. In 1977 Tony Kieu and other Amerasians were expelled from public school without official explanation, branded as "disruptors" of the classroom. Already bilingual, in English and Vietnamese, Tony did not miss the regimen of class, but he was wounded by the new rejection, by the further proof of *difference*. He grew accustomed to the insults of his former classmates, sometimes fighting back, more often running home to hide inside his one-room flat.

Lin Kieu took up the education of her son as best she could, insisting that he practice English, drilling him with ancient copies of forbidden magazines. When left alone to study, Tony stared in fascination at the photographs and advertisements, drinking in the essence of America, from tantalizing push-up bras to flashy cars, celebrities whose names meant nothing to him, alternately mugging, posturing, and scowling for the cameras. His mother's lessons were inevitably punctuated with reminders that their present lowly state was brought about by the Americans who had abandoned Vietnam, and most especially by the lone American who had deserted wife and child in favor of his life in the United States. She spoke his name as if it were a curse, describing his small-town home in Indiana as if she had been there herself.

Lin Kieu was unemployable within the new regime, unskilled, unwanted by the ruling powers of the socialist republic. She reverted to a life of prostitution, outlawed now but tolerated by authorities within narrowly circumscribed limits. Still attractive, she became a favorite of certain minor politicians, union officers, policemen, and they joined her in the bed where she had previously entertained Americans. On the occasions when she was abused, Lin bore her wounds in stoic silence and attempted to conceal them from her son.

Excluded from the classroom, with his mother entertaining "guests" by night and sleeping days, young Tony Kieu was free to come and go at will. He ran the streets, alone at first and later with selected others like himself. Outsiders. Castoffs of the new society. They stole from vendors on the streets and ran from the

police when they were interrupted, scattering like mice before a
terrier. Sometimes they clashed with other street tribes, waging
guerrilla warfare in the alleyways and side streets. For the first
time Tony heard himself referred to as *bui doi*, "the dust of
life."

Coming home one night to the apartment in Cholon, he froze
with one hand on the doorknob, startled by the sound of sobbing
from within. Although she did not speak, he recognized his
mother's sound from other nights when she had wept, but it had
never been like this. He stepped inside and found her kneeling,
naked, in the middle of the room. Before her, fingers of his left
hand tangled in her raven hair, his right hand raised to strike
with open palm, stood a policeman Tony recognized from run-ins
on the street. A bully, overweight and balding, he was fond of
slapping *bui doi* children on the rare occasions when he caught
one. This night he stood before Lin Kieu with pants around his
ankles, stubby, turgid penis thrusting toward her face. She wept
and tried to fend him off, one eye already swollen shut, a palm
print livid on her cheek.

The officer turned and saw Tony. He grinned wickedly,
revealing crooked yellow teeth. He did not strike again, but
pulled Lin Kieu against his loins and held her there, still watching Tony's face. Smiling.

Tony rushed at him without a conscious plan, surrendering to
pure blind rage. He saw the big, scarred fist, could not avoid it
as momentum carried him on a collision course. The impact
broke his nose and pitched him backward, stunned, already
losing consciousness before he hit the floor. He never saw the
officer hitch up his trousers, scarcely felt the boots that drummed
against his ribs.

When he returned to consciousness, his mother had him tucked
in bed, but Tony threw the covers back and staggered to his
sleeping pallet in the corner, pushing her away when she reached
out to help him. Sickened by their life, the casual indignities that
she accepted as her due, he drew the blanket-screen between
them, closed her out. Beyond the curtain, he could hear her
weeping softly as he drifted into troubled sleep.

Tony's maternal grandfather died in the spring of 1979, and
Lin Kieu, uninvited, led her son to pay his last respects for
someone he had never seen. Religious services were now forbid-

den by the communist regime, but gatherings in honor of the dead were tolerated as a necessary evil. Tony's grandfather had lain in state at home. His wife received relatives and friends who came to offer food, condolences, and gifts. Lin Kieu and son had entered unobserved, retreating to a corner of the room while others passed before the bier or huddled with the widow and her daughters. Nearly half an hour passed before Lin's younger sister noticed her and whispered something to their mother. When the older woman rose, attended by the children who had not betrayed her, Tony thought that she might welcome them. Instead, she passed them by without a glance, escorted from the room by daughters who refused to look at Tony or his mother. After they were gone, Lin Kieu approached her father's coffin, and whispered something in the dead man's ear. Then she led her son from that house of mourning.

On the street, after they had traveled several blocks in silence, Tony tugged her sleeve and asked if everyone had stared at them because he was *bui doi*. Lin spun on him and slapped his face, a stinging blow that rocked him on his heels. Instantly remorseful, she had clutched him to her, whispering that he must never use such language to describe himself. His *father* was to blame for all their troubles. Someday God would punish the American who had deserted them.

At twenty-seven, Lin Doan Kieu was hardened, her youth spent. When liquor was available, she drank too much, and Tony knew instinctively that she was drinking to forget. She slept through morning, into afternoon, and plied her solitary trade by night. Sometimes, when business had been slack, she lured their landlord into bed, her body offered up in lieu of rent. The first pale strands of gray were visible among her raven tresses; she pretended not to notice, but within a year she had stemmed the spreading tide with dye that made her look brittle and synthetic. Tony watched her age before his eyes and was afraid.

While Lin slept late, or drank and "entertained," her son took to the streets. His closest friend and confidant was Charley Nhu, another Amerasian, who had been abandoned by his mother when she fled the city. He slept in parks, cellars, alleyways, and Tony sometimes spent the night with him, returning home in daylight. It was an adventure, like the clashes with their rivals or the petty thefts of food and cash they practiced on the side, a twisted semblance of childhood on the streets.

Returning home one night through driving rain, Tony spied a figure huddled in the entryway of their run-down apartment house. A man in uniform. The figure glanced in each direction, furtively, as if he was engaged in some activity that badge and gun might not defend. Retreating into shadow, Tony watched the man emerge, recognizing the officer who had beat him so badly.

His stomach was a knot of apprehension as he waited for the officer to disappear. Secure at last, he ran the final twenty yards and ducked inside his building, taking the steps two at a time in his haste. Before he reached the door of his apartment, Tony knew it would be unlocked.

He burst inside, surprised at first to find his mother not at home. A second glance revealed her naked, crumpled form behind the bed, and Tony moved to kneel beside her. Lin Kieu's eyes were swollen shut and she bled from the nose, her face and body a mottled patchwork of bruises and abrasions. Tony tried to help her, discovered that she could not stand alone, and finally lifted her onto the bed. He covered her with blankets, wet a cloth and bathed her face, unable to perform the same ablution on her battered body. Through the night he sat with her.

When she did not return to consciousness next morning, Tony knew he would need assistance. Lacking money for a doctor, certain that the newly socialized practitioners would not extend their services on credit to a Cholon prostitute, he racked his brain for a solution. When it came to him at last, he knew it was his only hope.

With grave misgivings, Tony Kieu retraced the path that he had traveled only once before. The home of his maternal grandmother was also in Cholon, but situated in a better district, several blocks from what had once been Saigon's red-light neighborhood. He recognized the house at once, for it had undergone no changes, other than dramatic aging, in the past four years. He climbed the narrow steps, expecting someone to emerge and challenge him before he reached the door. Instead, the house was silent. He knocked, and then a second time, less timidly. He waited through what felt like an eternity, aware that it must only have been moments.

He was not prepared to face the shrunken apparition in the

doorway. In the years since he had seen her for the first and only time, his grandmother had shriveled to a shadow. Her eyes were sunken, cheekbones prominent beneath the facial skin stretched as taut and dry as parchment. One hand braced against the doorjamb, she appeared to be in danger of collapsing on the threshold, but she did not tremble. There was instant recognition in the sunken eyes, but no surprise.

He launched at once into a sanitized recital of the injuries sustained by Lin Doan Kieu. Tony thought he saw a flicker of emotion as he spoke his mother's name, but it was quickly stifled. He explained the need for medical attention, finally apologized for troubling the woman in her home. She heard him out in utter silence, and when Tony finished, there were teardrops in her eyes. He tasted victory, transformed at once to bitter gall as the old woman shook her head, stepped back, and firmly closed the door.

He had no other recourse now; his failure was complete. His mother needed him, and Tony turned for home, alone, aware at fourteen years that he could do nothing to help her by himself. He might recruit his friends to raid a pharmacy, but he was not a doctor and might easily compound the problem, even poison her. The best he could do was make her comfortable now, provide for nourishment in case she struggled back to consciousness and found her appetite along the way. Returning home, he found that she had soiled herself. Tony wept with rage to see the blood that glistened darkly on the sheets.

Lin Kieu survived for two more days, and Tony did not sleep in all that time. He sat beside her bed and waited on her, bathing her swollen face when she began to moan and mutter in her sleep. He knew that she was dying, and he dared not leave her side. The neighbors could do nothing; no one could do anything to help her now. When she stopped breathing on the third night after the attack, her son experienced a fleeting moment of relief, immediately banished by an overwhelming shame.

Without his mother's income, Tony had no hope of keeping the apartment. Turned out on the street within a week, he found a home of sorts with Charley Nhu. What had once been an occasional adventure became a way of life. He began to steal in earnest now, for food and merchandise to trade on the thriving black market. Wherever possible, he memorized the patterns of police patrols in self-defense, and he learned the name of one particular patrolman, studying his routine until he knew the moves by heart.

The killer's name was Phuong Van Minh. An eight-year veteran of the local force, he drank too much and had a reputation for brutality in handling arrests. He was Lao Dong, and thus protected from the normal discipline that might have fallen on another officer who turned up drunk on duty and abused his prisoners. Officially untouchable, he still had certain weaknesses that Tony thought he might be able to exploit in time.

Surviving on the streets of Saigon, Tony and his comrade, Charley Nhu, attracted others like themselves, the hard-core *bui doi* orphans who possessed no family of any kind. Their faces bore the stamp of fathers who had left the Asian killing fields behind; some of their mothers had been lost to war or illness, some to the reeducation camps, while others merely jettisoned their children, seeking to escape the living cross that they were called upon to bear. In leisure time—between the street fights, thefts of food, and helter-skelter flights from the police—they traded stories of their absent fathers, passing around the photographs that were their sole inheritance. Without exception, save for Charley Nhu, the children of the streets had managed to delude themselves that they were wanted, loved, by men who had abandoned them years earlier without a second thought.

In 1982, a decade after the withdrawal of its combat troops from Vietnam, the U.S. government had launched an "Orderly Departure Program," theoretically designed to rescue 16,000 Amerasian children from the communist regime. Anything but orderly in fact, the program forced potential emigrants to file repeated and redundant applications, starting at the local level and progressing to the nation's capital. Between official fees and mandatory bribes, the average cost of an escape from Vietnam amounted to three taels of gold—a thousand U.S. dollars—far beyond the reach of any orphan on the streets. Likewise, Orderly Departure bogged down absolutely in the case of children with no family waiting to receive them on the other end. An average of one flight every month left Vietnam for Bangkok under Orderly Departure, bearing forty children to the staging areas that so resembled cattle pens, but Tony Kieu and his companions knew that they would not escape that way.

The plan was Tony's brainchild from the start, but Charley Nhu agreed to it at once and threw himself behind it with a missionary's zeal. The others, they agreed, would never willingly cooperate and might obstruct them if they were included in the scheme. It would be necessary to deceive them, play upon their hopeless fantasies of family reunions to enlist their aid. With luck his friends would never know they had become unwitting instruments of Tony's vengeance.

Tony's plan was simplicity itself. With Charley Nhu he would secure transportation to America, seek out his father, and destroy the arrogant American who had condemned his mother and himself to hell on earth. As time and opportunity permitted, they would stalk the others, bring the war home to their doorsteps and destroy the lives that they had built upon the suffering of their abandoned children in Saigon.

Aware of all the obstacles that stood before him, Tony had proceeded cautiously, one slow step at a time. The trip to Bangkok, and from there to the United States, would not be inexpensive or devoid of risk. The first leg would be traveled overland, on foot if need be, but they could not walk or swim from Thailand to America. Their passage, even on the meanest tramp, would cost more money than they stood to earn inside a year of working dead-end jobs around Cholon. They would be forced to range more widely, growing more aggressive in their raids against the local merchants, hoarding cash and other valuables that might be used to pay their way.

A doctored version of the scheme was cautiously presented to their fellow children of the streets. As Tony laid it out, his plan would circumvent the labyrinth of Orderly Departure. He would travel to America with Charley Nhu, make private contact with the absent fathers of his friends, arranging reunions that would make their dreams come true. A larger delegation would attract unwelcome notice from the moment they set foot on shore, resulting in immediate arrest and deportation back to Vietnam. Cooperation from the others would be vital; the alternative could only be a lifetime wasted on the streets of Saigon.

The others fell in line with a pathetic eagerness that might have broken Tony's heart had he not hardened it with dreams of sweet revenge. They gave up precious snapshots, told him everything they knew about the soldiers who had sired them in the midst of war. He memorized the scanty details, drilled himself until they had become second nature. With the photographs to guide him, he would recognize his prey.

He stole an atlas of the world and calculated distances, directions. Bangkok lay five hundred miles northwest of Saigon, most of that in jungle, but the first leg of their trip would be the least of it. America was vast, as Tony realized when he began to plot his targets on the map. It might take months—or years—to find the individuals he sought. If any one of them had moved to other cities in the intervening decade, he might never find them. Still, he owed the effort to his mother.

And he owed it to himself.

An arbitrary six-month deadline was established for departure. By then they would either have the necessary funds or would leave with what they had.

Disaster overtook them three weeks short of their goal. The raid, against a baker's shop on Quang Ho Street, had been routine: two girls would tip a rack of fresh-baked goods, distracting the proprietor while Charley Nhu cleaned out the till. It had been Tony's lot this time to stand watch outside, and he was waiting when the girls emerged running for safety, the angry baker on their heels demanding that they stop and pay him for the damaged items. He was braced to move when Charley Nhu exploded from the doorway, clipped the baker with an elbow, and broke in the opposite direction, straight for Tony Kieu.

He was not ready for the uniformed patrolman, slender, sallow as the khaki that he wore, who emerged that moment from a tobacconist's shop across the street. Without a second thought the officer whipped out his automatic pistol, sighting down the barrel as he called for Charley to surrender.

Charley Nhu was grinning when the bullet struck him from behind, drilled through a lung, and punched a blowhole in his chest. The runner lost his stride, slack-jawed, the look of triumph fading as he stumbled and fell at Tony's feet. He lay with both eyes open, staring skyward, as a pool of crimson spread beneath him on the sidewalk.

Tony stooped to take the money from his outstretched hand, ignoring a command to halt or die. He ran, aware that he might feel a bullet slap between his shoulder blades at any moment, conscious of the fact that he was risking everything, his mission, for a sum equivalent to seven U.S. dollars. Charley Nhu had died to earn that money for their journey to America, and Tony would not leave it lying in the street, not even if it cost his life.

He ran for what seemed hours, through the twisting alleys of Cholon, aware that other officers had joined the chase behind him. Tony ducked in through the front of shops and out the back, confounding patrons and proprietors. He toppled trash cans in his wake and finally scrambled up a fire escape to lose the last of his pursuers. Huddled on a rooftop blocks from where the desperate race had begun, he paused to gasp for breath and wept for Charley Nhu, the only living soul who shared his secret and his vision.

Tony Kieu was finally alone.

As three weeks would make no difference, he decided not to wait. Before he left Saigon, however, there was unfinished business to be settled. . . . Tony spent three nights observing Phuong Van Minh, refreshing memories of his patrol routine. He was a silent shadow on the killer's track, inexorable, tireless. On the fourth night Tony waited for him outside the apartment of a prostitute, a length of pipe tucked underneath his flimsy jacket. When the officer emerged, he faded back into the shadows of an alleyway adjacent to the house and lay down on the filthy ground.

He heard Phuong approaching, made the first groan barely audible. The footsteps faltered, slowed, and Tony moaned again, a little louder this time, reeling in the line. His back was to the street, but he could track his quarry by the sound of bootheels on the pavement drawing nearer. Phuong called out to him, received a muffled whimper in response, and bent closer, one hand settling on Tony's shoulder.

Striking like a cobra, Tony whipped his pipe around and struck Phuong a solid blow across cheek and jaw. Bone snapped on impact, and the killer sat down, hard, his rancid breath escaping in a rush. Before Phuong could reach the pistol in his holster, Tony scrambled to his feet and brought his weapon down across the big man's collarbone with force enough to leave his right arm hanging useless at his side.

Phuong struggled to rise. Tony hit him with a solid backhand, careful not to lay the pipe across his skull with lethal force. He had considered killing Phuong Van Minh, but over time he had decided on a different measure of revenge. The killer would survive . . . but at a price.

As Phuong lay stunned before him, Tony took the automatic pistol from his holster, dropping it in a trash bin. Working swiftly, conscious that he might be disturbed at any time, he used his pipe to shatter elbows, ankles, knuckles, knees. Phuong offered no resistance, whimpering as Tony struck the first few blows, then slipping into deep unconsciousness.

There would be pain enough when he revived, a lifetime to consider what had happened, *why* he had been singled out. Determined that he should not miss the point, Tony took a snapshot of his mother—one of only two that he possessed—and stuffed it in a pocket of Phuong's tunic, buttoning the flap for safety's sake. It might be days or weeks before the photograph was found, but when it was discovered, Phuong would understand.

Tony left Saigon that night, his business finished. Daybreak overtook him in Baqueo, and he slept that morning in the woods outside of town, emerging in the afternoon to purchase food. He walked by night the next two days, until he realized that no one had the slightest interest in his movements or his destination. There was no pursuit from Saigon; no one spared the ragged boy a second glance. He was *bui doi* and thus invisible.

Crossing the border into Kampuchea on the sixth day of his journey, Tony felt more vulnerable, more exposed. As an Amerasian, he had plainly come from Vietnam, and many of the locals still had scores to settle from the early days of the Vietnamese occupation. Moving with the flow of refugees along the highway leading to Phnom Penh, he still felt totally alone. No one molested him, although he grew accustomed to suspicious stares and muttered curses from the Kampuchean natives. Tony fretted more about the roving gangs of bandits and Khmer Rouge guerrillas who controlled the countryside, extorting food and money from the peasants to support themselves. He kept the major portion of his money hidden, doling out small change reluctantly when food was unavailable by any other means.

The Kampuchean capital, once roughly equal to Saigon in population, had been ravaged by civil war and occupation. The resulting glut of refugees jammed the streets, existing—where they managed to survive at all—in abject poverty. Wherever Tony looked, the shops were either closed or doing business on a bargain-basement, close-out basis. Stately homes had been converted into tenements and filthy hovels were the order of the day, but thousands had no roof to call their own. Tony Kieu spent two weeks in Phnom Penh in a fruitless search for menial employment, finally moving on. He had accomplished nothing in the city and had spent the rough equivalent of thirty U.S. dollars, precious time and money wasted.

The second leg of Tony's trek across the Kampuchean countryside consumed three weeks. He spent the night in roadside ditches or abandoned huts, avoiding military convoys when they rattled past him on the highway, churning dust clouds in their wake. The occupation forces, harsh enough in dealing with the natives, were positively brutal when they stumbled onto refugees from Vietnam. More than once Tony watched from hiding while patrols accosted transients on the highway, robbing them, manhandling the men, occasionally dragging women off the road to rape them in the forest.

Crossing into Thailand, Tony traveled through the forest, shunning highways with their checkpoints and patrols. He watched for snakes, and for opium traffickers who claimed the jungle as their own. More ruthless than the Kampuchean bandits or Khmer Rouge, they would kill him out of hand if they suspected he was spying.

In nine more days Tony was in Bangkok, teeming anthill of the Chao Phraya river delta, where he settled into perfect anonymity among the Asian nationalities who jammed the waterfront. And in Bangkok, Tony met Captain Esquivel, the master of the *Corazón de Oro*.

6

SAN FRANCISCO, 1986

Some days he woke up angry; other days he wondered why he bothered waking up at all. This morning, LeRoy Gadsden Duckworth woke up frightened, bathed in perspiration, eyes wide open in an instant, staring at the ceiling of his tiny bedroom in the artificial darkness. Tinfoil on the windows kept the bedroom dark and relatively cool all day, but it could not keep out the street sounds or the dream that still haunted him after all this time.

The dream was nothing special, when you thought about it. He was riding in a jeep outside Da Nang with Tommy Cotton at the wheel and Skeeter Robinson in back. The three of them, wisecracking, were secure in the knowledge that the worst was all behind. No matter that Da Nang was known as Boomtown for the frequency with which it was shelled. They were young, alive, invulnerable. It was party time.

Each time the dream unrolled, no matter how he tried to brace himself, the jerk-off on his goddamned motorcycle still came out of nowhere, swerving right across their lane and losing traction on the muddy surface of the highway. Tommy tried to miss him, but the crazy bastard never had a chance; the off-side fender clipped him hard, and LeRoy saw him airborne, like a human pinwheel, in the heartbeat that was left before the impact drove them to the left across oncoming traffic. Duckworth saw the armored transport looming like a mountain on wheels and knew there was no frigging way the juggernaut could stop in time.

Tommy Cotton threw his hands up to protect his face. When they hit, he hurtled forward like a rag doll, shearing off the wheel on impact, skewering himself on the jagged steering column. Blood exploded from his nose and mouth, across the shattered windshield.

Duckworth tried to brace himself, but it was no damned use. He hit the dash with stunning force and slithered under it, one leg twisted beneath him at an impossible angle. In his dream he *heard* the femur snap but felt no pain, not even when the spear of bone erupted through his flesh. He was anesthetized, somehow, immune to physical sensation as he saw the nightmare through to its predestined end.

Above him, Skeeter Robinson came sailing forward like a human javelin, striking the windshield with his skull. He kept on going, punching through with enough force to shred his face before reactive force took over, hurling Skeeter backward once again. The broken glass had closed around him like a collar, ripping his head off on the rebound. Duckworth heard it bouncing on the hood before the dead man toppled back into his seat, blood spouting from the torn carotid artery. Aware that he was weeping, Duckworth raised his face to greet the crimson rain.

The dream invariably cut away at this point to an antiseptic ward where Duckworth lay with ranks of mummies swathed in bloody bandages. A doctor with a long, sad face stood over him, enumerating injuries and promising that all would heal in time, returning Duckworth to roughly his original condition. There might be a limp, of course, but he was lucky all the same. The doctor smiled awkwardly and said, "You're going home."

Duckworth came awake at this point, his body slick with perspiration, rigid as a board. He had to suffer through the dream a dozen times before he realized that it was *going home* that terrified him. Going home was worse than being wounded, worse than being killed in Nam. Going home was worse than *anything*, because he knew precisely how the dream turned out, and there was no such thing as a happy ending.

Duckworth threw the rumpled bedding back and padded to the bathroom, naked in the darkness, finally turning on a light above the sink to keep himself from watering the toilet seat. He did not have to check the clock beside his bed to know that it was almost noon; he woke each day within five minutes of 11:45, regardless of the time he went to sleep. It was a pain sometimes, but it was something he had learned to live with, like his middle name.

His family was from Alabama. None of them had ever strayed more than a hundred miles from Gadsden, in the Black Belt, and they liked it that way. They were settled, as secure as any blacks could ever be when they were farming cotton in the heart of Ku Klux land and even whites with bigger farms were scratching to survive. When he was born, they must have seen a hint of wanderlust in LeRoy even then, and they had tagged him Gadsden in the hope that it might anchor him somehow. It might have worked except for Vietnam, and at the time he had been thankful for an opportunity to serve his country anywhere outside of freakin' Alabama. Never mind that he might get his ass shot off for reasons that he did not understand. If Duckworth didn't make it home . . . well, he had seen enough of old Etowah County.

He joined the Corps because they advertised their skill at building men. Boot camp had been hell, but Duckworth had come out feeling like a man all right, not like the faggots you saw everywhere these days. The Corps was building life takers and heart breakers in those days, unashamed of training killers. LeRoy had taken to the martial training like a hog to slop, and when the call went out for volunteers to serve in Vietnam, he did not hesitate.

Above all else, he was not LeRoy Gadsden any more. Within the Corps he was L.G., or simply LeRoy, with the hated geographic middle name forgotten, save for payroll records and his confidential personnel file. He felt reborn, as if he had been favored with a second chance.

Emerging from the tiny bathroom, Duckworth found himself a wadded pair of jeans and struggled into them before proceeding to the kitchen. Seldom hungry when he woke, he ate from force of habit—two eggs, fried, with bacon on the side and hot, black coffee. Concentrating on his food, he gave the old familiar nightmare time to fade away.

Duckworth did not blame his problems on the service or the war. All things considered, Vietnam had been the high point of his life. Within the standard military limitations he was free—to drink and fuck and fight and kill without remorse, and he was getting paid for it. There were no jobs like that for black boys back in Alabama, or in any other state that Duckworth knew about. There was a decent chance that he might get his ticket punched, but for the moment he was *living*.

Duckworth had experienced some second thoughts, especially around Khe Sanh in '68 when Charlie and the northern regulars were everywhere and there was no place for a man to take a crap without artillery and mortars raining hellfire all around him. Duckworth had believed he was dying at Khe Sanh, and he was startled to discover that the prospect held no terror for him. He did not enjoy the thought of checking out with shrapnel burning in his guts, but neither did he cherish any superstitious fear of the unknown. To him, the heaven trip was nothing but a crock of shit, and if there was no heaven, then it stood to reason there could be no hell. If he was wrong . . . well, Duckworth figured he could stand the heat as well as he could stand another forty years in Gadsden.

He surprised himself by coming out of Khe Sanh without a scratch. After all the heavy rounds that Charlie threw into a tiny piece of real estate, and all the guys who got shipped out in body bags, it had to be a freakin' miracle. When the offensive broke and Ho Chi Minh decided to cut his losses, Duckworth was among the survivors who received a four-day pass for R & R. He drew Da Nang, with Tommy Cotton and an okay white boy, Skeeter Robinson, and they were on their way, already celebrating on the road and getting lubricated when some jerk-off on a motorcycle cut the joyride short and landed Duckworth in emergency receiving.

A gimpy private had no future in the Corps, but Duckworth took the news in stride. He did not blame the service, did not even blame the gooks, who never laid a finger on him during

fourteen months of combat. There was no point blaming dead
men, either, so he shined it on with Tommy Cotton and the
jerk-off biker, who, it turned out, had been carrying dispatches
for the freakin' CIA. There seemed no point in blaming anyone,
but Duckworth could not shake the hunch that someone, somewhere, was responsible. In time he came to place the blame upon
himself.

The drugs came later. He had done a fair amount of grass in
Gadsden prior to entering the Corps, and ample shit was around
in Nam, but he could handle it. The ganja never interfered with
his performance on patrols; he pulled his weight. Duckworth
could be relied upon when it came to do or die. LeRoy had
stayed away from pills and skag and all the rest when overseas,
though not because of any moral qualms. In simple terms, he did
not need a bigger fix; he was already high on war, the heady mix
of life and death that kept a soldier on the edge, alert to every
new sensation. He was wired and running with his throttle open.

LeRoy had not expected bands and banners when he hobbled
off the plane in San Francisco, but he had not been prepared for
jeering insults, either. Long-haired bastards screaming at him
that he was a baby-killer. They spit at him from behind a cordon
of police. Impossible at first to understand, gradually, over time,
it came to him: They were afraid to go where he had gone and do
what he had done. Their jealousy had driven them to strike a
pose of protest, drawing courage from their numbers, sublimat-
ing envy in the guise of righteous indignation. Duckworth hated
them at first, until he realized that they were empty, hollow, that
they had never looked deeply into the abyss. After that, he
settled down to hate himself for just that.

It had not been a conscious choice. The self-condemnation
crept up on him by degrees as Duckworth realized he was fit for
nothing. He had never finished high school, never learned a
trade, and had no special skills aside from killing other men. A
ruptured lumbar disc prevented him from seeking other battle-
fields, from recapturing the thrill of combat. He communicated
briefly with a handful of his friends from Nam and lived vicari-
ously through their letters. But none of them kept in touch for
long, and Duckworth finally realized he had become a living
symbol of defeat, a bad-luck omen best avoided if you gave a
damn about the future.

San Francisco in the early seventies had been the seat of Flower Power and a wasted generation heeding the command to "tune in, turn on, drop out." The drugs were everywhere, available to anyone, and if you couldn't pull the cash together, there was always some fool trying to improve his karma by handing out "love grass" on the street. In time, LeRoy's suspicions of the flower generation were confirmed: they made a lot of noise about their hatred for the war, but they could never get enough of hearing combat stories from a veteran, especially a black man who had suffered in the cause. His stories of Khe Sanh were good for grub and grass at any commune in the Haight. Duckworth smiled to think of all the white chicks he had bedded just by pouring on the pity. LeRoy knew that underneath their quest for peace and justice they were looking for a chance to writhe on the black man's snake, and he helped them out whenever possible. A veteran of countless bureaucratic screwings, Duckworth knew that when it came to fucking it was infinitely better to give than to receive.

Somewhere along the line, drugs had taken precedence over fucking and all the rest, and Duckworth had acknowledged his dependence on chemicals to get him through. He started racking up a record of arrests in San Francisco, Alameda, Berkeley. Though he was loaded *all* the time, so wired that he could rarely satisfy the groupies anymore, one of them had liked him well enough to marry him, and Duckworth had been stoned enough or fool enough to play along. They had been doomed from the beginning, but in the interim they had a daughter. She was eight months old when Duckworth and his lady recognized their error. LeRoy had not seen her since. She would be eleven in July.

He cleared the dining table, left his dishes in the sink for later. He spent an hour tidying his two small rooms, more out of habit than necessity, then cracked the first of half a dozen beers he would consume throughout the afternoon and settled down before his aging Zenith for the game shows. Duckworth favored *Tic Tac Dough* and *Wheel of Fortune,* but he watched them all, from *Sale of the Century* to the *$25,000 Pyramid.* With two or three more beers inside him, LeRoy would begin to see himself as a contestant, matching wits against a housewife from Duluth or a professor from Manhattan, smiling as they handed over money, cars, and any other thing a man could want.

At four o'clock he drained his final beer and turned the television off. He showered, dressed for work in denim shirt and chinos, locked the door behind him as he left. His studio apartment sat atop a single-car garage, with the adjacent house divided into several other rentals. As the garage was used for common storage by the tenants, all of them were forced to park their cars along the street, discomfiting the neighbors. Duckworth had no car—in fact, he had no license, thanks to three DWI arrests—so the lack of a garage had never struck him as an inconvenience. Someday, when his ship came in, he would have cash enough to buy himself a house with a garage attached, and he would live there alone.

Unless his ship turned out to be another freakin' garbage scow, as always.

Walking south on Shotwell, Duckworth came to Twenty-fourth Street, hung a right, and covered three more blocks to Mission and the underground. He waited seven minutes for the train and used the time to examine other passengers already waiting on the platform. Two career-girl types, well dressed and whispering to one another, pointedly ignoring him and everybody else. Their loss. A kid in denims and an army jacket, vaguely Hispanic in appearance; though he was inoffensive on the surface, you had to watch the quiet ones. A solitary girl done up in punk was studying the kid with interest, but he wasn't giving her the time of day. A pair of faggots sporting makeup and the latest styles in unisex, holding hands.

The gender benders did not startle Duckworth anymore, and he was able to resist sarcastic comment for the most part, if his day had not been too depressing and he wasn't too drunk. The changes wrought in San Francisco had required some getting used to, everybody hopping out of closets all at once that way, but Duckworth told himself he did not mind a homosexual, as long as the guy wasn't recruiting. It didn't happen much these days, provided that you did not wander into gay bars by mistake, or try to take some steam at one of the establishments euphemistically referred to as bathhouses. One of them had tried to hit on LeRoy in a Mission Street saloon some years ago; the guy was drunk enough to think that "no" meant "maybe," and he followed Duckworth to the men's room, looking for an easy score. Instead, he ended up with reconstructive facial surgery, and it was one time that the cops had fallen out on Duckworth's side. You couldn't even count on that, these days, and he was hearing rumors on the street that many of the *cops* were gay.

The ride downtown always took thirteen minutes. He disembarked at Civic Center station, noting that the grungy girl and inoffensive kid also got off. They were not together yet, but she was eyeing him the way a starving man might scrutinize a steak. The way men used to look at women, before somebody started switching all the roles around. He wished the poor, dumb bastard luck and struck off to the west on Grove. He walked four blocks to catch Van Ness, and then another eight due north to reach the Feldsheim Building, where he worked five nights a week as a custodian.

He checked in with a guard who looked as if he was twenty, going on sixteen, and rode the service elevator to the basement, where he punched in seven minutes early. There would be no extra pay for clocking in ahead of time, but who cared? If he was forced to quibble over minutes, he would have to brood about the time he spent commuting every night, and none of it was worth his time. It was a job, no more, no less, and as jobs went, he found it relatively easy. Some nights he made it through a whole damned shift without once working up a sweat.

He ran the Power Wand, a vacuum cleaner with attachments that could suck up anything. Assigned three floors—four, five and six—he cleaned each weeknight after the offices were closed. He didn't mess with emptying the ashtrays, taking out the trash, or any shit like that; his job was floors. Sometimes, when he was toking, he imagined he was back in Nam operating a minesweeper, checking the paddies for any surprise packages Charlie might have left. Nobody ever tried to shoot your ass off working Feldsheim's, though, which was certainly a bonus. Granted, it was not entertaining or adventurous, but he was a janitor, not Indiana Fucking Jones. Nine floors meant three men on Power Wands, five men on mopping, buffing, shit like that. The women emptied trash and cleaned the johns from top to bottom, making sure the business world had a decent place to shit.

If LeRoy paced himself, he would be halfway through his second floor when dinnertime arrived at nine o'clock. He seldom packed a lunch, preferring to select from a bank of vending machines in the employee's lounge. There was a microwave if you wanted something heated, but he usually went with chicken salad, knowing the burritos gave him gas and anything with "cheese-food" on it tasted like rubber. Duckworth ate alone whenever possible and spoke only when spoken to. The others may have thought him strange, standoffish, but it didn't phase him. After working with him for a year they knew no more about him than any stranger on the street, and Duckworth liked it that way.

After a quick bite, he headed back to five and settled in a men's room stall to smoke a joint. He didn't do the hard stuff anymore, no 'ludes or crystal now in better than a year. Grass was harmless. Better, it was beneficial. When he started dragging on the downside of a shift, bored shitless by the same old, tired routine, a little smoke helped keep him mellow. Tonight he had two joints, but he was saving one for later in case the first one let him down.

As Duckworth smoked, he felt himself unwind. Grass did not make him hyper, as it did others. The more he smoked the more LeRoy relaxed, until he felt that he could scarcely lift a finger if his life depended on it. But he never did *that* much anymore. It wasn't economical and Feldsheim's would be happy to replace him if he couldn't wag the Power Wand.

I got your Power Wand right here, he thought, and grinned.

Suitably relaxed and running out of break time, Duckworth flushed the roach and ambled back to work. No matter if he left the men's room smelling like a commune in the Haight; the fans would clear it out before the women made it up to five, and if they didn't, what the hell? No one had anything on Duckworth, and if someone on the crew should beef, it would be their word against his.

The Power Wand responded to his touch and Duckworth finished five in record time. If you punched out early, you were losing pay, and if the crew chief caught you stroking it he might assign you extra duties—so he took his time on six and did it right. He finished up with fifteen minutes to spare, just time to ride the service elevator down and stow his gear before he hit the clock. He was outside and buttoning his jacket up against the fog before he realized he had not smoked the second joint.

No longer mellow, LeRoy Duckworth walked south on Van Ness, his thoughts reaching back across the years and miles to

Vietnam, returning to the moment when he had truly been alive. He did not see the slender shadow that fell into step behind him half a block from Feldsheim's, keeping pace. If he was conscious of the footsteps echoing his own, he gave no sign. Together, man and shadow passed along the street and were devoured by the fog.

7

Tony waited for the lights at 720 A to be extinguished, for his prey to fall asleep. Though he did not plan to go inside, it had become a ritual, this waiting to be certain Duckworth would not venture out again.

Alone in misty darkness, Tony closed his eyes and felt the neighborhood around him. It was lower-middle class at best, an ethnic stew composed primarily of couples and small families who let their children run at will throughout the day, their broken toys accumulating in the scruffy yards of aging duplex homes. It did not have the crowded feel of Chinatown, but Tony sensed a trace of desperation in the air. The families huddled here thought they were merely passing through. They told themselves that they were upward bound, but in reality the vast majority were going nowhere fast.

A bachelor who lived alone, his target was a local oddity. His small apartment, stacked above an old garage, rarely heard the sound of other footsteps, other voices. Tony had been watching his mark for seven days, and in that time no other person crossed the threshold into 720 A. His quarry was as isolated from his neighbors as a hermit in a cave.

A week of following his target told him Duckworth worked
five days a week at Feldsheim's after everybod, else had gone
home. He left for work about four o'clock each day, returning
sometime after two A.M. On weekends he was more erratic, less
predictable; he visited saloons and drank a lot of beer and wine,
once loitering around the toilets for a muttered conversation with
another patron who acted as if he had been expecting Duckworth.
Money was exchanged, and something else. LeRoy was buying
drugs.

The bars had been a problem. Tony still had no ID, and
doormen at a number of the dives had refused to let him enter.
When that happened, he would wait for Duckworth on the street,
aware that sooner or later his man must emerge. In roughly half
the bars, proprietors appeared to flout the law in their pursuit of
profit, failing to request ID, content with Tony's money as he
ordered beer and nursed it slowly, observing every move
Duckworth made, endeavoring to understand the man.

Duckworth was going through the motions of his life, devoid
of purpose. Wasted. With his liquor and his drugs he sought
forgetfulness, which he could never finally achieve. But what,
precisely, was he trying to forget? As Tony followed him he
wondered whether Duckworth was consumed with guilt about
the woman and the child he had abandoned in Saigon. He hoped
the black man suffered terribly, remembering the lives that he
had ruined, but he saw no evidence of inner pain on Duckworth's
face. If anything, his quarry seemed perpetually bored, burned
out, waiting for the end.

So be it. Tony Kieu would help him on his way, but first he
would remind the former soldier of his crime, make certain that
he understood why death had sought him out.

But not tonight.

The neighborhood was risky, residents departing and returning throughout the night, as if none of them had a job to go to in
the morning. Some of Duckworth's neighbors in the big, old house
attached to the garage appeared to leave their lights on all night,
and he had no wish to disturb them, run the risk that one
might summon the police. Inside the small apartment, Duckworth
might have weapons. He would certainly possess the great advantage of familiar ground on which to fight, if Tony failed,
somehow, to catch him in his sleep.

The alternative plan presented special problems of its own, which he was not prepared to deal with just yet. As Tony turned toward Mission Street and BART, he was preoccupied with more immediate concerns. Three weeks in San Francisco had come close to wiping out his cash reserves, and rent was due again tomorrow. He could just afford the room, but he'd have no money left for food or transportation.

He could not go looking for a job. In the first place, regular employment would deprive him of mobility, defeat his purpose. Furthermore, he realized that an employer must keep records; if he found a merchant who was willing to employ him without ID, his employment would create a paper trail for the authorities to follow when he left San Francisco.

The answer came to him in bed that night with sudden crystal clarity. On two occasions while he waited outside bars for Duckworth to emerge, he had been propositioned by aggressive homosexuals. He had rejected them each time, but he had also noticed other youths, his age and younger, who were not so quick to turn the offers down. Male prostitutes were nothing new in Tony Kieu's experience, not after Bangkok, but at the thought of offering himself for sale, Tony's stomach twisted into knots.

You gonna love this town. Your kind of people here.

The sneering mate was wrong. He would devise a variation of the game, make certain that this time the odds were in his favor. Tony had already given everything he could afford to lose. This time, he would *take*.

Next morning, after paying Mrs. Soo for one more week, he had four dollars left. He would not eat again until his cash had been replenished, whether it required one day or seven. Hunger could be inspirational, and Tony needed every ounce of motivation for the part he must play.

That afternoon he hiked to Market Street and spent two hours searching out a neighborhood of bars and "niteclubs" catering to homosexuals. The various saloons were unimportant to him at the moment; Tony spent his time examining the streets and alleys, memorizing alternate escape routes. If he failed tonight, it would not be through lack of preparation.

Dusk was closing in when Tony walked back to his room on Mason Street. He showered, dressed, and slipped on the pea coat in preference to his army-surplus jacket. He had slit the lining to create a makeshift pocket for the bolo knife and sheath. Before departing, Tony tucked the weapon in its hiding place and spent a moment practicing his draw, becoming gradually accustomed to the extra weight. The knife dragged slightly on the left side of his jacket, but the bars he had selected would be dark enough to hide it.

His first stop was a bar called the Acropolis. A number of the local gay bars seemed to draw their names or their decor from ancient Greece, but the significance was lost on Tony Kieu. The doorman looked him over, seemed about to ask him for ID, then reconsidered. As he entered, Tony was acutely conscious of the knife inside his coat, the tiny bankroll in his pocket. He had four dollars, and the first beer cost him two.

He found a table near the door. From past experience, acquired while tailing Duckworth, Tony knew that patrons seated at the bar were pressured into buying drinks more frequently. The tables seemed to be a kind of neutral ground where cocktail waiters did their job halfheartedly, more interested in flirting with the customers than selling alcohol. With any luck a single beer might see him through the first phase of his hunt.

As the bar filled up, Tony scanned the new arrivals for a likely target. His prey would have to make the contact, but it would not hurt for Tony to appear alluring, available. He sipped his beer and waited, scrutinizing the men, many of them in business suits, who collected at the bar.

"Alone?"

Surprised, Tony almost jumped, but caught himself and turned to find a slender young man standing at his elbow.

"Are you alone?" the man repeated.

Tony nodded. "Yes."

"I'm Vince. Mind if I join you?" He was settled in a chair before he got the question out, scooting it around until his knee was pressing Tony's underneath the table. "First time out?"

Uncertain of his meaning, Tony was content to nod and smile.

"I thought so." Beaming at his own imagined cleverness, he scooted several inches closer. Both his knees were touching Tony now, imprisoning one leg. "I've got a talent that way. I can always spot first-timers."

"So, you come here often?"

Sipping at his drink, Vince dismissed his question with an airy wave. "I make the scene when I'm between relationships, you understand? I'm basically monogamous . . . but then again, it doesn't hurt to play the field occasionally."

"No."

"How long have you been out?"

Tony thought about the question, saw no need to lie. "Since six o'clock."

Vince giggled, leaning closer, placing one hand on his captured thigh. His touch made Tony's flesh crawl, reminding him of Esquivel.

"No, silly. I mean, how long have you been out of the closet?"

Tony hoped that his bewilderment was not too readily apparent. "I was never in the closet."

Vince seemed impressed. "My God, I wish I'd had the courage of the youngsters coming out today. I mean, you can't imagine what it's like to hide your light beneath a bushel all through school. I didn't come out of the closet until I was *twenty-three*."

Convinced that he was in the presence of a madman, Tony thought it best to smile and hold his tongue.

"I'm really glad we met," Vince said. "But gracious, I just prattle on. I haven't even asked your name."

"It's Anthony."

"How absolutely perfect. Anthony and Cleopatra. Are you looking for a piece of *asp*, by any chance?"

Delighted with his jokes, Vince squeezed Tony's thigh. Tony forced a smile and wondered what the man found so amusing. He concluded that the cocktail Vince was sipping must not be his first this evening.

"I simply *must* know everything about you," Vince continued. "Come on, now, tell me all about yourself."

"Well—"

"Can we go somewhere? I mean, the atmosphere is so *frenetic*, and I feel the need to just *relax*. You understand?"

Tony understood. He finished his beer in one long swallow. He felt a tingling in his face but knew that it would pass. One beer was not enough to make him drunk, and he was steady on his feet once Vince released his leg and let him stand. Tony realized that Vince was several inches taller, but it made no difference to his plan. The other man was slender, obviously weak; his every movement was effeminate. As Tony rose, he felt the bolo's reassuring weight beneath his jacket.

"You have a car?" Vince grinned as Tony shook his head. "No matter. Mine's outside. Your chariot awaits, fair Anthony!"

They left the bar together, Vince with one arm looped through Tony's, snuggling closer as they hit the sidewalk. They reached his car—an early-model Mustang, lovingly maintained—and Vince played chauffeur, opening the door for Tony with a flourish. As he settled in and waited for his prey to climb behind the wheel, his mind was racing.

When they had traveled several blocks from the Acropolis, Tony turned to Vince and said, "Please, stop the car."

Vince hesitated, glanced at him suspiciously. "What's wrong?"

"I want you now."

"My God, you *are* impetuous." A slim hand rested on Tony's thigh.

They passed a park, mist-shrouded in the darkness, seemingly deserted. Vince drove once around the block to satisfy himself that no police were lurking in the shadows, then he parked beneath a weeping willow tree and killed the headlights. Fumbling with his belt and zipper in the dark, Vince had his slacks around his knees when Tony laid the bolo's razor edge against his throat.

"Oh, Jesus." Instant tears, without a heartbeat's hesitation. Tony was unmoved. Vince clutched his small erection in one hand and whined, "Don't hurt me. *Please*."

"I want your money."

"Money?" Vince seemed confused, as if he did not speak the language. "You want my money?"

"Money." For a moment Tony could have sworn the man was disappointed, even outraged.

"In my wallet." Limp hands fluttered toward the slacks, now pooled around his ankles.

"Get it."

Moving cautiously, avoiding any sudden pressure on the blade beneath his chin, Vince found the wallet. Tony slipped it in a pocket of his coat without a second glance.

"The rest."

"It's all I have, I swear. Don't *hurt* me."

Tony reached across his prisoner and took the Mustang's keys from the ignition, dropping them in his pocket with the billfold.

"Don't follow me."

"I won't. I swear to God."

"I'll kill you if you follow me."

Vince moaned and shuddered like a dying man, but Tony realized that he was on the verge of climax, somehow stimulated by the threat of violence. Cheating him, he drew the knife away and said, "Relax, you're safe now." Tony did not close the Mustang's door behind him, leaving Vince crouching underneath the dome light, pants around his ankles, tugging at his flaccid cock.

"You little *bitch*!"

Leaving the park behind, Tony covered two more blocks before he dropped the car keys in a mailbox, standing beneath a streetlight to examine Vince's wallet. Tony knew the credit cards could betray him, even though he did not understand precisely how. Looking for cash instead, he came up with half a dozen twenty-dollar bills, three singles, and a crisp new fifty. Satisfied, he put the wallet in the mailbox with the keys and started home.

That night in bed he realized that he had stumbled onto a bonanza. He could not return to the Acropolis for fear of meeting Vince again, but there were countless other bars in San Francisco, patronized by homosexuals who might respond to his apparent innocence. He had already earned enough to live for two more weeks, if he was careful with his money, and he should be finished in the city long before then. Of course, there was the matter of ID, still unresolved, and Tony knew that he would have to spend more cash to get the documents he needed. This time, though, he would be careful and refuse to pay "up front."

He hunted on successive nights, encountering a local dentist and a stodgy businessman from out of town, relieving them of over seven hundred dollars. Neither evidenced the excitement shown by Vince, and neither offered him resistance. Each accepted the humiliation of the robbery as if it were his due.

He learned to choose his hunting grounds, avoiding the

saloons that catered to men in leather. After traipsing into one such bar by accident, he understood that these men did not fit the pattern of his chosen victims; they were tough and unintimidated, more inclined to violence. For Tony's purposes, he needed weak men who would tremble in the face of danger. Men with everything to lose.

Each afternoon he checked the local papers, searching for some evidence that he was being hunted by police. He understood that in America, unlike Saigon, reports of crime were commonplace, a kind of entertainment for the working class. As the days went by, he wondered whether the police had been informed at all, or if his victims were too embarrassed to report the crimes.

He understood that each new crime increased his chances of arrest, but Tony could not stop. Not yet. Another robbery or two and he would have a thousand dollars—cash enough, he thought, to purchase suitable ID and still have money left to travel after he was done with Duckworth. Once he had killed in San Francisco there would be no time to waste. The police could not ignore a murder.

His fourth night out he chose—or let himself be picked up by—an artist who appeared to be insulted that his name was not well-known to Tony.

Mollified by Tony's promise to become his model for a night, he led the way on foot, back to a tiny loft crammed full of poor, half-finished portraits. He resisted the demand for money, full of arrogance and pride, and Tony had to strike him with the bolo, careful to employ the flat side of the blade. Thus chastened, streaming blood from lacerations in his scalp, he revealed a wall safe, opened it, and handed Tony nineteen hundred dollars, pleading for his life. Elated, Tony shut the artist up inside a closet and braced a chair beneath the knob, using his bolo knife to slash the telephone cord before he left.

At an all-night deli he stopped to celebrate before catching the next train back to Chinatown. He had almost three thousand dollars now, three times the goal that he had set.

He was halfway through a corned beef sandwich, sipping at his Coca-Cola, when a young blond man in denim sat down at his table, opposite, without an invitation.

"I know you," the stranger said, and the short hairs rose involuntarily on Tony's neck.

"I don't know you."

"I'm Jerry. And you are . . . ?"

"I'm Vince."

"Hi, Vince. I seen you working the Acropolis a few nights back," the blond declared. "And then last night in Papa Bear's."

The latter was a gay bar where he had encountered the dentist. Tony stiffened, sensing trouble, wondering if he could reach the bolo knife in time to save himself, if anyone would try to stop him as he sprinted for the door.

"I don't believe in accidents, ya know?" The blond was prattling on. "I figure meeting you like this is fate or something, dig it? Like, we're soul mates."

"Soul mates?"

"I admire your style," the stranger told him, changing subjects without warning. "You don't even have to work at it, man. You're a natural."

"Natural?"

"Sure. I should know. I've got some a these old farts eating out of my hand, or wherever. The minute I saw you, I knew we could get something on."

It was dawning on Tony and he had begun to relax by degrees, recognizing the young man for what he was. "You are a prostitute?"

"Puh-*leeze*." The blond put on a pouting face. "You must be newer in the business than I thought. I hustle, sure—like you. But no one—*no one*, darling—calls it pros-tee-tution anymore."

"You hustle."

"Right." The saucy smile was back in place. "I figure we could pool our assets, make some decent coin, ya know?"

"I will be leaving San Francisco soon."

"Okay, no point in wasting time then, is there? Gimme two weeks, tops, an' you'll be sitting on a decent nest egg when you leave."

He had no interest in poultry, but a sudden thought occurred to Tony Kieu. If Jerry was a veteran "hustler," he might have access to illicit documents. There was risk, of course, but Tony saw no obvious alternative. He dared not shun a golden opportunity.

"I have a proposition for you," Tony said.

They struck a bargain swiftly. Jerry knew a guy who knew a guy, and he agreed to make some calls. He spent ten minutes on the pay phone and another twenty waiting for the call back. When he finished with the second call, he came back to the table, looking satisfied.

"We're in. I toldja, Vince, I got connections."

"Will I have to pay up front?"

The blond looked horrified. "That's sucker bait." He grimaced. "Figure on a small deposit, maybe ten percent. The rest is strictly COD."

Afraid to ask for further explanations, Tony nodded. "Shall we go?"

"Too early, man. This guy does business from a pawn shop, dig it? We can be there when he opens up at eight."

It was approaching one A.M. according to a clock behind the deli's counter. Seven hours. Tony frowned and pushed his plate away.

"If you will give me the address—"

"Hey, not so fast there, Vince. We need to get acquainted if we're going into business, dig it? Now, it just so happens I'm invited to a party, and I know they wouldn't mind another pretty face."

He thought about it, weighing the risks if he should try to draw out the address by force. "How far?"

"It's just around the corner, can you dig it?"

"Dig it." Tony smiled with a false enthusiasm.

Jerry made a show of studying the cold cuts, letting Tony pay the check. Outside, Tony found that "just around the corner" meant a walk of several blocks through twisting, darkened streets. He tried to keep the names in mind, in case he had to find his way back alone.

He heard the party well before they reached the ancient house that stood apart from sleeping neighbors, every window lighted, music rattling the walls. Tony followed Jerry up the steps and through tall, oaken doors. Inside, the music blaring from the stereo was deafening.

"Enjoy!" his blond companion shouted, barely audible above

the din, before he disappeared in the direction of the bar. Young people milled about the parlor, lounging on the staircase, legs like frail stalactites dangling from a catwalk overhead as Tony entered. Though it was warm, Tony kept his coat on, conscious of his nineteen hundred dollars and the bolo knife. Working his way around the edges of the crowded, makeshift dance floor, he ducked through the open doorway of a study he had noticed on the far side of the room. Inside the study Tony found a couple stretched out on the sofa, making sluggish love beneath a blanket. They ignored him as he entered, paid no more attention to him as he crossed the room and passed out through another door.

A more or less secluded pantry off the kitchen was as quiet as he might expect. Curling up in a corner, he was fast asleep within a moment, closing off the surrounding noise. Brief moments might have passed, or hours, when a gentle hand upon his shoulder roused him from a troubled dream of Vietnam.

"Hey, man, I thought you split." There was a rueful smile on Jerry's face. "We better shag it, man. It's almost time."

Tony stood up stiffly, following Jerry back through a crowd that had not thinned appreciably while he had slept. Outside he was surprised by morning light that hurt his eyes.

"What is the time?"

"I'd call it seven, give or take. We got a ways to go."

In fact they walked two miles or more before they reached the tiny shop on Quane, near Twenty-fourth Street. He was relieved to see familiar street signs and to realize that he was only blocks from a familiar BART station.

The shop windows held a glittering array of knives and razors, carelessly displayed around a drum set and guitars, with saxophones hanging from bent hangers overhead. Inside, the narrow aisles were blocked with television sets and amplifiers, stereos and battered luggage, each item with a tag proclaiming it to be a "Super Bargain." Glass showcases held more knives, displays of jewelry, and handguns by the score.

A balding man with three chins stood behind the register, regarding them suspiciously through rimless spectacles. "I help you, gentlemen?"

Jerry smiled and lounged against the counter. "Ziggy sent us."

"So?"

"My friend here needs some paperwork."

"Your friend there got a tongue?"

"I need ID."

"How much you wanna spend?"

"Two hundred?"

"Please, the doctor says I ain't supposed to laugh this early in the morning."

Jerry made a sour face. "Let's cut the bull, okay? You gotta price in mind, let's hear it."

"Four yards gets ya born and sets ya up with Uncle Sam. Another two'll put ya on the road."

Jerry translated. "It's four hundred for a birth certificate and Social Security. Two hundred more for a driver's license."

"Ain't that what I said?"

" No driver's license," Tony answered.

"Great. A bona fide pee-destrian. Four bills it is."

"How much up front?"

"The standard ten percent. Let's call it fifty, shall we?"

"Better check your calculator," Jerry sneered. "We'll call it forty."

"Hey, I'm easy."

Tony slid two twenty-dollar bills across the counter and pinned them there as the proprietor reached out to claim them. "How long?"

"This time on Monday." Pocketing the twenties, he produced a pen and a scrap of paper. "Lemme have the name you wanna use, the same for parents. We make up the addresses ourselves, all part of the service."

Tony took the pen and wrote down "Vincent" for a start, then cast around for a surname. He scanned the shelves of radios, computer hardware, telephones, and finally wrote down "Tandy." He would call his nonexistent father Charles, out of respect for Charley Nhu. His mother's name was "Lynn."

"That oughta do it. Monday morning, gentlemen . . . unless you've got your eye on something special?"

"Monday morning," Tony answered, turning for the door with Jerry at his heels.

Outside he made excuses, promising to meet Jerry at Papa Bear's that night, aware that he would never keep the date. Jerry was a liability from this point on, and Tony was determined to be rid of him before he let some secret slip. If Jerry learned Tony's name or address, he would have to die.

Tony waited, feigning patience, while Jerry wrote his phone number on a matchbook, pressing it into Tony's hand. "You'll call me, huh?"

"I'll call you," Tony lied.

They parted, Tony moving slowly along the street, waiting until he was sure that he had not been followed, turning finally for the underground and home. He needed sleep, and time to make his final plans for LeRoy Duckworth. Much remained to be done, and Tony was determined that there should be no omissions, no mistakes. Perfection was the very least that he was willing to accept. It was the very least his absent friends deserved.

8

On Monday morning Tony rode the train from Chinatown to Twenty-fourth Street, disembarking there and walking over to the pawn shop on Quane. He spent the better part of half an hour watching from a block away, alert for any sign of tricks or ambush. Jerry did not show, presumably discouraged by the fact that Tony had not called him since Friday night, and there were no police in the vicinity. He crossed the street, pushed through the swinging doors, and found the same bald man with triple chins behind the register.

His documents were ready, and he studied them before he paid. The birth certificate described him as a citizen of the United States born in San Francisco during 1965. His Social Security number was 570-91-9345, and while he did not understand the system, Tony knew that it would help him find employment if the need arose. Satisfied, Tony paid the fat proprietor $360 and pocketed his treasures.

With time to kill, Tony rode the subway back to Civic Center, roaming the concrete canyons from United Nations Plaza to the Opera House. At noon he ate his lunch at a corner sandwich shop across the street from Hastings Law College, watching earnest students as they made their way about the campus. Tony marveled that people so advanced in age were still permitted to remain in school. In Vietnam, such sluggish scholars would have been compelled to find employment with the state.

At half past three he entered Feldsheim's on Van Ness. Another ninety minutes remained till closing time, but Tony had not been inside the building previously, and he wanted time to scout its several floors, examining the exits and potential hiding places. Just inside the revolving door was an information booth, but Tony passed it by as if he knew precisely where he had to go. By night, a guard in uniform would occupy the booth. From observation, Tony knew the guard made rounds at sixty-minute intervals, being absent from his post for ten or fifteen minutes at a time.

Tony moved on past the elevators, past the public rest rooms, noting that the doors appeared to have no locks. He scanned the offices that lined the corridor on either side. The first floor housed an advertising agency, a tax accountant, several lawyers— none overrun with clients at the moment.

At the far end of the corridor he found the service stairs and slipped through the EMPLOYEES ONLY door. He climbed two flights to reach the second floor, stepped out into another corridor, examining the carbon-copy offices. More accountants, more attorneys, empty waiting rooms behind tall windows. Tony retraced his footsteps to the service stairs, repeating his examination of each floor until he reached the ninth and uppermost, where several of the offices were vacant. Confident that he had overlooked nothing of importance, Tony rode the elevator down to three and got off.

The Feldsheim Building had public rest rooms on alternating floors: the first, third, fifth, and so on. There were also toilets for employees on the fifth floor, but finding no others, he assumed the several offices must hide small bathrooms of their own. None of the rest rooms were equipped with locks. Tony devised a plan.

He stepped inside the third-floor men's room, moved along the row of empty stalls, and settled on the final one in line. Inside the cubicle, he closed and latched the door behind him, sat down on the toilet, and attempted to relax.

It was a simple plan, and nearly foolproof. Tony would

remain inside the rest room when the various employees left for the day. No guard was on duty at the moment, and employees on the day shift would have little interest in the toilet stalls. The clean-up crew was coming on at five, but logic told him they would not be starting on the middle floors, and by the time they reached his hiding place he would be on the move, perhaps already finished with his task.

The rest room door hissed open, and Tony braced his feet against the door, presenting the appearance of an empty stall. It was not closing time, and no one would think twice about the toilets being occupied, but Tony saw no point in taking chances, leaving any witness who might recall a stranger in the rest room. He held his breath and listened as the new arrival noisily disturbed the water in a urinal, then washed his hands. Alone once more, Tony let his pent-up breath escape and wished again that he had taken time to buy himself a watch.

Disturbed twice more within the next half hour, he lifted up his feet each time, praying that the new arrival would not single out his ''empty'' stall. When offices began to close at five o'clock, he heard employees in the corridor outside, an exodus directed toward the elevators.

Tony listened as the building quieted. Below him somewhere, Duckworth and the others would already be preparing for their shift. Eyes closed, he reached inside his pea coat, closed one fist around the handle of the bolo knife, and smiled.

Although he could not be precisely sure, Duckworth believed it was the worst hangover of his life. He had been drinking hard the past two days, and it was catching up with him. Riding in to work had been a nightmare, with a couple of the young brothers trying out their ghetto blaster on the train. Around the time Aretha started screaming for some R-E-S-P-E-C-T, LeRoy had thought his freakin' head was going to explode.

Some grass would take the edge off, but he couldn't risk it yet. If he could stick it out till dinnertime, he would forgo the normal chicken salad, make a beeline for the crapper up on five, and score himself some sweet relief.

Duckworth punched the clock and grimaced as it echoed inside his skull. He got his Power Wand and wheeled it to the service elevator, climbing in with Escobar and Lopez, riding in

silence while they chattered back and forth in Spanish. Escobar
got off on one and that shut Lopez up, thank God.

He didn't mind the vacuum's noise so much. Accustomed to
it as he was, he found it almost soothing, like a mind massage. It
couldn't beat the grass, of course, but that would have to wait.
He put the Power Wand on automatic pilot, shutting down his
brain. The evening stretched before him like a wasteland.

Satisfied that fifteen minutes had elapsed, Tony left the toilet
stall. He listened for footsteps in the corridor outside, hearing
nothing but the soft, insistent thrumming of the blood that filled
his veins. Thus far he was alone.

About to leave the rest room, Tony spied a plastic bucket
underneath the sink, the handle of a scrub brush resting inside.
Apparently forgotten by the cleaning crew last night, the pail
was still half full of murky water, giving off a vaguely antiseptic
smell. He hesitated for a moment, finally picked the bucket up.
Though a poor enough disguise, he might, at a glance, appear to
be a member of the crew.

He glanced both ways along the corridor before emerging.
No sign of Duckworth yet, or any of his fellow workers. Tony
knew that on a normal evening the crew consisted of two women
and eight men. With nine floors and approximately sixty offices
to clean, it stood to reason that there must be some established
system. Without knowing their set routine, Tony would have to
search each floor until he found his prey.

He opted to begin on nine, descending to check each floor in
turn. That way, if Tony were surprised, he would be headed in
the right direction: toward the street and escape.

The ninth floor was deserted; likewise the eighth. On seven,
Tony found a short Hispanic man waddling along behind a
vacuum sweeper, singing to himself, oblivious to his surroundings. At the far end of the corridor, a black man wearing
headphones was preoccupied with wringing out a mop.

He was not Duckworth.

Two more flights, the water sloshing in his pail, and Tony
was about to poke his head out of the stairwell onto six when he
was startled by the jangling of keys nearby. Closing the door, he
leaned his weight against it, braced to stand and fight if someone
tried the knob, the bolo knife in his hand.

He counted sixty seconds, listened to the jangling recede, and risked a glance along the corridor. The uniformed guard, a pistol riding on his hip, was disappearing into the elevator. Tony's breath escaped through gritted teeth as he waited for the double doors to close.

He should have forty minutes, minimum, before the guard patrolled another floor. With any luck he might have Duckworth isolated by then and ready for the kill. Three quarters of an hour was a lifetime, but he still had eight employees unaccounted for, one of them the man he sought.

On five, one of the women was emerging from an office, trundling a cart before her. Ducking back, he avoided her as she rumbled past.

Switching the bucket to his other hand, he flexed his fingers, bringing back the circulation. Every floor he eliminated raised the odds against encountering his quarry in a suitable position. If he found no more employees till he reached the first or second floors, he would be forced to scrub the mission, find a way out past the guard.

Two flights, the bucket dragging at his arm now, and he poked his head out of the stairwell onto four. He recognized his prey at once, despite the fact that Duckworth's back was turned, his shoulders hunched as he propelled the vacuum sweeper back and forth across the corridor.

His heart hammering against his ribs, Tony watched as Duckworth reached the nearest office door, opened it, and wheeled the sweeper on inside. Tony seized the chance, moving swiftly, water slopping out from the bucket in a trail behind him.

After hesitating briefly in the office doorway, Tony pushed through and set the bucket down inside. He drew the bolo from its sheath as Duckworth fired the sweeper up again. Circling a secretary's desk in the reception room, Tony held the knife blade flat against his leg, stepping into the center of the room.

Aware that he was wasting precious time, aware that other members of the crew might wander in at any moment, Tony studied Duckworth for the moment, memorized his every movement in the final seconds of his life.

Alerted by some primal sense, Duckworth shut the sweeper off and turned around. "Hey, man, what it is?"

"LeRoy Duckworth?"

"Might be. Who's askin'?"

Tony took a long stride toward the desk. "I have a message from your daughter."

Something sparked behind the black man's eyes. A trace of hope? Or an awareness of the death that was about to overtake him?

"Celia?"

Tony frowned, his fingers tightening around the bolo's grip. "Mai Linh."

The ebony face went blank. Tony Kieu was stunned to realize that Duckworth did not know his daughter's name.

"What kinda mind-fuck is this, man? I oughta kick your sorry ass for jerkin' me around." He took a step toward Tony, hesitating as the bolo knife came into view, its polished blade reflecting light from the fluorescent fixtures overhead. "Hey, man—"

"Your daughter sends you greetings from Saigon."

"You're crazy, man. There must be some mistake."

The move was telegraphed through Duckworth's eyes, and Tony saw it coming, braced himself to meet the rush. He stood his ground and brought the bolo hissing down, surprising Duckworth, who had hoped to benefit from surprise. Too late to save himself entirely, Duckworth raised an open palm to take the blow, recoiling as the heavy blade sheared off three fingers. He staggered backward, brandishing the bloody stump, colliding with the secretary's desk. Panic pinched his vocal cords and bottled up the rising scream.

The wounded man retreated and Tony followed him. Duckworth feinted to his left and Tony struck out in the opposite direction, cold steel opening the denim shirt, the flesh beneath. His prey was cornered now. LeRoy knew that he must either charge or kneel and wait for death.

He charged.

It was a clumsy move at best, made doubly so by shock and loss of blood. Head down, hands outstretched, he stumbled blindly toward his adversary. Tony sidestepped like a matador and brought the heavy bolo down across his shoulders, opening another rent in flesh and fabric.

This time Duckworth's own momentum took him down, and Tony was upon him, straddling his prostrate form before he could rise. The bolo whispered as it fell, and Duckworth suddenly went limp, death erasing every vestige of resistance.

Tony spent a few more moments with the body, finishing his work, then wiped the bolo clean on Duckworth's shirttail and returned it to its sheath. He took the snapshot of a smiling man from his pocket, tore the face diagonally across, and tucked the pieces into Duckworth's open palm.

There were bloodstains on his clothes, as there had been with Esquivel, but with the pea coat buttoned they would be invisible. He calculated that the guard downstairs would be preparing for his rounds by now. If he was quick enough, he had a chance to make the street and exit unobserved.

He took the stairs in leaps and bounds, aware that he was flirting with disaster. One misstep would bring him crashing down. Desperation gave him speed, but there was something else as well: a flash of pure exhilaration as he cleared the final steps and narrowly avoided colliding with the wall.

Tony crossed the lobby, a vacant no-man's-land, in a breathless rush. He reached the tall revolving door—and found it locked. A rapid search disclosed the latch—low down, against the floor—and Tony cleared it on his second try.

The door refused to budge.

A further search disclosed the second latch, directly overhead. He twisted, pulled the latch bar free, and threw his weight against the door. He emerged into darkness with a brisk wind in his face.

Walking southward on Van Ness, he resisted the desire to break and run. The guard would not be at his post again for several minutes yet, and hours might elapse before the corpse of LeRoy Duckworth was discovered. Even then, he thought, a search would begin in the building while police were summoned from outside.

One task remained before he could leave San Francisco. Such a simple thing, but crucial to him.

The misty darkness covered Tony Kieu's retreat and saw him safely back to Chinatown.

9

SOUTHERN INDIANA

Snow had fallen in the night. Gray trees, their branches flecked with frost, stood out in stark relief against the sugar-dusted hills. Above, gunmetal clouds threatened another snowfall for the early afternoon. The wind had grown new teeth and learned to bite.

Buttoning his sheepskin jacket, tucking hands inside the fleece-lined pockets, Anthony Patterson struck off along the curving gravel drive. He loved the woods in every season, but winter was his favorite time of year. Despite the inconveniences of icy roads and frozen pipes, there was a special magic to the season, when the hills and valleys were transformed into a pure crystal snowscape, dazzling the eye and mind.

They were isolated here, three miles from Calvary, the cabin barely visible from Galesburg Road, and Anthony liked it that way. He could walk to town during decent weather, but he had no neighbors breathing down his neck and watching every move he made. A man who had already seen enough of crowded cities for a lifetime, he was protective of his privacy.

His leg was worse this morning, as it often was in colder weather. Hobbling along the drive, he felt decrepit, though in fact the limp was unrelated to his age. At thirty-eight, he was as vigorous as anyone could logically expect from someone who had been blown up and then stitched back together by a team of combat surgeons.

He was younger then, and youth as much as anything had granted him the will to live. It still amazed him sometimes when he stood before the mirror after showering and saw the scars that twined around his hip and buttocks, etching abstract patterns on his thigh. A few more inches and the shrapnel would have disemboweled him.

They had been fighting for the ruined town of Hue, above Da Nang. For reasons he had never clearly understood, Hue had become a major target of the Tet offensive in January 1968. The Cong and NVA had overrun three quarters of the town in their initial push, driving ARVN troops and dispossessed civilians through the streets like frightened sheep. The first few days, before artillery and bombers were deployed to raze the stronghold, the fighting had been house-to-house.

Anthony Patterson had been in the thick of it, a sergeant with the Special Forces, pulled from duty on the DMZ with other members of his team to join the fight for a town suddenly invested with great strategic value. On their second night they had dug in downtown with a Marine detachment on their flank when seven hundred screaming NLF commandos in black pajamas had attacked from nowhere, breaking like a human wave around their forward outpost. Pouring automatic fire into the hostile shadows, hurling hand grenades and sometimes fighting hand to hand, they broke the first assault, then beat back a second before pale dawn lit the killing ground. Four members of their team were down, but they had stacked two hundred corpses in the ruins around their position.

You never hear the shot that kills you. Patterson had heard it said a hundred times. While the soldier's aphorism was demonstrably untrue, it lent confidence in combat situations. If you heard the bastards firing at you, you were still alive, still able to return that fire and pull it out, regardless of the odds.

That morning, in the second week of January, he had heard the rocket coming. It was hard to miss; the RPG's distinctive rattle seemed to shake the houses for a block around. He had been scrambling for cover when the earth dissolved beneath his feet. The pain came later, when he had awakened on a stretcher, airborne, with an IV in his arm. His lower body was on fire, and he had known he was dying.

He was wrong, but for a time it had been touch and go. The combat surgeons at a nearby M.A.S.H. unit saved his life and his legs, but they were frankly pessimistic in their prognosis. Three of them believed he would never walk again; a fourth had been more hopeful: he believed that Patterson might learn to use a walker, if he applied himself. Four years in VA hospitals had finally proved them wrong, but there was still the limp, along with psychic scars that gradually, so slowly, had begun to fade.

He rarely thought about the war these days, despite the painful limp in winter, but it had been on his mind the past two weeks. No . . . eighteen days to be precise. He had been counting in his mind, unconsciously, since the arrival of the envelope from San Francisco.

In the absence of a return address, he had checked the postmark prior to opening the envelope. He knew no one in San Francisco, could not understand why anyone in California would be writing to him. It was not computer-generated junk mail; he could tell that much from the handwritten address in a childlike script. He did not recognize the writing.

There had been no letter, nothing to explain the photograph. He recognized the woman instantly. It had been half a lifetime since he last laid eyes on Lin Doan Kieu, but in the faded snapshot she was still as young and fresh as ever, smiling timidly across the gulf of time.

He had replaced the snapshot in its envelope, blocking out the flood of images it brought to mind, examining the address in an effort to retain his grasp on here-and-now reality.

Anthony Patterson
Galesburg Road
Calvary, Indiana 47448

No route or box number, though it scarcely mattered in a town the size of Calvary. The incomplete address was interesting, not because the photo had arrived—postmen knew precisely where to find their seven hundred customers and letters rarely went astray—but because the anonymous sender had traced Patterson to Calvary without obtaining his exact address.

It never crossed his mind that Lin herself had sent the photograph. If she had tried to reach him after all this time, she would have surely written something, anything, to let him know that she was still alive and well. The snapshot was a cryptic message, but he could not read its meaning in her eyes.

They had been thrown together by the war, by loneliness, while Patterson was stationed in Saigon. When they first made love, he had not been surprised to learn she was a virgin; it was simply one of the countless incongruities he faced in Vietnam, where children were assassins, priests were terrorists, and Viet Cong guerrillas were on the payroll of the CIA. Patterson had missed her when his team was ordered north to fight along the DMZ. Two weeks later he was wounded, airlifted out of Hue with IV needles in his arm.

He seldom thought of Lin throughout the next two years. The shrinks had called it blocking and they helped him to remember, but by then there had been little point in dredging up the memories. His Cholon virgin was a world away. She would certainly have found herself another man, perhaps another Green Beret, to keep her warm at night. . . .

And there was Jan.

She was his nurse when Tony had undergone yet more therapy at yet another VA hospital, this one in southern California. He had been on the verge of giving up and settling for the walker, possibly a wheelchair, but there had been something in Jan's eyes, her attitude, that made him want to stand and fight it out. Reluctantly at first, he had applied himself with greater vigor to his exercises, straining to the limit when he knew that she was watching, conscious of a need to please her by succeeding. It took a while for him to realize that she was giving up her own time, logging extra hours on the ward to talk him through the screaming nightmares, see him through the worst. He came to love her for it, for herself. He owed her everything he was, would ever be.

He had been discharged from the VA as an outpatient in April 1972, two weeks after the American troop withdrawals from Saigon. The news meant nothing to him then; he had his legs, and in a few more months he would throw away the cane. Jan had given him her number, a going-away present, but a bitter week had passed before he finally called her. He was surprised when she seemed glad to hear from him, cautiously hopeful when she agreed to see him, relieved when she offered to cook dinner for him at home.

Her small apartment near the hospital was warm and homey, very different from the room that he had rented for the duration of his therapy. There was no pressure, no demand upon him to perform. She cooked spaghetti, they drank wine together, and he helped her with the dishes afterward. He found himself at ease with her, at peace within himself. She did not ask about the war, perhaps because she knew the worst of it already. More than anyone he'd met who had not been in Vietnam, she understood the fears of soldiers coming home in bits and pieces.

Anthony had known she was attractive, knew he missed her after checking out of the VA, but not until that evening had he wanted her so badly that the need became almost purely a physical sensation. Frightened by the sheer intensity of his emotion, worried when his hands began to shake, he had excused himself, but Jan stopped him at the door. Without a word she came into his arms. She led him silently to the bedroom, and they did not fall asleep until the first thin light of dawn broke through the window.

Several weeks later Jan broached the subject of his moving in. Her logic was impeccable: she wanted him full-time, and he was wasting money on his small apartment since he hardly every slept there as it was. Despite the need for her, which had become a kind of physical addiction, he had hesitated, worried that he might become a burden to her, something to be pitied. When he found the nerve to tell her so, she laughed, but without derision.

He had moved in the next day, but several months elapsed before they spoke of marriage. His father's death in February 1973 had brought him home to southern Indiana for a week, and Jan had come along to offer her support. She had been dazzled by the snowfields as they motored south from Indianapolis, enchanted by the wooded hills of Forrest County when they reached his childhood home. A lifelong California girl, she fell in love with winter at a glance.

Anthony's sole inheritance had been an ancient house in downtown Calvary, which was the only private dwelling on a street of thriving shops. He had been startled by the offers he received from local merchants anxious to acquire more property, and he consulted Jan.

"I think you ought to sell," she said. "But first I want to show you something."

While he dealt with funeral arrangements and the details of his father's small estate, she had been scouring the county in their rental car, exploring narrow back roads, nosing into private drives. That afternoon she drove him three miles out from town on Galesburg Road and turned the rental down a gravel drive-way, coasting to a stop outside a weathered cabin crowned with snow.

"Somebody lives here," he protested.

"No. It's listed with a local realtor."

She already had the keys, and she had led him on a whirl-wind tour of the place: two bedrooms, each with an adjoining bath; a spacious country kitchen–dining room; the parlor with its massive ceiling beams and fireplace of native stone.

"Of course, it needs some work," she said when she had finished guiding him from room to room. "Especially in the basement."

"I'd need help," he told her, getting in the spirit.

"That could be arranged."

"The price—"

"Is roughly half what you've been offered for the house downtown."

Moving to a window, he spent a moment studying the trees. "I can't quite see the beach from here."

"I've seen the beach already."

"Jan—"

"I think it's time you made an honest woman of me, Mr. Patterson. Don't you?"

"Yes."

"All right, it's settled then. Just one more thing, before we go . . ."

Her hands were at his belt and he laughed, his breath a frosty plume that hung between them.

They had been married nine days later in Los Angeles, and Jan had given three weeks notice at the VA. Bundling their worldly goods into a Chevy Blazer, they took seven leisurely days to drive from L.A. to their new home in Forrest County. It was a honeymoon of sorts, and Anthony imagined he could feel his old vitality returning with each day that brought him closer to Indiana.

He loved the woods, so different from the claustrophobic, decaying forests in Vietnam. By night he was content to sit outside the house and watch the ghostly silhouettes of deer parading through the trees no more than twenty paces from the porch swing where he sat. Jan loved the forest, too. Everything was new to her, and her enthusiasm for discovery knew no bounds.

They spent a month "fixing up" the cabin, knowing that it might take years to finish off the job, before the small-town grapevine heralded construction of a local clinic. Anxious to preserve their savings, Jan secured a daytime nursing job, while Anthony began to build his reputation as an artisan. Within a year, his furniture was offered on consignment in a number of the local shops, and the money he made with his hands supplemented his disability check. Already comfortable by the end of their second year in Calvary, the Pattersons were locally considered "well-to-do."

They had postponed a family for the first four years of marriage, then spent three more years attempting to produce a child. When Jerod had arrived in 1980, he possessed his mother's golden hair and china blue eyes. He had Anthony's mouth, which would set in grim recognition of a problem to be overcome, an obstacle to be defeated. Nearly six years old, Jerod would be starting school next fall. He could already read the funnies, with a little help, and Anthony wondered how his first-grade teacher would respond when Jerod started quoting Garfield or, worse yet, *The Far Side*.

For all that they had been through, Jan knew relatively little of Anthony's time in Vietnam, and nothing whatsoever of his brief relationship with Lin Doan Kieu. Anthony meant to keep it that way if he could. He had immediately burned the snapshot and its envelope.

The nightmares had not reappeared yet, and there was hope that he might fend them off this time. He told himself the snapshot was a part of some elaborate joke. If he did not respond, the prankster would grow weary and turn to someone else. It seemed impossible that Lin was in America, that there was any danger to himself or to his family.

And yet, who else had known about his brief affair with Lin? A member of his unit? Someone from her family? Her Cholon neighborhood? And how had they obtained the photograph? *How had they found him*?

He reached the mailbox and sorted through the dozen pieces it contained. The normal bills and advertisements, junk mail— and a slim, white envelope, addressed in the same childish script. Another San Francisco postmark. No return address.

He opened the envelope slowly, as if it might explode. Reluctantly extracting a newspaper clipping, he recognized it as an obituary. Someone using a blue ballpoint pen had dated the piece in its margin: Feb. 18. He read it through twice.

LeRoy Duckworth

LeRoy Gadsden Duckworth, 39, died yesterday at his place of employment. A veteran of the United States Marine Corps, Duckworth is survived by his former wife, Yolanda Green, and by their daughter, Cecelia. No services or visitations are planned. Beamer's Mortuary is handling the arrangements. Mourners are asked not to send flowers.

The name meant nothing to Patterson, and he saw no significance in the dead man's having been a veteran. Countless men had served their time in uniform and there was nothing in the clip to indicate that the deceased had been in Vietnam. The age was right, but that proved nothing in itself.

What was he looking for? A link between Lin Kieu, the dead Marine, and his new life in Indiana? He would never find it in the brief obituary, and he was about to crumple up the scrap of newsprint, burn it with its envelope, when something stayed his hand. Irrationally, he put the clipping in a pocket of his shirt. Later he transferred it to his wallet, tucking it away behind the least-used credit cards, and he would wait. He destroyed the envelope that afternoon with other trash that had been waiting for the fire.

He would say nothing of the incident to Jan. Not yet. She was no part of what had happened in Saigon; there was no reason to disturb her with a pointless, idiotic prank.

10

LOS ANGELES

The weather in America would never cease to puzzle Tony Kieu. It had been cold and damp in San Francisco, with the chilling fog at night, but in Los Angeles the climate was more temperate. Although the sun was visible, you could not say the sky was clear. A dingy sort of haze hung over everything, and it has bothered Tony's eyes at first, until he had become accustomed to it.

Moving north on Cleveland Street, he fell into an easy stride, conserving energy, alert to every nuance of the city that surrounded him. He was an alien once more, uprooted before he had a chance to really savor San Francisco. He could not complain. The choice was his. His mission would not wait.

He had obtained a map of greater Los Angeles and a state map before departing San Francisco, picking out a general target area in advance. He shied away from public transportation on his journey south, concerned that the police might somehow find a way to trace his movements if he took the bus. Instead, he became a hitchhiker.

Securing a ride had been ridiculously easy. He had spent a quarter of an hour watching other transients, observing their techniques, before he took a place along the shoulder of Highway 101, southbound, and stuck out his thumb. Twenty minutes later he was on his way, befriended by a group of would-be rock 'n' roll stars in an ancient van. When they dropped him at an off-ramp seven miles above Salinas, bearing west toward Monterey and "bitchin' gigs," Tony had almost been sorry to see them go.

His next ride was a youngish salesman—farm equipment and supplies—who talked about his job while driving through the flat Salinas Valley. Orchards, cultivated fields, and pastured livestock flanked the road on either side and stretched away to hazy mountains that defined the valley, east and west. Regaled with agricultural statistics, Tony marveled at the quantity and diversity of food that California must produce. It made the hunger he left behind in Vietnam more painful.

The salesman dropped him in San Luis Obispo, and Tony made a meal of greasy tacos at a roadside diner. Forty minutes later he was picked up by a dour Pentecostal minister who tried to save his soul en route to Santa Barbara, leaving Tony with a pocketful of tracts and a solemn injunction to set his feet in the "One True Way." He ditched the pamphlets, having no use whatsoever for religion, and was ready with a smile when three girls in a station wagon stopped to offer him a ride.

They chattered all the way from Santa Barbara to Los Angeles, flirting shamelessly with Tony, making him uncomfortable with their easy smiles, their very presence. A tawny blonde named Sandra sat beside him in the backseat, her perfume almost overpowering, and when she spoke to him she let her warm hand come to rest on Tony's thigh. It would have been unseemly in his native land for girls to act this way with strangers, but he knew that in America such behavior was considered "sociable." They let him off near Dodger Stadium at his request, left him with a parting joke about getting to first base, which Tony did not understand. He watched them drive away and wondered at a land in which such things were possible.

He had selected Dodger Stadium deliberately. Near his destination, it would provide police with no address if Sandra and her friends reported him in days to come. With luck, they would forget him by the time the afternoon was out.

Dodger Stadium was just a quarter mile from Chinatown, a

half mile from the teeming city's Civic Center. He did not intend to stay in Chinatown this time, but he would be nearby, as would the source of information that he needed to pursue his hunt.

The local Asian ghetto was reminiscent of its counterpart in San Francisco, boasting the obligatory shops and temples, restaurants and laundries. Bounded on the north by College Street and on the south by Alpine, on the west by Yale and on the east by Broadway—yet another imitation!—L.A.'s Chinatown appeared to be a carbon copy of the neighborhood in which he had recently lived. As he moved along the crowded sidewalks, watching lights come on in restaurants and theaters that featured Chinese-language films, the young man was again acutely conscious of his *difference* from those around him. There were numerous Vietnamese in evidence, but Tony felt no kinship with them. He was a tourist, simply passing through, and this was not his home.

He compromised and found a small apartment one block west of Chinatown on Cleveland Street. It cost him three hundred dollars a month, furnished, and he was forced to pay the first and last months in advance, together with a cleaning and damage deposit that ran the total bill up to eight hundred dollars. Most of that was simply wasted, but Tony was not worried, yet, about the money. Never mind that he had no intention of remaining in the small apartment for a month, let alone two. He still had better than a thousand dollars in his jeans, and he had learned that there were ways of making more when that ran low. In any case the flat was worth it to him, symbolizing as it did his break with Chinatown, a recognition that he did not need the Asian cover anymore.

Of one thing Tony Kieu was certain now: by local standards he was white enough to "pass," and then some. Staring in the mirror, he had always previously looked for traces of his mother, but now, increasingly, he saw the hated features of his father. The eyes, more round than almond, hinted at his link to Asia rather than proclaiming it. The nose, more prominent than normally expected in an Oriental face, surmounted lips that verged on sensuous.

He meant to kill his father when they met, but other duties remained. He had responsibilities that reached beyond himself,

transcending private pain, and if he flinched from the performance of that duty, Tony knew his mission would be doomed.

The small apartment featured what the manager had called a
kitchenette—apparently referring to a hot plate, tiny sink, and
squat refrigerator roughly two feet square that occupied a corner
of the living room. He could save money, Tony thought, by
cooking in his room, but he was hungry *now*, his stomach growling and the greasy tacos long forgotten. There were restaurants
nearby, and he could shop for groceries in the morning.

Tony shrugged his army-surplus jacket on and locked the
door behind him. He was unarmed, the bolo knife pushed through
a sidewalk grating to the storm drains on his final night in San
Francisco. If they found it, which he thought unlikely, mud and
water would have cleansed the blood and fingerprints away. Not
that it mattered. Since his fingerprints were not on file anywhere,
he had no fear of being identified.

Local papers had been sparing in their recitation of the facts
surrounding Duckworth's death. He had been forced to search
the pages diligently, finally turning up a three-inch article with
the headline "Custodian Murdered." The piece contained a passing reference to mutilations and hinted that police had "several
leads." That much, at least, was plainly false, and Tony wondered if police were lying to the press, anxious to appease the
public. There might well be other stories in the days to come,
but Tony had no time to waste. He clipped a small obituary,
leaving out the sketchy article describing the cause of Duckworth's
death, and mailed it first thing in the morning on his way to
Highway 101.

Despite his hunger Tony did not turn toward the familiar
sights and smells of Chinatown. In San Francisco he had first
become acquainted with the wonders of fast food, and prior to
renting his apartment he had spied a drive-in just around the
corner. He dined that night on burgers, onion rings, and fried
burritos, washing the conglomeration down with Coca-Cola while
he watched the car hops in their skimpy uniforms enduring
suggestive comments from the mostly teenage, mostly male
clientele.

Noticing he was finished, one of the waitresses swung by his
table on her way back to the kitchen. "Anything else I can
getcha?"

He smiled contentedly, aware of the correct response.

"Not unless you're on the menu, sweetness."

Inexplicably, her face went cold. "Grow up, whydon'tcha," she suggested. She stalked away from Tony, leaving him confused.

Had he ignored some nuance in the phrasing of his compliment? Had she been subtly conscious of his *difference* from the other brash young men who patronized the drive-in?

He stood up hurriedly, anxious to be gone. The car hops were assembled at the order window, giggling among themselves, and Tony felt the sudden color flaming in his cheeks. None of them so much as glanced in his direction as he left.

He roamed through Chinatown for better than an hour, finding sanctuary there. He was a simple tourist, window-shopping with the rest, and nothing made him stand apart.

When he tired of Chinatown, he walked down Broadway to the terminus of Sunset Boulevard and headed west, examining the faces that he passed along the way. The people of the night were much the same in dress and hairstyles as those he had seen in San Francisco, but their movements seemed more urgent, the intensity suggesting that they thought this night might be their last. The open doors of nightclubs blared apocalyptic music as he passed them by, and barkers shrilly challenged him to stop and take a load off, see the girls, the boys, the show. Tony was content to move among the night people like a shadow, perfectly anonymous.

About midnight he felt tired and turned for home. He doubled back on Sunset, took a left on Hill, and walked due north until he reached the fringe of Chinatown. He was a block from his apartment building, headed west on Alpine, when he was distracted from his private thoughts by the sounds of a struggle from a nearby alley.

A woman's voice beseeched someone to relax and take it easy. A man answered, his curses slurred by drink and anger. Then there was scuffling and the sound of the impact of an open palm on flesh.

The alleyway was like an open throat, prepared to swallow Tony Kieu alive. He hesitated on the threshold of the shadows, poised to fight or flee if someone sprang upon him from the darkness. He could hear the words of the invisible combatants more clearly now.

The woman: "You don't haveta get excited, man. We're almost there."

The man: "I've fucking waited long enough."

She grew angry. "Maybe we should just forget the whole damned thing."

He was furious. "Forget, my ass. I'm getting what I paid for, bitch!"

An image came to mind of Tony's mother, kneeling at the feet of Phuong Van Minh. He stepped into the alley, following the sound of the voices to their source.

He found them huddled near a garbage dumpster halfway back, the man a hulking shadow, standing with his arms flexed like a wrestler. The "woman," Tony saw, was no more than seventeen or eighteen years of age. She stood her ground, with nowhere left to run, her back against the filthy wall. She held a shoe in one hand raised to shoulder height, the tall spiked heel her only defense.

"You like that shoe so much," the man said, "I'm gonna shove it up your ass when I get through."

"Back off, you bastard, or I swear to God I'll put your eyes out!"

Tony stumbled on a weapon, stooping to retrieve the brick before he lost the slim advantage of surprise. Too late, the big man was aware of scuffling footsteps on his flank. He turned to pierce the dark with narrowed eyes and took the brick along his hairline, staggered by the impact, crimson streamers pouring down across his face. He gasped in pain, rebounding from the garbage bin as Tony struck again and drove him to his knees.

Tony was prepared to finish it, but suddenly the girl had thrust herself between them, snarling at him, pushing him away. She hobbled on one foot with the other shoe held high, prepared to strike.

"Goddamn it, you, back off!" she hissed.

He stared at her, dumbfounded by the spirited defense of her attacker.

"I can take care of myself," she said. "I don't need anybody's help." Behind her on the ground, the man who was prepared to rape her moments earlier was whining like a puppy, one arm thrown around her legs.

"Don't let him hurt me, baby."

"No one's gonna hurt you, man. Relax." Her eyes burned into Tony's and despite the darkness he could see that they were glistening with angry tears.

"Forget it, kid," she said. "Somebody shoulda told you the Lone Ranger's dead. I hear he got AIDS."

She was deranged; he saw that now, and there was nothing he could do to help her. Tony dropped the brick and turned away without a backward glance. It was another valuable lesson to be filed away for future reference: contact with unstable strangers must be minimized and nothing volunteered at any time. Exposure jeopardized his mission.

Tony pushed his mother's image out of mind and concentrated on the sidewalk underneath his feet. It was secure, solid. It would take him where he had to go, if he had strength enough to concentrate, ignoring all diversions. It would take him to his prey.

11

Next morning Tony caught the southbound bus on Grand Avenue. The surly driver glared at him when he produced a dollar bill, pointing imperiously to a cardboard sign that demanded EXACT CHANGE ONLY. The big man drummed his fingers on the steering wheel and scowled as Tony sorted through coins in his pocket. As Tony took a seat, he felt that every other passenger was staring at him. He pressed his face against the window, studying the city that would soon become his hunting ground.

They rode through steel and concrete canyons with the buildings of glass piled high on either side. The County Courthouse on his left. Dorothy Chandler Pavilion on his right. Row upon row of office buildings, lavish stores, and multiscreen theaters—none of which advertised "Triple X" features or seemed to be Open All Nite. Tony felt he had crossed an invisible boundary to a different world from Sunset Boulevard.

He disembarked at Grand and Fifth Street, walking west for half a block to the Central Library. It was roughly twice the size of San Francisco's, but he found a detailed map inside the lobby. After only one false start, he found the reference department on his own. A young librarian pointed him toward the city directories, but he was not prepared to face the nightmare that awaited him on neatly ordered shelves.

Los Angeles, he understood at last, was more than a gigantic city crammed to overflowing with nine million souls. It was a network of communities and suburbs—some 243 of them in all—that sprawled across four counties, covering 465 square miles. The telephone directories stretched out before him in a wall of silence, daring him to seek the puny piece of trivia he required.

He started with Los Angeles proper, the White Pages, working his way through East and West L.A. before he tried a change of strategy. Retreating to a rank of vending machines in the lobby, Tony fortified himself with candy bars and a can of Pepsi before he attacked the suburban directories in alphabetical order, beginning with Alhambra. He was doggedly determined to examine Yorba Linda, if it came to that, but he got lucky. Tony had examined the directories for only eighty-six communities when he found it.

Hollywood.

He was conscious of the fact that rich Americans made motion pictures here, that actresses and actors were designated "stars" and were worshipped by their slavish public and he understood the Hollywood mystique. But presently, his mind focused on the tiny printed letters that identified his prey.

PRICE Evan . . . . . . 1330 Barton Av

He wrote down the address, including the telephone number as an afterthought. That done, he consulted the Los Angeles Yellow Pages, searching for pawn shops, and discovered that a number of them could be found on Wilshire Boulevard. Tony did not bother copying addresses, confident that he could find them tomorrow.

Afternoon was fading into early dusk as Tony reached the sidewalk, and he realized that he had spent the best part of the day inside. His search had been rewarding, but fatigue and hunger fell upon him now. It had been hours since he'd dined on candy bars, and now the growling of his stomach was distinctly audible. A sandwich shop was nearby, but Tony turned away from it, retracing his steps to the bus stop. He would celebrate this evening, before the second hunt began, with a traditional Vietnamese meal, prepared by his own hand. The grocery shops in Chinatown should still be open and would have everything he required.

Throughout the bus ride north on Grand, his mind was occupied with images of Evan Price. He had no need to scrutinize his snapshot of the enemy; he knew the face by heart. The photographs were for insurance, and they were a message to the others. None of them would understand . . . except, perhaps, his father.

Tony hoped he would. The knowledge of implacable revenge descending like a sword from heaven would destroy the soldier's will to fight before they ever met. It would make Tony's final piece of business so much easier.

But all of that lay ahead of him, and Tony cleared his mind of any thoughts beyond the here and now. He left the bus at Alpine and North Broadway, leaving metropolitan Los Angeles behind and stepping into Chinatown. Walking past the first two groceries unsatisfied with what he saw, he stopped in at the third and purchased rice, green vegetables, a pound of fish, assorted spices. Two years on the street in Bangkok and Saigon had taught him rudimentary survival skills, and while his cooking would not pass for *cordon bleu*, it was sufficient for his needs.

Four long blocks to Cleveland Street, but Tony Kieu had scarcely left the grocery when he realized he was being followed. Intuition, some sixth sense perhaps, alerted him to eyes that followed him along the sidewalk, marking every move he made, and Tony knew, without quite understanding *how*, that his pursuers would be keeping pace. He slowed deliberately, as if to window-shop, and shot a cautious glance back.

Half a block behind him two young toughs were suddenly immersed in conversation, talking with their hands, ignoring him with great determination. On the far side of the street, a third was propped against a lamppost, smoking. All three wore the nylon jackets of a local fighting gang, the Thunder Dragons.

He had seen them lounging near the grocery when he entered, garbed in sullen silence, but he had not given them a second thought. Had there been more than three? He wished now

hat he had paid attention. If there were others, if they had been
ent ahead, he might already be cut off.

He wasted no time wondering about their motives. His very
resence on the street might be enough to spark resentment, or
hey might intend to rob him. Unarmed, with a thousand dollars
n his pocket, Tony was an easy mark, but if they meant to take
his money, they would have to fight.

He passed a gift shop with swords and ornate razors in the
window, but he did not stop. If they attacked him, Tony would
ely on speed, evade them if he could. It would be suicide to
orce a confrontation when the numbers were against him. Better
o escape, if possible, and avoid the neighborhood in the future.

Three blocks, and he was bearing west on Alpine, almost
clear of Chinatown, when Tony heard them closing in. He
started walking faster, feigning nonchalance until he spied a
break in traffic and abruptly crossed the street. Behind him,
Tony heard a muffled curse, drowned out by blaring horns as his
pursuers followed.

Two blocks. Would they dare follow him to his apartment
building? Or would they abandon the pursuit when he was out of
Chinatown, beyond their turf? A narrow side street opened on
his right and Tony took it, opting for the shortcut. After traveling
less than fifty feet, he realized he had made a serious mistake.

Three youths in matching nylon jackets waited for him,
standing shoulder to shoulder across the sidewalk. Behind him,
he could hear the others drawing closer. He was trapped. The
tallest of the three in front of him stepped forward.

"You in a hurry, man?"

"I'm going home."

"You must be lost. This street belongs to us. You gotta pay
a tax to walk through here."

He was familiar with the system. In Saigon and Bangkok
fighting gangs had extorted money from the merchants on "their"
streets. He understood the way these young men operated, how
they thought, but he was not inclined to confront them at the
moment.

"I understood that streets were free for use by everyone," he
said.

The tall boy scowled at Tony, eyes invisible behind oversize
sunglasses. "Man, you must be F.O.B."

Behind him, one of the pursuers echoed, "F.O.B. He's gotta be."

"If you will please excuse me . . ."

"Sure, man, we'll ex*cuse* you. But you gotta pay your tax before you go."

He saw that it was hopeless. Though they might be satisfied with pocket change, once they saw the roll of bills he carried, they would want it all. Aware that he would have to fight, he chose his moment, smiled again, and hurled his bag of groceries at the tall boy's face.

They closed on him immediately as their leader ducked a spray of flying rice and vegetables, losing his balance, going down on hands and knees. He came up cursing, but the others were circling Tony like a pack of hungry dogs.

The danger lay behind him, first, and Tony spun in that direction, kicking out with all his strength, his heel connecting with a kneecap. Bleating out in pain, a youth staggered and fell, his place immediately taken by another, who threw a lighting jab at Tony's face.

The knuckles grazed him as he ducked and counterpunched. The stiffened fingers of his right hand sank to the second knuckle in the solar plexus of his enemy. Untutored in the martial arts, he knew enough about survival on the streets to fight effectively, no quarter asked or granted, but the odds were against him here.

A forearm slammed across his shoulders, and he staggered into a looping blow that opened up one eyebrow in a bloody gash. The impact drove him to his knees. Tony knew that he was finished even before the boots began to hammer him from every side. He knew that they could kill him if they wanted to, and no one on the street would intervene.

And still he fought. When one of his assailants stepped in close to kick him in the ribs, he grabbed the denim-covered legs and threw his weight against them, bringing the street thug down with an awkward rolling tackle. He could see astonishment behind the young man's eyes, and every ounce of Tony's anger, every trace of hatred trapped inside him, was directed toward that face. His fingers locked around the screaming throat. If they killed him now, Tony would be satisfied that he had taken one of them at least.

A solid blow behind the ear stunned Tony Kieu but did not

knock him out. He was conscious of the boots that drummed against his back and ribs and thighs. Desperate hands pried his fingers loose and saved his adversary's life with seconds to spare. They turned out his pockets and he recognized the whistle of appreciation when they found his bankroll.

"Hey, the fucker's loaded."

"Lemme have it."

"Fuck you, man. I found it."

They began to fight among themselves, forgetting Tony. Only one of them remained beside his prostrate form, a thin young man who held one hand against his throat and spoke in rasping whispers.

"*Our* street, man."

Kicks and curses alternated as a kind of punctuation.

"*Our* street, motherfucker. *Ours!*"

12

"Hey, man, are you all right?"

The voice was distant and distorted by the pain inside his skull. Someone was shaking Tony, cautiously at first, and then with more insistence when the gentle touch got no response.

"You in there, man?"

A face swam into focus, inches from his own as he regained consciousness. It was familiar to him, but he could not place it at the moment. Someone from the Cleveland Street apartment house, perhaps. A woman.

His memory returned in harsh, disjointed flashes. Fists and boots and pain exploding into darkness as the street thugs beat him, turned his pockets inside out. He tried to reach the precious oilcloth packet inside the waistband of his jeans, but cool fingers circled his wrists, restraining him without apparent effort.

"Easy, hey? You've taken quite a beating, man. No acrobatics for a while."

She crouched beside him in the alley while he tried to place her. He had seen her recently, he was convinced of it, but she had changed since then in some way he could not define. He almost had it when her voice cut through his jumbled thoughts again.

"Can you stand up? You really need a doctor."

Loud alarm bells in his mind competed with the killer headache. Doctors meant questions Tony Kieu was not prepared to answer.

"No." He feebly tried to push her hand away. "No money. Robbed."

"Well, Jesus, County General doesn't charge if you can prove you're broke. I'd say you qualify."

"No hospital."

The woman studied Tony's battered face for several moments, and she seemed to understand.

"You got a place to stay?"

"Cleveland Street."

"You live alone? No good. For all I know, you've got internal injuries or something. You really shouldn't be alone."

He tried to rise, falling back before he made it to his hands and knees. She helped him on the second try. The sidewalk tilted, but a few more seconds brought a passable return to equilibrium. The young woman stood beside him, serving as a crutch, her perfume filling his nostrils, and he recognized her now. He had seen her before in an alleyway, and she had been prepared to blind him with her shoe.

"Thank you," he said, when he felt steady on his feet.

"You're coming home with me, all right? I ought to have my head examined, but—"

"I have a room."

"On Cleveland Street, I know. Your room's not going anywhere, okay? So trust me. What've you got to lose?"

He let her slip one arm through his, guiding him along a sidewalk littered with his trampled groceries. They hobbled on for blocks that felt like miles until they reached a duplex on a darkened residential street. Propping Tony up against the door frame, the girl searched her purse for keys, and then they were inside.

She led him to the sofa. He lowered himself awkwardly onto the cushions. Tony's head was swimming, and a droning in his ears would not go away. Returning from the kitchen with a pan of water and some towels, she knelt before him, dabbing at his battered face with gentle strokes, removing grime and crusted blood.

"Hey, listen, man . . . about last night—"

"It's not important."

"I'm Wendy Nash. You got a name?"

He thought of lying to her, falling back upon his fake ID, but finally saw no point.

"Tony Kieu."

"Is that like P-Q-R?"

He spelled it for her, wincing as she cleaned the gash above his eye.

"What kind of name is that?"

"Vietnamese."

"You kidding me? I never woulda guessed."

"My father was American."

"Oh, yeah? Hey, I don't mean to pry. It's cool."

She was unbuttoning his shirt, and Tony grabbed her wrists to stop her, easing off the pressure when she winced in pain.

"I've gotta check you out, okay? I do all right with Band-Aids and Merthiolate, but broken ribs are something else. A broken rib can kill you, dig?"

He took a deep breath, held it, slowly let it out again. "My ribs aren't broken."

"Just like that?"

He tried to rise, but sudden dizziness swept over him and turned his legs to rubber. Wendy made a beeline for the kitchen, returning with a glass of amber liquid that she held to Tony's lips.

"Drink this," she ordered. "It'll help you settle down."

The whiskey burned his throat, and Tony came up spluttering for air. The second swallow was a little easier, and by the time he drained the glass a pleasant warmth was spreading out from Tony's stomach to his tingling limbs.

"You need a good night's sleep. I've got some extra sheets and things."

"Where is the bathroom, please?"

"The first door on your left. You need a hand?"

"No, thank you."

But he did, and Wendy helped him off the sofa, staying close beside him as he tottered to the bathroom door and pushed it shut behind him. Tony's bladder felt as if it might explode; he urinated long and loudly, embarrassed and vaguely aroused by the thought of Wendy standing just outside the door. When he was finished, Tony spent a moment before the mirror, deciding that it might have been a great deal worse.

Clean sheets, a pillow, and a lightweight blanket were waiting for him on the couch when he returned. Wendy had shed her knee-length coat, revealing a sheer halter top and thigh-high leather skirt with dark net stockings underneath. The spike-heeled shoes she wore were only too familiar from their first encounter.

"Get some sleep," she said. "I'll see you in the morning."

"Why are you doing this?"

She shrugged uneasily. "I've always been a sucker for a stray. Or maybe I was wrong about the Lone Ranger. Could be he was just out of town for a while."

Tony woke next morning to the smell of eggs and bacon cooking in the kitchen. Sitting up was painful, but he managed. He was on his feet when Wendy emerged from the adjacent kitchen dressed in a T-shirt and faded jeans. Her breasts were small and well-proportioned, and the denim fit her like a second skin. Her face was not made up, and her streaked blond hair was tied back in a ponytail that emphasized her youth.

"I hope you're hungry."

"Yes. Thank you."

"You like 'em scrambled? Any way I try, they come out scrambled when I'm finished."

"I like scrambled," Tony answered, not having any idea what it meant.

"You've still got time to catch a shower, if you want."

A see-through bra and pair of black lace underpants were hanging on the bathroom towel rod, but Tony worked around them. Emerging from the shower clean and more or less refreshed, he stood before the mirror once again, examining the patchwork of his face and torso. He would live, but it would be some time before he could play pretty boy around the local gay bars. After his encounter with the Thunder Dragons, he had forty-seven cents, the snapshots wrapped in oilcloth, and the documents that named him Vincent Tandy. He would need more cash, soon, if he was to pursue the hunt. Rummaging through pockets, he discovered that the slip with Evan Price's address was gone, but Tony had not forgotten 1330 Barton Avenue.

Wendy was putting breakfast on the table when he emerged from the bathroom, damp hair slicked back from his face and plastered against his skull. "You look like Rudolph Valentino," she said, smiling in a way that let him know a compliment had been intended.

"What is F.O.B.?" he asked, when he was nearly finished with his eggs and bacon.

"What?"

"The boys who robbed me called me F.O.B. What does it mean?"

"Oh, yeah. It's like a nickname that they use for greenhorns. Fresh off the boat."

He had been right. The Thunder Dragons had discerned his *difference*.

"You're looking better," Wendy told him. "Well, the bruises might look worse, but that's a good sign, really. In a few more days you'll be as good as new."

"I cannot afford to pay you."

"Pay for what? You helped me out with Captain Hormones. Call it square."

"He was a friend of yours, this captain?"

Wendy shook her head. "He was a john." She saw incomprehension on his face. "A trick, okay? A *customer*."

When Tony looked across the breakfast table now, he saw his mother, young as she had never been within his memory.

"That freaks you out?" she asked. "I'm self-employed: no pimp. A lot of ladies working on the streets today will tell you that they're waiting for a movie break. Guys, too. It's all a crock, you know? I'm in the life three years come April, and I've never seen a hooker make it in the reels. Not once. The hard-core pros can't even make it into skin flicks these days. Too much amateur competition from the suburbs."

She hesitated, drained her coffee. "Do I shock you?"

"No."

For just an instant, Tony thought his answer might have disappointed her. Her face went blank, and then the smile came back by slow degrees, a little tentative around the edges. For no particular reason he told her briefly of his life in Saigon and his mother's death, omitting anything that might have hinted at his mission in America. When he was finished, Wendy Nash regarded him with something very much like awe.

"You traveled all this way alone? How come?"

"I have no life in Vietnam," he told her simply. "I am half American. My home is here now."

"But you're still illegal, right? Hey, I don't care. There's more illegals in L.A. than anywhere, I guess. I read somewhere we've got a million from Mexico alone. Throw in the Cubans, Haitians, Nicaraguans—Jesus, half the town's illegal."

Tony pushed away his empty plate. "You have been most generous. If there is any way I can repay your kindness—"

"Wait a second, where's the fire? You're leaving?"

"Yes."

"Just because you're feeling better doesn't mean you're out of the woods," Wendy said. "I mean, suppose you have some kinda relapse when you're home alone? You haven't got enough bread left to buy yourself a hot dog."

"I will find a job."

"Like *that*? Let's face it, Tony, you look like the poster child for hit-and-run, you know? You want a decent job, you're gonna have to get yourself in shape."

"I have a place to rest."

"Okay. And food? I noticed that the Dragons did a tap dance on your groceries last night."

He knew where she was headed, and his mind was both attracted and repelled by the idea.

"I cannot stay here."

"Give me one good reason."

"It would shame you."

Wendy stared at him, dumbfounded for a moment, then she giggled to herself. "You're worried about my reputation? That's a classic."

"It would not be seemly."

"Maybe not, but it would sure as hell be practical."

Attraction slowly triumphed over indecision, and he finally agreed to stay with Wendy for a few more days, until he was presentable enough to find a job.

Toward evening, Wendy disappeared into the bedroom to ready herself for work. If Tony had not been prepared, he would scarcely have recognized the end result. The ponytail was gone, replaced by flaxen curls that fell about her shoulders. Her eyes and lips were painted; there was glitter on her cheeks and in her cleavage, which a low-cut mini-dress exposed. Her legs were bare, her slender ankles sheathed in high-topped boots. The cut and the sheer material of Wendy's dress led Tony to believe that she was wearing nothing underneath.

Another image of his mother came to mind, impossible to shake. He pictured Wendy "working," and he was embarrassed for her, even as he was aroused.

"I'll probably be late," she said. "Don't wait up. You need more rest."

"Okay."

He watched her through the window, walking south toward Sunset Boulevard, four blocks away. Within a moment she was lost to sight, and Tony pulled the curtains shut against the creeping darkness.

He washed the day's accumulated dishes, dried them, and replaced them in the cupboards. Afterward he made himself a sandwich and ate standing up, over the sink. Confused at first by *TV Guide*, he switched the television channels aimlessly until he found a Western under way. He recognized the story from his long-ago school days: it was about the cavalry and Indians. Outnumbered white men poured rapid fire from never-empty weapons into screaming ranks of savages intent upon assisting in their own annihilation.

Tony was nodding as the credits rolled across a body-littered battlefield, and he went to fetch his sheets and blankets. Wendy kept them in her bedroom closet, and Tony hesitated for a moment on the threshold. He entered cautiously.

Perfume and cosmetics mingled with another, more disturbing, scent that he could not define. Her queen-size bed was still unmade, and he imagined he could see the outline of her body on the sheets. The closet held a staggering array of clothing, jeans and T-shirts on the left, assorted dresses—Wendy's working clothes—on the right. He counted thirteen pairs of shoes and wondered how such opulence was possible. His mother, in similar circumstances, had sometimes been without the rent for their apartment in Saigon, and Lin Kieu's wardrobe had consisted of three dresses, carefully repaired whenever they were torn by eager, drunken hands.

Without disturbing them, he felt the soft material of Wendy's dresses, nervous fingers sampling silk and satin, velvet and velour. Inside the closet Wendy's scent was overpowering, and Tony Kieu imagined he could hear the whisper of expensive fabrics over flesh.

Breaking the spell, he pulled his bedding down, retreating to the sofa where he lay in darkness, waiting for his mind to clear. His thoughts were jumbled and confused; he had revealed his true name to a stranger, placed himself entirely in her hands, and yet he felt secure for the first time since he landed in America. He was aroused by Wendy Nash and simultaneously sickened by his knowledge of the life she led. His sense of urgency about the hunt had slackened, and Tony found that to be the most distressing fact of all.

He told himself that he was merely groggy from his injuries; when he recovered fully, he would find the old vitality restored, his deep rage intact. The time he spent with Wendy would be a simple respite from his private war. When it was time for him to go, she would not hinder him in accomplishing his mission.

Tony came awake in darkness, without being conscious of the fact that he had slept. A sound had roused him, someone moving in the room, close by. He sat up on the sofa, groping blindly for the bolo knife, remembering too late that he was unarmed. Braced to spring upon his enemy, he recognized the scent of Wendy's perfume.

"I didn't mean to wake you. Sorry."

"It's all right." His heart was hammering against his ribs, and Tony wondered whether she could hear it.

"See you in the morning."

He was awake before her, fixing breakfast in the kitchen when she joined him, looking sleepy in her quilted bathrobe, woolly slippers on her feet.

"What are you making?"

"A surprise."

He added cheese and hot sauce to the omelette, strips of bacon on the side, and laid the plate before her. Wendy tried the eggs and smiled.

"Not bad. I didn't know you were a chef."

"When there is no one else, you learn to cook or else eat raw food."

"I guess." She ate a strip of bacon, watching Tony all the while. "Your mother cook?"

"Sometimes, but mostly rice and vegetables."

"Oh, yeah. A health food kind of thing." She used a fork to push the eggs around her plate. "My mother used to cook a lot, when she was sober. When her live-ins didn't have her on her back, they had her in the kitchen."

"Live-ins?"

"Yeah, you know . . . her boyfriends. She used to call them fiancés, but none of them were interested in getting married. When the last one started getting interested in *me,* I figured it was time to split."

"How old are you?"

She smiled. "A woman doesn't like to tell her age."

"I'm sorry."

"It's okay. Eighteen." She must have seen the disbelief in Tony's eyes. "Okay, I'll *be* eighteen in August."

"So young."

"You think so? Some days I feel like I'm ninety, goin' on a thousand."

He could think of no response and concentrated on his omlette.

"You always wear that outfit?"

Tony had worn the same blue jeans and shirt the past three days. "I have some other things at my apartment."

"We'll check 'em out today, and if they don't pass muster, we can get you something new."

"I have no money," he reminded her.

"So, you can owe me. Anyway, I had a decent night, the rent's all covered—"

Tony's silence stopped her cold. He cleared the plates away and poured more coffee. Wendy took her cup and headed for the bedroom.

"Give me ten," she said, "and we'll be on our way."

Tony was surprised to learn that Wendy had a car. It was an old Camaro, beautifully maintained, in a private garage.

She drove him to the Cleveland Street apartment, followed him inside. The furnished rooms looked dingy in comparison with Wendy's, and Tony felt embarrassed.

The shirt and jeans, identical to those he wore, did not pass Wendy's muster, but she took a fancy to his stolen pea coat. "Might as well bring everything," she said, retreating toward the door. Enchanted and confused, he dutifully obeyed.

Outside she lounged against the Camaro's fender, toying with her keys. "You wanna drive?"

He felt the color rising in his cheeks again. "I can't."

"Why not?"

"I don't know how."

"How the hell do you expect to live here if you're not on wheels?"

She drove him to Dodger Stadium. There were no games in winter, and the parking lot was a vast asphalt desert. Wendy traded places with him and talked him through the process.

"Take your time, and *stay the hell away from light poles*. Got it?"

"Got it."

Within an hour Tony was wheeling like a veteran, putting the Camaro through a chain of figure eights and driving circles in reverse. He loved it, but the thrill of motion could not hold a candle to the smile in Wendy's eyes.

They spent another twenty minutes practicing on nearby residential streets, but Wendy took the wheel for their excursion to the shopping mall. "Downtown's a different ball game," she explained.

They visited several stores where Tony tried on shirts and slacks and shoes. He would have settled gladly for a simple shirt, another pair of jeans, but Wendy was insistent that he must present a certain "image."

"Clothes make the man," she said. "Well, anyway, they *help*. And don't believe the jerks that tell you different."

He spent $250 of her money in three short hours, feeling more indebted, more dependent, by the moment. She visibly delighted in remaking him from scratch.

"You need a haircut, but we'll have to wait on that," she said. "I have to get to work."

He watched TV while Wendy showered, dressed, and made up for the streets. He tried to concentrate on the movie, which involved a giant reptile crushing Tokyo, but Tony's mind was on the night ahead and what he must do. When Wendy reappeared, a sexy waif in silk and sequins, Tony saw her off and watched from the window until she disappeared from view.

Her car keys hung from a nail beside the kitchen telephone. With the extra house key on the ring, Tony locked the door behind him when he left, emerging into semidarkness. Backing out of the garage was easy, but Tony felt a rising apprehension as he wound through residential streets, at last emerging onto Figueroa in the midst of evening traffic.

He avoided Sunset Boulevard. His map, open on the seat beside him, he did not need. He had already memorized the street names and their approximate relation to each other. North on Temple. West on Beverly. Then north again on Vine.

Barton Avenue was two blocks long. It ran from east to west, between Gower and Vine, bisected by Centro. Tony had no difficulty finding 1330. It was a private home. He found a parking place across the street and backed into it awkwardly, afraid of scratching Wendy's car. When he was reasonably squared away, he settled down to watch and wait.

The house was lighted from within, and two cars were in the driveway. Tony palmed the photograph of Evan Price, refreshing his memory as he sat waiting in the dark. He could feel his prey close by.

A quarter of an hour passed before a porch light blazed to life, and Tony slouched down in the driver's seat.

The door of 1330 opened and a tall, attractive blonde emerged. She lingered on the doorstep, saying something to someone who remained invisible inside the house. As she left, Evan Price emerged and called her back.

The years had changed him, adding lines around his eyes and silver to his hair, but there could be no mistake. He was the smiling, self-confident soldier from the photograph. Tony watched him as he slid his arms around the blonde and drew her to him for a parting kiss. They lingered, locked together for a moment, finally breaking with an obvious reluctance. She headed for her car, a sporty red convertible.

"I'll see you Saturday," she called when she was belted in behind the wheel. Tony realized now that Evan Price was not a married man. That meant his quarry would be spending time at home alone.

Tony put the car in motion and spent a few more moments

circling the neighborhood, discovering an alleyway that ran behind the homes on Barton Avenue, apparently for convenient
trash collection. Finished with his crude reconnaissance, he turned
for home . . . and was surprised to find himself considering the
teenage hooker's duplex in those terms.

He was awake when Wendy entered, lying in the darkness
with his eyes wide open, but he made no sound. She called his
name once in a whisper and was satisfied when there was no
response. He waited, lying motionless until he heard the shower
running, then sat up and swung his feet onto the floor. The
rhythmic drumbeat of his pulse was deafening, eclipsing every
other sound as Wendy turned off the shower.

He heard the door ease open though, her bare feet on the
carpet in the hallway. Thinking him asleep, she had not bothered with a robe or towel. She turned on the bedroom light. He
saw one breast in profile, the suggestion of a curly thatch below
her smooth, flat stomach, thighs and buttocks rippling with the
muscles of an athlete.

Wendy turned to glance across her shoulder. With the light
behind her, Tony could not see her eyes, but he could *feel* them.
Cringing, frightened that she would be angry if she caught him
watched her, he didn't move. He held his breath, afraid to
exhale, and his lungs were burning by the time she finally closed
her bedroom door.

Five days later, on Sunday, Wendy rose late, informing Tony
that she would not work that evening. He was relieved, for
reasons that he could not explain, and he insisted on preparing
dinner. He drove her to Chinatown where they bought the ingre-
dients for the dishes Tony had in mind. Wendy seemed to enjoy
herself, and Tony matched her smile for smile, but he was
constantly alert for roving members of the Thunder Dragons.
When they started home, with Tony at the wheel, he felt relief
and disappointment. They were safely out of hostile territory, but
he almost wished he had confronted his enemies.

Wendy loved the meal and the wine, and when they finished
it was late. Tony piled the dishes in the sink and promised he
would deal with them tomorrow, when his stomach was not quite
so full. She brought his sheets and blankets from the bedroom,
left them on the sofa.

"You have everything you need?"

He nodded yes.

Wendy stood with eyes downcast. "I thought you might be tired of sleeping on the couch."

He felt a sudden pang of apprehension. "Do you wish me to go?"

"Are you for real?" She smiled, then sobered. "Never mind. It was just a thought. G'night."

Bewildered, Tony waited for the bedroom door to close behind her before going for a shower. As he stood beneath the spray and soaped himself, he wondered if somehow he had overstayed his welcome.

He did not hear the opening or closing of the bathroom door. Surrounded by the hissing water, lost in thought, he jumped as Wendy pulled the shower curtain back and stepped inside to join him. She was sleek and naked.

She did not speak. She took the soap from Tony's hand and languidly began to wash herself, the froth adhering to her breasts and clinging in the down between her thighs. She captured one of Tony's hands in both of hers and brought it to her, using palm and fingertips to spread the lather on her body, guiding him until she felt secure enough to turn her back. He bathed her tenderly and watched her pirouette beneath the shower, rinsing every trace of lather away. Embarrassed by the thrust of his erection, he was dizzy from the shower's heat, the sudden blood-rush to his groin.

Then it was his turn, and Wendy scrubbed him with a mounting sense of urgency, her sharp nails tracing lines on his chest and stomach. Concentrating on his genitals, she soaped his shaft, ran her fingers up and down its length until he felt he would explode.

"Not yet." She stood aside to let the drumming jets of water rinse him clean.

She knelt before him in the shower, water streaming off her shoulders as she took his penis in her mouth. Tony closed his eyes, surrendering to the sensation of her lips and tongue, her teeth strategically applied. No virgin, he had played the childish sex games of the streets in Saigon, but his limited experience did not encompass anything like this, a pleasure so intense it was more akin to pain.

"Not yet," she said again, and clenched one hand around the

base of Tony's shaft, insistent pressure bringing him back from the brink like a slap in the face. She rose and drew him toward her, her shoulders pressed against the sweating tile. She slipped one arm around his neck, allowed him to support her weight as both feet locked around his hips. Her free hand found his cock and led it home.

"Inside me. Now."

They moved together, lazily at first, with greater speed as the heat between them intensified. Her flesh was like a velvet glove, enfolding Tony, milking him, and neither of them struggled to prolong the moment. Wendy was already gasping when he came, and Tony felt his knees give way beneath him, hopelessly entangled with her arms and legs as he began to slide. They ended in a crouch, Wendy straddling his hips, her teeth imbedded in his shoulder as she trembled in the fading throes of climax.

Afterward they dried each other gently, basking in the heat that they had generated in their coupling.

"I thought you might be tired of sleeping on the couch," she said again.

"I am."

13

Evan Price hung his robe on a hook behind the bedroom door. Completely naked, skin still tingling from his shower, he stretched out on the king-size mattress with a wireless remote control device on either side. One set controlled the twenty-two-inch Sony mounted on a dresser at the foot of Price's bed; the other gave commands to an Hitachi VCR and thereby fed the Sony images that dreams were made of.

Tonight, Price thought, it would be Ginger Lynn. She was his favorite actress, and he had collected half a dozen of her recent features on cassette. She might not be especially adept at the delivery of dialogue, but she delivered when it counted, and he did not watch the hard-core reels in search of overlooked Academy Award performances.

The VCR was new. He hoped to add a camera soon and maybe shoot some features of his own, if Mandy was amenable. And if she wasn't . . . well, Price had a pretty good idea that he could find another starlet when the time was right. With Mandy gone so much, she would not need to know the bedroom had been turned into a sound stage. Not unless he chose to let her see the tapes some night when they were high and he did not particularly give a shit.

This weekend she was on a layover in Sydney. Price had seen Australia, had enjoyed the beaches and the suntanned women bursting out of their bikinis, but he did not think about it often now. To think about Australia meant that he would have to think about the rest of it, and too damned much was happening in Price's present to wallow in morbid visits to the past. He had survived and learned a trade. The rest of it was bullshit, best forgotten.

Now was all that mattered, when you really thought about it. Now, and with a little luck, *tomorrow*. Evan Price was satisfied with now, the first time in his thirty-seven years that he could make that statement honestly. And for perhaps the first time in his life, he did not dread tomorrow.

In a crazy kind of way, he owed the Sony and the new Hitachi and his peace of mind to Vietnam. He had been twenty-one and terrified of combat when the draft caught up with him in 1969. You couldn't turn a television on in those days without seeing images of body bags and flag-draped coffins containing men his age and younger, coming home to stay. The junior college gig had been specifically designed to keep him out of uniform, but he had hung around the freshman courses too damned long, and a report of insufficient progress from the dean had upped his 2-S rating to a big 1-A. The "Greetings" note from Uncle Sam had hit him like a dropkick to the family jewels.

All things considered, it could have been a great deal worse. If Price had not revealed an unexpected aptitude for flying, he would almost certainly have landed in the fucking infantry with jungle lice and Charlie crawling up his ass. It had been bad enough flying med-evac, retrieving shattered bodies in dust-off operations and ferrying them back to surgeons who were waiting for a few more human jigsaw puzzles to assemble. Seven months of that and he had transferred into gunships, learning all about a different kind of terror, scanning new horizons of man's inhumanity to man.

One morning they had taken up a team of Green Berets with VC prisoners in tow. As they hovered a thousand feet above the treetops, there had been questions, which the Cong had stubbornly refused to answer. Two of them had been ejected from the chopper, screaming all the way to impact, before the third had broken down and spilled his guts. The grim inquisitors had listened, and when he finished, they had thrown him out to join his friends. No witnesses. The pilots, being soldiers and Caucasians, did not count.

Price had returned to southern California with recurring nightmares and the skills required for a commercial pilot's license. After half a dozen airlines turned him down, he got the point and started shopping locally. The charter market was a thriving business in L.A., and for the next few years he had been reasonably happy making border hops and flying losers into Vegas for the weekend. Gradually it had dawned on Price that he could make more money as a solo act instead of working on commission for a boss he rarely saw.

The start-up loan had been no problem; Price was deep enough in debt by then that *everybody* wanted him to borrow money. He had started with a Piper Cub, a rented hangar, and a cut-rate advertisement that had somehow failed to lure heavy customers. He had survived on Palm Springs junkets, flying horny kids to Catalina, barely getting by before the Cuban had dropped in one afternoon.

The Cuban called himself Herrera, and you didn't need a Ph.D. to know the name was an alias. He wore dark glasses day and night, but Price had been more interested in his car—a sleek Mercedes—and the diamonds on his hands. The hulking bodyguards required some getting used to, but Herrera came with cash in hand, and Price had never been inclined to look a gift horse in the mouth.

Three times a month on average he flew Herrera, or Herrera's friends, to Mexico, sometimes to destinations farther south. They filed a flight plan listing Ensenada as their destination, but in fact they seldom landed there, detouring along the way to *ranchos* fitted out with airstrips of their own. Price did not ask about the cargo that was loaded on those border runs; he had been paid to fly and keep his mouth shut.

Association with Herrera meant more cash on hand, and while he was not wealthy yet, Price had begun to think that he was comfortable. There were certain benefits as well. On overnight excursions his employer covered all expenses, and he had been known to spring for playmates who would entertain the staff. Sometimes, when he was feeling generous, Herrera tipped the pilot with an ounce or two of coke, enough to keep him flying high with Mandy when the leggy stewardess had time to stay and play.

Like Nam, flying for Herrera involved risks. Smuggling was relatively simple in itself, with DEA spread out so thin the narcs could never hope to cover every airstrip in the L.A. area. A bust was possible, but Price had been assured that lawyers stood by in case a beef went down. A more immediate concern was competition from Herrera's assorted rivals—especially the tough Colombians. He was familiar with the stories of their cruelty, the grisly trademark that they sometimes left upon their victims. Dubbed "the Colombian necktie," it consisted of a throat, slit open, with the tongue pulled down and out to dangle beneath the victim's chin. Price had not seen this piece of native art firsthand, but he could do without it.

He might grow wealthy with Herrera, but it never hurt to use initiative, and on a recent visit to Jalisco, Price had bought himself a kilo of cocaine. The Cuban did not seem to mind, and if he played his cards right, Price could earn his money back times ten. He needed contacts he could trust, and he was working on it a step at a time. In another year or so, Price might not be working for Herrera anymore. Hell, he might *be* Herrera.

Turning the Sony on, he keyed the VCR, fast-forwarding through credits and preliminaries to the good stuff: Ginger, kneeling on a bed, one man in front of her, another at the rear. Price never ceased to marvel at her flexibility and energy.

His erection rose before him, like a supplicant before the Sony shrine. Price took it lovingly in hand. If Mandy was available, they might have watched the film together, trying out a few of the positions on their own. They did that sometimes after snorting several lines to set the mood. The thing was, he could never concentrate on Ginger once they started, and they always ended up with static hissing at them from the television screen, as if the Trinitron were rating their performance.

Stroking, Price could feel the old excitement mounting, pressure building toward the detonation point. His free hand found the Sony's remote control, muting the sound track. Next time Ginger spoke he could imagine that her words were meant for him. She would be dazzled by his size, the jutting proof of

Evan's admiration for her talent. She would worship at his feet, a willing slave, and when her eyes rolled up in supplication, it would be *his* face she saw, *his* love she was begging for.

His heavy breathing nearly covered the subtle noise and he almost missed it. Almost.

Price released his rigid organ, killing the Sony and Hitachi with their separate remotes. His bedroom door was open. The noise had issued from downstairs. The living room; perhaps the dining room.

Price froze. *The den.*

He vaulted off the bed, erection wilting by the time his naked feet touched deep shag carpeting. His mind raced as he found the Browning automatic pistol in his nightstand drawer and eased the safety off.

It would not be Herrera. They were too tight. He had scored his recent kilo with the Cuban's blessing.

The Colombians? It seemed unlikely, but the very thought made his scrotum shrivel as he padded toward the open bedroom door. Along the way he snared his robe and shrugged it on, not bothering to tie it at the waist. It didn't matter if the prowler caught a glimpse of man's best friend; together with the muzzle of his Browning, it would be the last damned thing the bastard ever saw.

He cleared the threshold, reaching back to kill the light behind him so as not to offer his enemy a silhouette. He took the stairs with caution, hoping that the fucker had not heard him when he scrambled out of bed.

Another sound, like shifting furniture. Definitely the den this time. No doubt about it. Could the prowler have been unaware that he was home? The lights, the open bedroom door, and the sounds of Ginger humping overtime should certainly have tipped him off .. . . which meant the fucker didn't care. He was prepared for confrontation, confident he would walk away with what he came for.

And there was no doubt about the "what" in Price's mind. His kilo, the foundation of his brave new world, was tucked away inside his wall safe in the den. If someone cracked the box and walked away with his investment, he was out three thousand dollars for a start, never mind the loss of face that he would suffer in Herrera's eyes.

He thumbed back the hammer of the Browning and grimaced at the sharp, metallic sound it made. He might as well be pounding on a goddamned drum to herald his approach, but there was no reaction from the den. The prowler was distracted by his search, and that might be all the edge Price would need.

Reaching the bottom of the stairs, he high-stepped toward the den, its door ajar. He was certain he had left it closed. He held the automatic in both hands, his elbows locked, braced to take the recoil.

The thought of killing did not worry Evan Price. He had been educated for it in the military, although the opportunity had never arisen. Tonight he had the purest motive in the world— self-interest—and he would not hesitate to drop the fucker if he got a decent shot. He paused on the threshold, breathing deeply to relax.

His bare heel struck the door dead-center, slammed it back against the wall with force enough to ding the plaster there. He entered in a crouch, the Browning primed to answer any challenge with the final word. His trigger finger ached and he was trembling.

The empty room ignored him, mocking his explosive entry with silence. Stunned to find himself alone, Price doubled back to check behind the door.

Nothing.

Cautiously he moved to the closet. For a moment he felt the urge to put a bullet through the door, but common sense prevailed and he reached out to grasp the knob instead, prepared to fire if anyone sprang out at him from ambush. Flinging back the door, he got the drop on golf clubs, tennis rackets, and a hunting rifle that he had not fired in years.

Price felt embarrassed. Had his own imagination run away with him this time? The sounds that he had heard might easily have been the old house settling, and he was almost certainly mistaken when he thought that he had closed the door.

But what about the *lights*?

No way in hell would he forget the fucking lights.

Somebody had been here, and they had not emerged while he was covering the door, but where the hell could they have gone?

He eased the Browning's hammer down and crossed the

room to stand before a Norman Rockwell print. He lifted the painting down and propped it on his desk. The safe was securely locked, but had the bastard been inside? Price spun the dial, first left, then right, then left again. The door came open at his touch, and when he peered inside, he found the plastic bag intact, apparently untouched.

But what if they had switched it on him? Clever bastards did that. You heard about it all the time. There was but one way to be sure.

He set the automatic pistol on his desk and reached inside the safe. Before he had a chance to lift the bag of flake, a scuffling sound behind him froze Price in his tracks.

Oh, shit!

He dropped the baggy, spun around, one hand reaching for the gun, and found grim death advancing on him from the rear.

Needing cash, Tony had worked Sunset Boulevard by night. He preyed on solitary drunks and wasted rockers, rolling them for pocket money until he had accumulated eighty-seven dollars.

One evening he rode the bus up Wilshire Boulevard to Alvarado Street. From there he walked beneath familiar neon lights to pawn shops advertising "easy-credit loans." He toured three, examining the pistols, and was told about the mandatory waiting period that would permit police to check his record. Tony bought a twelve-inch bowie knife instead, complete with leather sheath, for thirty dollars. As an afterthought, he also bought himself a folding balisong knife for $11.95.

On Thursday, after Wendy left for work, he borrowed her car again and drove to Hollywood. This time he parked the old Camaro on a side street and walked a half block over to the alleyway that ran behind the homes facing Barton Avenue. The darkened gravel corridor was no more than two blocks long, and Tony knew precisely where to find his quarry. Twice he was surprised by dogs that hurled themselves against the wooden fences, snarling at imagined adversaries in the darkness. Tony ignored them and hoped their masters would do likewise. If police were summoned, he would have no explanation for his presence. His car might be discovered, even seized, and how would he explain all that to Wendy?

He had shared her bed for five nights running, but they made love only in the daytime, after Wendy had a chance to rest and wash away the touch of strangers. Sometimes Tony helped her bathe, but when she came home in the early morning hours, he would simply hold her while she fell asleep. He never asked about her work, her tricks, the things she did for money.

He was amazed and fascinated by the sharp duality of Wendy's character, the child who lived within the cynical woman of the streets. In quiet moments Tony looked at Wendy Nash and saw his mother as she might have been, without a child to feed, without the shame of having been abandoned by the baby's father. Other times, as Wendy regaled him with her stories of the streets, of "burns" and "rip-offs," her eyes were cold, her tongue as sharp as tempered steel. He saw another side of Lin Doan Kieu in Wendy then and knew she was doomed. . . .

He reached the gate that opened on the yard of 1330 Barton Avenue and found it locked. Certain no dog was in residence, he covered all his bets by rattling the gate softly, waiting. Tony used the time to study Price's home. It was dark except for an illuminated second-story window facing the yard.

A drive by on the street had reassured him that the woman would not be with Price tonight. Perhaps she would return in time to find the body, and he smiled to think of her reaction. She had spread her legs to please a man who had deserted wife and children in Saigon, uncaring of the misery he had caused. That she should share his punishment seemed appropriate.

Tony had no trouble climbing over the gate. A concrete path crossed new-mown grass and led him to the back door. He crouched, straining to detect any sounds that would betray an ambush, catching only muted television noises from upstairs. With his bowie knife he snapped the lock and stepped inside.

The kitchen was immaculate, likewise the living room. Upstairs the bedroom door was open, spilling light across the landing, down the stairs, but Tony made no move in that direction. Evan Price must come to him, and so he moved along the downstairs corridor until he reached the den. A glance told him this was his target's private sanctuary, his retreat, and Tony knew at once that it would also be his killing ground.

He checked the room for hiding places. The windows were locked and screened, with a three-foot drop to thorny shrubbery below. He would lose the minimal advantage of surprise if he was forced to scramble in and out through windows while his prey stood watch inside. The closet seemed too obvious, a death trap if his enemy was armed with anything more lethal than a kitchen knife.

The answer, when it came to him, was preposterously simple. Shoved against one wall was a massive desk, and he realized the spacious kneehole would accommodate him with room to spare. If Price did not immediately glance beneath the desk on entering, Tony might take his adversary unaware.

No sounds of television from the upstairs bedroom now. He moved around the den, deliberately making noise. He rolled the desk drawers in and out. Turned on the IBM Selectric. Turned it off again. He settled into Price's chair, complete with rollers, and propelled himself across the carpet, digging with his heels for traction.

Footsteps overhead. He waited, listening, imagining his enemy above him doing the same. When Price was halfway down the stairs, Tony pedaled back across the floor, slipped in beneath the desk, and pulled the chair in after him. In his hidey-hole, he drew the twelve-inch bowie from its sheath and ran his thumb along the edge, which he had honed to razor sharpness using Wendy's electric sharpener.

Price entered his sanctum like a soldier on patrol. He slammed the door wide open, entered in a crouch, a pistol in his hands. He checked the windows, searched the closet, even peered behind the open door as if a cardboard cutout of the prowler might be lurking there, pressed flat against the wall.

He did not look beneath the desk.

Instead, Price stood beside it, out of Tony's view. Tony heard Price set his pistol on the desktop. He took a painting down and propped it on the desk, directly over Tony's hideout. Soft, metallic clicks sounded, as of a locking mechanism being set or disengaged.

Price heaved a sigh of obvious relief, and Tony knew it was time to move. He shoved the desk chair back and scrambled from his niche, the bowie in his hand. Price turned from the open wall safe as Tony wobbled to his feet, reaching for the pistol as Tony struck. The keen blade opened a second narrow mouth below the one that tried, in vain, to scream.

Price staggered back against the wall, hands pressed against his throat, dark blood escaping between his fingers. He was naked underneath the robe, completely vulnerable. Tony followed up on his advantage, striking low and fast, the bowie slicing home beneath his target's sternum, pinning him against the wall.

Price took another minute and a half to die, and Tony waited, wrenching loose his blade when every sign of life had vanished from the glassy eyes. Released, Price slithered down the wall, his passage leaving rusty trails along the plaster as he crumpled in a heap against the desk. Tony took the snapshot of a smiling soldier from his pocket, tore it right across, and placed the halves in Price's upturned palm.

The open safe gave up a bag of white powder and a thousand dollars in fifty-dollar bills. The bag and currency went into Tony's pockets. He tucked the automatic pistol in his belt and returned the bowie to its sheath inside his pea coat. He could use the money for the next leg of his journey, sell the drugs for more, if necessary. There was nothing else of interest here.

The crosstown drive was uneventful, but he felt emotionally exhausted as he navigated through the evening traffic, steering clear of Sunset Boulevard. Before leaving, he had another day or two with Wendy, and Tony wondered how he would explain.

He parked her car in the garage and entered the apartment through the kitchen. Replacing her car keys on their hook, he went to the living room, found the light switch, flicked it on . . . and froze. Wendy was waiting for him on the couch. She stared at the blood that stained his shirt.

"I think we need to have a little talk," she said.

14

SOUTHERN INDIANA

The dreams were coming back. Three nights running he woke before dawn, sweat-drenched despite the freezing temperature outside. The nightmares had been mercifully obscure, but they had left him with headaches, a sour stomach, and transient paranoia—all the classic symptoms of battlefield stress. Without remembering the details, he knew precisely what was happening inside his mind when he lay down to sleep.

But on the fourth night, Anthony remembered everything.

The third envelope had turned up in his mail box a week ago, postmarked Los Angeles. Another obituary, heralding the death of yet another stranger. Evan Price, age thirty-seven. Found dead at home. No services and no survivors.

The dead man was a U.S. Army veteran, but the name meant nothing to Anthony Patterson. How many thousands served their time in Vietnam? It would be folly to expect that he should recognize two names, selected randomly in California, miles and years removed from his involvement in the war.

The latest envelope informed him his pen pal had moved south, but otherwise it offered no useful clues. A date, March 5, was written in the margin of the clipping, indicating Price had died or had been discovered on the fourth. The date held no significance for Patterson, and he had finally given up playing Sherlock Holmes. He burned the envelope and clipping, as he had the other two, and tried hopelessly to put the matter out of mind.

If Jan had noticed anything unusual in his behavior, she kept it to herself, but he could not go on deceiving her for long. She knew him better than he knew himself, had seen him at his worst, when Nam was with him every moment of the day and night. She was bound to notice something soon, no matter how he tried to hide his apprehension. He imagined she was watching him already, at the breakfast table, as he worked around the house.

He fired up the chain saw and let it idle for a moment, breathing in the sharp exhaust fumes. Though they were not short of wood, Anthony had volunteered to cut some anyway and thus be alone. The sudden urge for solitude was troubling. In the old days, in and out of the VA, he was obsessed with privacy—an obsession that had eased as his relationship with Jan grew stronger. In thirteen years since they had married, Anthony had never felt the burning need to be away from her.

Until today.

He braced one foot against the log, let the saw bite deep, and closed his eyes against the spray of chips and dust that blew back in his face. The engine's grumble escalated to a scream as he depressed the trigger. He felt the vibration in his arms and shoulders. With his eyes shut tight, ears deafened by the whining saw, he might have been a world away.

He might have been in Saigon.

In his dream he walked the Cholon streets and searched for Lin Doan Kieu. She called his name but would not show herself. Though he was desperate to find her, the dream was always well advanced before he recognized the source of mounting urgency.

Cholon was burning.

In the middle distance he could hear the rattle of small-arms fire. He knew that Charlie would be coming for him soon, once all the forward outposts had been overrun, and he was nearly out of ammunition. If he did not find Lin before the shock troops overtook him, it would all have been for nothing.

After a sudden movement in a shop downrange, Patterson

abandoned caution, calling out to Lin and sprinting down the middle of the blasted street with flames on either side. Behind him, other voices sounded the alarm as he was sighted by the enemy, but Patterson ignored them, ducking through an open doorway into smoky darkness.

Stairs rose before him in the murk, ascending to a second floor. Lin called to him from the darkness overhead, a plaintive, childlike voice. Patterson began to climb. His M-16 was growing heavy and he let it drop, uncaring, heard it clatter on the stairs behind him as it fell.

Smoke shrouded the upper floor. He called to Lin, his own voice baffled by the walls, and felt a surge of panic when she did not answer him at once. He called again and heard her this time, as she spoke in a whisper.

"Tony?"

Stepping from the shadows like a wraith, Lin stood before him. She was painfully thin, almost skeletal, the tattered silk dress hanging from her shoulders like a shroud. The hands that she stretched out to him had bony fingers, broken nails. Her eyes were deeply sunken, cheeks devoid of flesh, so that her face took on the aspect of a skull.

"Tony, stay with me this time."

Heart hammering against his rib cage like a captive animal, he took a long stride toward her, hands outstretched, and then the rotten floor gave way beneath him. Pinned at the knees, he struggled savagely to free himself, unmindful of the rusty nails and splintered boards that tore his flesh. One leg was almost free when a commotion on the stairs distracted him.

A dozen VC burst into the room, all jabbering at once, gesticulating with their weapons. Lin was speaking to them in Vietnamese, pleading for a second chance. Her supplications fell on deaf ears. A dozen automatic weapons roared as one. Converging streams of fire propelled Lin Kieu backward into darkness.

Now the Cong surrounded Patterson, their AK-47s leveled at his face. He felt absurdly small, a midget trapped by angry giants, and the more he fought to free himself, the deeper the nails and jagged slivers gouged into his legs.

"Now, you," the leader of the strike team said, and somehow Patterson was not surprised to hear himself addressed in English.

He gave another violent heave and felt the rotting boards yield. In desperation, nothing left to lose, he hammered at them with his fists . . . and suddenly the floor collapsed. He was in free-fall, spinning dizzily, the rattle of the firing squad above him fading into distance, lost. He fell—

—and hit the stony ground with all the grace of laundry sliding down a chute. He was amazed the fall had not awakened him. It was an axiom of clinical psychology that falling dreams invariably terminate before the point of impact. But not this dream. He knew that he was still asleep because Lin Kieu stood over him, her body sieved by automatic fire, a long knife in her hand.

"You left me," she declared, and there was nothing he could say in self-defense before she fell upon him, hacking at his face.

That woke him, and he just had time to bite the scream off, swallow it before it could escape. As panic faded, guilt crept in to fill the void.

You left me.

It had not been his fault. He had not planned to get himself blown up. The years in VA hospitals had not been part of any scheme to get away from Lin. He had enjoyed their time together, reveled in the passion they had shared, but he had been too young to think in terms of a lifetime commitment. He had not seduced her with promises of anything beyond the moment. There could certainly be nothing left between them now after all this time.

The cryptic mailings made no sense. Lin's photo might have been intended as a warning, a reminder, even as a threat. Of blackmail? Of revenge?

Some days he managed to forget about the puzzle, put it out of mind for hours at a time. The workshop kept him busy, and he had a list of orders to be filled by early March. And yet the intricacy of his work was not enough to keep Lin's face from drifting into view at unexpected moments, flanked by the obituaries of two men Patterson had never known.

There was no point in calling the police, since he had not been overtly threatened. There was no crime in mailing snapshots or obituaries to total strangers, and the Forrest County sheriff's office had more pressing matters to contend with than a run of junk mail.

He would tough it out, and he would keep it to himself for now. Jan had her hands full with Jerod and the household. He could share the riddle with her later, if he thought it necessary. In the meantime . . .

Shutting down the saw, he straightened slowly, wincing as the muscles in his back began to cramp. Ears numbed by the incessant growling of the saw, he nearly missed the sound of footsteps closing on his flank. A snapping twig was all that saved him, triggering the ancient combat reflex in his mind.

He dropped the chain saw, pivoting into a crouch, knees cracking as he found the hatchet, cocked his arm—and froze. Across the clearing, Jerod stared at him wide-eyed, rooted in his tracks. Jan stood behind him, one hand on the boy's shoulder, the color draining from her face.

"I didn't mean to scare you, Daddy."

"It's all right. I'm sorry." Putting down the ax, he crossed the little clearing, kissing Jerod first, then Jan. Her lips were cold.

"It's getting late," she said.

He had lost track of time, unaware of shadows closing in among the trees. It would be dark soon, and the clouds were threatening another snowfall. They had come to fetch him home, and he had treated them like enemies.

"I'm sorry, Jan," he said again.

"Come on."

He laid a fire with Jerod's help while Jan was busy in the kitchen. Supper was her famous stew, a rich concoction thick with meat and vegetables, hot enough to light a fire inside regardless of the weather. Afterward he helped Jan with the dishes and they read to Jerod from his favorite storybook before they packed him off to bed.

"I must be getting old," Jan said, emerging from the bathroom in her quilted robe, a towel wound turbanlike around her head. "I can't believe he's starting school this fall."

She pulled the towel away, began to brush her hair, still damp and glossy from the shower.

"You look pretty good to me," he said.

"You're prejudiced."

"I am?"

"You'd better be."

"Okay."

"I didn't mean to startle you this evening," she said.

"Forget it."

She set the brush aside and considered her reflection in the mirror. "Two gray hairs this week. That proves it."

Kneeling at her side, he slid an arm around her waist. "I've got a thing for older women."

"Pervert." But she had to catch her breath as he nibbled on her earlobe, nuzzling the soft curve of her neck. "That's nice."

He slipped his hand inside her robe and cupped one pliant breast, the nipple coming to attention in his palm. He teased it with his thumb and felt her shiver at his touch.

"You're not so old."

"I'm feeling younger all the time."

His hand slid between her thighs until she clamped her legs around his wrist and held it captive.

"Now I've got you."

"Not a chance. The hand is quicker than the eye."

"You'll have to prove it, mister. Oh . . . oh, yes . . . right there." He brought her to the edge, then drew his hand away. "Where are you going?"

"Bed. We old folks need our sleep."

"Too late." She followed him, her robe forgotten on the chair.

Much later, when her cries had given way to rhythmic breathing and she slept within the cradle of his arms, he lay awake and listened to the wind that played around their house, beneath the eaves. In his imagination there were voices, whispering beyond the windowpane, but they were still too faint, too far away, and he could not make out their words.

15

LAS VEGAS, NEVADA

Tony stood on Fremont Street, beneath a giant cowboy with a nervous arm. The cowboy waved incessantly to passersby, his smile unwavering, a cigarette protruding from the corner of his mouth. Across the street his giant girlfriend perched atop the roof of the Las Vegas Club, legs crossed demurely, waving back. Beneath the neon giants pedestrians flowed up and down the street like rivers of ants, the banks of colored lights imparting crazy hues and shadows to their faces.

A Friday night on Fremont. Locals called it Glitter Gulch, an apt description for the eight short blocks in the heart of town. From where he stood, a glance to the right took in the Fremont, Golden Nugget, and the Sundance hotel-casinos. To his left, the Mint, the Union Plaza, the Las Vegas Club, and half a dozen smaller gambling dens spilled light and noise into the street through perpetually open doors.

Traffic on Freemont was bumper-to-bumper. Tony crossed to the north side in front of a blonde in a new red convertible, catching a smile as he passed. She reminded him vaguely of Wendy, and that made him lower his eyes as a dull pang of guilt pierced his chest.

He had lied to her back in Los Angeles when she had caught him returning from Price's apartment. Unable to explain away the blood that had soaked through his shirt, he confessed to the murder, accusing the pilot of raping his mother in Saigon years earlier. He was astonished when Wendy accepted the story. She was worried, but she did not denounce him or order him out of her home. She had warned him the pistol was traceable, and he had promised to throw it away, though he had no intention of doing so. When he had shown her the money and drugs, Wendy's eyes had gone wide with amazement.

"That's coke," she informed him after tasting a few grains of powder from the fat plastic bag. "I'm no judge, but I'd guess that it hasn't been stepped on. He just had this lying around?"

"In the wall." Tony wondered why someone would step on narcotics.

"That figures. A kilo like this, cut and packaged, might bring fifty K on the street."

"What is fifty K?"

"Fifty thousand dollars."

"You can do this?"

"Not here. Someone loses a gold mine like this and they look for it, dig? Never mind that the holder's on ice. He'll have partners, and they'll want their piece."

He knew what to say next: "Would we have better luck in Las Vegas?"

She smiled. "We just might."

She had been all for packing and leaving that night, but he stalled her, explaining that he was concerned about witnesses, worried he might have been seen as he left Price's home. Wendy argued that it was the best time to leave, while detectives were still picking over the scene, but he hung on until Sunday evening, when telecasts first carried news of the murder in Hollywood.

In the morning while Wendy was packing, he walked to the corner and purchased the *Herald-Examiner*. He clipped the obit for Price. After writing the date in the margin, he sealed the clip in his third prestamped envelope, wrote the address with meticulous care, and consigned his message to a curbside mailbox. Wendy was already waiting for him when he got back to the duplex, her belongings crammed into the trunk of the Camaro.

"The place came furnished," she informed him. "I'm paid up through March, but what the hell, I'm ready for a change."

"Me, too." It would be good to have her with him in Las Vegas, but he dared not think of what came afterward, when it was time to move again.

Despite his reading, nothing had prepared him for the desert. Vast and empty, desolate beyond belief. The only "trees" were stunted, twisted things, with bristling trunks and leaves like bayonets. The smaller shrubs were so impoverished that in places they had pulled up roots and rolled across the highway in the face of arid, driving winds. Where sandy topsoil had been blown away, the earth was cracked and peeling like a mummy's flesh.

They took turns driving, listening to hard rock on the radio, and stopped for lunch in Baker, where the several restaurants were all controlled by someone known as Bun Boy. Tony took the wheel at Baker, pushing on another fifty miles before he felt a sudden urge to stop the car. Beside him, Wendy had been dozing, but she awoke as Tony killed the engine.

"What's the matter?"

"Nothing."

"Do you feel okay?"

"I'll be right back."

He walked a hundred yards into the desert, feeling Wendy's eyes upon him. When the car had dwindled in the distance, Tony stopped and looked around, examining the soil, the thorny shrubs, the crystal sky. High up, a thousand feet or more above his head, a vulture rode the thermal updrafts, circling lazily in search of carrion. Around his feet, ants made their endless circuit of the stones and sage, retrieving fallen seeds or dead insects.

Tony realized that he was not surrounded by a wasteland after all. The desert was alive; its denizens performed their survival rituals upon a hostile stage. A lizard, squat and thorny as the stunted Joshua trees, emerged from the concealment of a stone and snapped up the ants as they paraded past, oblivious to sudden death beyond the range of their myopic eyes.

He watched the shadow of a cloud gliding eerily across the desert floor. It reached him, swallowed him alive, passed on, and Tony was amazed to feel a spattering of rain against his upturned face. Around him, scattered drops left tiny dust rings

on the soil, evaporating even as he watched. Reluctantly, aware
that he was wasting time, he turned back toward the car.

"Is everything all right?"

"I'm fine," he said.

"It's something, isn't it? I mean, I couldn't live out here, the
way some people do . . . but still, it's something."

"Yes."

They reached Las Vegas in the afternoon, and Wendy guided
him along The Strip, past the palacial hulks of grand hotel-
casinos, each with names that conjured up some erotic fantasy.
The Tropicana. Caesars Palace. Stardust. Silver Slipper. The
Flamingo. Miles of neon tubing, tinted glass and tile.

"Hey, this is nothing," Wendy told him. "We'll come back
and check it out tonight when all the lights are on. You won't
believe it."

They had bypassed the great hotels, proceeding north along
Las Vegas Boulevard toward downtown, skirting the casino
center as they searched for inexpensive lodgings. Wendy chose a
place on Bridger where the weekly rates were reasonable by Las
Vegas standards, and they settled in a cubicle constructed of
cinder blocks. She assured him that the place was temporary, but
he did not mind. In Tony's scheme of things the *town* was
temporary. He saw no need for shelling out a deposit on an
apartment.

That night they drove along The Strip and visited a number
of the swank casinos. Tony was intrigued at first by all the lights
and noise, the constant action, but he gradually understood that
all of the casinos were essentially the same. One boasted circus
acts around the clock, another featured Roman art and architec-
ture, yet another housed a shopping mall beneath its roof—but in
the ways that mattered they were all identical. Their restaurants
and shops and lounge shows were designed to cycle players past
the slot machines and tables where their money would be swiftly,
systematically, appropriated by the house. Tony was amazed
that seemingly intelligent Americans would travel here from
every corner of the nation to be fleeced by experts.

Shortly after nine o'clock they drove back to their digs and
parked the car, then walked two blocks to Fremont for a bargain
meal of steak and lobster at El Cortez.

"It's gonna take some time to move the coke," Wendy said,

when they were halfway through the tossed green salad. "I can't just walk in someplace and drop that baggy on the table."

"All right."

He did not care about the drugs, except that the money from their sale would keep him on the road to other cities, other targets. In the meantime he had cash enough for food and lodging. If Wendy moved the drugs, he was prepared to give her half the money—more if she received enough to send him comfortably on his way. He had not yet decided if he would ask Wendy to accompany him beyond Las Vegas when his task was finished there.

"I'm gonna try and get a job," she told him, while they waited for dessert.

"A job?"

"They've got some heavy escort services around this town, you know? I could be picking up some money here, instead of wasting time."

"What is an escort service?"

"You know . . . like L.A., except it's all computerized in Vegas. Operators take the calls and fix the dates. They tell you where to go and take a flat base rate. The gravy's for the girl."

"A pimp."

"A business."

"We have money. You don't need to work."

"I *want* a job, okay?" She looked disgruntled as the apple pie and ice cream finally arrived. "Besides, the guys who run these services have juice, you understand? If they can't move that kilo for us, no one can."

In their motel room he riffled through the yellow pages of the telephone directory while Wendy took a shower. There were advertisements for a dozen different escort services with names like Dreamdates, Satin Touch, and Swinging Cindy's. All of them accepted major credit cards, and several promised "satisfaction guaranteed." Accompanying photographs depicted women posing, kneeling, offering themselves in postures that left little doubt about the services available on such "distinctive dates."

Even though the room was air-conditioned Tony's cheeks burned and he had a sour taste in his mouth. He did not analyze the feeling or understand why he felt ill when he imagined

Wendy as one of the girls in the advertisements. He cared for her, but the decision was her own.

He closed the phone book, then reopened it to the white pages, working backward through the Cains and Butlers, Browns and Briscoes, till he found the name he sought. Mitchell Breen lived on Pennwood Avenue. Tony dialed the number, hoping Wendy would not catch him on the phone. He waited through five rings. A female voice came on the line.

"Hello?"

"Is Mitchell Breen at home?"

"Who's calling, please?"

Thinking fast, Tony fell back on his fake I.D. "Vince Tandy. I knew Mitchell in the army."

"Oh . . . I'm sorry, he's not here right now, but if you want to leave a message—"

"No. We haven't seen each other since the war, and I was hoping to surprise him."

"Sure, I understand. You might try catching him at work."

"Where's work?"

"The Horseshoe, down on Fremont. Mitch deals twenty-one five nights a week. You oughta check it out."

"I will. And thank you."

"Hey, no sweat. You sure you don't want me to tell him you're in town?"

"I want to see his face when he finds out."

"Okay. Maybe I'll see ya later."

Tony cradled the receiver. *Maybe*. Breen was his intended target in Las Vegas, and he had no quarrel with the soldier's woman.

His quarry worked close at hand. The Horseshoe was in Glitter Gulch, a five-minute walk from the motel, and while Tony was not quite sure what "twenty-one" was, he knew any game with dealers must involve a deck of cards. Despite the size of the casino, it should not be difficult to locate Breen and watch him from a distance, get to know the man before he made his move.

An obese Hispanic woman perched precariously on a stool to Tony's left, feeding three slot machines at once, while her companion, an emaciated Oriental man, stood back and watched, a dazed expression on his face. Close by, an ancient crone was talking to her pet machine, cajoling it to loosen up and pay. She wore a pair of leather work gloves to protect her hands from blisters.

Tables on the gaming floor were delegated to specific games, with dice and roulette off to one side and kidney-shaped card tables ranged along a strip of open carpet. The several armed guards in uniform appeared to take no notice of Tony as he moved among the tables, glancing at the cards in play, his attention focused on the faces of the dealers. He passed a dozen tables before he spotted Mitchell Breen.

There could be no mistake, but Tony palmed the thumb-worn photograph to satisfy himself. The living, breathing face was older, showing more wear around the mouth, but he could still make out the scattered freckles, slightly crooked teeth, the receding line of Breen's curly red hair. If further proof was necessary, Tony's target wore a nameplate on his shirt, identifying him to one and all as "Mitch."

After watching Mitchell deal for several hands, Tony saw that "twenty-one" was similar to baccarat, a popular attraction in the Bangkok gaming parlors. Here, instead of drawing cards to total nine, the players tried to reach a count of twenty-one, which was described as "blackjack" when an ace and face card made the perfect total on a deal. Instead of cash, the players bet with colored plastic chips, which were obtained by paying money to the dealer. Different colors signified various amounts.

A blue-haired dowager gave up her seat and Tony slid into her place, directly opposite Mitchell Breen. He dug a wad of crumpled twenty-dollar bills out of his pocket, pushed a couple of them toward the dealer, and received his chips. Tony's heart hammered against his ribs and his mouth was parched. A cocktail waitress hovered near his elbow, and he ordered a beer.

"What's happening?" Breen asked.

"I'm playing cards."

The dealer looked amused, and other players at his table snickered. "Fair enough," Mitchell Breen said. "Bets down."

Tony pushed two chips forward and Breen dealt the cards, facedown to players, one card concealed and one showing for himself. A one-eyed jack stared back at Tony from the tabletop.

He made a shelter of his hands and checked his own cards, smiling at the queen and ace of diamonds.

"Blackjack."

"Hey, another lucky winner."

Breen played on around the table, breaking Tony's three companions with a twenty of his own before surrendering two chips.

"The house pays two."

He dealt again, and this time turned up an eight of spades. Tony held a five of diamonds and a deuce of clubs.

"Another card."

The ten of diamonds lay before him. Seventeen. From the instructions printed on the green felt tabletop, he knew Breen was required to draw if his cards totaled less than seventeen; conversely, if he held a seventeen or better, rules prohibited the dealer from attempting to improve his score.

"Again."

He drew another deuce, making it nineteen.

"No more."

The woman on his right had drawn a blackjack and was preening now, as if the draw had been determined by her skill instead of pure, dumb luck. On Tony's left a black man in a wrinkled suit drew twenty-three and busted, cursing beneath his breath.

Breen turned to Tony Kieu. "It's you and me."

The dealer turned his hole card, revealing another eight. Sixteen.

"Dealer takes a card."

The ace of spades glared up at Mitchell like a baleful eye.

"Seventeen. The house pays."

One more hand, and Tony stood on twenty, watching as the dealer busted with a twenty-six. He felt light-headed, almost giddy from the beer and victory.

"Bets up."

Supremely confident, he pushed four chips across the table, drew nineteen, and waved away the opportunity to draw another card. It did not matter that the dealer had a face card showing, not until he turned the ace and made it blackjack, raking Tony's chips away and adding them to his collection with a sympathetic smile.

"Bets up."

Eighteen, and Mitchell had another face card showing. Tony drew a ten of hearts to make it twenty-eight, watching another four chips disappear. The dealer beat him with a sorry twelve.

"Bets up."

His hands were trembling as he pushed a stack of chips, uncounted, toward the center of the table. He was dealt a seventeen, the very worst that it could be, and felt compelled to draw. A three of spades made up the twenty, and he settled back as Breen revealed his cards. Fourteen. The dealer would be forced to draw.

"The house draws seven. Twenty-one." His stomach churning, Tony watched his last chips disappear.

"Bets up."

He pushed back from the table, trying not to hurry as he turned away. The gaming room had grown somehow, and Tony seemed to walk forever as he sought the exit onto Fremont Street. Behind him, he could hear the mocking voice of Mitchell Breen.

"Another lucky winner. Hey, what's happening?"

Outside he told himself the game meant nothing, less than nothing. The odds were stacked by the house. His early luck had been a fluke, completely unrelated to his mission and his chances for success. When next he faced the red-haired dealer, Tony Kieu would have the odds behind him, and he would not have to stand on seventeen.

16

Mitchell Breen was worried. The pit boss, Leno, had been giving him the eye again, and that was never good. It made him nervous when the guy just stood there like a mountain, staring at him. You never knew exactly what was on the bastard's mind.

At worst they might suspect that he was cheating, dealing seconds so that one of his acquaintances could make a killing at the table. That would be the worst because they locked you up for that, took away your work permits and put you on the blacklist. If you were lucky. If the house got pissed enough . . . well, things could be a damn sight worse.

Breen was an adequate mechanic with the cards. In dealer's school they taught you how to spot a cheat, and that meant that you had to know the moves yourself. You weren't supposed to practice them, of course, but what a student did at home was no damned business of the teacher's. He could probably have pulled it off—they all said that—but he would never have assumed the risks involved. It had not been that long since two of the casino's men in uniform had been indicted after beating up a couple of suspected cheats. And those were *customers*, for Christ's sake.

Mitchell didn't even want to think about what might have happened to an employee.

You still heard stories from the old days, and they were enough to make your blood run cold. When old Gus Greenbaum ran the Fabulous Flamingo after Benny Siegel bought the farm, he used to interview suspected dealers in the soundproof counting room. Once they were in there, safe from prying eyes, their cheating hands were crushed to pulp with pipes or loaded baseball bats. That done, they would be driven to the city limits, relieved of shoes and socks, and given their marching orders: Walk to Barstow. Barstow was 150 miles from Vegas as the buzzard flies, and it was desert all the way.

If he was lucky, maybe it was just another layoff in the making. Dealers had no job security at all, which didn't make a hell of a lot of sense when you thought about their crucial function in the state's economy. If gambling ever folded, you could scrape Nevada into the crapper and forget that shit about Lake Mead and scenic off-road trails. Without casinos two-thirds of the population would dry up and blow away. Yet the dealers had no contracts, no union, in a town that had been built from bedrock up with Teamsters money. Fucking janitors and cocktail waitresses were in a union that could shut the city down on half an hour's notice, but the dealers? Screw 'em. Dealers didn't count.

So maybe, if his luck was holding, he would only be laid off awhile. It could be worse. He could be sitting in the counting room, damned right, while some gorilla turned his hands to pulp or tickled his *cojones* with a cattle prod.

Breen knew he was getting paranoid. Las Vegas did that to you sometimes. Working Vegas was like a stroll on the high wire, knowing that your safety net was full of gaping holes. Vegas topped the charts in suicides, and never mind that PR crap about how all the guys who ate their guns were transients, losers suffering from postroulette depression. Plenty of the dead and walking wounded were his neighbors, regulars. The fast lane had its share of casualties and then some.

Breen punched his time card. Seven minutes overtime, and fuck 'em if they couldn't take a joke. Sometimes they acted like an hour's overtime would break the house, when everybody knew that they could pull a million out of petty cash and never feel the bite. A million bucks was chump change to the house, but they would fight you for a lousy dime.

It had been different in the military. Breen had served his tour in the Navy with the SEALs—the Sea, Air, Land commandos—and no sooner had he finished all the in-depth training with its emphasis upon economy, than they had packed him off to Vietnam where no one seemed to give a damn. Each night the Mekong delta base camps set aside "mad minutes" during which the personnel were actively encouraged to expend their ordnance in random fashion, one eye on the clock. It could be pretty damned spectacular, a couple hundred guys all cranking loose at once, full-auto, none of them with any special target, tracers burning through the night like comets. No one said too much about it when they started finding bullocks and civilians afterward. They were occasionally recognizable, but any human dead were written off as Cong infiltrators. Before his hitch was done, a couple of the delta base commanders had revised their sport from "mad minutes" to "happy hours," blasting everything that moved within their designated free-fire zones for sixty minutes at a stretch. But there was never any ammo shortage on the line. Breen suspected that the manufacturers back home had thought up "happy hour" on their own. God knows it had been good for business, and it gave the grunts a way to let off steam.

For all of that, when Mitchell Breen looked back upon his hitch in Vietnam, he did so with pride. He felt they had accomplished something positive, although he could not always put his finger on precisely what it was. Their fight had finally been a losing one, but that had been the fault of politicians. Combat troops in Vietnam had never lost a major battle with the enemy, no matter what the reds had thrown against them, and it was a goddamned shame that they had been pulled out before they had a chance to win the war.

Some of the other veterans he knew would disagree, violently, with Breen's perspective on the war. Embittered by their personal experience in Nam, pissed off because society had not been handing out blank checks when they returned, a number of his fellow vets were sounding more and more like left-wing activists these days. It was a funny thing, but Breen could not remember hearing any gripes about U.S. foreign policy when he was serving time in Vietnam. There had been constant bitching about the food, the bugs, and barmaids who were carrying a dozen different strains of clap, but those were staples of a soldier's life. In Nam he could not remember anyone's debating the necessity of standing firm against the communists. It was accepted, understood . . . until the troops came home.

As for himself, Breen still had no regrets. There had been moments, sure, when he was terrified, and all the training didn't help for shit. They told a story in the SEALs about a squad, on duty in the delta, that was cut off and enclosed by a superior detachment of the enemy. The numbers grew each time the story went around, till it was something like a hundred gooks for each American, but no one ever tampered with the punch line. Breen could still remember how he used to stomp the floor and howl along with everybody else when they were told how the commander of the squad had looked around at all those slanty eyes and smiled. "They've got us surrounded," the lieutenant said, according to the legend. "Jesus, I feel sorry for the bastards."

Nam had not been totally without its compensations. He had been a virgin when he joined the Navy. Saigon had changed all that. The SEALs had taught him how to kill, and Cholon's finest had instructed him in ways to pass the time between engagements with the enemy. Before he wrapped his tour, Mitchell Breen had become proficient in both fighting and fucking. After a while they both seemed pretty much the same.

Nam had been on his mind these past few days, since Patty let it slip that someone from the service had been trying to connect. She had asked him how he liked his big surprise, and when he questioned her, she turned apologetic. Vince had called, she said, and he had asked her not to tell. It took some effort to convince her that she had not spoiled the big reunion; if and when Vince showed, Breen told her, he would act surprised.

Except that it wouldn't be an act.

Because he had never known a soldier named Vince. . . .

The Horseshoe's underground garage maintained a section for employees—on the lowest level, naturally, and limited in size. Though a hassle, at least the space was free, and he was spared the two-block hike to city parking where they charged you by the hour. Theoretically, the parking guards were on duty round the clock. In practice, you could find them hanging out around the lot attendant's booth for roughly seven hours every shift, intent on making time with the bimbos who accepted validation slips from guests and logged the fees on drop-ins.

Mitchell seldom locked his car. The ancient Nova was not worth a real thief's time, and he would no more think of leaving valuables inside than he would dump them out on Fremont Street. In Vegas you thought of rip-offs all the time, aware that if you did not look out for yourself, nobody else would do it for you.

Breen removed his clip-on bow tie, opening his collar button as he slid behind the Nova's wheel. Another day, and he had done all right in tips. Approximately sixty bucks, of which he would declare no more than ten. He had his key in the ignition when he heard a movement in the seat behind him. Before he had a chance to turn around, the cold muzzle of a gun was pressing against the skin behind his ear.

Breen flicked a glance in the direction of the rear-view mirror, catching eyes like chips of flint. He could not see the moving lips as his assailant spoke.

"I bring you greetings from your son."

The underground garage had been his second choice. He would have much preferred to face the enemy at home, but it was not to be. There was the woman to consider, a potential witness, but he would kill her, too, if necessary. The decision, finally, had been removed from Tony's hands by circumstance.

The third night in Las Vegas he was left alone while Wendy drove to her first date for the escort service. She had gone with Satin Touch for reasons that eluded Tony, and he did his best to put the whole thing out of mind. He had walked to Fremont Street and waited for a bus with stops on West Sahara, confident, from studying his map, that he could reach his destination easily if he disembarked on Arville. But finding Mitchell Breen's address turned out to the least of Tony's problems.

In the end, his target's residence turned out to be a large apartment complex—labeled Woodcreek on the sign out front—that covered several acres, adjacent to a high school and a Mormon church. Without a number for the unit occupied by Breen, he realized that he might be reduced to wandering around the complex endlessly in hopes their paths would ultimately cross. Tony knew that he was doomed if he could not devise another angle of attack.

Retreating to the neighborhood convenience store, he found a pay phone, thumbing through the dog-eared yellow pages for the number of the Woodcreek rental office. The lethargic, disembodied voice had no apparent interest in the problems of a long-lost relative intent on pulling off a joyous family reunion; the release of individual apartment numbers was categorically forbidden. Had he considered speaking with his brother personally? Surely Mr. Breen would be only too pleased to give the number out himself.

It was a hopeless stalemate. He could not call Breen without alerting his intended target, and the woman might become suspicious if he called again. Even if she gave him the address, she might have second thoughts and alert his enemy before he had a chance to strike.

The answer came to him that night as he was riding back to Fremont Street. If Breen did not rely upon the bus for transportation, he would have a car. And if his target had a car, that meant he had to park it somewhere while he worked his shift. Simple. . . .

Next evening Tony walked back to the Horseshoe, circling the block before he finally determined that the only parking lot was underground. He passed the exit ramp, deciding that there had to be an entrance other than from the street. Entering the casino proper, he dropped several quarters in a slot machine for appearance's sake, then made a beeline for the elevators.

Emerging from the elevator, Tony found himself inside a man-made cavern, split up into several levels. On Level 1, Tony kept himself in shadow as he hurried down the sloping ramp, his back turned toward the lot attendant and the guard in case they glanced in his direction.

On the second level there were endless lines of cars with license plates from half a dozen states. Tony was wasting precious time. Level 3 was the same, and he was on the verge of giving up when he hit pay dirt at the bottom of the pit, on Level 4. Sequestered in a corner of the concrete barn was a section where the parking spaces had been marked in yellow paint, not white, with stenciled warnings on the wall reserving some two hundred spaces for EMPLOYEES ONLY.

Tony saw that each employee vehicle displayed a special sticker resembling a horseshoe, with a number printed on the arch. Each car had been assigned a different number, almost certainly on file with the employee's other records in a special office somewhere overhead.

He had no hope of penetrating the security upstairs, but it would not be necessary if he found a place to wait until Breen showed himself. It should be relatively simple to observe which car he drove and memorize the details for another day. It was what the Americans would call a piece of cake.

Tony launched his vigil at a quarter past eleven. Three long hours later his target finally appeared. Breen walked with several other Horseshoe dealers, chatting easily and laughing at a joke that one of them was telling. Tony squatted between a station wagon and a British sports car as the members of the little group dispersed to their separate vehicles.

Emerging from his cover, he passed within a yard of his intended target, casually watching as Breen slid behind the wheel of a Chevy Nova. He memorized the Nevada license plate, noting that Breen had not used a key to open the door. If he was in the habit of leaving the car unlocked, it could make Tony's job that much easier.

It was after three A.M. when he returned to the motel on Bridger. Still no sign of Wendy. He showered and went to bed, but he was still awake when she came in an hour later.

"Tony? You awake?"

He sat up in the bed, said nothing. She looked tired, but she was smiling. Tony looked away from the disheveled hair, the open blouse, his full attention concentrated on the floral pattern of the inexpensive bedspread.

"I let Gino have a sample of the coke. You know, my boss? He figures he can move it for us in a coupla days. Course, he'll be taking ten percent, like for a finder's fee, but even so . . ."

"That's good."

"Are you all right?"

"A little tired."

"Me, too. I've gotta catch a shower, okay?"

"Yes, sure."

He lay awake and listened to the water hissing in the bathroom, gurgling down the drain. She came to bed with nothing on and wriggled up against him.

"G'night."

He was aroused as he had never been before, but Tony could not bring himself to touch her. When he closed his eyes, he pictured Wendy smiling, telling shameless lies to strangers. Again her face was blurred, subtly changing into the face of Lin Doan Kieu, and Tony felt his stiff erection wilting like a candle in the summer sun.

The next night, Friday, Wendy was called to meet a date. Tony stayed in the room by himself. He watched the television news, which seemed preoccupied with gambling and violent crime, then flipped the dial until he found a monster movie, hosted by a woman with tremendous breasts and long, black hair who called herself Elvira, Mistress of the Dark. While priests and villagers pursued a werewolf through the moonlit woods of Transylvania, Tony stripped the magazine from Evan Price's automatic pistol and studied the weapon.

The movie's closing credits rolled at half past one. Tony carefully replaced the pistol's magazine, then worked the slide to put a cartridge in the firing chamber. Lowering the hammer gently with his thumb, he set the safety lever, tucked the Browning in his belt, and zipped his jacket halfway up to keep it hidden.

Tony returned to the Horseshoe and loitered at the slot machines for several moments, dropping quarters. This time he won back a dollar and a half before he struck off for the elevators. Beating the machine was a propitious omen. As he rode down to the garage, he felt invincible, protected by some higher power that had smiled upon his mission.

Emerging from the elevator, Tony spared a glance for the attendant and her man in uniform. Neither of them noticed Tony as he scuttled down the ramp to Level 2 and disappeared from sight.

Breen's Nova was not parked where it had been last night, and Tony realized that spaces were not individually reserved. He found it all the same, a four-door with the paint job faded to a sort of khaki color from neglect and long exposure to the desert sun. He tried the back door on the driver's side and found it locked. His stomach knotted painfully.

The driver's door came open at his touch, and Tony slid behind the wheel, relieved. He scrambled over the seat, snagging his gun in the process, cursing as he worked it free. The lumpy floorboard was unyielding, painful on his knees, and Tony wormed his way around to a more comfortable posture, seated with his back against the doorpost. He eased the pistol's safety off and wedged the gun between his thighs, its muzzle pointed at the floor. While Tony waited, he took out the photograph of Mitchell Breen and tore it once on a diagonal across the smiling face.

Three quarters of an hour passed before the guard came by to make a cursory examination of the bottom level. Tony heard his footsteps on the concrete ramp. He felt a sudden urge to urinate and clamped his knees around the pistol, trying to distract himself with thoughts of other things.

It did no good to think of Wendy. She inspired a different kind of burning in his groin, but the desire was tempered now with sharp anxiety. Before much longer he would have to make a choice, and Tony was not sure if he was ready.

Someone else was coming now. He checked the inexpensive watch that he had purchased at a nearby gift shop, Trader Bill's. He heard voices echoing in the garage. Not many—four or five at most—but it was still enough to spoil Tony's plans if his timing was not perfect.

They had stopped a few yards from the car. He thought he recognized Breen's voice, but he could not be sure.

"Heard anything about a layoff?"

"No, have you?"

"That bastard Leno's giving me the fisheye every time I turn around."

"What's bugging him?"

"Since when does Leno need a reason?"

"I hate the prick."

"The walls have ears, my man."

"So, screw the walls."

"I heard that."

"Hey, listen, if you *do* hear something—"

"Never fear."

"Okay. I'll catch you Monday."

"Solid."

"Later, man."

Doors slamming, engines turning over, Tony felt his stomach knotting. Had his prey changed shifts? Might he have hours yet to wait before the dealer showed himself?

As if in answer to his thoughts, the driver's door opened and Breen slid behind the wheel. No matter what the cause of the delay, it had worked to Tony Kieu's advantage. The other vehicles were moving out as Breen got settled, put his key in the ignition.

Tony clutched the nearest seat belt, using it to haul himself erect, the muscles in his back and legs protesting painfully. No time to check for witnesses. No time for anything as Tony pressed the Browning's muzzle against the skin behind Breen's ear.

"I bring you greetings from your son."

A pair of startled eyes were reflected in the rearview mirror. Breen considered grabbing for the gun, thought better of it as he heard the hammer clicking into place.

"There must be some mistake."

"No mistake," Tony snapped.

"But I don't *have* a son! I don't have any children."

Tony felt the old familiar rage assert itself. He thought of Charley Nhu and saw him dying in the street.

"You *had* a son."

"I don't know what—"

The bullet entered half an inch behind Breen's ear, exploding through the mastoid process at 1,100 feet per second. The impact hammered Breen's face against the steering wheel. Thin rivulets of blood were painted on the inside of the windshield, others dribbling off the padded dash. A foul, pervasive odor filled the car as dying sphincter muscles released their load. Breen's body sagged, but hung suspended on the wheel.

His ears still ringing, Tony craned his neck to search for witnesses. No sign of movement, but for all he knew the gunshot had been audible on other levels, even on the street. The guard might be calling for reinforcements while he sat there wasting precious time.

He dropped the pistol next to Mitchell Breen, withdrew the mutilated snapshot from a pocket of his coat, and propped the pieces on the dead man's shoulder, screwing up his nose against the fecal stench. It seemed appropriate that Breen should soil himself in death, as he had lived without a trace of honor or compassion for his only son.

Moving up the ramp, Tony hesitated as he cleared each level in succession, listening for sounds of an alarm. When he reached Level 1 and found the guard still flirting with the blond attendant, Tony knew he was safe.

Emerging from the Horseshoe onto Fremont Street, he felt elated. He had played against the house, and he was walking out a winner. He had beaten all the odds.

17

A change girl at the Horseshoe discovered Breen's body shortly after 2 A.M. on Saturday. It made the *News at Noon* on Channel 8 that day. Tony watched the team of bleary-eyed forensics officers and homicide detectives scouring the scene, their efforts captured from a distance by the station's "live-eye" Minicam. A spokesman for the metropolitan police reported that the slaying had been carried out in gangland-execution style. With no apparent evidence of robbery, he speculated that narcotics were involved.

The killing made both Sunday papers, with a headline in the more sensational *Las Vegas Sun*. As with the televised reports, there was no mention of a photograph recovered at the scene. Authorities were optimistic that a pistol, thought to be the murder weapon, might be traced through an examination of its serial number. Tony read the articles and smiled. The gun would lead them back to Evan Price and nowhere else.

He clipped a short obituary from the *Review-Journal* and mailed it that afternoon from a postbox on Fremont. Wendy spent the afternoon "with friends," presumably from Satin Touch, but she returned to the motel in early evening, smelling heavily of alcohol and marijuana. Tony did not like her distant, dreamy attitude, but he decided nothing was to be gained by putting off the inevitable.

"I'd like to go away," he said while she was dressing, checking out a brand-new outfit in the full-length mirror.

She seemed confused. "Leave *Vegas*?"

"As soon as possible."

"How come?"

"I have no business here."

She giggled, tugging at the neckline of her blouse to show more cleavage. "Nobody has *business* here. It's like a great big party, dig it? A big hustle."

"I don't like it here."

"I do."

"You won't come with me, then?"

She turned away from the mirror, frowning. "We just *got* here."

Tony knew he was losing. "I'm tired of this place."

Wendy smiled. "We can get better digs. Hey, I'm working now. We can afford an apartment."

He weakened. "How long?"

She relaxed, sensing victory. "Gino's still trying to lay off the coke. I can't leave till he closes the deal."

Tony knew she was stalling for time. Once the drugs had been sold, there would be something else. She would trap him and hold him forever if he was not strong.

"How much longer?"

"Two weeks, give or take."

Tony felt himself weaken. "All right."

Wendy knelt on the mattress beside him, one hand on his thigh. "You'll get used to it, babe. It's a rat race at first, but you just have to kick back and learn to enjoy it."

"Like you?"

"Right. Like me."

She leaned forward, soft strands of her hair on his face as she kissed him, lips parting to welcome his tongue. She was stroking the swell of his fly, nimble fingers attacking the zipper and setting him free. Tony reached for her breasts, found them bare beneath loose-fitting silk.

Wendy glanced at the clock on the nightstand.

"We don't have much time."

She crouched over him, working with fingers and tongue while he lay on his back. Tony tried to resist her at first, but he had no strength left. When she straddled him, naked and wet underneath her short skirt, he was lost. Wendy rode him until he exploded. Even after he finished, she clung to him, grinding her hips till she stiffened and shuddered, breath hissing between her clenched teeth.

"Christ, I'm late!"

She emerged from the bathroom a few moments later, adjusting her skirt, hair brushed back and away from her face.

"Talk to Gino," he said.

"First thing Monday, I promise."

It was early when Wendy returned. She was waiting when Tony got back from McDonald's with Chicken McNuggets and fries in a bag. He was startled but happy to see her, until he observed the pallor beneath her cosmetics.

"You bastard." Her tone was emotionless, flat.

"What's the matter?"

"You did it, you shit."

Tony felt the first tingling of dread, like a draft on his neck.

"I don't know what you're talking about."

Wendy stared at him, hollow-eyed, numb. "Did you think that I wouldn't find out? Did you think I was stupid?"

Unable to think of an answer, he said nothing.

"You're cool, I'll say that for you. Sitting there, watching TV like you didn't know what they were talking about, with the blood on your hands all the time."

"Wendy—"

"No!" Spotty patches of color were back in her cheeks. "If it wasn't for Carla at work, I might never have known. But she's balling a cop, dig it? He doesn't know what she does on the side, so it's cool, and he tells her things. Things like the picture they found on that stiff at the Horseshoe."

"I see." He felt empty inside.

"They were holding it back, just in case someone copped to the job, get it? Something to weed out the freaks who confess every time there's a squeal. I remembered, because it was the same as in L.A."

"They won't catch me."

"You say." She was rigid with anger. "It isn't the cops, don't you see that? You *lied* to me. All of that shit about Price and your mother. You conned me. You made me look stupid."

"You were good to me."

"My first mistake."

Tony said, "I've got business in Denver."

"No business of mine."

"Let me tell you a story."

"You've done that already."

"The truth, then."

Reluctantly. "Sure, I'll try anything once."

Tony told her the truth, sparing nothing. She winced when he told her about Esquivel and the price of his passage; she wept when he describing his mother's death in Saigon. He did not name the others to come, but he mentioned the cities where they lived.

As he finished, she sat with her eyes downcast on the edge of the bed. Tony sat beside her with daylight between them, avoiding contact. A part of him wanted to reach for her, but he could sense her uncertainty, tempered with fear and revulsion. It struck him that he had succeeded in shocking her, finally cracking the cool mask of streetwise omniscience.

"Come with me," he said, when the silence between them had stretched tissue-thin.

Wendy shook her head. "I can't."

"I'll protect you."

"From what?"

"From the world."

"I don't need your protection, okay?" He was stunned to see tears in her eyes. "I don't need to be part of your fantasy."

Tony could feel himself shrivel inside. She was utterly, hopelessly lost to him now. He could picture her ten, fifteen years down the road when she would be reduced to the low-budget trade, marking time while she waited to die. It was not in his power to save her. But he might still be able to spare her some measure of suffering, some of the shame.

"Will you go for a ride with me?"

"Why?"

Tony shrugged. "I'll be leaving tomorrow for Denver. I thought we might spend a few hours together, before."

Wendy dabbed at her eyes. "I don't feel like a party."

"No parties," he promised, retrieving her purse from the nightstand, extracting her keys. "Let me show you the night."

Tony drove. West on Charleston to Rainbow, then south to the Blue Diamond Highway. West again, the landscape rising steadily until it crested at a point called Mountain Springs. He found a scenic turnout, pulled well off the road, extinguished lights and engine. To the east below them, Vegas pulsed and shimmered like a cooling lava flow. The sky above was velvet, pricked with stars.

"It's beautiful from here," she said. "Like something from another world."

"It *is* another world."

She hesitated, working up to it. "About the coke—if you could let me have an address, I could send your share when Gino pays me."

"I don't need the money."

"What?"

"You keep it."

"But it's yours."

"I took it from a dead man."

"Even so . . . I mean, unless you're *really* sure . . ."

He closed the door behind him as he got out of the car. Two thousand feet above the desert floor, it was already cool, but Tony shrugged his jacket off and left it wadded up on the Camaro's hood. He leaned against the fender, closed his yes, and let the darkness enter, breathing it deeply into his lungs. Behind him, he heard Wendy's footsteps on the gravel, and she nestled beside him, radiating body heat that could not cut his chill. His heart was crystalline, a lump of ice.

He reached for Wendy in the darkness and she offered no resistance. She was shivering as Tony pressed her back across the still-warm hood. His hands, beneath her skirt, found prickly gooseflesh on her inner thighs. The grill was rough against his knees as Tony entered her, still standing up, his sneakers slipping on the gravel.

Wendy arched her back and thrust against him, climaxed swiftly, with a kind of desperate ardor that surprised him. Overhead the silent galaxies bore witness to their coupling. When

Tony strangled her, her life was like a captive bird that fluttered briefly in his hands and then flew free.

He carried Wendy a hundred yards into the trees until he found a picnic area. He placed her on the rough-hewn table, smoothed her skirt, and brushed the hair back from her face. He thought she would be safe enough from animals, and Tony could not bring himself to take her back and leave her on the street. Retreating toward the parking area, he felt a heavy burden lifted off his shoulders. The world had no power over Wendy now.

18

SOUTHERN INDIANA

Patterson received the third obituary on March 17th. The plain white envelope was postmarked four days earlier. A stranger by the name of Mitchell Breen was dead in Las Vegas, cause of death predictably unspecified. A marginal notation indicated the obituary had been run on March 13th.

His pen pal had moved closer. In a week he had covered 200-plus miles from southern California to Las Vegas and arrived in time for yet another death, which seemed to carry some obscure significance. Breen was a veteran—U.S. Navy—so the three had that in common, even though the clip did not refer to time in Vietnam. The age was right; he could have been in-country at the same time Patterson was there.

So what?

Here were three deaths connected—theoretically at least—to Vietnam and Lin Doan Kieu. He knew that he was stretching with the last assumption, but the snapshot that had started all of this must have some significance. If only he could find the common link. . . .

He woke next morning from a restless sleep, exhausted, unrefreshed. He could remember almost everything about the nightmares now, and that was reassuring in a way. He knew precisely what his problem was, and while he had no ready-made solution, it was still a damn sight better than his years of groping in the dark for answers.

That morning over breakfast he told Jan that he would spend the afternoon in Bloomington. He needed saw blades to complete a set of cabinets, and the local hardware store was all sold out. When Jan suggested that they make a day of it, he put her off, explaining that he might be forced to visit several stores before he found the quantity and quality of blades required.

Though disappointed, she had bought the lie. Of late she had been buying them with frequency, as he had lied about his dreams—"I really can't remember, honestly"—and his state of mind—"I'm fine, don't worry." This would be the first time he had lied to her about his movements. He felt a pang of guilt but recognized the necessity of his deception.

The I.U. campus was a labyrinth of one-way, dead-end streets, apparently designed to snare unwary motorists and hold them prisoner forever. Years before, he and Jan had mistakenly turned off Third too soon and spent a harried thirty minutes trying to get back again. They had passed an ancient cemetery, headstones sprouting in the shadow of a Gothic lecture hall, and Jan had joked about the tenants of the graveyard being wayward travelers. It wasn't quite so bad if you took time to learn your way around, but he brought along a street map just in case.

Climbing the broad stone steps of the library, he passed a group of laughing coeds, impossibly young, impossibly beautiful. He felt decrepit, understanding Jan's anxiety about her age. Had *he* once been so young?

Inside the lobby Patterson made his way to the periodical reading room. He had already called ahead, confirming that they carried both the San Francisco *Chronicle* and L.A. *Times*. No papers from Las Vegas, sorry. But that did not matter. If he could not find a pattern in two cases out of three, the pattern simply was not there.

An anorexic-looking redhead tore herself away from Calculus 100 long enough to show him through the stacks. The papers were arranged alphabetically, and they were kept for roughly thirty days before conversion onto microfilm. He was in luck;

the microform division had been running several weeks behind, and February's papers were still available.

He pulled the *Times* for Wednesday, March fourth, along with issues for the next three days, repeating the procedure with the *Chronicle* for February eighteenth through the twenty-first. With papers tucked beneath each arm, he found an isolated carrel and settled in to scan the rumpled pages in a quest for . . . what? An absolution from his fears? Or confirmation of the worst?

He found the first account of LeRoy Duckworth's death on page nineteen, a simple item, buried near the back.

On Thursday, February nineteenth, LeRoy made page one. He did not rate a headline, but there was a grainy photograph below the fold, and this time there were details. Jesus, were there ever.

Feldsheim Janitor Found
Murdered, Mutilated

FEB. 18—LeRoy Gadsden Ducksworth, employed as a night custodian at the Feldsheim Bldg. on Van Ness, was murdered Tuesday night, according to Detective Harvey Stokes, and the body mutilated by the killer.

"Without going into too much detail, I can tell you that the victim was decapitated," Stokes informed the *Chronicle*. "There were some other injuries as well. We're working on a final cause of death right now."

Duckworth, 37, a decorated veteran of Vietnam, had several prior arrests for public drunkenness, disorderly conduct, and possession of controlled substances. His last recorded brush with the law occurred in 1983, and homicide investigators see no link between his past arrests and the circumstances of his death on Tuesday night.

"I wouldn't rule it out," Stokes said in an exclusive interview, "but at the moment we have nothing to suggest a tie-in."

Duckworth's body was discovered by a fellow worker in a fourth-floor office of the Feldsheim Bldg., which he had apparently been cleaning when the killer struck. "I thought it must have been some kind of joke," Juanita Lopez told the *Chronicle*. "A rubber head or something else, you know? But then I recognized the face, and it was LeRoy."

While police refused to comment, Mrs. Lopez said the victim's severed head was sitting on a secretary's desk, positioned to face the office door. His body was discovered on the floor beside the desk.

"I know it's crazy," Mrs. Lopez said, "but for a second there I thought that he was smiling."

Patterson felt sick as he put the Thursday *Chronicle* aside and picked up Friday's late edition. Duckworth's murder had been relegated to page four, and the police reported no new leads. A confidential source reported that a photograph had been discovered with the body, but Detective Stokes would not confirm the rumor.

Turning to the *Times,* Patterson scanned March 4th, found nothing for the day of Evan Price's death, and moved on quickly through the next two issues. Nothing. He was into Monday, March 7th, when the story leapt out at him from the front page of the Metro section.

Pilot Slain in Hollywood

MARCH 7—Charter pilot Evan Price was found dead in his home on Barton Ave. in Hollywood last night, the victim of a homicide. According to a coroner's report, the victim had been killed at least two days before his body was discovered. The report confirms that "certain mutilations" were performed upon the body after death.

Price, 38, was sole proprietor of Dream Flight Charter Service, based in Santa Monica. A veteran of the U.S. Army, he was decorated for his service as a helicopter pilot during the Vietnam War. He was unmarried and leaves no survivors.

Price's body was discovered by his fiancée, Amanda Ketring, 29, who shared his residence on Barton Ave. Ms. Ketring is a flight attendant for United Airlines. She was working in Australia at the time of the victim's death.

According to the coroner's report, Price suffered lacerations to the throat, together with a stab wound in the chest.

Spokesmen for the medical examiner declined to comment on reports that Price's body had been mutilated sexually after death.

"There were additional, nonlethal wounds," said Dr. Gary Sundberg, "but I'm not at liberty to deal with the specifics at the present time."

Investigators for the LAPD Homicide Division noted that a photograph was found on Price's body. "It appeared to be a snapshot of the victim taken during military service," said Det. Raymond Oxley. "Someone tore the photograph in half and placed it in the victim's hand. Presumably, that someone was the murderer."

According to Ms. Ketring, Price had no known enemies who might have wished him harm. "He was a sweetheart," she said. "Everybody loved him."

Guess again, thought Patterson, as he read the story through a second time. He concentrated on the paragraph about the snapshot, feeling cold inside.

Photos of the dead from Vietnam.

A photograph of Lin Doan Kieu.

And what the hell was the connection? He had never heard of Price or Duckworth or the latest victim, Breen. He did not have to guess about the cause of death in Vegas, either. Whether he was stabbed or shot or strangled scarcely mattered. Patterson was betting Breen had not died peacefully.

He had been receiving photographs and clippings from a murderer, or at the very least, someone who had knowledge of three homicides in widely separated cities. Was he being warned, or threatened? Was he on the killer's list? Or was some stranger trying to alert him, keeping him apprised of the assassin's movements?

Patterson knew that he should contact the police, for self-protection if for no other reason, but he hesitated. How much could he really tell them? He had burned the photograph, the clippings, envelopes. No evidence remained for the detectives to examine, nothing for the labs to analyze. It was his unsupported word, and he could tell them nothing of the distant crimes that they did not already know—except that someone with a deep, abiding interest in the homicides was also interested in *him*.

For Jan's sake, and for Jerod's, he must take some action to protect them from the faceless enemy. If they were in no danger at the moment, still, it might be coming, and he had to be prepared. He was not ready yet to share the story with his wife, but it was time to seek professional advice. He thought at once of Amos Swift, the Forrest County sheriff.

So caught up was he in the mental argument that he forgot his saw blades, had to double back and buy a set at Sears. He didn't need them, but he could not let Jan catch him in a lie. It troubled him, but she was not the target, and the enemy was still a thousand miles away.

Or was he?

Mitchell Breen had been murdered in Las Vegas six days ago. Time enough to drive crosscountry certainly, and if the killer chose to fly, he could be back and forth across the continent in hours. For all of that, Patterson felt no sense of urgency. The danger signals he had learned in Vietnam, the chills and the bristling of the short hairs on his neck, were silent now. An unfocused restlessness had made his stomach queasy for the past few days. It was a sign, but he was still prepared to trust his instincts. He would know when the time was right.

He pushed the Blazer on the homeward drive, suddenly anxious to see Jan's face again, to take Jerod in his arms. One final stop to make in Calvary, and then he would be finished for the day.

The sheriff's office was tucked away behind the courthouse in the Forrest County Law Enforcement Building. Parking was a bitch, with thirty spaces set aside to serve no less than twice as many cars. Patterson eventually found a space against the curb a block away. The deputy on duty glanced up from the latest *True Detective*, grinned, and buzzed him through.

"What brings you in? No, let me guess." Swift leaned back in the tall reclining chair behind his desk, arms folded on the wide expanse of his chest. "Parking ticket? Jaywalk? I believe I'm lookin' at a one-man crime wave."

They had been friends for years, since Patterson had joined the local dragnet for a missing child. The story had a happy ending all around: the little girl had been recovered safely, Patterson had come out of his shell a little more, and he had made a friend in Amos Swift. A dozen years his senior, Swift was the antithesis of Patterson in almost every way: outspoken, even boisterous, while Anthony was quiet and reserved; an activist in local politics, where Patterson was happy to observe things from the sidelines; a roguish bachelor with a string of women, while Anthony was content with Jan. The two men were as different, physically, as they were temperamentally dissimilar. Where Patterson was lean and muscular, the sheriff might have been constructed out of rough-hewn wooden blocks. He was a mountain of a man, without an ounce of fat on his massive frame.

Patterson shut the office door behind him, took a seat across the desk from Amos Swift. He had built the desk, commissioned by the sheriff after Swift had seen some of his other work.

"I've got a problem, Amos."

Instantly the jaunty smile was wiped away, replaced by concern. "Let's hear it."

"This is confidential, off the record."

"If you say so."

He began with the photograph, alluding briefly to his wartime tryst with Lin Doan Kieu. He caught a flash of interest in the sheriff's eyes and felt vulnerable. But Amos was a friend and would not use it as a weapon. Patterson continued with the three obituaries, and his own discovery that two of the deceased had been the victims of particularly brutal homicides.

"All strangers?"

"Absolutely."

"Well, I'd guess you're right about the guy in Vegas being murdered like the other two. You figure it's the killer sending you these clippings?"

"How the hell should I know?"

Amos shrugged. "Too bad you burned 'em. Might have had the sucker's fingerprints or something. Save the next one—if there *is* a next one—and I'll see what I can do."

"But in the meantime . . ."

"California and Nevada are a mite beyond my jurisdiction. I can make some calls, but someone's bound to wanna know my interest in their open cases."

"Never mind."

Swift thought about the problem for another moment, smiling thinly as he came up with a possible solution. "Say the

killer's working interstate. We *know* the letters crossed a few
state lines to get here. That's federal business, last I heard. You
might try talking to the FBI.''

"I don't know, Amos.''

"It was just a thought.''

"I've got no proof that any of it even happened. By the time
I lay it out, they'll think I'm shell-shocked.''

"*I* don't think you're shell-shocked.''

"You don't count.''

"Well, I sure as hell can't make you call the feds, but I'd be
on the phone right now, if it was me.''

"I'll think about it.''

"Sure. And in the meantime, if you get another love note
from your pen pal, keep me posted.''

"You'll be the first to know.''

"You might consider leveling with Jan,'' Amos said.

He thought about it for perhaps the thousandth time that day.
"Not yet,'' Patterson said.

19

DENVER

The rooming house on West Eleventh was adjacent to a park. From Tony's bedroom window on the second floor he watched the teenage boys who gathered there to practice football after school. They seemed more interested in posing for the girls who followed them around, and Tony was amused at the clumsy courtship rituals.

One of the girls, a slender blonde, resembled Wendy from a distance. Tony wondered why Wendy had not struggled harder in her final moments, why she had surrendered. Perhaps she had welcomed death because she recognized that life devoid of honor was no life at all.

Denver's civic center was a short half mile from Tony's rooming house, but he took his time, proceeding north and east on foot, crossing Cherry Creek at Thirteenth Avenue, encroaching on the heart of Colorado's mile-high city. Tony passed the U.S. Mint. He had read that cash was printed there, and also burned. It seemed a wasteful system. He carried all the money that he needed in a pocket of his jeans.

He had paid a month's rent at the rooming house, but there was still enough cash left from Evan Price's safe to see him safely through St. Louis, possibly beyond. He might not have to work the bars again until he reached Chicago. Meanwhile, he had other business.

He had been lucky with the ride from Las Vegas. After picking up his things at the motel, he had parked the old Camaro at McCarran Airport, tearing up the ticket as he left the cavernous garage. In darkness he had walked back to The Strip, trudging west along Flamingo Road until he reached the freeway. Crouching in the darkness with his pea coat wrapped around him, Tony had been waiting less than fifteen minutes when a motorist stopped to offer him a ride.

The driver was a middle-aged Vietnamese named Luan Nol, who traveled widely as a salesman. Flying would have saved him time, but he was a thrifty man terrified of airplanes. His evacuation from Saigon had been traumatic; VC rockets had destroyed a transport just behind him on the runway, and the flight to Honolulu had been stricken twice by savage storms. While airborne over the Pacific he had promised God that he would keep his feet on Mother Earth forever if his family was allowed to reach the promised land in safety. They had settled in St. Louis, he had found a job through fellow countrymen, and he had been a freeway nomad ever since.

Luan Nol immediately recognized Tony Kieu for what he was: *bui doi*. The story Tony offered was plausible enough: a laundered version of his trip to the United States, his hope for a reunion with the father he had never seen. He did not mention Esquivel or Duckworth, Price, or Breen. He fabricated letters from his father, quoting them as if from memory. Luan Nol sympathized; he understood the plight of war-torn families, having left behind innumerable relatives in Vietnam.

Nol was homeward bound, his business finished for the moment, and he readily agreed to drop his passenger in Denver. They stopped for breakfast in St. George, pushed on from there across the Utah desert, taking turns behind the wheel of Nol's vintage Cadillac. They stopped again for gas and tacos in Grand Junction, entering the Denver suburbs just as night fell over the Rockies. Nol, napping throughout the afternoon while Tony drove, was refreshed and ready to continue on his own when Tony disembarked in front of Union Station. Tony took the pair of twenty-dollar bills his benefactor offered him and palmed the business card that listed Nol's address in St. Louis. He had business in Missouri, and while he had no intention of renewing contact with the salesman, Tony tucked the card inside a pocket of his coat.

It might be days or even weeks before authorities in Vegas got around to checking Wendy's car at the airport. And days more while California license plates were checked against her last address, and they would still have no idea where Wendy Nash had gone. Discovery of her body would complete the superficial picture, but homicide detectives would be at a loss to name her killer or identify his motive. Nothing to connect her death with Mitchell Breen's. After spending seven days around Las Vegas, Tony knew that homicides were fairly commonplace and frequently unsolved. He had no fear of being linked with either crime. His face and fingerprints were not on file in the United States, and no one living in Nevada knew he existed.

Denver was different from the other cities he had visited. For one thing, it was much cleaner. Another oddity was the predominance of Western garb, worn by citizens of every age and nationality. In Vegas, "cowboy clothes" had been a costume worn by the employees of casinos with "historical" motifs, occasionally by Texans come to risk their oil wells on the cards and dice. In Denver, though, the outfits seemed to be a way of life, as were pickup trucks that carried gun racks in the windows, sprouting CB aerials like giant insect antennae.

Tony had already bought a map to help him find his way around the city, and he recognized the major landmarks as he passed City Hall, the Denver Art Museum, the public library. He did not stop until he found a phone booth with directory intact, outside the State Judicial Building. Tony found his target listed in the book and ripped out the page.

Aaron Mathers lived on Kendall in suburban Wheat Ridge, roughly three miles from Tony's rooming house. His faded photograph revealed a blue-eyed blond with classic cheekbones, smiling hesitantly for the camera in full dress uniform. He had been very young, but old enough to spawn a son, Li Trang, before he had returned to civilian life in the United States. Li Trang had been abandoned at an early age in Saigon, living alone on Cholon's meanest streets until he met Tony Kieu. Li Trang had seen the worst life has to offer in an Asian slum, and still he clung to fantasies of life in the United States. He had been quick to grasp at Tony's plan for organizing a reunion, eager to supply the photograph that would identify his father when they met in Colorado.

Soon, Li Trang would have his justice. If it was not all that he had hoped for, it was still the best that Tony Kieu could offer.

The morning of his third day in Denver, Tony struck off through residential neighborhoods of tract homes, naked trees, and reasonably tended lawns dappled with snow. He crossed the South Platte River via Colfax Avenue, not far from Mile High Stadium, and passed by several hospitals before he entered Sloan Lake Park. The grass was brown from weeks of frost and snow. He bought two hot dogs and a cup of coffee from a vendor, took them to the water's edge, and had his pick of empty benches facing the lake. A chilling wind from off the water cut through Tony's pea coat like a knife through cheesecloth, but he did not mind. It was a clean wind, and it stiffened his resolve.

When he was finished in Denver, Tony would be more than halfway through his list. Two cities left before he met the father who had never cared to look upon his face. Two targets after Mathers—opportunities to hone his skills, perfect himself before his meeting with the man who had created and destroyed his life.

He finished the second hot dog, burning his tongue with scalding coffee as he tried to wash it down. The sudden pain brought Tony's mind back to reality. He focused on his duty, understood that he had taken on a grave responsibility when he had formed his pact with Charley Nhu and the rest.

Shivering, he tried another sip of coffee. Still too hot to drink, it left Tony with the taste of tinfoil on his smarting tongue. He dropped the cup and the hot dog wrappers in a trash can, bearing west from lakeside, hiking through more residential streets until he reached his destination twenty minutes later. Kendall Street ran north and south, from Colfax Avenue to West Thirtieth, bisecting suburbs in the process. Aaron Mathers lived in the 2600 block, and Tony walked north after catching the street at West Twenty-second.

Like its neighbors, the house was drab and unremarkable, in need of painting. Tony loitered on the curb, reluctant to approach during daylight hours. Inside his coat the bowie knife was heavy in its leather sheath, reminding Tony of his mission, but he was a stranger here and dared not linger too long in the neighborhood. From where he stood, he saw enough to satisfy his curiosity: the open yard in front with chain-link fencing in the rear; no sign of dogs or children; ancient Chevrolet sedan parked in the open, single-car garage. The drapes were drawn in front, and Tony had no view of the interior.

He felt as if the neighborhood were watching him, a living, sentient thing, suspicious, hostile. On a nearby lamppost hung the laminated portrait of a bloodhound in a trench coat standing upright like a man. The hound's lapel button proclaimed his intention to "Take a Bite out of Crime," and just in case a would-be burglar missed the point, the logo for Neighborhood Watch was stamped beneath his feet in Day-Glo letters.

Next morning Tony left his room at half past six beneath a brooding sky that threatened snow. He wore the army-surplus jacket rather than his pea coat, a concession to the possibility that he had been observed the day before. The bowie knife was tucked inside his belt, its hilt uncomfortable in the small of Tony's back, but he took solace from its reassuring weight.

The curbs on either side of Kendall Street were lined with garbage cans this morning, lids askew or lying in the gutter, battered by the careless handling of trash collectors. When he was almost opposite the Mathers house, observing it peripherally, the front door opened and a woman started down the walk to fetch her cans. He watched her as she made two trips to carry them around the side of the garage.

He would have said that she was slender, though a quilted robe effectively concealed the outlines of her body. There were fuzzy slippers on her feet, and crew socks covered her ankles where they showed beneath the hemline of her robe. Dark hair was brushed back from her face and tied behind her head with what appeared to be a piece of yarn, but straggling wisps escaped to fall across her cheeks. She wore no makeup and her face was pale, except for sooty shadows underneath her eyes. Her narrow lips were welded together in a frown.

A screen door slammed behind him and he turned to find a chunky, red-faced woman glaring at him from her porch. Tony held her gaze just long enough to see it falter, then he moved on. If Mathers was inside the house, he would be safe today.

That night emotional exhaustion struck him like a fist between the eyes, nearly bringing him down before he reached the bed in his lonely rented room. He had tried to telephone the Mathers home, but there had been no answer, so he showered and crawled into bed.

Tony fell asleep with Aaron Mathers on his mind and woke the same way hours later. It was dark and cold outside, but he was drenched with perspiration. His fever had returned. The sheets were plastered to his body and he threw them back, preferring chills to the experience of lying in a shroud.

There was no point in going back to sleep. Mathers followed him into his dreams and mocked him there, conducting Tony on a frenzied chase through labyrinthine corridors, remaining just ahead of him, beyond his reach. At times he lost his quarry altogether, lost himself, and then a taunting voice would call him back into the game. He had no choice but to continue, running on until he dropped from sheer exhaustion, helpless to defend himself. . . .

He checked the watch that he had purchased in Las Vegas. Three-fifteen. Too early for the hunt, but he could not go back to sleep.

Today. Regardless of the risk, he would not rest until he dealt with Aaron Mathers. If it meant invasion of his target's home, so be it.

At six o'clock the day began to show the first, faint signs of brightening. The clouds had thinned since yesterday; there would be spotty blue skies overhead for Tony's walk to Kendall Street.

Familiar with the streets and houses now, he knew which dogs would bare their teeth or bark at him as he passed, which would press themselves against their chain-link fences, wagging tails and waiting to be petted by a friendly hand. In the United States the dogs ate better and more regularly than the peasants of his native land.

Full light fell on Kendall Street as Tony made the turn off Twenty-sixth and started pacing off the final blocks. At his destination, curtains fluttered briefly behind him as he crossed the sloping lawn. He felt the red-faced woman watching him and wondered how long she would wait before she telephoned police. No matter. There would still be time.

Tony stood alone on Aaron Mathers's porch, one finger resting lightly on the doorbell. Part of him longed to cut and run, but he refused to let his nerves betray him now. He wore the pea coat this time, and the bowie in its sheath anchored Tony to the spot and gave him no alternative.

He pressed the button, listened to the muffled chimes inside. It took a moment, and he was about to try again when he heard footsteps. Tony slipped the buttons on his pea coat open, braced to draw the knife and strike as soon as Mathers showed himself. Before the woman on the far side of the street could reach her telephone, he would drop the torn snapshot and run for his life.

Tony froze. After a fumbling with the double locks, the door was open. He scarcely recognized the woman; she had fixed her hair, applied cosmetics, though her face was still unnaturally pale. A haunted look was in her eyes, deep lines etched around her mouth. She wore a blue, snug-fitting dress that revealed her body to be painfully thin.

The haunted eyes were locked on Tony's face. "Can I help you?"

"Aaron Mathers?" He could think of nothing else to say.

The final vestiges of color evaporated from her cheeks. "Aaron?"

Tony nodded, feeling like an idiot, aware that he would have to kill her now. She was a witness.

"May I speak to him?"

For a moment he thought that she was choking. When she found her voice at last, it sounded faint and faraway.

"He isn't here."

"I have a message for him, from a friend in Vietnam."

She placed one hand against the doorjamb—whether to support herself or bar the way he could not tell. Then she turned away, her movements those of someone twice her age.

"Come in," she offered. "Please."

20

The living room was dark and mildew was in the air. He closed the door behind him, waiting for a moment while his eyes adjusted to the darkness. For an instant Tony felt as if he might have stepped into a cave . . . or a mausoleum.

His hostess made it to the couch and turned on a lamp, obviously more for his sake than her own. He felt she could navigate the house by instinct and touch. As she waved him to an easy chair, he wondered why she craved the darkness. Was she hiding? If so, from what? From whom?

The living room was unremarkable. Indoor plants had suffered from the darkness—two were dying over by the windows where the heavy drapes had permanently cut off their light—but otherwise the Mathers home seemed fairly well-maintained. The lady wore a ring that told him she was married, and a wedding picture on the mantel showed a smiling Aaron Mathers with his arm around a younger, gayer version of the woman seated across from Tony.

"I'm sorry," she began, "but I don't even know your name."

"Li Trang," he told her with a smile. Poetic justice.

"Oh, you're Asian?"

Tony kept the plastic smile in place. "Vietnamese. My father is American. I'm on my way to see him now, but first I have a personal message to deliver to Aaron Mathers."

"He's gone."

"Where may I find him, please?"

She stared at Tony, *through* him, with a strange expression on her face. At last she found her voice and said, "My husband died eight weeks ago."

Tony felt his stomach knotting. For a moment everything appeared to tilt around him, slipping out of line and back again before his senses could incorporate the shift. He felt as if the floor might open up beneath his chair and swallow him alive.

"If I may ask, how did he . . ."

"Die? It's funny you should ask. It's funny you should *be* here, when you think about it. Aaron was a casualty of war. Your country killed him, with a little help from Uncle Sam. Oh, he survived the fighting; he was never even wounded. But the damned war killed him all the same."

A pack of cigarettes was lying on the coffee table. Tony's hostess took one for herself and lit it, offered him the pack, and shrugged when he declined. His legs were trembling. He did not know if they would function on command, but Tony wanted out of there. It was enough to know that he had come too late for Mathers. He did not wish to share the other's life.

But there was no escape.

"You never met my husband? That's too bad." She had not waited for an answer, uninterested in his response. "You would have liked him. Everybody liked him."

Tony nodded mutely. Li Trang's mother had been one of those who liked the young American.

"He didn't have to go to Vietnam, you know. I told him that. We could have married earlier, he could have brought his grades up at the junior college . . . but he *wanted* to. He wouldn't have enlisted on his own, but once he got that 1-A notice, it was like he turned into a superpatriot or something. He was going to save the world. Turns out, he couldn't even save himself."

Her voice was bitter, brittle, on the verge of cracking.

"Mrs. Mathers—"

"Reena. I'm not Mrs. Mathers anymore." She took a long drag on her cigarette and blew a plume of smoke at the ceiling. "When Aaron was in Vietnam, I used to write him every day. Of course, he didn't have a chance to write back very often. He was part of what they used to call the lurp team. That's long-range reconnaissance patrol. He spent a lot of time in the jungle, fighting."

And some time in Saigon, too, Tony thought.

"I knew a little bit about his job, how dangerous it was. He couldn't tell me most of it, and he was never much on writing letters anyway. I used to pray each night that God would keep him safe and send him home again." The bitter, mocking smile was back. "So, maybe He was only listening with one ear."

He did not want to hear this, but he felt as if his body had been rooted to the chair. "I don't know."

Her smile softened around the edges, but her voice was no less bitter when she said, "I don't believe He listens to a thing we say. Oh, maybe He's in tune with Billy Graham, I don't know, but who the hell could listen to a zillion prayers a day and still remember anything? I mean, He can't be everywhere at once, you know?"

She stubbed her cigarette out in an ashtray on the coffee table, lit another one.

"The lurp teams didn't mind the jungle," she informed him, "but it was a problem for the base camps. Hard to see exactly who you're killing with all those trees in the way. So, someone says the trees have got to go, and they come up with Operation Ranch Hand. Aaron told me all about it after he came home. Their motto was, 'Only you can prevent forests.' "

Tony glanced in the direction of the door. It seemed a million miles away.

"They used to spray the forests with a chemical called Agent Orange. That's dichlorophenoxyacetic acid to you and me." She smiled again. "I used to get straight C's in chemistry, but now I'm motivated. I've been doing homework.

"Anyway, the word was out that Agent Orange was harmless. Never mind the way it stripped the trees and killed the fish in lakes and streams. 'No danger to civilians or to military personnel.' The brass forgot to mention lab tests where the rats got cancer. Nobody noticed that the animals exposed to Agent

Orange produced defective fetuses ninety percent of the time. Rats are cheap. Grunts are cheap.''

She was weeping now, the tracks of silent, angry tears etched darkly in mascara on her cheeks.

"Aaron came home in July of '71, and we were married two months later. He was happy to be home. He didn't brood about the war and jump at little noises like so many of the other boys. He didn't wake up screaming in the middle of the night. He *handled* it, you know? He made me proud.

"We wanted children right away. He was an only child; I've got a sister nine years older, and we both felt like we'd missed a lot as kids, not growing up in larger families. Some say the opposite, but Aaron wanted kids. I wanted kids.''

He had a son, thought Tony Kieu. *He* has *a son*. The dead man smiled down at him from the mantelpiece.

"It took six months to plant the seed," she said, "but what the hell, they say that trying's half the fun. I don't know why, but both of us expected it to be a boy.'' She paused to light another cigarette. "When I miscarried in the fourth month, Aaron took it like a curse from God. He didn't know that God was out to lunch. He didn't know about the rats.''

"I should be going now," Tony said.

She did not seem to hear him, and he could not find the strength to leave.

"Over the next eight years, I miscarried five times. Every time the doctors did their song and dance: 'There's nothing we can put our finger on.' ''

Sneaking a glance at his watch, Tony found that he had been inside the Mathers home for thirty minutes. Time enough for nosy neighbors to start worrying and call police.

"In '84, when I got pregnant for the seventh time, we never thought we had a chance. I'd never made it past five months before, but this time I went all the way. You should have seen how Aaron followed me around the house. He wouldn't let me get a glass of water by myself. I even gave up smoking just to give the kid a fighting chance.''

"I really ought to—''

"Aaron thought that it might be a girl this time. I didn't care, as long as it was healthy.'' Reena Mathers shook her head and chuckled to herself, a dry, dead sound. "By now you've guessed the punch line. It was a girl, all right, but she was stillborn. They wouldn't let me see her afterward, but Aaron saw. He couldn't talk about it, but it was the first time that I'd ever seen him cry.

"The doctors checked me out again a few weeks later. Nothing. Aaron had a few tests run himself, and that was when they found the cancer. It was too damned late already. There was nothing they could do, but Aaron had insurance and the bastards had a field day. Chemotherapy and radiation treatments, marrow transplants and exploratory surgery. I still don't know which finished him, the cancer or the cure."

"I'm sorry."

"Are you?" Reena's eyes swam into focus for a moment, and she studied Tony's face. "Yes, I believe you are. By early '85, there was a lot of news about the lawsuits over Agent Orange. So many veterans with cancer, kids with birth defects. The government denied it all. They can't admit that kind of error . . . if it *was* an error. Personally, I'm inclined to think they knew from the beginning, and they didn't give a damn. But then again, I'm rather cynical these days."

The silence stretched between them for a moment and he realized, with sudden clarity, why Reena Mathers had been living in the darkness with her blinds drawn. She was hiding from her memories. She had been hiding from herself.

"You said you had a message for my husband?"

Taken by surprise, Tony swallowed hard and dredged his voice up from the cellar of his soul. "A message, yes."

"What was it?"

Greetings from his son, in Vietnam. The only son he would ever have. The son you will never see.

He could not bring himself to speak the words. Instead he said, "Your husband was a friend to many people in the war. He helped the people of my village and defended them against the Viet Cong. Now, communists have everything, but people still remember the Americans. The headman of my village knew that I was coming to America. I promised him that I would stop and thank your husband for his kindness to our people."

Tony was embarrassed by the lie, but he had no grudge against this woman. She had suffered. He saw no reason to compound her pain by telling her the man she loved was the father of a half-breed child halfway around the world.

"It seems a shame," she said. "You've traveled all this way for nothing. Would you like to see him?"

"See him?"

"He's at Crown Hill Cemetery, half a mile from here. Ten minutes, if we catch the lights."

"Well—"

"Good. I didn't feel like going in to work this morning anyway. I'll give my boss a call. He's used to it by now."

In the kitchen Reena Mathers spoke briefly then slammed down the telephone. Angry color was in her cheeks when she returned, but she attempted to conceal it with a smile.

"I shouldn't get so angry. Honestly, I wonder they've put up with me this long." She lit another cigarette, retrieved her purse. "You ready?"

As they backed out of the driveway, Reena waved in the direction of her neighbor's silent, watching house, responding with a snort of laughter as the puckered bedroom drapes fell back into place.

"That's Mrs. Carmody, the nosy bitch. She hasn't spoken to me in a month of Sundays, but she watches me like the CIA. This ought to give her something for the gossip mill."

She laughed again, and Tony thought it made her look years younger. She had been attractive once, he guessed, before her life had fallen apart.

The sprawling grounds of Crown Hill Cemetery had been tended lovingly through snow and biting frost, with hearty winter grass still green in most places. Preparations for a graveside ceremony were underway near the entrance, and he watched the diggers in their overalls, preparing strips of artificial turf to hide the open pit from mourners who would be arriving shortly.

The cemetery covered many acres, but Reena made her way along the narrow, winding road unerringly. Five minutes after passing through the vaulted, wrought-iron gates, she parked the Chevrolet with two wheels on the grassy shoulder.

"Come on," she urged, and Tony followed her reluctantly across the rolling lawn, past stones of every shape and size, from simple plaques and crosses to elaborate cherubim and pillars bearing graven likenesses of the deceased. En route Reena pointed

out the graves of governors and mayors, military heros from the
Civil War to Vietnam, a gangster from the 1930s. Death had
brought them all together.

The grave of Aaron Mathers bore a simple, wedge-shaped
marker, canted to display a photograph of the deceased that had
been inlaid in the marble, covered with protecting plastic. Tony
felt the lifeless eyes upon him as he studied the inscription:

Aaron Robert Mathers
Loving Husband
1951–1985

A small bouquet of withered flowers rested on the grave, a
token of remembrance. Reena and Tony stood in silence, one
loving, one at war within himself.

"I'll see you at the car." Reena turned away, a slender
figure, out of place among the monuments to death. Tony was
alone with Mathers; he could curse the dead man if he wished or
spit upon his grave. It all seemed pointless now. The dead man
was beyond his reach.

Still, he could not leave without some gesture, an expression
of his personal contempt. He drew the mutilated snapshot from
his pocket, stooped to prop its crumpled halves against the
marble gravestone. Straightening, he spent another moment studying the different faces of the enemy. Before and after. Life and
death. The hero and the corpse.

It was enough. He backtracked to the car, found Reena
waiting for him, silent as a mannequin behind the wheel. Without a word she put the Chevy through a U-turn, following the
blacktop ribbon back through the wrought-iron gates.

"Can I drop you somewhere?"

"What about your job?"

"I'm late already. What's the difference?"

As it turned out, Tony's rooming house was more or less en
route to Reena's job. She was a salesclerk at a clothing store in
downtown Denver, but she made it sound as if her services were
rarely needed. The proprietor had been a friend of Aaron's from
before the war.

"He's getting fed up," she said. "Can't say I blame him.

I'm a bitch to work with. Always late. Some days I don't go in at all. He'll have to can me soon."

They drove the last two miles in silence, and she parked outside the rooming house on West Eleventh Street, the Chevy's engine idling roughly. Tony felt as if he should say something, but he was at a loss for words.

"I'm glad you came today," she said at last. "It does me good to talk things out sometimes, but no one wants to hear it anymore."

She turned to face him, and he forced himself to meet her eyes.

"You're lucky, kid. You've got somebody waiting for you, someone you can care about, who cares right back."

Tony thought of Charley Nhu, Li Trang, the others he had left behind in Vietnam, and forced a smile. "I guess you're right."

He closed the door behind him, stepping back onto the curb as Reena pulled away. He watched her as she turned the corner onto Mariposa, southbound, waving through her open window as she disappeared from sight.

He was alone. The lucky one.

21

ON THE ROAD

By eight o'clock the railroad yard was bustling with activity. The engineers and workmen were preparing several trains at once. Tony had already picked the one he wanted: it was east-bound for St. Louis.

He had passed a sleepless night, beset by doubts, compelled to reexamine every action he had taken since he left Saigon. The death of Aaron Mathers and his meeting with the veteran's wife had left him shaken, questioning his mission. No black-and-white solutions existed anymore, and it occurred to him that some of those he meant to kill had suffered in the war as much—or more—than the children they had left behind. Some of them might already be condemned, like Aaron Mathers, to a slow and agonizing death. If anything, his plan to end their lives might be a premature release from suffering. He had no wish to do them any favors. For hours Tony wrestled with the thought of giving up his quest for vengeance.

Then he realized that he was playing foolish mind games, wasting precious time. It did not matter if his prey had suffered in the war. It was preordained, a part of life in uniform, and nothing that had happened to his targets could expiate their sins against their children.

In the end his trip to Crown Hill Cemetery and the meeting with Mathers's widow only strengthened Tony Kieu's resolve. It did not matter, finally, if Nature had preempted him in Denver. Rather, it confirmed the righteousness of his errand. The death of Aaron Mathers was a sign, a confirmation of his self-appointed role as judge and executioner.

Before dawn Tony left his rented room on West Eleventh, dropping his key without a note of explanation on a table in the hall. Without a new obituary for his father's small collection, he was forced to improvise, but in the end he thought his choice appropriate.

He dropped the envelope into a mailbox near a neighborhood convenience store. Inside he purchased bread, canned ham, candy bars, two cans of Coca-Cola. All of these went into Tony's duffel bag, beside his bowie knife, the meager stock of extra clothing, and the "Vincent Tandy" ID. In his pockets Tony carried nothing but the dwindling supply of cash from a dead man's safe in Hollywood, nine hundred dollars, give or take.

He had decided the railroad would keep him off the highways for a while, reducing risks of contact with police. A ticket would be costly, so he would ride for free. In Vietnam and Thailand, stowaways on trains were an accepted part of life, and Tony figured it would be the same here in America.

A bloodshot sun was rising in the east as Tony reached the staging yard of the Union Pacific on Blake Street west of Twenty-ninth. He scaled a chain-link fence that was designed to keep out dogs and children rather than determined interlopers. He moved like a shadow past the flatcars and the boxcars on their sidings. There were hundreds of them. He had a specific destination in mind, and while he might be forced to settle for a fair approximation, he was not prepared to waste his time, meandering for days across the countryside.

In fact, the choice was easier than he had dared imagine. Schedules of arrivals and departures were posted on the wall outside the stationmaster's office, and he had a chance to scan the listing after three abortive tries. Number 35 was scheduled to depart for St. Louis at nine A.M., and finding the train that bore his lucky number had been a simple task.

Four diesel engines coupled in a line would power him across the plains. Other cars were being added as he watched: the open hopper cars; long, silver tankers; flatcars, some of them with cargo lashed down under canvas; boxcars, jammed with freight or waiting to be loaded at their destination; stock cars, empty now, but smelling richly of sheep and cattle.

Hiding in a damaged sidelined boxcar, Tony watched the yardmen move along the line of cars, inspecting each, securing the locks on those already loaded, checking out the empties for uninvited passengers. He waited until the inspection team had passed out of sight, clutching his duffel bag tightly as he prepared to make his move.

No more than thirty feet of open ground lay between his hiding place and his goal, but the yardmen and doubtless other workers would be close at hand. Tony knew all his planning would be wasted if he was seen boarding the train. . . .

No!

His imagination was his worst enemy. He couldn't allow it to destroy his confidence. His target, a stock car, was one of three that stood nearby, the sliding doors left open by the yardmen after their inspection.

Tony held his breath and listened to the voices as they faded. Swinging his legs across the threshold of the car, he pushed off and landed lightly on his toes. With a final glance in each direction he saw the yardmen on his left a hundred yards away, distracted in conversation. He crossed the empty no-man's-land in loping strides. Pitching his duffel bag inside the car, he scrambled after it, scraping his palms and knees. Once inside, he grabbed his bundle, scurried to the darkest corner of the car, and huddled there, intent on blending with the dappled shadows.

The stock car reminded Tony of a night he had spent in Thailand, hiding in a farmer's tiny barn with bullocks crowded all around. Though the car was cleaned at frequent intervals, ancient dung was crusted between the floorboards, impervious to hose or broom.

At half past eight another yardman came along the tracks, whistling discordantly, a clipboard tucked beneath his arm. Pausing, he slid shut the door on Tony's car before continuing his rounds. He did not latch it, but the sudden shutting off of air and daylight made the car seem claustrophobic. Scowling in the darkness, Tony made his mind up to reopen the offending door as soon as they were safely under way.

They did not leave on time. At 9:15 Tony felt the shudder of the diesel engines warming up, and a quarter hour later they started creeping slowly from the yard. Tony felt a tingle of excitement in his stomach, swallowed hard, and held his breath until it went away.

The train seemed to take a lifetime to clear the staging yard, but finally they picked up momentum, whistling through intersections, leaving Denver, rolling through suburban Commerce City and beyond. According to his map, their route ran hard beside the Rocky Mountain Arsenal, but Tony saw nothing but the desert scrub that seemed to stretch forever.

He had carefully studied highway maps of Colorado and adjacent states before deciding on the train. It was at least 860 miles from Denver to St. Louis, open country all the way. The journey would take about sixteen hours. The car was dry and relatively warm, and he had sufficient food to last the trip, although he knew his stomach would be growling by the time they reached Missouri.

It was growling now in fact, and Tony made a meal of bread and ham, two candy bars, washed down with Coke the temperature of urine. His belly filled if not precisely satisfied, he stowed the can and wrappers in his duffel bag, then wandered down the car to try the sliding door. On his second try it opened halfway, groaning on its runners.

Sitting in the open doorway well back from the threshold, Tony watched the hurtling landscape. They left the Rocky Mountains in their wake, outran the arid Colorado basin, bored a path across the fallow heartland of Nebraska. Hours passed, and Tony watched, enchanted, rising only to relieve his bladder at the far end of the car.

They took on freight in Julesburg and again in Paxton. Each time Tony felt the train decelerate, he closed the stock car's door, retreated to his corner, prayed they would not be loading livestock. When they shuddered to a halt outside of Callaway in Custer County, Denver lay 320 miles behind.

In Callaway his bowels betrayed him. Urinating in the car was one thing; shitting there and riding with it for the next five hundred miles was something else. Tony knew he would have to take his chances, there and then.

No security precautions had been evident at either of their previous stops, and Tony had not closed the stock car's door completely as they rumbled into Callaway. He risked a glance along the track, left and right, saw railroad workers near the forward engines, others toward the rear, off-loading a boxcar.

He edged through the opening and dropped to the ground. No one was watching. So far, the whistle-stops had lasted roughly thirty minutes each, but the quicker Tony was back inside, hidden from the world, the better.

The tiny station house, thirty yards away, probably had public rest rooms, but he dared not risk a chance encounter with the stationmaster. A larger, corrugated metal building—apparently a combination storehouse and garage—stood out back. Tony skirted the perimeter, finding some cardboard cartons standing near a trash bin at the rear. The dumpster had recently been emptied but still contained some ancient rags that he grabbed for toilet paper. Using several of the larger cartons to form a screen for privacy, Tony crouched beneath the open sky, his jeans around his ankles, praying that he would not be discovered.

He was not, but the physical relief that Tony felt was coupled with a new anxiety. Returning to the stock car would be twice as dangerous as getting off. If he was spotted as he tried to board the train, the stationmaster would pursue him. At the very least he could expect to lose his duffel bag. At worst . . .

He pressed himself against the corrugated steel and craned his neck around the corner. At the far end of the train a pickup truck was being loaded with assorted crates and cartons. Seeing no one near the engines, no one loitering outside the station, he made his move.

Across the yards of open gravel welcome darkness beckoned him to sanctuary inside the car. Was the door opened a little wider than when he left? Impossible. He closed the gap to thirty feet. Now twenty. Ten. He leapt to catch the narrow handrail welded to the doorframe and lifted himself across the rusty threshold.

Safe!

The fist came out of nowhere, striking with sufficient force to lift him off his feet. He tried to grab the doorframe as he toppled backward, missed it, saw the world tilt crazily through one good eye. He landed on his back. The impact emptied his lungs, and pain exploded in his skull. For several panicked seconds Tony thought he must be dying, then his lungs again worked, and he could focus on the burly man who stood above him in the open doorway of the stock car.

"Fuckin' tramps. I thought we'd seen the last of your kind. Seems like you bastards never learn."

He climbed down nimbly for a man his size and seized a wad of Tony's jacket in his fist. One tug and Tony Kieu was on his feet, but his knees were rubber.

"I oughta kick yer ass," the big man snarled. "Too bad we gotta let the sheriff's boys have all the fun. You come along with me now, quiet like, or I just might forget my orders."

Tony was propelled along the trackside on shaky legs. It occurred to him that he should make a break for freedom, but he realized that he was in no shape to run. Until he got his wind back, he was at the big man's mercy.

A cautious glance across his shoulder verified the first impression that his captor had missed the duffel bag containing Tony's knife, extra clothing, food, and false ID. The bag was lost, but perhaps it was just as well. Who knows what trouble he'd face if he was caught with bogus papers and a weapon.

Inside the station Tony was directed to a wooden bench. "You budge from there," his captor cautioned, "an' I'll have to rearrange your parts."

The yardman ducked behind the counter, poked his head inside an office door, and reemerged a moment later with a shorter, older man in tow.

"We got another 'bo here, Mr. Sykes. I caught him tryin' to beg a ride on Number 35."

The old man studied Tony's face. "You work him over, Steve?"

"No, sir. The little bastard tried to deck me when I found him in the stock car. Ain't that right, boy?"

Tony glowered at him in silence.

The older man seemed unconvinced, but he was not prepared to argue in Tony's defense. "I'll call the sheriff. Keep him here, and keep those mallets to yourself, Steve, hear me?"

"Yessir." When they were alone, the yardman moved to

stand in front of Tony, hands on hips, a crooked smile upon his face. "I wish you'd try to rabbit, boy, I surely do. I need my daily workout."

"Steve!"

The bully turned, still grinning. "Yessir?"

"Seems I recollect you've got some work to do outside."

"I gotta watch this boy here, Mr. Sykes."

"I'll call you if I need you."

The screen door slammed behind Steve, and his bootheels clomped across the wooden platform. Tony watched the old man as he came around the counter, beckoning him with a crooked index finger.

"Rise and shine, son. Sheriff says I should pat you down for weapons. I don't want no trouble here, but I can call Steve back to do it for me, if I have to."

Tony rose and stood immobile, arms extended, as the old man frisked him. Somehow he missed the precious oilcloth packet, thinner now and tucked inside a secret pocket of the pea coat, but he found the wad of cash immediately, palmed it, counting off the bills.

"A roll like this, how come you're bummin'?"

Tony kept his mouth shut. His one, small hope lay with the poor defense of silence.

"You got a name?"

Tony said nothing.

"Suit yourself." His money disappeared into the old man's pocket. "Have a seat. The deputy should be along anytime."

Another quarter hour passed. Tony watched the train depart with his belongings while he waited for the squad car. Somewhere down the line another stowaway might find his duffel bag and be amazed that anyone would jettison such treasures on the road.

At the sound of tires on gravel, Tony turned to find a black-and-white patrol car outside the station house. The driver was a tall man dressed in khaki, heavy even for his height. His belly almost hid the buckle of his gun belt, and his double chins looked pinched in the confines of his collar. Khaki trouser legs were tucked into calf-length boots. He wore a rolled-brim Stetson, mirrored glasses, and he kept a toothpick in his mouth, occasionally shifting it from side to side. The tarnished nameplate on his breast identified the deputy as "Kehoe."

"Jack?" The old man looked surprised. "I reckoned you were on vacation."

"Change of plans." The toothpick grin was sour. "McMurtrey's wife run off again, and he went lookin' for her. Screws the rest of us, but there you go. You got a little somethin' for me?"

"There he sits. Steve caught him in a stock car on the U.P. 35. No papers, and he won't say boo to me."

"He clean?"

The old man slid a roll of bills across the counter. Tony noticed its size had dwindled since it left his custody.

"Six hunnerd bucks?" The deputy was turning toward him now. "You steal this money, boy?"

He studied his reflection in the mirrored lenses and held his tongue.

"Smart ass, huh?"

The old man retreated toward his office. "He's all yours, Jack."

"Don't you worry. I know how to handle trash like this. C'mon, boy, get your ass outside."

He was across the threshold, moving toward the car, when Kehoe caught him with a boot that sent him sprawling. Bleeding where the gravel had scuffed his palms, Tony scrambled to his feet and faced the lawman. Jack Kehoe kept one hand on his revolver, pointing with his other toward the squad car.

"Spread 'em, boy. Keep your legs well back. I have to tell you twice, I'll open up your skull."

Tony pressed his bloody palms against the cruiser's roof and spread his feet. The handcuffs closed around one wrist with startling rapidity; before he could protest, Kehoe hit him with an open hand between the shoulder blades and forced his chin against the car. The shackled arm went behind his back, the other followed, and his wrists were locked together. Steel bands cut off the circulation. A rough hand on his collar drew him upright, and he saw the bloody handprints he left behind.

His keeper had the back door of the cruiser open, waving him inside. "You watch your head, now." Kehoe shoved him so that Tony's forehead struck the doorframe, helping with another boot as Tony slumped inside, arms twisted painfully behind him.

Kehoe slammed the door. Tony was in a tiny cage, wire mesh preventing any contact with the driver.

They drove in silence through the narrow, dusty streets of Callaway. The jail and courthouse were inside a single red-brick structure at the heart of town. Inside the booking room a gray-haired deputy in a rumpled uniform removed the handcuffs, then took his fingerprints and photograph. He stood in silence when they asked his name and address. Tony watched as Kehoe counted out his money, dropping it in a plain manila envelope.

"Three hunnerd dollars," Kehoe told the booking officer.

Tony spent two hours in a tiny cell before Jack Kehoe reappeared with keys in hand. "J.P.'ll see you now. If you're smart, you'll tell the man your name. Make him mad—you're fucked, and that's a fact."

He had expected to be cuffed again, but Kehoe settled for a solid grip around one arm, thick fingers sinking deep into his biceps. Tony moved up a dingy flight of stairs and into the court. The room, including benches for the curious—all vacant now— was smaller than the railroad station's public waiting area.

The justice of the peace waiting for them was brown and wizened from a lifetime in the sun, his face was like a raisin crowned with tufts of graying hair. His eyes were small, but quick and bright. His teeth were yellow stumps.

"Let's hear the charges."

"Vagrancy and loiterin', your honor. Tryin' to defraud the railroad."

"Hobo?"

"Yessir."

"What's your name, boy?"

Tony stood in silence.

"What's his name?"

"Can't say, Your Honor. Got no papers."

"Well, now, is that so? I can't pass sentence on a man without a name. I'll have to think on this a spell. Meanwhile, I'd say this hobo was a juvenile. You think so, Officer?"

"I'd guess that's right, Your Honor."

"Fair enough. We'll see if Noah can't find somethin' that'll keep him out of trouble while I take this case under advisement. You're a ward of the court, boy. Take him away."

The gavel rapped perfunctorily, and Jack Kehoe led him back

downstairs. Instead of returning him to the cell block, Tony's captor led him to the parking lot and pushed him into the squad car. Kehoe wedged himself behind the steering wheel and slipped his mirrored glasses on.

"I told you you were fucked, boy. Ain't no fault of mine you wouldn't listen. Maybe you'll think better on it once you've spent a couple weeks at Noah's Ark."

22

INDIANAPOLIS

Anthony Patterson parked behind the Federal Building in a
space reserved for those who had OFFICIAL BUSINESS ONLY. He sat
behind the Blazer's wheel for several moments in the drizzling
rain and listened to the engine cooling, reminding himself once
more than this was absolutely necessary. He had stalled too long
already. It was time to place his problem in the hands of trained
professionals.

He stood outside the office of the Federal Bureau of Investigation, staring at the seal of Justice, part of him insisting he
could still turn back.

Like hell.

The FBI receptionist resembled *Playboy*'s Miss October, but
her smile was cautious.

"Special Agent Hackett will be with you shortly, if you'd care
to have a seat." The cautious smile switched off; she turned
back to her typing. He had been dismissed.

The magazines were standard office fare, outdated *Time*s and
*Newsweek*s, with a scattering of *Law Enforcement Bulletin*s. He
chose a *Newsweek* with Qaddafi sneering on the cover, opened it

at random to an article about pornography in Scandinavia, began to read. A wasted effort, he gave it up in under thirty seconds.

The latest mailing from his secret correspondent, postmarked Denver, had been different from the others. Curious. Confusing. Patterson had not known what to make of it. The implications were unsettling, but he could not deal with them. Not yet.

"Mr. Patterson?"

He glanced up, startled, from his magazine. The man who stood before him did not fit his image of a federal agent. Fiftyish and heavyset, in shirtsleeves, with a thin tie that was several seasons out of date. The short revolver on his hip weighed just enough to drag his slacks down, making him appear lopsided.

"Yes."

"Ben Hackett." Patterson was pleased to find Hackett's handshake firm and dry. "This way, please."

Miss October buzzed them through a door designed with terrorists in mind, and Hackett led the way along a corridor with offices on either side. The room reserved for interviews was small and spartan. There was a GI desk and swivel chair for the interrogator, and directly opposite, a straight-backed wooden chair to keep his guest from dozing off. A yellow legal pad was centered on the desk top, flanked by telephone and intercom. The President, the FBI director, and the late J. Edgar Hoover alternately smiled and glowered from the walls.

"Please, have a seat." The chair was every bit as comfortable as it looked. "I know we've spoken briefly on the phone, but now I'd like to hear your story from the top."

"All right." He began at the beginning, with the photograph of Lin Doan Kieu, alluding to their brief relationship in Vietnam. He noted the arrival of the three obituaries, heralding the death of strangers, and his own discovery that two at least were murder victims. Hackett scribbled on the legal pad and interjected when he felt the need.

"You kept these clippings?"

"No. I burned them."

Hackett raised an eyebrow, scribbled something else, and waited for him to proceed.

"Two days ago I got another envelope. From Denver. Just before I called your office."

"An obituary?"

"No. It's something else."

"You kept it this time? May I see it?"

Patterson withdrew the slim, white envelope with its meticulous inscription from an inside pocket of his sport coat. Grudgingly he handed it across the desk and was surprised to feel a portion of his anxiety evaporate as Hackett took delivery.

"You've read the contents? Handled it?"

"Yes, sir."

"Okay. It's probably too late for any decent fingerprints, but we can always try."

He took a pair of forceps from a drawer and used them to extract the contents of the envelope. Placing the single sheet of paper on the desk in front of him, he unfolded it gently, weighting the corners with his forceps and a ballpoint pen.

"I'm sorry, I don't read Vietnamese. Does this mean anything to you?"

"It's torn from a traditional *Ho Kau*, a kind of family register. The page you're looking at is something like a birth certificate."

"I see. This name on top would be . . ."

"The mother. Lin Doan Kieu." In Saigon in another life he had considered it important that he learn to write her name. He had not thought of it in years.

"This empty space?"

"The father's name. Omission indicates he wasn't known, or else he was considered an embarrassment, a family disgrace."

"Mmm hmm. And here?"

"The child's name."

"Can you translate for me?"

"No, I'm sorry."

"Never mind. I'd like to keep this, if I may."

"Of course."

"There's still an outside chance for latent prints, and I can run it by the Bureau linguists, find out if there's anything significant about that name or in the text."

"What will you do about the killings?"

Hackett frowned. "You have to understand that murder is a purely local crime. Unless the victim is a government employee or the crime takes place on federal land, the Bureau has no jurisdiction."

"What about state lines?"

"We handle certain interstate offenses, but our powers are defined and limited by federal statute. If there was a warrant on your killer, we might have an angle with unlawful flight, but as it is . . ." He spread his hands, a gesture of helplessness.

"I've been told you have a program aimed specifically at murderers who roam around the country."

"VICAP," Hackett said. "The Violent Criminal Apprehension Program. It's a new idea, just getting started really. It's designed to target serial killers, the repeaters like Bundy who travel and kill as they go."

"There you are, then. This fits."

"Maybe so, maybe not. I'll need more information on each of the crimes for a start. Then, you've got to remember that VICAP has eight or nine agents right now. Most of them are in Washington trying to get the computers on line."

"I've been threatened by mail. Now, I *know* that's a crime."

"Yes, it is. But it's not in the Bureau's domain."

"Come again?"

"It's confusing, I know. If the clippings and whatnot were finally judged to be threats, they'd be handled by postal inspectors. Of course, since you burned all the evidence . . ."

"Damn it! You're saying that no one can help me?"

"Not quite. I can talk to police in the various cities where murders took place. If we make any prints from your pen pal, they may fit a crime scene. We'd still need a name for the warrants, of course, but if one man looks good for all three . . . well, it's something to run with."

"I see."

"Is there anything else I should know?"

Feeling cornerèd, he turned to a lie. "I'm not sure what you mean."

"Well, this whole thing began with a woman. Now, three bodies later, she crops up again. I don't put that much faith in coincidence."

"No. I don't, either."

"Okay, so we've got a potential connection. The dead men were strangers, you say?"

"They were strangers to *me*. I can't say if they knew one another."

"All right, I can check on that later. They may have known Lin . . . was it Kieu?"

"Yes, it was. And they may have, of course. I don't know."

"Have you heard from the lady at all, since your time in Saigon?"

"No, I told you that once."

"So you did. Any word from her family?"

"No."

"Any relatives stateside, let's say?"

"I was never in touch with her family. She was afraid of her father's reaction, I think."

"Was he anti-American?"

Patterson shrugged. "He was hard-core traditional. Politics never came into it."

"*Mmm.* You've kept this from your wife?"

"So far."

"Your choice, of course." There was a healthy dose of disapproval in the agent's frown. "Unless you have something to add, any questions, I think that we're just about finished."

"That's it?"

"If I come up with anything, I'll let you know."

"Don't call us, we'll call you?"

Hackett rose, shoved his hands in his pockets. "I'll do what I can, Mr. Patterson. Understand, please, that your own slow response in this matter, plus the destruction of evidence, makes it impossible for me to guarantee anything. *If* we find prints, *if* they match any crime scenes or suspects, *if* local agencies want to play ball, I'll get back to you."

"Sure. And the next time he writes?"

"If you hear from your pen pal again, you should forward the letter, unopened, to me. We can run it for prints straightaway, before anyone muddies the water."

"All right."

"In the meantime, relax. Denver's over a thousand miles west, and we don't have a body confirmed there so far."

"That's what bothers me. *Why?*"

"I don't have any answers, yet. First, let me sort out the questions."

"You'll call me?" He hated the vague desperation he heard in his voice.

"When I have something, yes, sir."

They shook hands again; Hackett's grip was as firm and dry as before, while his own hand felt clammy and soft. Hackett walked with him back to the bulletproof door, thanked him solemnly for his assistance, and closed the door firmly behind him. Miss October never glanced up from her typing as he passed.

Outside, the drizzle had evolved into a driving rain, and he was soaked before he reached the Blazer. He cranked the engine over, let it idle while the heater drove his chills away, and tried to bring some order from the chaos of his thoughts.

Frustration topped the list, a feeling that he had accomplished nothing through his conversation with the G-man. Hackett operated in a narrow world defined by bureaucratic rules and regulations, handcuffed by the very laws he was commissioned to enforce.

Among his other jumbled feelings, Patterson was startled to discover that he felt relief. If nothing else, his secret burden had been shared, diminished in the sharing.

23

CHICAGO

Ben Hackett hated flying coach. The seats were cramped, and he invariably found himself sandwiched between snotty children whose mothers concentrated on their snacks and magazines. This time he had a pair of them in front of him, towheaded twins who had been whining constantly since takeoff. Mama had the aisle seat. She was working on her makeup now, attempting to correct a mess that plastic surgeons might have found intimidating.

Next time when he put in for an upgrade and the Bureau turned him down—which they inevitably would—he just might fool the bastards, take it out of pocket for a change and ride first-class. They still had asshole kids up there, but most of them were wearing ties, and drinks were on the house.

A disembodied voice, allegedly the captain's, cautioned one and all that they were seven minutes from O'Hare. At least the flight had been a relatively short one; last time he had done the red-eye number, back and forth to San Diego on a case involving Cuban gangs.

Another voice from midair, feminine this time, commanded everyone to place their seats and trays in upright, locked position. Hackett followed orders, looked around for someone to relieve him of his empty plastic cup, and finally stuffed it in the pocket of the seat in front of him.

Hackett had no luggage, and he waited for the aisle to clear before he made his move. The twins were ragging Mama, pulling on her skirt and whining that they wanted to go home. He smiled. Sometimes you get what you deserve.

He had no problem picking out the agent assigned to meet him. The guy looked like a poster child for the "new FBI" —hair playing tag with his collar and grazing the tops of his ears, thick mustache, a pastel-colored shirt and stylish silk tie. Old Hoover would have shit a cinder block before he shot the kid on sight, but that was ancient history.

And so, Ben Hackett thought, *am I.*

The youngster must have been expecting Efrem Zimbalist. He looked confused when Hackett introduced himself. He also looked a bit intimidated, which was fine.

"I'm Devon Cramer, sir. The SAC selected me to back you up."

"That's nifty, Devon." *Devon?* Gentry would be laughing up his sleeve, no doubt about it. Hackett made a mental note to plan a special greeting for Chicago's agent-in-charge, next time Gentry visited Indianapolis.

"Do you want to claim your luggage?"

"What you see is what you get. I won't be here that long."

He trailed his escort through the terminal and out into the parking lot. The "unmarked" Plymouth never would have been mistaken for civilian wheels by anyone with half a brain, but it was standard Bureau issue. Hackett didn't mind. His mission in Chicago was not undercover.

Cramer made an unsuccessful stab at small talk, finally discouraged by monosyllabic replies, and after half a mile or so Ben Hackett was allowed to think in peace.

It was four days since he had met with Patterson, and Hackett had been on the horn to homicide detectives in the cities where the various obituaries had originated. San Francisco confirmed that LeRoy Duckworth had been decapitated, his head propped upright on a desk inside the office he was cleaning. Hackett had a list of all his priors, and he readily agreed that nothing on the dead man's record seemed significant enough to justify his end.

There were no prints, no witnesses, no suspects, but a wartime snapshot of the victim, torn in two, had been discovered on his body.

L.A.'s finest filled him in on Evan Price, a one-time Army chopper jockey, recently the owner-operator of a one-man charter service catering to short-hop high rollers. Reports on file with Vice connected him to Manuel Herrera, one of Castro's rejects from the 1980 boat lift and a known cocaine importer. Price, his throat cut and his wall safe empty, was believed to be the victim of a drug burn. There were still loose ends, of course. The body was emasculated, and a mutilated photo of the victim, smiling for the lens in better days, had been discovered in one lifeless hand. The print technician had recovered decent partials from the scene, but they were not on file.

Las Vegas had the scoop on Mitchell Breen, a dealer at the Horseshoe, ambushed in the hotel parking lot by someone waiting in the backseat of his car. *You should have locked it up, man.* Death had been instantaneous: one shot fired into the skull at point-blank range. The shooter used a Browning automatic, which had been abandoned at the scene in classic gangland style.

With Vegas, he had played a hunch. "And where'd you find the photograph?"

After a momentary silence on the other end, his contact finally answered, plainly pissed, "You're not supposed to know that, mister."

But he did know, and they told him. Torn in half, the snapshot had been resting on the dead man's shoulder, some kind of message from the killer.

Unraveling that message was the problem. Hackett had a theory in the works, and while some gaps remained, it seemed to cover all the facts, so far. He was convinced that Duckworth, Price, and Breen would show up as connected, somehow, when a rundown on their military service records was completed. They had been involved in something over there—perhaps narcotics, the black market, even crimes against civilians—that was coming back to haunt them. Someone was settling a score. He could not put a finger on the Patterson connection yet; nothing indicated that the other victims had been warned or threatened, but he could not prove they *weren't*. It would be worth a closer look, but in the meantime, Hackett thought that he could trim the list of suspects. His theory, and the notion that he might prevent another killing, were the reasons for his visit to Chicago.

It was the kind of slick "creative thinking" that had been a Hackett trademark over thirty years of service with the Bureau, and it landed him in trouble on occasion. As a bright-eyed youngster in the fifties, prior to JFK and Bobby, he had pushed for an investigation of the syndicate while Hoover's top priority was still domestic communists. Assigned to work Detroit, he had ignored the not-so-subtle warnings from his SAC to shadow members of the Angelino family on his off-time. After several admonitions he had finally provoked a confrontation with the don himself, and he had slapped the old man's face. A transfer to "Siberia"—translated Butte, Montana—had probably saved his life, but it had taken years to work his way back up the ladder to a major urban office. Hoover's death had saved him from oblivion, and Hackett had been working in Indianapolis since 1974. His maverick reputation lingered on, however; old-line G-men still remembered Hackett as a rebel under Hoover, while the newer breed ironically regarded him as part of the conservative old guard. He wondered, sometimes, if they might not both be right.

They took a right on Lake Shore Drive, past Lincoln Park, Lake Michigan on one side, looming office towers on the other. Many of them had been built with money earned in Prohibition, in the labor wars and the narcotics trade, a cash bonanza endlessly recycled through legitimate concerns until the stains of blood and misery were hardly visible. You couldn't breathe inside the city limits of Chicago without smelling dirty money, and the richer suburbs had an odor all their own. The mob had burrowed deeply here, resisting every effort made by law enforcement to uproot illicit enterprise, but now the old, established dons were facing competition from a different quarter. After fifty years of uncontested rule, they were confronted with a revolution in the streets.

It was the good old, bad old days all over. Ethnic gangs and recent immigrants were rising from the urban gutters, challenging the power structure for a piece of the action. Cubans and Colombians, the Japanese, Chinese, Vietnamese, the Haitians, Puerto Ricans, home-grown blacks. They dealt in drugs and prostitution, ran protection rackets in their neighborhoods, annihilated their competitors. For anyone who knew the history of syndicated crime in the United States, the 1980s were a mirror image of the roaring twenties. It was like turning back the calendar and watching evolution start from scratch.

"We're here," Cramer said.

The office tower was a monolith of steel and glass, impervious to damage from the lakeshore weather. Law firms, advertising agencies, and retail chains had suites therein, but they were merely renting. The proprietor, who occupied the top three floors exclusively, was Le Chuan Duc, an Asian "businessman" whose pockets were reputed to be bottomless. That his assorted businesses included heroin, pornography, and prostitution was unrecognized by most of those with whom he came in daily contact. Local journalists and civic groups had showered him with kudos for his efforts to improve the lot of Southeast Asian immigrants in Illinois. No matter that he sold their daughters into slavery, poisoned thousands more with China white. He was a man of means and thus deserving of respect.

Hackett planned to speak with the private Le Chuan Duc this Monday morning. Devon Cramer parked the Plymouth, was about to follow him inside when Hackett placed a restraining hand upon his arm.

"I'll play this out alone."

"But I'm supposed to back you up."

"That won't be necessary."

"You don't know that. We have information linking Chuan with seven hits last year. That's seven dead we *know* about. He's not exactly Mr. Nice Guy."

"Any badges on your body count?"

"Well—"

"Look, he knows I'm with the Bureau, and he's got to know you're sitting down here waiting for me. I'll bet my life he's not an idiot. Okay?"

"Under protest."

"Fair enough."

The three floors occupied by Le Chuan Duc were serviced by a private elevator. Hackett was expected, and the car was waiting for him; so were three of Le Duc's men when he prepared to disembark. One of them tried to pat him down, and Hackett hit him with a solid straight-arm to the chest.

"Get real," he growled, prepared to punch the greasy bastard's ticket if he made another hostile move. He might not have the speed required to take all three, but he was betting two of them, at least, would never play the violin again.

The honcho's "private secretary" was a bruiser. Hackett figured he could stop him with a .38 between the eyes, but he was hoping it would not come to that. In fact, the walking slab of muscle greeted him with smiles and smooth apologies for any discourtesy he might have suffered. Those responsible, he promised, would be sternly disciplined. From the expression on the houseboy's face, Ben Hackett gathered that it was no idle threat.

The head man's office was approximately half the size of Hackett's home in Greenwood, Indiana. One whole wall was glass, which heightened the effect of size and almost made the visitor believe that he could make an easy swan dive to the lake. Le Duc, by contrast, was a slender, compact figure with a hundred-dollar haircut and a thousand-dollar suit. His hands were soft and neatly manicured, but there was granite in his eyes.

"Mr. Hackett, welcome to Chicago."

"Thank you. I appreciate your taking time to see me."

He accepted bourbon and declined cigars. When they were seated on opposite sides of Le Duc's massive desk, the Asian asked, "How may I be of service to the FBI?"

"We have a problem that may fall within your special area of expertise."

"Go on."

"Three men—Americans, all veterans of Vietnam—have, within the past six weeks, been murdered under similar circumstances."

"What have these crimes to do with me?"

"In each case, photographs of the deceased in military uniform were planted on or near their bodies by the murderer.

"We are convinced that each was killed as the result of a vendetta, dating from the war. They may have been involved in smuggling contraband from Vietnam to the United States."

"I am aware, of course, that such things happen. It is most unfortunate."

"We think the executioner is Asian, probably Vietnamese. Perhaps a refugee, more probably a syndicate enforcer acting under orders.

"The Bureau wants it stopped. We want the killer out of circulation, off the streets."

"Why come to me?"

"You have extensive contacts in the immigrant community, and more importantly, you are a man of vision. You can recognize how something of this nature might be bad for business."

"Oh?"

"A thing like this, with veterans being killed, it makes some people crazy. From the top on down you understand? If we can't isolate the killer . . . well, the heat may go down somewhere else. Chicago, for example."

Le Chuan Duc was silent for a moment, but he never lost his smile. "I have some contacts, as you say, among the refugees from communist oppression. I am not convinced that any of their number are involved in these unhappy incidents, but as a civic-minded citizen, I feel compelled to help you if I can."

Ben Hackett smiled. The little slug was neither civic-minded nor a citizen, but he had eyes and ears in places the FBI, for all of its technology, could never penetrate.

"I'm sure you'll think of something. And your efforts will be most appreciated."

"I must have specific details of the incidents."

Hackett rattled off the places, names, and dates. Le Duc did not take notes.

"Inquiries will be made."

There were amenities to be observed, but five more minutes saw Ben Hackett in the outer hall, accompanied by an escort to the private elevator. He observed with some amusement that his late antagonist had been replaced by someone more congenial. He hit the ground floor and hiked back to the waiting Plymouth and an anxious Devon Cramer.

"How'd it go?"

"It went." He cranked his window down to take advantage of the breeze. "Let's find someplace to eat."

24

NOAH'S ARK

Tony Kieu was wide-awake when the noise began at six A.M. His thirteenth morning of captivity, he had grown accustomed to the ritual of shouting, sheets and blankets snatched away from huddled bodies, slaps and curses. He was staring at the bedsprings of the bunk above him when Pug Stancell grabbed his blankets, whipped them down around his ankles, shouting, "C'mon, No-name, rise and shine!"

"I'm up."

The grinning boy was plainly disappointed by the mild reaction, but he turned the situation quickly to his own advantage.

"So, you're up, huh? Hey, he's up! You other faggots better watch your asses. No-name's up!" Pug straightened, jerked the covers off Skinny Jarvis, bellowing directly in his ear, "Hey, Porko! Shake a leg. Your buddy's up."

Pug's attention span had never been excessive, and he was already tiring of the game. He moved along, continuing his rounds with cries of, "C'mon assholes, rise and shine!"

The day began with sunrise at the Chalmers Home for Boys, known locally as Noah's Ark. Conceived originally as a last-chance school and sanctuary for the "wayward youth" of Callaway and other nearby towns, in practice the facility was neither. Classes in the basic grade-school subjects were irregularly offered, taught by randomly selected born-again believers who had volunteered their time. The Ark could not afford credentialed teachers, and the volunteers were prone to mix religion with their academic lessons, reading psalms in English class or teaching history from Genesis, with only passing reference to "the sinful, modern world."

As for the sanctuary notion, Noah's Ark provided nothing in the way of refuge from emotional or physical privation. Sixty-seven boys were housed in space built to accommodate fewer than forty. Funds for food and clothing were perpetually at a minimum, although the county kicked in thirty dollars every month per head in recognition of the fact that it could offer nothing better. Otherwise the Ark was self-supporting, selling vegetables in season and providing youthful labor for the town's odd jobs year-round. Aside from daily prayers, there were no rehabilitation programs, nothing in the way of therapy. A boy who entered Noah's Ark with problems generally took them with him when he left. If he was very lucky, he would not have picked up any new ones.

The Ark derived its nickname from its founder and headmaster, Rev. Noah Chalmers. A fundamentalist of the hellfire and brimstone school, Chalmers was stern but fair, a kindly man at heart. Of late, however, he was suffering from progressive senility. Within an hour of his own arrival, Tony Kieu had realized that Chalmers was the master of his house in name only. The power lay with others, and the aging minister had only vague ideas of how it was employed.

The afternoon of his arrival Tony had been ushered into Chalmers's office by Jack Kehoe. Lost behind his cluttered desk, a shriveled figure in an all-white suit at least three sizes too large, the reverend smiled at Tony and his escort, dentures clicking. At his elbow stood a muscular young man in faded jeans and denim work shirt.

"Thank you, Officer." The reverend's voice was dry and paper-thin. "I know you must be busy."

"This here's a tough one, Reverend. Tried to deck a fella at the railroad station, and he won't give up his name."

"I think we'll manage."

"I could stick around, in case—"

"No. Thank you."

Kehoe shot a sour glance at Tony and retreated from the office. Chalmers waited for the door to close before he spoke again.

"No name? Well, that's all right. We'll have to call you something, won't we? Let me see . . . I think I'll call you John, a small voice crying in the wilderness. I'm Reverend Chalmers, owner and administrator of the house in which you stand. And this"—he swept a gnarled, arthritic hand in the direction of the younger man—"is Stoney Burke, my chief assistant and a prime example of the final product we strive for at the Chalmers Home for Boys."

The final product scowled at Tony.

"We are a private institution," Chalmers told him, "open to referrals from the courts. My sacred mission is to mold the lives of troubled youths and set their feet upon the straight and narrow path of righteousness. With your cooperation, John, it is entirely possible that we can turn your life around. Without it . . . well, let's not anticipate the worst. Christian values. Personal responsibility. The only true foundation for a valuable, productive life."

The reverend paused, as if expecting some response from Tony. Drawing none, he nodded somberly and leaned back in his ancient, high-backed chair. "Stoney will escort you to your quarters and explain our simple rules. Tomorrow, you will receive your work assignment."

So far Tony had not spoken, but a single question had been nagging at him, preying on his mind.

"How long?"

The reverend looked surprised. "I beg your pardon?"

"How long will I stay?"

"Why, that depends upon the court's decision. And to some extent, it may depend on *you*."

He read the message loud and clear. Unless he told his name, supplied a verifiable identity, he might be there indefinitely. On the other hand, if he complied, he could be subject to arrest and deportation. His fingerprints were now on file in Callaway, and further contact with the courts would only heighten chances of his being connected with the homicides in California and Nevada. Silence was his only refuge . . . and his curse.

"Let's go."

He followed his escort from the office, through a musty parlor, then up a flight of polished hardwood stairs to the second floor. Their destination was a sleeping room that held four double-deck bunks and one large chest of drawers.

"Your bed," Burke told him, pointing to a lower berth against the east wall. "You get an underwear allowance by the month, and everybody shares the dresser. Everybody pulls a work assignment, like the reverend told you. Everybody eats together. Breakfast at six-thirty, lunch at noon, supper at six. Any questions?"

"No."

Burke hit him low and hard, a sucker punch that dropped him to his knees.

"No, *sir*! Let's try it one more time."

Tony gasped for breath. "No, sir."

"That's better." Grabbing Tony by the hair, Burke wrenched his head back, sending bolts of pain through Tony's neck and shoulders. "Tough guy, huh? You look like shit to me. I step on you, I'd have to clean my shoes."

He twisted Tony's hair for emphasis, eliciting a gasp of pain that put a sparkle in his eyes.

"You can forget about the old man's milk and honey, dig it, asshole? *I* run Noah's Ark, and *I* decide what goes. No one fucks with me."

A sudden shove slammed Tony's head against the wall. He was about to raise a hand and trace the swelling bump behind his ear, but he thought better of it.

"John, my ass. You're No-name, far as I'm concerned. You wanna be a man of mystery, go on ahead. It don't mean shit, because you ain't no man at all. You're zero on a scale of one to ten, you sorry fuck, and don't forget it."

Satisfied, Burke stepped away from Tony, pausing in the doorway. "Six o'clock for supper, on the dot. You show up late, you're outa luck till breakfast."

Tony struggled to his feet and braced himself against the nearest bunks until the room quit reeling. Pain from Tony's skull and stomach merged with the incessant throbbing of his swollen cheek where Steve had slugged him as he climbed aboard the train. His hands and knees were raw from scrabbling on the trackside gravel, and his back felt tender from the impact of his tumble from the stock car.

When the floor finally stabilized beneath his feet, Tony moved to stand before the windows, drawing back the flimsy curtains. In the open fields behind the house several dozen boys in matching denim churned the soil with hoes and rakes. A set of metal bars mounted on the outside of the windows, bolted to the wall, precluded any possible escape.

"Like the view?"

Surprised, he pivoted to face the voice and found himself confronted by a chunky youth with double chins, a crew cut, horn-rimmed glasses held together at one corner by a Band-Aid. He was smiling, hesitantly, carrying a broom.

"I see you've had your one-on-one with Stoney. Welcome to the club."

"Is he like that with everyone?"

"I'd say he's a consistent asshole, yeah. What are you in for?"

"I was picked up at the railroad station."

"You got a name?"

"Of course."

"Okay." The fat boy shook his head and said, "I'm Skinny. We'll, I'm obviously *not,* but it's my handle. Skinny Jarvis. Did you get a bunk assignment?"

Tony pointed at the berth that Stoney Burke had designated for him. "There."

"All right! We're bunkies. I'm on top . . . if that's okay?"

"Fine."

His bunkmate looked relieved. "It's almost time for supper."

The common mess hall at the Chalmers Home for Boys had been a formal dining room at one time, decades earlier. The furnishings and finery had been replaced by folding chairs and tables to create a seedy sort of cafeteria. Hardwood floors were clean but deeply scarred from years of abuse. The bill of fare was long on starch and short on protein, bland enough to satisfy the strictest salt-free diet. By the time that the Reverend Noah Chalmers finished saying grace the food was cold, but Tony wolfed it down, listening attentively as Skinny Jarvis filled him in on basics of survival in the Ark.

For openers, he pointed out the bullyboys who served as

Stoney Burke's enforcers. Eddie Green, a sneering youth with greasy hair and flaming acne on his cheeks, who giggled frequently without apparent cause. Pug Stancell, short and square-built, nicknamed for his piggy, turned-up nose. Mike Warkentin, potentially most dangerous of all, his throat encircled by a scar where he had narrowly escaped decapitation at age two by an alcoholic father. All three had histories of run-ins with the law; all three had been committed to the Ark as juvenile delinquents and had found a haven there beneath the wing of Stoney Burke. They were his personal gestapo, as described by Skinny Jarvis, and they carried out his orders to the letter.

"They've got it easy," Skinny whispered, studying the older boys. "Outside they'd go to jail for all the shit they pull in here. The reverend figures Stoney's 'saved.' His great success, you know? The poor old bastard also thinks *he* runs the place, which gives you some idea of his condition."

"Stoney runs it?"

"Pretty much. I figure there are folks in Callaway who know what's going on. I *know* some of them get a special price for work around their shops and shit like that. The difference goes in Stoney's pocket."

"How can you be sure?"

His bunkmate grinned. "I keep the books. It saves them paying an accountant, and I'm good with numbers."

Tony scraped his plate and downed a final bite of mashed potatoes. Skinny Jarvis was a stranger, but not an enemy. He took a chance. "I'm getting out of here."

"Good luck." The fat boy looked around, afraid they might be overheard. None of the other boys seemed to notice them at all. "You've seen the grillwork on the windows, right? The doors are locked at night. No one gets in or out without a key, and Stoney never lets it out of hand. You draw an outside work assignment, one of *them* is watching all the time. Whichever way you run, it's ten or fifteen miles of open country where a gopher couldn't hide."

"I'm getting out. I don't know how, but I'm not staying," Tony Kieu said.

As a new arrival and presumed escape risk, Tony drew an inside work assignment, helping keep the massive house in order. Skinny Jarvis also worked inside, along with half a dozen other boys who were precluded from assignment to the fields by their health or stature. All of them were subject to incessant verbal gibes from Stancell or his sidekick, Eddie Green, throughout the day. Most managed to ignore the insults—Skinny Jarvis even laughed along with his tormentors on occasion—but the worst abuse habitually fell upon slender Stanley Porter.

As the only nonwhite tenant of the Ark, he had inevitably been rechristened Sambo by the bullyboys. He could not share a room with Stoney Burke and company without attracting racial slurs or aspersions on his masculinity. He had a tendency to weep in public at the slightest provocation, and his tears invariably resulted in a torrent of renewed abuse. He was, Skinny Jarvis pointed out, "a few quarts low." The pointless cruelty sickened Tony Kieu, but he remained deliberately aloof, minding his own business. Until his seventh afternoon at Noah's Ark.

That day he was assigned to clean the large, communal bathrooms, one on each floor. He had been chosen personally by Pug Stancell. "Go easy on that chocolate, No-name," Pug grinned maliciously as he announced the day's assignments. "Wouldn't wanna spoil your appetite."

Tony had no idea what Stanley Porter might have done to earn the beating. Porter's bleating cries for help were audible throughout the house as Tony Kieu approached the bathroom door, mop and bucket in hand.

Inside the bathroom, Porter knelt between his persecutors, Green and Stancell, both hands raised above his head to ward off further blows. A smear of blood obscured his lower face; his cheeks were slick with tears.

"Leave him alone."

"Say what?" Pug Stancell seemed confused. Green chuckled at a joke that no one else could hear. "You got a problem, No-name?"

"Let him go."

"You wanna take his place?" For emphasis, Pug slapped the back of Porter's head, eliciting another squeal of fear.

Tony set his bucket down and stepped away from it. He kept the mop in hand. "He's had enough."

"I'll tell you when he's had enough," Pug growled. "You better shag ass outa here while I'm in a forgiving mood."

"Let's go, Stan."

"Sambo isn't goin' anywhere until we're finished teachin' him some manners."

"Manners," Eddie giggled, still amused.

Tony could have let it go at that, endured a few days of harassment as a new boy who forgot his place, but Tony was committed now. For reasons he could not begin to understand, he knew that he could not leave Stanley there. He moved forward.

Pug was in his face, all onion breath and body odor, cursing him. Eddie Green had moved to stand behind his stumpy side-kick, watching Tony with a curious expression on his pimply face. He was not laughing now.

With no way around them, Tony knew that any move he made from this point on would have to be decisive. Stancell stood no more than five foot six, but he was stocky, solid. Green would be surprised by any move that took Pug down, and that surprise might work to Tony Kieu's advantage.

"You *hear* me, No-name?"

"Sure."

He stepped back half a pace as if retreating, and the distance gave him room enough to slam a sneaker into Stancell's crotch. The bully doubled over, clutching his genitals.

Before Green could recover from shock, the sodden mop head struck him full across the face and sent him reeling. Tony followed up his advantage, clubbing Green across the head and shoulders with the handle of his mop. Once. Twice. A third time. On the fourth two-handed swing, he broke the handle over Eddie's back. That left him with a soggy pom-pom on a jagged, two-foot spike, and Tony was prepared to skewer Green if he made any hostile move. Instead of fighting back, however, Eddie made a run for daylight, veering wide around Pug Stancell as he vanished through the door.

"Come on, Stan." Tony held his hand out, helped the trembling adolescent to his feet. "Go to your room. And wash your face."

Stancell groaned from the sidelines, hunched over a sink for support. "You're a dead motherfucker," he hissed. "This ain't finished by half. Stoney won't let this go."

Over lunch, Skinny Jarvis was all eyes and ears, watching Tony as if he expected his bunkmate might sprout wings and fly. Other boys whispered to him, en route to the tables. *Good work. Way to go. Beautiful job.* At Burke's table the usual laughter was missing. Four cold pairs of eyes met his own when Tony looked up from his plate.

"You've got more balls than brains," Skinny told him, pretending to stare at his hot dog and beans. "Now they'll want you *and* Stanley. They always get even, man. Always."

He worked through the rest of the day, half expecting an ambush that never took place. Over supper, when Tony turned up in apparent good health, Skinny Jarvis seemed confused. Through the course of the meal he kept glancing at Tony as if he were sharing his place with an alien life-form.

The showers were "open" from seven to nine, though hot water most often ran out before eight. Tony usually waited for others to finish, but this night he needed the warmth to relax, and nobody argued or tried to cut in on his place in the line. As long as they left him alone, he was fine.

He had been in the shower ten minutes, was just rinsing down, when Tony's mind registered silence. No laughter. No sound of bare feet on the ancient linoleum. Slowly, he turned off the water, stepped out of the stall.

Stoney Burke and the others were waiting. Each carried a towel, sopping wet, with a knot at one end.

"You fucked up," Stancell told him, all smiles now that he had some support. "Fucked up *bad*."

Stoney Burke shook his head almost sadly. "I swear to God, No-name, I thought you were smarter than this."

"Guess we all make mistakes."

Tony charged, saw the ranks of his enemies melt, falling out to surround him. A move they had practiced and used more than once. Knotted towels stung his flanks, drummed his shoulders and ribs.

He was reeling, protecting his face with both hands while his enemies flogged him and ran him in circles. He slipped on the soppy linoleum, barely recovered his balance before a wet lash stung his testicles. Gasping, he dropped to his knees, curling into a fetal position as Burke and the others continued to lash him, each blow leaving red, angry welts on his flesh. With precision, they worked on his buttocks and thighs, on his kidneys and shoulders.

"That's enough." Stancell got in another few licks before Stoney Burke pushed him away. "That's *enough!*"

"Stoney, hey—"

Burke ignored him. He knelt beside Tony, knees damp from the floor, bending close so that even a whisper was audible.

"Tough guys don't make it. I told you that once. Maybe this time you'll listen."

For the next several days Green and Stancell went out of their way to make Tony's life miserable. He was assigned to the bathrooms or kitchen each day for a week, and the watchers made certain that there was a noxious mess waiting each time he reported for work. Backed-up toilets, apparently used several times without flushing, had to be pumped out by hand. Greasy pans were somehow misplaced, then "found" after Tony had finished the dishes and cleaned out the sinks. Plastic trash bags with bottoms slit open scattered their contents over the floor and his shoes. Tony took it in stride, uncomplaining, awaiting the day when a new job would take him outside. Away from the house. He would wait for the right time. He would escape.

But not today. This thirteenth morning, Tony drew the laundry detail. Each morning as he watched the others trooping out to work the fields, he felt an urge to fall in line behind them, take his chances, make his break as soon as they had cleared the fence. It looked so easy. Freedom was a hundred yards away.

It might as well have been a hundred miles.

The laundry room had three old washers and a single dryer. Dirty clothes were collected for a week and washed on Saturday. Unacquainted with the mysteries of Maytag, Tony listened carefully as Skinny briefed him on the workings of the various machines. He was alone, the first three loads already chugging merrily along, when he became aware of angry voices coming from the nearby kitchen.

A glance through the connecting door revealed Pug Stancell, hands on hips, confronting Stanley Porter. Stan was backed against the sink, his apron sopping and his hands all suds, recoiling as the bully shook a platter in his face.

"You call this clean? I wouldn't let a pig eat offa this. You gotta be the dumbest fuckin' nigger in the world."

"Don't call me that."

Though but a whisper, it might as well have been a shout. Pug Stancell's eyes went wide, his mouth fell open, color flaring in his cheeks. He swung, the platter shattering on impact, spraying jagged shrapnel. Stanley shrieked and threw his hands up, blood streaming from his lacerated scalp. He staggered, fell.

Tony saw the skillet on the counter and scooped it up before he had a chance to think. It would destroy the ruddy face before its twisted lips could utter one more hateful word.

Pug heard him coming, pivoted to take the blow head-on. Unlike in a cartoon, the skillet did not mold itself to Stancell's face. Instead, it finished off the job of flattening his nose—along with cheekbones, lips and chin. The bully's splayed and crooked teeth were not a problem anymore.

One blow would probably have done the job, but Pug was on his feet, still fighting to retain his balance, staring piggishly through eyes already swelling shut. The second blow broke Pug's jaw in three separate places, put a brand-new dimple in his cheek, and dropped him in his tracks, unconscious.

Stanley Porter was disoriented, groggy, rivulets of crimson tracing abstract patterns on his face. After a moment his eyes focused and he seemed to stare through Tony, facing down the adversary who had wounded him.

"Don't call me that," he whimpered.

Tony got him on his feet and held a folded rag against his scalp to stanch the bleeding. Stanley winced and tried to pull away at first, but finally held the compress on his own. Ignoring Stancell, caring little if he lived or died, Tony guided Porter up the stairs and saw him settled in his bunk, a clean towel pressed against his seeping wound, before he set off to confront the master of the house.

He found the Reverend Noah Chalmers nodding at his desk, a well-thumbed Bible open in his lap. If he had not been snoring softly, Tony might have taken him for dead. He closed the door behind him, crossed the room, and roused the old man with a gentle nudge.

The rheumy eyes were slow to recognize him. "John? You really should have knocked, my boy. A bit of common courtesy." He scanned the room. "Is Stoney here?"

"No, sir."

"What can I do for you, my boy?"

"It's Stanley Porter, sir."

"The nigra boy?"

"He needs a doctor."

"Doctor? What's the matter with him?"

"He's been beaten."

"What? Impossible!"

"By one of Stoney's friends."

"Is Stoney here?"

"No, sir, but—"

"He has been my great success, you understand. Of all the boys I've sheltered, all I've tried to set upon the narrow path of righteousness, none ever chose to stay and help me with my burden. None but Stoney."

"He's been using you to help himself."

"You should be thankful. We would all be lost without him."

"Stealing from you."

"The devil is a prince of thieves and liars."

Tony saw that it was hopeless. Noah Chalmers had retreated to a world where earthly problems were remote. If he understood what Tony had been saying, he could not accept it.

"You're wondering why I called you here, of course." The reverend looked puzzled, frowning at his Bible, searching for an answer to the riddle in Leviticus. "A moment, please, and it will come to me."

Eddie Green was waiting in the hall when Tony left the office.

"Stoney had you pegged, all right. He figured you'd run squealin' to the Man. I guess you need another shower, No-name."

"I think you need another mopping, Eddie."

Green retreated several paces, giggling nervously. "Forget it, asshole. Stoney's got your number. Better hope you grow some extra eyes to watch your back from here on out."

"I'll smell you coming."

Tony took a step in Green's direction and the boy bolted. Skinny Jarvis was already waiting for him when he got back to their room.

"Christ's sake, I figured you'd be dead by now."

"Not yet."

"You really did it, didn't you? I mean, you freaking *did* it."

"Yes."

"They had to take him into Callaway. You *smashed* him, man."

Tony lay down on the bunk and closed his eyes to think. His exit from the Ark was urgent. Skinny seemed to echo Tony's thoughts as he crouched down beside the lower berth.

"You've gotta find a way to make it outa here. You stick around, they'll kill you, sure as hell."

"I doubt it."

"Oh, you *do*? Well, let me tell you something, smart ass. It's been done before."

Tony listened as Skinny told the story.

"About a year ago, there was a new kid. Tough, like you. He wouldn't take the usual shit from Stoney and his friends. Not like *you;* he never put one of them in the freaking hospital, but he was cool.

"One night he up and disappeared. The story got around about him jimmying a lock and sneaking out, but it was bullshit. Couple of the guys he roomed with told me Stoney and the others came and got him in the middle of the night. He fought 'em, but he couldn't handle four-to-one. They took him, then they came back later for his stuff. You read me?"

"I'll be careful."

"Yeah, you do that," Skinny cautioned. "Be damned careful."

It was three for dinner at the captain's table. Stoney Burke, Mike Warkentin, and Eddie Green sat quietly, each glaring daggers at Tony through the meal. Around the table where he sat with Skinny Jarvis, silence radiated like ripples in a pond of apprehension. Those who sat the nearest to him finished with their supper quickly, clearing out as if the unadulterated hatred of the Burke brigade might be contagious.

Outside the dusk was deepened by a bank of storm clouds, moving in from the east with a rising wind. Before the boys of Noah's Ark had finished supper, rain was lashing down around the house, and bright sheets of lightning flared in advance of rolling thunderclaps. It was a night for violence, and the boys retreated to their rooms immediately after the Reverend Noah Chalmers's rambling benediction, passing up the hour of TV they were allowed on Saturdays.

Skinny Jarvis was tucked in by eight o'clock, reading by a night-light. Their other roommates feigned exhaustion, one of them snoring theatrically within seconds of resting his head on the pillow. Tony wondered how long he could keep up the act.

Fully clothed, his pea coat wrapped around him, Tony crawled under his sheets, taking care with the knife. He had lifted it during the meal, slipped it into the sleeve of his work shirt, returning a spoon and a fork with his half-eaten food. It was dull, but it would serve.

Darkness.

"Oh, shit."

Skinny Jarvis clicked the switch on his night-light in vain. From the hall, startled voices confirmed that the power had failed. Tony threw back his blankets, sat up in his bunk with the knife in his hand.

"Holy shit! You awake, man?"

"Right here."

"They'll be coming, the bastards. They knocked out the lights."

"Could be lightning," the voice of a sleeper responded. The snoring had stopped when the light was extinguished.

"My ass," Skinny hissed. "When's the last time we blacked out from lightning?"

A sound in the corridor: fumbling hands on the doorknob.

"Get a *flashlight*, goddamn it! Come on!"

"No," Tony ordered. He shifted the knife to his left hand and wiped his palm dry, took it back in his right.

The door opened swiftly, and three black-clad figures burst into the room. They went straight for Tony's bed.

Tony rose to his feet . . . and staggered as Skinny lunged past him, a hurtling butterball launched from on high. Eddie Green took the weight on his shoulders and folded, his knees slamming painfully into the floor. He was cursing and gasping as Skinny lit into him, gouging and biting, his bulk driving Green to all fours.

Which left two, and Tony braced himself, holding the knife at his side as they tackled him, hammering at him with table legs cut in the woodshop. He fought back as best he could, ducking beneath their clubs, taking the blows on his shoulders and back. Someone kneed Tony's chest and he clutched the leg, held it, his knife pumping in and out, blood-slick before it was wrenched from his hand.

Someone screamed. It might have been Skinny. Tony broke for the door, found its edge with his face in the darkness and

stumbled. Pain exploded in his shoulder as someone connected,
a blow from above and behind that was numbing. He lurched
through the door, crabbed into the hallway on hands and knees,
knowing that this was the end.

"I'll kill you, you bastard!"

Behind him, a silhouette etched by the lightning outside,
Stoney Burke filled the doorway, his bludgeon upraised to deliver the finishing blow.

A wailing, unlike any sound the combatants had made up to
now, stayed his hand. Tony pivoted, losing his balance completely. From out of the darkness a fireball was racing to meet
them, erratically weaving from wall to wall, keening in rage.

Tony recognized Stanley, the kerosene lamp, and he knew
what was coming. On elbows and knees, like a lizard, he
wriggled away from ground zero.

"Don't you call me that!"

Spinning, the lamp made a full turn before it exploded above
Stoney Burke, raining fire on his head from above. He was
screaming and dancing as Porter slammed into him, melding
their bodies together in flame.

Tony ran, with the fire at his heels. Ancient walls, floor, and
ceiling went up like a tinderbox, dark clouds of smoke churning
thick in the stairwells. Above him, more screams—the bars on
the windows prevented escape. Tony stumbled, fell headlong,
then scrambled to his feet again.

In the parlor he wrenched at the door, gave it up when the
lock resisted. Doubling back to the cold fireplace, he snatched
up a poker, renewed his assault. Boys were hammering past him
in search of an exit, and others were grouping around him, some
hurling their weight at the door, when it gave. Tony hurdled the
threshold, pushing past the others. He fell on the steps, skinned
his hands, kept on running. Behind him the house was a tower of
fire.

He would hear the screams after he knew it was no longer
possible for him to hear them. The screams, and the roar of the
flames.

Tony ran into the darkness and safety. He ran for his life.

25

SOUTHERN INDIANA

"You have my number?"

"Yes."

Jan Patterson felt foolish. She had asked the question twice already. She must look ridiculous, and yet . . .

"If you have any problems—"

"You'll be notified, of course. He seems quite happy with the other children."

Jerod *did* look happy, following a pair of new acquaintances around a course of child-size obstacles. His laughter sounded bittersweet and far away.

Would she have been more comfortable with a tearful scene, his tiny hands clutching her skirt, refusing to let go? *Of course I would,* she thought. *He could at least* pretend *to miss me.*

Jan was being selfish and she knew it, but the understanding did not soothe her wounded feelings. It was still too soon for her to cut the apron strings.

She had agreed with Anthony that preschool would be good for Jerod. It would let him grow accustomed to a new environment, make new friends, develop independence. At the same

time, it would help them get used to the idea that he was starting
school this fall. In five short months. Too soon.

Of course she was not losing Jerod. That was silly. He was
spending half the day at preschool, nothing more. And come
September, he would spend a longer portion of the day in class.
But he would still be *hers,* and there were years to go before he
went to college. Moved away. Got married.

God she felt so old!

Perhaps the only thing she needed at the moment was a
pick-me-up, Jan thought. She had a few ideas on how to beat the
old-age blues, if Anthony could tear himself away from work.
This afternoon would be the first time they had been alone
together in the house for almost six years.

Her thoughts of Anthony brought back to mind a different
concern. She was convinced his nightmares of the war had been
recurring, though he had not said as much. The past three
months or so he had appeared increasingly preoccupied. She
recognized the symptoms, having seen him through the worst of
it when he'd been a patient with the Veteran's Administration.
She had hoped that he would never have to deal with it again. So
far, they had been lucky.

She could love him out of it, she was convinced of that, if
only he would share his pain. By shielding her he could only
harm himself, but it was not a subject she could raise without an
invitation. It would never do for her to trespass in his private
hell.

She was surprised to find him waiting for her, seated in the
front porch swing. He smiled and raised a hand as Jan pulled up
beside the Blazer; swallowing her apprehension, she responded
in kind.

"You on a coffee break?"

"I didn't feel like working."

"Super." That would make it easy. "We can spend the
afternoon together."

"Want to take a walk?"

"Sure thing." The smile came easily. She wasn't *really*
worried yet. "Just let me change my shoes."

She put on a pair of comfortable walkers and joined him in
the yard.

"I'm glad you're home," he said.

He took her hand and led the way around the house, across a sloping meadow that concealed their septic system. Soon it would be bright with flowers. Jan had done the landscaping herself, and she was justly proud of her creation.

The meadow ended, and a deer trail wound through woods that thickened near the bottom of the grade. They had a string of feeding stations along the trail, supplied with salt licks and alfalfa. Sometimes deer came close enough for her to watch from the kitchen window as they grazed around the fringes of her meadow.

Jan, a city girl, had fallen for the woods with all a convert's zeal. She loved the animals and birds, the trees and flowers in their season, the dramatic difference from city living. Here, your closest neighbor might be half a mile away, but he would more than likely be your friend. In southern California, you were constantly surrounded, put upon by others, but you seldom really knew your neighbor, or wanted to.

The forest had intimidated her at first. Its strangeness and its silence—actually alive with tiny sounds, once she had learned to listen—had been almost frightening, but she had taken to the challenge with enthusiasm. Gradually she had learned the names of trees and birds and animals, their habits and their sounds. She knew that there was nothing more ferocious in the woods of Forrest County than the stray raccoon who liked to topple garbage cans at midnight. There were copperheads and rattlers, of course, but they were timid, secretive, and no one in the county had succumbed to snakebite in the past two decades. In the wildlands, man would always be his own worst enemy, and they had posted signs around the boundaries of their property to keep human predators at bay.

She knew before they reached it that his destination was their secret place. The hidden meadow was a geographical anomaly, a clearing in the woods where there was sign of neither fire nor flood. No fallen trees attested to a freakish windstorm or the ravages of man. No sign of lightning strikes. No barren rock that would deny trees their daily sustenance. No reason for the forest to surrender open ground equivalent to half a football field in size. But there it was, surrounded, overshadowed by the trees.

They had not visited the spot in a year or more, but it still looked the same to Jan. The knee-high grass would soon be green again, and any flowers blooming here had not been planted by the hands of men. From where they stood, the high end of the meadow, she could almost see the narrow stream that crossed it lower quarter, flowing from the trees and back again, emerging here to catch a bit of sun.

They found a point of high ground near the trees, and Anthony sat down. She joined him, looped her arm through his content to wait until he settled on precisely what he wished to say.

At length he said, "I have to tell you something, but I don't know where to start."

Oh, God, she thought, *it's bad.*

"Why don't you start at the beginning?"

"It's about the war. Some of it."

"I'm listening."

He told her everything. About the girl he had met in Saigon, prior to being wounded in the Tet offensive. Their relationship. It's sudden, violent end.

I can't be jealous. It was years before we met. There had been other men before she walked into the VA ward and saw him scowling out the window. If the truth be told, there had been others after, in the months before she came to realize how much she cared for Anthony.

He told her all about the faded photograph and how he had destroyed it to prevent her finding out. It was an act of love, she knew, but somehow Jan could not help wishing he had trusted her in the beginning. The obituaries puzzled and frightened her a little. More, when he explained that two of them referred to murder victims. When he got around to the *Ho Kau,* his visit with the FBI, she was confused again.

"What does it mean?"

He shook his head. "I haven't got the foggiest idea. The agent I talked to seemed to think it might be a vendetta, dating from the war."

"But if the other men were strangers . . ."

"I don't know." She read frustration, anger, in his voice. "I might have met them. Had a drink or something. Who the hell can say? It's eighteen years ago, for Christ's sake! I met lots of people. Some of them came home alive."

She slipped an arm around his shoulders, pulled him closer.

He did not respond at first, but then she felt him starting to relax. She heard a question forming in her mind, but she could not ask it.

"Does he think we're in danger?" It did not occur to her that Anthony might have to stand alone. Her life was inextricably entwined with his, and she could tolerate no thought of separation.

"No. He doesn't think the killer would be sending me these things, these warnings, if he meant to take me by surprise."

"But why, then?"

"Well, if I knew that—"

"We'll be all right," she said. "I love you."

He came into her arms with only momentary hesitation, bore her to the ground beneath his welcome weight.

"I'm sorry that I didn't tell you sooner."

He was kissing her, touching her. Her lips were opening to greet his tongue; her legs were open to accommodate the hand he slid beneath her knee-length skirt. She was on fire, and when he tried to slide her panties off, she made it easy for him, buttocks lifting off the ground.

"I love you, Jan."

He moved between her open thighs and entered her, their bodies welded in an instant as he pinned her to the ground. She locked her arms and legs around him, hung on for the ride, unconscious of the silent tears.

A single white-tailed deer stood watching from the shadow of the trees. He had been drawn by sounds and scents he did not recognize, surprised to find the man and woman rutting in his meadow. He sensed they were too preoccupied to do him harm.

The graceful forest creature watched them for a few more moments, curious, then turned and vanished.

26

ST. LOUIS

Tony Kieu approached St. Louis from the west on Highway
70 with the unearthly sound of steel guitars reverberating in his
skull. A long-haul trucker named Jerry had supplied him with a
ride from Kansas City, country-western stations fading in and
out across the miles. Jerry sang along and talked about the little
woman who was waiting for him in Centralia. Tony gave his
name as Vince and mentioned "family" in St. Louis, leaving
out the details that would certainly have sent his benefactor
racing for a telephone to call the police.

The run from Kansas City, better than two hundred miles,
had been the softest part of Tony's journey from Nebraska. He
had come away from Noah's Ark with only his precious photos
and the clothing on his back. No maps. No cash. No weapons.
Nothing. In the rainy hours prior to dawn, he had discovered an
abandoned barn and crept inside, stripping his sopping garments
off and letting them dry. He had awakened cold and ravenous,
his clothing stiff and brittle, but at least the rain had stopped.
The empty fields were steaming in the first pale light of dawn as
he set off again on foot.

Outside of Litchfield he was picked up by a farmer on his

way to market. Early morning news was on the radio, about a fire that had destroyed the Chalmers Home for Boys in Custer County. Thirteen boys were dead, and volunteers were sifting through the rubble in a search for other bodies. The Reverend Noah Chalmers had survived, but no one seemed to know precisely how or why.

That afternoon Tony robbed a henhouse near Ravenna, making off with half a dozen eggs, which he devoured raw to ease the gnawing hunger. Though he was not looking forward to another night without real food and shelter, motels were few and far between, and all of them demanded money. He was searching for a viable alternative, and getting nowhere, when he came upon the farmhouse north of Cairo.

Large and well-kept, a broad expanse of open farmland set it apart from neighbors. Best of all, a brief reconnaissance revealed that no one was home. He broke in through the rear and hit the kitchen first, constructing sandwiches of ham and cheese, with corn chips on the side, washed down with cans of Orange Crush from the refrigerator. Having appeased his hunger, he launched a systematic search for items that would help him on the road. Finding a set of luggage in the bedroom closet, he chose a laundry bag instead. From dressers and the closet he selected pairs of jeans that fit him, more or less, some extra socks, a plain white shirt. The kitchen drawers gave up a box of wooden matches, candles, and an eight-inch carving knife. He cut two strips of cardboard from a cracker box and made a homely sheath with masking tape before slipping the knife inside his pea coat. Digging in a cookie jar, Tony was delighted to discover fifty-seven dollars, folded once and anchored with a paper clip. He pocketed the money, topped his bundle off with dry salami, half a loaf of bread, a jar of baked beans, and struck off eastward.

Close to dusk he caught a ride as far as Bradshaw, where a fatherly motel proprietor examined Tony's luggage, adding five more dollars to the nightly rate. The room was worth it, cramped and seedy as it was; he took his first hot shower in three days and fell asleep immediately after in the sagging single bed.

The motel's checkout time was noon, but Tony Kieu was up and out by eight o'clock next morning. He breakfasted in a nearby coffee shop and was on the road by nine. He did not think they would be looking for him yet, but he would take no chances. Driven by a need to make up for lost time, he chose a highway ramp and stuck his thumb out.

East on Highway 80 into Council Bluffs, then south on Highway 2 to Kansas City. Tony rode with long-faced, sunburned farmers for the most part, listening to stories of their crops and families, the lives they led, the ways in which their faith had been tested. A balding Bible salesman picked him up in Fremont County . . . and immediately put him out again when Tony showed no interest in the laying on of hands. A college student, homeward bound for Easter break, had nearly deafened him with heavy-metal music screaming from his tape deck. Finally, in the flat lands east of Kansas City, there was Jerry in his Peterbilt, the long run over Highway 70 with Johnny Cash and Willie Nelson keeping time.

The trucker dropped him off on Market Street near Union Station in a neighborhood where drifters came to wait for likely prospects and the ragged homeless begged for change. Before he could attend to business in St. Louis, Tony required a base. His remaining cache of less than thirty dollars would not last the night.

He thought about Luan Nol, his casual offer of assistance if their paths should ever cross again. He had not kept the salesman's business card, had scarcely given him a second thought since Denver, but the memory returned now, offering at least a hope of sanctuary in the cold, forbidding city.

Inside the station Tony found a bank of phone booths, two with their directories intact. Luan Nol was listed and he ripped out the page, folding it into a pocket of his pea coat. Thumbing backward through the dog-eared pages, he pocketed a second flimsy sheet for future reference. He bought a city map for fifty cents, studied it, went back outside to hail a taxi.

Tony could have found a bus stop, searched the schedule until he found a drop-off point within a mile or so of his intended destination, but the hour was approaching twilight, storm clouds threatening another night of rain. He did not relish the idea of hiking through the suburbs in a downpour, laundry bag across one shoulder, searching for an address in the darkness. Should the salesman be away on business or unwilling to receive him . . .

The third cab out, a Checker, stopped for Tony Kieu. The red-faced driver cranked a window down.

"How much to Compton Avenue?"

"What part?"

"By Marquette Park."

The driver ran a tally in his mind, computing time and mileage. "Roughly seventeen, without the tip."

He was already climbing in the back. "Let's go."

The ride took thirteen minutes. Tony disembarked upon a residential avenue with streetlights spotted on the corners, paid the driver.

"That was seventeen *without* the tip."

"Right."

"Smart ass!"

After an angry squeal of rubber, Tony was alone. The park lay behind him, darkness shrouding empty tennis courts. The first, fat drops of rain were pattering around him as he struck off to the north in search of Luan Nol's home.

It was a decent neighborhood of large houses. Vehicles along the curb and in the sloping driveways indicated money spent with more attention to performance than fickle style.

If Luan Nol's house was any indication, he had been very successful in America. Two stories tall, painted white and gray, with manicured shrubbery, it spoke of quiet elegance. The vintage Cadillac was nowhere in sight, but an expensive station wagon occupied the driveway. Tony had expected less, and he was apprehensive as he moved along the pebbled walkway to the porch.

He took a breath and tried to calm himself. At worst he would be asked to leave. He still had time enough and cash enough to find himself a gay bar, if it should come to that, and try the game that he had played in California.

He pressed the doorbell. Waited. Nothing. Should he try again, or simply leave before the neighbors got suspicious? There were lights on inside the house, but that did not mean anyone was home. He had his finger on the doorbell when an ornate porch light blazed to life and momentarily blinded him. He was still blinking when the door swung open and a soft voice asked, "May I help you?"

He had not been conscious of the girl's approach. Her footsteps were muffled by the deep-pile carpeting. She was attractive in an understated way, and seemed shy. A child of Asia, planted in the New World by mistake.

He had a sudden urge to bolt. Instead he cleared his throat and said, "Luan Nol?"

"Please, wait."

She closed the door in Tony's face and threw the dead bolt. Standing in the porch light's glare, he felt conspicuous and vulnerable—a stationary target.

He made a conscious effort to relax. No one was looking for him in Missouri. And they probably would not be looking for him in Nebraska, either. What was one more missing boy, especially when he had no name? Another burden on the state removed, as if by magic.

Tony stiffened as the dead bolt opened once again. This time an older woman stood upon the threshold, studying his face without expression on her own. The girl—her daughter?—hovered in the background, sneaking bashful glances at him when she thought he would not notice.

"Yes?"

"I wish to see Luan Nol."

"My husband has been called away on business. He will be home later, if you care to leave a message."

Thinking about the long walk back to Union Station, Tony decided it was worth a try. "I met your husband in Las Vegas. He was kind enough to offer me a ride. In Denver, where we parted, he invited me to visit him when I was in St. Louis."

"You come so far, from Denver, just to see my husband?"

"No." He bowed his head, the image of humility. "I have been traveling to see my father. He is an American. I am *bui doi*."

The woman studied Tony for another moment, but he did not meet her eyes. "I understand," she said at last. "My husband would not wish for you to leave before he speaks with you. He should be home within the hour. Please, come in."

She took his coat, the carving knife securely hidden in its lining, and she stowed it in a closet with his makeshift duffel bag. He followed Luan Nol's wife into a comfortable parlor, sat down in the chair she indicated.

"I am Chao Ying Nol. And you are?"

"Tony Kieu." There seemed to be no point in lying, since the salesman knew his name.

"Mai Lin, our daughter."

Tony's smile brought color to her cheeks. She whispered

something to her mother, turned, and vanished through a doorway that apparently connected with the kitchen. Tony caught the rich aromas of a meal in preparation, and his stomach grumbled softly.

"You have been in the United States a short time?"

"Yes."

He had a story ready for Luan Nol, but he was not prepared to share it with the woman. Discussing such matters with a housewife in her husband's absence would be a breach of etiquette and tradition. Chao Ying Nol would understand.

"Have you enjoyed your travels?"

Tony thought of Wendy Nash, his days and nights at Noah's Ark, and forced a smile. "I have."

"In Vietnam," she said, "my husband was a merchant with a business of his own. In the United States he works for others, and we live like Madame Nhu." She spread her hands to indicate the living room, its furnishings, the house itself. "For all of this, we have to thank America. It is a country of surprises."

"Yes."

"Here, I think that we are very lucky, but I wish my husband did not have to be away from home so much."

Her eyes grew nervous. She was embarrassed by her indiscretion, having shared the secret of her feelings with a total stranger. Tony saw her weakness as another mark of how America had changed Nol's family. Along with the expensive cars and the grand suburban home came the erosion of tradition. Historically, Asian woman were expected to preserve decorum, speak their minds in private, if at all, and only with advance permission of their husbands.

Awkward silence hung between them for a moment, broken by a splash of light across the windows as a car pulled up into the driveway. Tony Kieu was on his feet before Nol's wife could rise.

"My husband."

Wife and daughter met the salesman as he entered, planting chaste suburban kisses on his cheeks. Mai Lin stepped close and whispered something to him, glancing once in the direction of the parlor. Nol frowned thoughtfully and handed a leather briefcase to his wife. Both women disappeared in the direction of the kitchen as he turned to deal with Tony Kieu.

"The young man from Las Vegas." Recognition turned the frown into a cautious smile of greeting. "Welcome to my house."

Humility was called for. Tony made a show of studying the carpet. "I apologize for coming to your home without an invitation."

"I believe you were invited. Please, sit down."

They faced each other from the depths of matching armchairs.

"Is your father well?"

"He has denied me," Tony said. It was a truth of sorts, and the embarrassment he felt was real enough.

"I see."

"There is no place for me in the United States. No place in Vietnam. I have a little money, but it will not be enough."

"You must stay here," Nol said. "Tomorrow, I will help you look for work."

"Your generosity is great."

"The loss of homeland is a bond between us. Say no more." Nol's wife appeared as if on cue. "We have a guest," he told her. "Mai Lin will prepare the spare room."

"As you wish."

He sat across from Luan Nol's daughter at the dining table. She refused to meet his eyes directly, blushing once when Tony caught her glancing at him surreptitiously. They dined on salad, pot roast, rice, string beans, and apple pie. Tony Kieu was ravenous, but he declined a second helping of the roast. He was a guest, and as such there were protocols to be observed.

Luan Nol conducted Tony to the guest room after dinner, pointing out the bathroom on the way. A narrow single bed was set aside for visitors, the mattress bare, but Mai Lin soon appeared with pillows, sheets, and blankets, working swiftly and efficiently until the bed was made. Luan Nol observed his daughter at her task, did not seem startled or concerned when she graced Tony with a smile in parting.

"Tomorrow," the older man reminded him, "we look for work."

27

On the second lap, Luis Briones realized that he was getting old. He felt it first in his legs, then in his chest, where lungs once accustomed to much longer runs had lately strained for wind within the first few miles. He would be panting by the time he hit lap six or seven.

Tomorrow was his birthday, thirty-seven big ones down the crapper, but he knew a lot of men his age who ran in marathons, for Christ's sake.

"Hey, coach!"

The coeds greeted him with smiles and upturned fannies as they did their stretching exercises. He made a point of sucking in his gut and picking up the pace until he left them well behind. A little motivation, that was all he needed, and Briones did not want to think about the fact that in another moment little girls with coltish legs and pear-shaped asses would be lapping him.

Lap this, he thought, and put a little something extra in his stride.

It was not time that threatened him, he realized; it was his lifestyle. Too much beer. Too many late-night parties stretching into morning. *Too much sex?* Not lately, damn it. Not since

Angela decided on a change of majors. There she was, the sweetest little graduate assistant he had ever seen, and she was humping Carstairs in the history department. What a waste!

Lap three. It was amazing what a little righteous anger did for the adrenaline. Still, you couldn't stay pissed *all* the time, and he resolved to cut back on the Michelob. Not cut it out entirely—he was no fanatic—but a little moderation would not kill him. He was still in decent shape for someone edging out of his thirties. Damn near fifteen years since he had left the service, and on good days he could still put in a seven-minute mile.

At least his job gave him an opportunity to stay in shape. Teaching physical education at Forest Park Community College would never make him rich, but tenure made it secure. It kept him outside much of the time, away from the confinement of a classroom, and he knew that it was safe. Not like the city schools, which had become a war zone in the past ten years. At least in Nam you were permitted to shoot back.

Briones had been drafted by the army late in 1967. It had been his own damned fault, of course. His freshman year in college he had screwed around and let his grades slip, kissing off his student deferment. Basic training had not been as bad as he expected—for a P.E. major anyway—but it had not prepared him for the grim realities of combat. The bottom line was his heritage had fucked him over; the Hispanic name had made him automatic infantry, and stature marked him as a perfect tunnel rat.

It had been filthy, terrifying work, despite the aura of adventure that barracks troopers tried to paint around the men who did their killing and their dying underground. V.C. were tunnel rats themselves, prepared to burrow anytime and anywhere. They buried weapons and supplies, constructed fortresses beneath the jungle floor that would have put a colony of ants to shame. They booby-trapped their tunnels with explosives, pungi stakes, and vipers cunningly suspended from the ceilings. There was only one damned way to root them out, and that was to pursue them underground, a KA-BAR in your teeth, a flashlight and an automatic pistol in your hands.

When it came down to killing in the tunnels, everything was right up close and personal. If Charlie met you in a narrow passage and you pulled his plug, you had a choice: back out the way that you came in, or push the corpse ahead of you until the tunnel widened out and you could roll it to the side. Incessant fear of cave-ins was a fact of life, along with fear of snakes and scorpions and spiders, fear of being killed or cut off underground. So many of his friends had gone down one dark hole too many, and Briones knew that he was lucky. He came away with transient claustrophobia, which he had learned to cope with over time, and partial hearing loss in one ear, the result of a grenade explosion. These disabilities brought him a check from Uncle Sam each month, as regular as clockwork.

It could have been a great deal worse, he realized, and combat had its compensations. Minh Nguyen, for instance. They had met in a Saigon saloon, with Briones coming off his second tour of the tunnels at Cu Chi. He had three kills behind him and a need to forget about the musty darkness for a while. Minh had been happy to oblige him for a price, and after they had come to know each other better it was on the house.

He seldom thought about their child these days. A spot on *60 Minutes* several months ago had served as a reminder of his living legacy in Vietnam, but any guilt he might have felt about returning home alone had burned out long ago. There had been college to complete, and student teaching, a career to build. Minh Nguyen would have held him back; she would have complicated things, prevented him from being all that he could be. A child, on top of that . . . well, it had been no contest.

When he thought about it afterward, Briones was convinced that his decision had been the best for all concerned. It was a kindness, sparing Minh from the embarrassment of living as an alien in the United States. Briones was no stranger to discrimination himself, and he would never put another soul through that if he could help it. She would thank him, if she only understood.

No matter. It was ancient history. Their little girl would be in high school now, assuming that they had high school in Vietnam, and it was too damned late to think about a change of plans at this stage in his life.

After the fourth lap Briones gave it up. A lousy mile, and he could hear the leggy coeds gaining on him, chatting back and forth without a trace of strain. It was humiliating, and he didn't need that kind of aggravation on a Monday afternoon.

He veered off course, saved something for the bleachers,

digging hard, and he was puffing by the time he reached the upper level of the stadium. Forget the image, he would walk back to the coaches' dressing room and take his own damned time about it. No practice was scheduled for today, and he should have the showers to himself.

Inside the locker room he stripped down, bagged his sweats and crew socks for the laundry, padded toward the showers with a towel across his shoulder. Steaming water helped his muscles, stiffening already from the final laps when he had pushed himself beyond his normal pace. No pain, no gain.

The students in his class were required, by law, to finish four semesters of P.E. Briones liked to think that he was popular enough, but in the absence of a state requirement, students would not have exactly beaten down his door to register for golf, gymnastics, and volleyball. If he was more like Carstairs, a pedantic, superannuated hippy, maybe Angela would still be working for him, showing him her moves.

He felt the first, small stirrings of desire and switched the shower onto cold immediately. Wandering around the showers with a boner was a no-no, even if he was alone. Of course, there was the time when Angela had shared the shower with him, for the hell of it, and they had—

No!

He made his mind a blank and concentrated on the icy water drumming on his chest, his groin. It worked, but he allowed himself another moment, working up a decent crop of goose bumps, banishing the hornies to a shadowed corner of his mind before he turned the shower off.

In the locker room Briones quickly dressed in slacks and sweater, filling pockets with his billfold, change, and keys. He had his socks on, was reaching for his Reeboks, when he heard the outer door scrape open, kiss the wall, and whisper closed.

"Who's that?"

Odds on, it would be Hoffman, still recovering from yet another drubbing of his tennis team. Most of his players couldn't serve for shit, although a couple of them had potential in the T & A department. Hoffman's racket-hounds had never won a match, but they were party animals who celebrated defeat in style.

"That you, Norm?"

Silence, and Briones felt the short hairs bristling on his neck.

It might be Janeway; he was always pulling some lame stunt, sneaking up on someone like the frigging Phantom. His idea of humor.

"Ed? You there? Don't screw around, now."

One shoe was on, but he was clumsy with the laces, barely managing an awkward bow. He bent to reach the other, and a shadow filled the narrow aisle between the rows of lockers. Startled, the instructor spun around then, immediately felt himself relax. Some kid.

"You're lost, I think. This is the *coaches'* dressing room."

"Luis Briones?"

"Yeah?"

"I have a message from your daughter."

Sudden shock, as if a fist had caught him in the solar plexus. No one stateside was supposed to know about Minh Nguyen or the child. They were his private secret.

"Sorry, you must be—"

He saw the knife and realized that there was no mistake, no wild coincidence. He saw his future in the young man's eyes and could not find a happy ending there.

"What is this?" Stalling, digging for the nerve to make his move. The kid was taller by a head and wiry, with his reach extended by the stainless blade. "What do you want?"

"Your life."

He bolted, past the lockers, toward the stairs. If he could make it to the office, he could lock the door and call security.

If he could make it.

If he couldn't . . . well, then, he would have to fight or die.

Like in the tunnels, right.

Like in the fucking tunnels.

Luan Nol had helped him find a job, as promised. By his second evening in St. Louis, Tony Kieu was working as a box boy at an all-night market, half a mile from Compton Avenue and Marquette Park. He would be staying with Nol's family until he earned enough to rent a room and feed himself, a circumstance that might take several weeks at Tony's current rate of pay. In any case, he did not plan to be around that long, and in his spare time he prepared to kill Luis Briones.

By the end of Tony's first week as a box boy, he knew

everything he had to know about his target. He could recognize Briones from the faded snapshot, and the St. Louis telephone directory had given him his prey's address on Kingsbury Place. He knew the car Briones drove—an eight-year-old Volkswagen Beetle with oxidized paint—and where he worked.

Tony knew so much, in fact, because he worked the supermarket's night shift with a doper by the name of Roger Foreman. Roger turned up wasted every night. Tenuous as Roger's contacts with reality might be, he recognized a friend, and he was glad to lend his car keys out one night when Tony had to run an errand on their dinner break.

"No sweat, man." He had grinned. "Take your time. You're late, I'll cover for you."

Tony had driven across town to Kingsbury Place. The house was a triplex, his target's name inscribed with felt pen on a numbered mailbox. The squat VW in its numbered parking place was branded with an FPCC staff parking sticker on the windshield. A simple phone call to the school next morning had provided him with details of Briones's daily schedule.

He had spent the weekend with Nol's family, helping out around the house. On Sunday afternoon he had accompanied Mai Lin to the zoo. Seeing the animals in pits and cages, sprawling listlessly or pacing back and forth behind the bars, made him nervous, but he pretended to enjoy himself.

Tony recognized that Mai Lin was developing a strong affection for him, and that made him nervous, too. He found her physically attractive, sometimes thought of her with lust, but he was vaguely frightened by her gentle family. Tony had no place in such a safe and placid world. His path had been determined in the womb, on the streets of Saigon.

They sat outside the aviary, sipping root beer, while she offered her condolences and tried to understand him. Tony did his best to be polite.

"You must be very lonely."

"No, not very."

"In a strange land, far from home."

He knew what she was searching for. "I feel that I have found a home with you, your family."

She blushed and glanced away. "I'm glad you came to stay with us."

"So am I," he said.

"Have you known many girls?"

"Not many." Tony pictured Wendy's face, her mouth half-open, choking on a silent scream.

"I'm afraid that I have led a very sheltered life."

"You're lucky."

"So my parents say, but I don't think so. I wish I had more . . . experience."

"You'll have it soon enough."

"Sometimes I think I never will." She made him feel much older than his years and very wise. "If I had someone who could teach me . . ."

"Teach you what?"

"Oh, things." She hesitated, hands clasped tightly in her lap. "Sometimes, I think of you. At night. When I'm in bed."

"Sometimes, I think of you."

"You *do*?"

"I am a guest within your father's house. He trusts me, and I will not steal from him."

Her shoulders sagged. "If you were not his guest?"

"Then I would not be stealing."

Mai Lin's eyes were shining as she faced him. "Have you saved much money yet?"

"A little," Tony teased her.

"You must be more frugal."

"I will try."

With a sparkling laugh she became a lovely child again. "Then you must see the monkeys next. They sometimes do outrageous things in public."

On Monday afternoon Tony left the household early with the explanation that he had to run some errands before work. His first stop was a phone booth, where he called in sick to the market.

He took a bus that stopped on Oakland near the junior college, and students directed him to the sports complex.

He waited in the shadow of the press box, watched Briones pace himself around the oval course. The man was not particularly fast for an instructor of athletics, and as Tony watched, he lost momentum, obviously tiring. In a quarter of an hour he was finished, plodding up the narrow concrete steps between the rows of bleachers, passing close by Tony as he headed for the showers.

Tony waited while his quarry bathed and dressed, unwilling to lay hands upon his naked body if it was avoidable. The man was one shoe short when Tony showed himself.

He could read the shock, the guilt, upon Briones's face at mention of the daughter he had left behind in Vietnam. The bastard *knew*, despite his lame charade of ignorance. Any second thoughts Tony might have entertained were banished in a heartbeat, replaced by grim resolve.

"What do you want?"

"Your life."

When Briones bolted, Tony was prepared. He dodged around the rumpled bag of dirty clothes, convinced that it would be no contest. Making for a narrow flight of stairs, Briones leapt to catch the banister and stumbled. Tony heard him panting and reached for his belt.

The kick surprised him—swift and powerful, a hammer stroke against his ribs. Briones was off-balance, out of practice, but it was a creditable effort. He staggered Tony, slammed him back against the wall and nearly spilled him down the stairs. He broke away and reached the office door, but Tony Kieu was after him again before the door hissed shut.

He threw himself against the door with force enough to wrench his shoulder, sprawled across the threshold as Briones staggered back against the nearest desk. Before Tony could regain his feet, the coach was charging, scooping up a metal trash can, slamming it across Tony's shoulders as he crouched on hands and knees.

The impact flattened Tony, but he struck back blindly, jabbing at the coach's feet and ankles with his carving knife. Briones danced away and hurled the trash can at him. It caught Tony on the head with force enough to knock him sprawling.

He heard Briones coming for him, scrambled to his knees and whipped the carving knife around to meet his enemy. Briones slithered to a halt, sidestepped, and plucked a basketball from a nearby filing cabinet. The short man put his weight behind it, aiming for his adversary's face. Tony flayed his knuckles with a punch that slammed the ball off-target, sent it skittering across two cluttered desks to smash the front of a display case filled with trophies.

Briones came at him again, kicked out, and knocked the knife out of his hand. It clattered on the floor and disappeared beneath a desk. He lunged to meet the coach and drove him back against the wall. Briones clubbed him with a fist that felt like stone. Tony's legs had turned to rubber; they would not support him as Briones stepped away and let him fall. The floor rushed up to meet his face, and Tony flickered on the edge of darkness. . . .

"Bastard."

He could hear Briones as the man turned away, retreating toward the nearest desk. He heard the telephone receiver lifted from its cradle.

Briones was calling the police.

Tony held his breath against the pain and dizziness, commanding arms and legs to function as he rose. All fours. Now, kneeling. One foot under him, then the other.

Timing was essential. He could never slug it out with his intended victim now in this condition. He required a genuine advantage, one which his opponent could not overcome.

No time to find the carving knife.

He moved on instinct before the thought took form, knowing that he had no time to waste. Briones was already speaking as his left hand slid around the coach's face to grip the telephone receiver, wrench it from his startled grasp, and wind the spiral cord around his throat. He clutched the cord in both hands with all his strength, his dead weight hauling on the noose and shutting off his adversary's wind.

Briones toppled backward, fingers clawing at the wire, bringing Tony down beneath him. Tony closed his eyes and clenched his teeth, ignoring heels that slammed against feet and shins. Briones was sprawled across his chest, and Tony wrenched his quarry to the left, rolled with him, staying in the saddle. Desperate, the coach was reaching for his face now, clawing at his lips and eyes, compelling him to twist his head away and out of reach.

It seemed incredible that anyone could hold his breath so long or function with the strangling wire around his throat. He could not see Briones's bulging eyes, the lips drawn back from gums gone purple as the tunnel rat made one last frantic effort to escape.

Unwilling to believe his senses, Tony held the wire garrote in place for several moments after his assailant ceased to struggle. When he smelled the acrid stench of urine, he knew then that it was truly over. He rolled clear and searched for his knife. He needed it. He still had work to do. . . .

The house was empty, but he had a key. Luan Nol had trusted him that much. Upstairs he cleaned his closet out and packed his laundry bag, removing nothing that had not been with him when he came. He would not rob this family after they had sheltered him.

Mai Lin was waiting for him at the bottom of the stairs, all smiles until she saw his face and his bundle.

"Tony, what happened to your face? Where are you going?"

"Time for me to go."

"Who hurt you?" She was halfway up the stairs, and Tony raised an open hand to warn her off. "I'll have my father talk to the police."

"No."

Her eyes grew wide with understanding. "What have you done?"

"My duty."

Tony passed her on the stairs and pressed his key into her hand. She stared at it.

"Don't go," she pleaded.

"You're a child. Enjoy it while you can."

The door swung shut behind him.

Tony's final stop before he caught the freeway was a curbside mailbox.

28

SOUTHERN INDIANA

Patterson was cleaning up a drift of sawdust, reaching for a dustpan, when the telephone began to ring. The basement workshop had its own extension, an annoyance he had grudgingly accepted after Jan pointed out that he would lose more work time running up and down the stairs.

Jan answered calls when he was working, disturbing him only if it was important, but she was away now delivering their son to preschool.

He considered playing deaf and dumb, then thought it might be Jan. The Volvo had been acting up the past few days; she might be stranded on the road.

"Hello?"

"Mr. Patterson? This is Agent Hackett. How are you, sir?"

"What can I do for you?"

"Well, I've just been on the horn to Chicago. Our field office there has recovered a '78 Volkswagen beetle. Missouri plates. Registered owner: Briones, Luis."

"In Chicago?"

"South Side. A municipal lot. It had been there two days, maybe three."

Call it 230 miles. Probably less.

"What's happening?"

"We're in sync with Chicago P.D. Latent prints from the bug match the scene in St. Louis, with tentative matchups in L.A. and Vegas. The down side is they're not in our files."

"What does that mean?"

"It tells me our boy has no outstanding warrants. He hasn't done time, hasn't been in the service. He hasn't been booked, that we know of, but NCIC has been running a little behind."

"What's the NCIC?"

Hackett cleared his throat. "The National Crime Information Center. Basically it's a computer clearing house containing records of arrests and bookings from around the country. Say your sheriff pops a transient on suspicion and he wants to check for pending warrants. The computer scans submitted prints and tells him if John Doe is wanted for a car theft down in Houston or a murder in L.A."

"Except?"

"Submission of material is voluntary. Some departments don't participate at all. With others, it's a one-way street: all take, no give."

"I see. And what about Chicago?"

"Well, I can't go into details of the operation, but I'm free to tell you that they've had no homicides as yet that fit the pattern. If he's hunting, chances are he won't know that we're on to him. Next time a squeal comes in, we'll be on top of it."

"Unless Chicago was a pit stop," Patterson retorted. "Two, three days, he could be here right now. He could be sitting on my doorstep."

"We think that's unlikely, sir. He could have driven straight on through and saved himself a hundred miles, instead of turning north and dropping off his wheels. It doesn't scan. I'd swear he's hunting in Chicago."

"Fine. And if you're wrong?"

"I'd have a talk with local law enforcement, see about protection."

"We've already had that talk. The sheriff's office can't spare any baby-sitters at the moment."

"Off the record, are you armed?"

"I will be, from now on."

"It couldn't hurt."

"You don't expect to catch him, do you?"

"I have every confidence . . . but in the meantime, watch yourself."

"I will. I appreciate the call."

"Least I could do. I'll keep you posted."

It was the second call from Hackett in the past four days. On Monday evening they were sitting down to dinner when he'd called to tell him of a murder in St. Louis. Luis Briones, gym coach at a junior college, had been strangled in his campus office. There were mutilations, signs of struggle, and a wartime snapshot of the victim had been torn in half, one portion of it thrust between his teeth.

The other half was missing until Wednesday afternoon, when Patterson retrieved his mail.

He finished sweeping up the sawdust, dumped it in the waste can, stowed the broom and dustpan in their proper places. From the shelves along one wall, he lifted down a heavy trunk, its half-inch layer of dust unmarked by fingerprints, and placed it on his workbench. It was double-locked, but he knew where to find the keys.

On top, two sets of camouflage fatigues were neatly folded along with his green beret. Beneath the jungle togs, his webbing: shoulder harness, pistol belt with ammo pouches, fighting KA-BAR in its scabbard, two canteens, a first-aid kit. A pair of jungle boots, size twelve.

The payload was concealed beneath a poncho at the bottom. Patterson removed a leather holster, the initials of his country branded on the flap, and drew the military-issue .45. It was a standard Colt, model 1911A1, like the sidearm he'd carried in Nam. It was not the same weapon. He had been in no shape to collect souvenirs when they posted him stateside, but after the VA released him, he'd gone on a shopping spree. Most of the items he purchased were legal, available over the counter from sporting goods dealers. The rest . . .

He extracted the Colt's empty magazine, laid it aside, checked for stray rounds that might have been left in the chamber. Methodically, Patterson fieldstripped the pistol, removing its slide and the recoil spring, pulling the barrel, examining each part for signs of corrosion. A chamois cloth treated with oil put a sheen on the pistol's components before reassembly. Each part snapped back into place with precision.

He rummaged around in the trunk, found a half box of .45 ACP cartridges, made a note to buy more. Seven rounds in the magazine, one in the chamber; the safety on, thinking of Jerod and Jan. He would hide it, along with the seventeen rounds still remaining, when he went upstairs.

The M-16 had been dismantled before it was packed, its components wrapped snugly in burlap and oilcloth. He opened each parcel in turn, wiped the contents with dry chamois cloth before laying them out on the bench. Reassembly took sixty-five seconds in all, but he thought he could better that time if he practiced.

With its twenty-round, staggered-box magazine empty, the rifle weighed six and a half pounds. The selective-fire option made it a machine gun in terms of the law, and possession alone was a federal offense. Four magazines used up his meager supply of .223-caliber ammo, with two more still empty, and rounds for the M-16 went on his mental shopping list.

Feeding a loaded clip into the magazine well, he raised the weapon to his shoulder, pivoting to bring imaginary targets under fire. Dead faces, conjured up by his imagination, were obliterated by the impact of imaginary bullets. In his mind, he felt the weapon's recoil, caught a whiff of cordite. In his soul, he heard the sound of automatic fire and screams.

Other sounds, above him, suggested someone's moving through the house. He froze.

"I'm home!"

He pulled the magazine, replaced it in the trunk, and quickly stripped the rifle down again. He did not need it yet. He still was not prepared to go to war.

He finished loading up the trunk with poncho, boots, and webbing, uniforms and green beret on top. He had not bothered checking the grenades, but they could wait.

He put the trunk back in its place, took one last look around the workshop, then started up the ladder. Patterson had customized bedroom closet, building in a trapdoor that would grant them access to the basement in emergencies. Tornadoes seldom struck in Forrest County, but it happened every thirty years or so, and it was best to be prepared.

He came up through the closet floor and closed the trap behind him, found the switch by feel and turned the light on overhead. He had already stashed the extra bullets in a shoe box and was looking for a place to hide the pistol when the door swung open. Startled, Jan leapt backward. The parcels spilled from her hands.

"Goddamn it, Anthony, you scared me half to death!"

"I'm sorry."

"Sorry? You could give someone a heart attack, the way you creep around and—"

She was staring at the pistol in his hand, her fright and anger suddenly forgotten.

"What's that for? You know I don't want that thing in the house."

"They think he's in Chicago, Jan."

She turned away from him without another word, retreating from the bedroom, leaving bags and packages where they had fallen on the floor. He heard her in the dining room a moment later, weeping.

For an instant Patterson was totally consumed by rage, a seething hatred for the stranger who was threatening to tear his life apart. He hoped they missed the bastard in Chicago. Hoped he made his way to Calvary somehow and forced a confrontation.

As swiftly as the moment came upon him, it was gone. Its passage left him cold and empty, suddenly aware of loneliness, of Jan's sobbing from the kitchen.

Burying the .45 behind a pair of boots he seldom wore, he killed the light and went to comfort her. If only he could find the proper words.

If only he could make himself believe them.

— 29

CHICAGO

Patience is a virtue of the saints, and Le Chuan Duc had never been a saintly man. He had acquired the trait through careful training, years of practice. Even now, in middle age, he retained a measure of youth's brash exuberance. A conscious effort was required for him to keep his head when things went badly, or when plans were unavoidably delayed.

The penthouse office and the home in Elmwood Park, the fleet of cars and membership in three prestigious country clubs, were symbols of his perserverance. Chicagoans were less concerned with race these days, and not at all concerned with how a man might earn his money, just so long as he possessed it in sufficient quantity. Too many business and political careers were rooted in the sins of Prohibition, shady deals with labor, management, the underworld, for any of the nouveau riche to waste time looking down their noses at a newer arrival.

Ironically, Le Duc had benefited from the fact that he was Asian, and specifically Vietnamese. A refugee from communist oppression in his homeland, he could count on a degree of sympathy from the conservative establishment, a helping hand from time to time. His efforts to improve the lot of fellow immigrants, endowing scholarships and so forth, were acclaimed as evidence of altruism. The deductability of his assorted gifts at tax time was beside the point. American philanthropists expected something for their trouble.

A peasant's son, Le Duc had traveled far from Quang Tri province, via Saigon, Bangkok, and Macao. His empire spanned the vast Pacific, anchored on the continents of North America and Asia, but his appetite was limitless, and there was ample room for growth. The drug trade was his staple, with connections in the fertile Golden Triangle, and while supply would never match demand, a cunning businessman could not afford to stake his hopes on one pursuit to the exclusion of all others. Prostitution had been lucrative, beginning with a stable of Vietnamese and branching out from there, until his stock included every color of the human rainbow. Films and videos had been a sideline of the prostitution racket, but their sales now earned him several million dollars every year. The Asian's love of gambling had launched him into the casino business, on a local scale, and now he bankrolled floating games from Kansas City to St. Paul. With gambling came debtors, and Le Duc was pleased to issue loans without collateral, provided that the borrower was willing to accept his interest terms of twenty-five percent per week.

Of course, there were legitimate concerns as well. Illicit dollars were reinvested in commodities and corporations, real estate, construction. Le Chuan Duc was the proprietor of several theaters, the high rise that contained his own plush offices, a cartage firm, and a recording company. If the recording equipment was occasionally used to crank out bootleg tapes and albums after hours, who was harmed? If the occasional gratuity bestowed on ICC inspectors saved his truckers from harassment on the highway, what was Le Duc's crime? If payoffs to the local unions won him sweetheart contracts on construction projects, he was only living up to the tradition that had built America.

A man of temper, he had little tolerance for threats, not even when they were delivered with finesse and style. The federal agent, Hackett, had been none too subtle, but Americans knew little of diplomacy, as evidenced by their recent humiliating failures in the world at large. Le Duc would help the federal man track down his prey because he could not fight the U.S. government and hope to win. Not yet. His organization was strong, but its roots were shallow. More time was required—perhaps a generation—before its structure was entrenched to the degree of the Mafia.

This favor to the FBI might even help, although Le Duc did not intend to grant it in the way Ben Hackett had desired. He would locate and neutralize the man in question to preserve his own interests, but he would not play informer for the government. He had no love of renegades, but neither did he serve the power structure. Possibly, when he was finished with the troublemaker, he could plant a trail and lead Ben Hackett to the corpse.

Already he had gathered information that the FBI did not possess. He knew the killer's name and his precise description. Word had been relayed across the Midwest after Hackett's visit, and the murder in St. Louis gave new focus to the search. A canvass of the usual contacts in Missouri turned up one Luan Nol, a runner for the syndicate who made his living in the transport business, hauling cash and "teal"—the fine gold leaf employed as currency by Asian mobsters nationwide—from one drop to another, interstate. Luan Nol had recently taken the murderer into his home as a guest.

By Tuesday evening Le Chuan Duc had known the killer's name was Tony Kieu. A homicide report, prepared by detectives in St. Louis, told him what the fugitive was driving and supplied him with the license number. Nol's description was relayed to hunters, who would bring the troublemaker down.

Now Tony Kieu was in Le Duc's backyard, the center of his web. The hot VW had been recovered from a South Side parking lot that morning. Word was on the street. The net was closing tight around their prey.

It was a matter of logistics now. There were hotels and rooming houses to be canvassed, hideouts to be searched, informers to be questioned. Le Chuan Duc had eyes and ears throughout Chicago, watching, listening for any trace of Tony Kieu.

The newsstand on North Clark Street carried magazines and paperbacks, along with the major daily papers. Tony Kieu picked

p a copy of the *Tribune*, paid in change, and made a show of
tudying the headline. His attention was focused on the posh
partment building opposite. He watched the burly doorman in
is regal uniform, who smiled as tenants came and went, ac-
epted tips for hailing taxis, glowered at solicitors and sent them
n their way.

There was a rear exit, but he had tried it several times and it
ad always been securely locked. The building had no fire
scapes. If he was going to invade this fortress, as he must, then
e would have to enter through the front—and that meant getting
ast the doorman.

His first night in Chicago, after ditching the car, renting a
oom in a small hotel, and changing clothes, he had found a
awn shop. There he purchased a ''survival knife'' with nine-
nch blade, hollow handle, and saw teeth on its spine. With
even dollars in his pocket, he had found himself a gay bar, paid
he cover charge, and settled down to nurse a beer. It took ten
ninutes for a live one to accept the bait.

He worked three bars that night, pocketing eleven hundred
ollars and a Rolex watch. On Tuesday afternoon he hiked back
o the pawn shop where he had acquired the knife. He spoke
vith the proprietor at length, convinced the old man finally that
e was not an undercover officer, and swapped the Rolex for a
Taurus .38 with eighteen rounds of ammunition.

On Tuesday night he worked the bars again and pocketed
another seven hundred dollars in an hour and a half. Next
morning he searched the classifieds for transportation, settling on
a tiny notice near the bottom of the page.

> MUST SELL. 1981 Chevette. Like
> new, w/ auto. trans, AM radio,
> htr. $800 or best offer.

The owner was a balding, chinless man with bifocals who
lived in Cicero. He haggled briefly over price, accompanied
Tony on a ride around the block, and finally let the Chevy go for
seven fifty. Tony thought he could have talked another hundred
dollars off the price if he had argued long enough, but it was
unimportant. He was mobile now, and he had cash enough to see
him through Chicago and on to Indiana.

On Thursday afternoon he left the car outside his hotel securely locked, and rode a bus to North Clark Street. His knife was hidden in the lining of his pea coat; the revolver weighted down one pocket, scarcely balanced by the extra ammunition he carried on the other side. He was prepared to strike immediately, but this was intended as a scouting expedition, laying down the groundwork for the kill.

His target, Ernesto Gigante, was a father of twins, one of whom still lived in Saigon. The other, along with the woman Gigante had promised to marry, was killed in a fire that demolished their plywood-and-tar-paper hovel. Gigante had not been aware of the tragedy. He had departed for the States on the day his two sons were born. And for that he would die.

The directory listing for Gigante, E., did not include an apartment number. Tony estimated that the high rise contained three hundred units, minimum, and he did not have the luxury of time to make a thorough search. There must be a directory somewhere inside. Past the tall, revolving doors. Beyond the doorman, with his uniform, his leather gloves and wary eyes.

He spent another quarter hour on the sidewalk, riffling aimlessly through the *Tribune,* observing the deliverymen who came and went from the apartment building in a steady stream. They carried groceries, furniture, appliances, and clothing from the cleaners. One man entered empty-handed and emerged with seven yapping dogs in tow. The doorman questioned each in turn, then passed them through.

In a sudden bolt of inspiration Tony knew precisely how to get inside. It was so simple when you thought about it.

He dropped his *Tribune* in a curbside trash can, walked two blocks, and caught a bus back to Forty-eighth Street and his lodgings. He would make his move tomorrow evening.

He walked around the Chevrolet, made certain it was still secure before he went inside. The ancient elevator wore an OUT OF ORDER sign, but he preferred the stairs anyway. In another moment Tony stood outside the numbered door of his room on the second floor, key in hand. Distracted by his thoughts, he missed the keyhole on his first attempt—and was surprised to see the door nudge open half an inch.

It had been locked when Tony left; he could remember double-checking it a scant two hours earlier. Someone had entered. Someone might still be inside.

His thoughts were racing as he pocketed his key and drew the Taurus .38. Like most revolvers, this one had no safety switch; for results, you merely aimed and squeezed the trigger.

Tony used one foot to nudge the door back. Six more inches. There was sudden, furtive movement in the gap between the hinges. In his panic, Tony thought he glimpsed polyester, oily hair, a single glaring eye.

Though he kicked the door with force enough to slam it back against the wall, something blocked it. Muffled curses came from behind the door. A shadow filled the doorway, and Tony put two bullets through the silhouette, then headed for the stairs.

He made the landing, heard the sounds of pursuit, knew that he would have to lose them now or risk being overtaken on the stairs. He swiveled, hit an awkward crouch, already squeezing off in rapid fire before he had a solid target.

Two men, both Asian, one with blood already speckled on his shirt, were gaining on him as he opened fire. The bleeder broke to Tony's left in search of cover, but he stumbled on a bullet, kissed the wall as gravity brought him down.

His partner's weapon had a silencer. It coughed at Tony, and the bullet whispered past his face, drilling plaster somewhere to the rear. The Taurus held three rounds, and Tony popped them off within a second's time, the hammer then snapping over empty chambers.

His target staggered, sat down on the threadbare carpet, squeezed off another silent round that gouged a furrow in the ceiling. Tony jammed the empty .38 into his pocket, hit the stairs, afraid there might be other gunmen in the building.

Moving through the lobby, he ignored the gaping desk clerk, scanning every corner of the dingy room in search of enemies. Outside, he half expected to be cut off from his car, but no one raised a hand against him. He slid behind the Chevy's wheel and fumbled with his keys before finding the ignition. On his second try the engine caught and he was rolling.

30

"Ernie?" Carla called.

"Yeah, a minute."

Scowling, he selected Seagram's, topped the shot glass off, and downed it in a single, fluid motion, waiting for the fire to settle in his stomach.

Ernesto Gigante was not used to failure, especially in bed. The last thing he had failed was high school, and that had not turned out so bad. He was making more money than all of the nerds in his class put together, and having more fun at it too.

Until lately.

He measured another shot, brimming the glass, drank it down. It was working now, slowly but surely, eroding the image of Carla all hungry and wanting while Ernie stayed limp as a noodle.

It happened to guys, hell, he knew that—but to *other* guys, never to Ernie Gigante. With him, sex had been an assembly-line process at which he would never mind putting in overtime. Anytime, anywhere, anything goes. Except here. In his own bed. Tonight.

He had things on his mind, that was it. Had to be. Competition was hurting his books, and the niggers were shaving his take on the numbers with some kind of crazy free-enterprise deal, like they thought they could go into business without an okay from the family.

If that wasn't bad enough, now they were fucking around with his love life as well as his income, and Ernie Gigante was damned if he'd tolerate that. He would have to exact retribution, as soon as he thought of a means that was simple and safe.

Ernie liked his life simple and safe. Let the muscle-heads do all your dirty work, take all the risks, while you sat back and counted your money in peace. If a problem arose, there were people to call who would handle it. From plumbing to leg-breaking, everything came with a price tag attached, but you got what you paid for.

Ernesto Gigante fought when he had to, got dirt on his hands when he had to, but he was a thinking man. Business took brains rather than muscle. A thinker could always find sluggers to weed out his enemies. There was no shame in the fact that a man liked his life to be safe and secure.

The war had been a hitch in his plans, but Gigante had come out all right in the end. On assignment to Nam, he had wangled a job as a general's driver in Saigon. The old man had no more intention of risking his ass in the field than he had of defecting to Poland, and Ernie became indispensable to him, supplying the women—and later the drugs— that he'd needed to get through the night. With some black-market deals on the side, he had come out ahead of the game.

Back in Chicago his family ties guaranteed he would never go hungry. As a cousin, twice removed, of the Liguori family, Ernesto served a brief apprenticeship as a shylock's leg-breaker, learning the usury trade inside out, leaving anything lethal for others to handle. In time he was granted a minuscule piece of the action in bookmaking, numbers, a couple of crap games. The money was flowing, and lately Gigante was looking at drugs as a possible channel for future investment. The problem, of course, would be street competition from blacks, Asians, and Hispanics. The bastards had their eyes on his gambling already, and he would be forced to subdue them before he could think of expansion.

One problem Gigante did not have was women. Whenever he wanted them, they were available, often for free. They had always been drawn to his boyish good looks—and now that he had money to burn . . . As a freshman in high school, Gigante had gladly surrendered his cherry to Paula McCloskey, a senior who gave him the night of his life. She had given him clap in the bargain, but what was a dose in the era of wonder drugs? Over in Nam, he had juggled as many as four at a time, fathered children with two of them that he was sure of. One went the abortion route; the other—well, he was here and she wasn't. Who the hell cared?

When he wanted a woman these days he just picked up the phone. There were dozens like Carla, dumb bitches who got off on giving themselves to a "gangster" and talking it up with their stupid-ass friends after. On occasion if one caught his eye, he would take her along in the Lincoln to visit his drops. She could service him while they were driving and *really* have something to talk about. If he was feeling beneficent, Ernie might give his chauffeur sloppy seconds. He had the best-satisfied driver in town.

"I'm waiting, Ernie."

It was working, Seagram's and a little relaxation, melting off the tension. Ernie felt himself responding, and he capped the bottle, set the glass aside.

"I'm coming, doll."

"Not yet, I hope."

The doorbell chimed.

Goddamn it! He was not expecting anyone this evening. If the doorman had allowed solicitors inside the building, it would be Gigante's pleasure to report him—after he had kicked his ass around the block a couple times.

"Hurry, Ernie, or I'll have to start without you."

"Jesus, just a second."

He would brush the asshole off in record time and think about the doorman later. Carla had his motor running now, and nothing was about to slow him down.

He looked through the peephole. The fish-eye lens revealed a kid, perhaps eighteen, bored-looking, with a basket full of flowers in his hands.

Gigante threw the double locks and faced the kid.

"What is it?"

*   *   *

Tony Kieu had chosen artificial flowers. They were cheaper, with a longer life expectancy in case he had to drive around with them for several days. He could not risk another rented room, nor could he count on Gigante's being home the first time that he called. If he was forced to make the run a second time, he did not care to waste his money on unnecessary stage props.

After driving aimlessly for several hours, waiting for his pulse to stabilize, his thoughts to clear, he wound up sleeping in his car outside a Rodeway Inn on Highway 94 in Lincolnwood. He awoke, stiff and cold, with hours to kill before he sought his quarry out. A squat-and-gobble breakfast from a fast-food restaurant left Tony's stomach grumbling, but he had more pressing problems on his mind.

The hunter had become the hunted in Chicago. Someone had traced him from Missouri to the cheap hotel on Forty-eighth where he had registered as "Vincent Tandy." That had puzzled him, until he realized they must be operating from an accurate description, canvassing hotels throughout the city, hunting him relentlessly. Finally, with a flash of insight, he knew the source.

Luan Nol.

The salesman was a law-abiding would-be citizen. Reports of the Briones murder, coupled with Mai Lin's report of Tony's brusque departure, must have driven Nol to notify police. He would have made the move reluctantly, perhaps delaying for a time, but in the end his conscience won out. There was no shame in Nol's behavior. Tony felt no anger at him for having alerted the authorities.

Except that his assailants at the hotel had not been police. By noon he was convinced of it. For one thing, the men he'd seen clearly were Asian—possibly Vietnamese—and while that might be normal in Saigon, Chicago was a different game.

But the silencer had finally convinced him. It was his experience—a feeling reinforced by American TV shows like *Mike Hammer* and *Miami Vice*—that the authorities were often arrogant and always noisy. Screeching tires and shouting orders, smashing doors and windows, shooting off their guns at any opportunity—they seemed to have no use for stealth. If the police had meant to gun him down at his hotel, they would have done the job with fanfare, probably with automatic weapons, bullhorns blaring in the background.

So, if the police were not pursuing him . . . then who was?

He searched his mind for other possibilities, came up with nothing plausible.

At last he gave it up, convinced that he would never crack the riddle. All he could do was take every possible precaution and go on about his business with resolve.

He found a florist on Diversey, bought the phony flowers in a wicker basket. Though not a funeral wreath, it would have to do. He chose a card—"For Old Times' Sake"—with no intention of inscribing it, and carefully addressed the tiny envelope to E. GIGANTE.

He topped the Chevy's gas tank and purchased lunch at Jackson Park. The sky above Lake Michigan was gray and stormy, but he scarcely noticed. He was busy scrutinizing motorists, pedestrians, assorted vagrants, fingering the weapon in his pocket, ready if his nameless adversaries made another move against him.

The twelve rounds left would have to be enough. There was no question of acquiring extra ammunition as the sun slid lower in the sky. Shortly after five o'clock he pulled the Chevrolet into a high-rise parking lot, not far from the apartment house on North Clark Street. He took a ticket from the automatic teller, left it on the dash, and found an empty space on Level Three. The elevator took him down and put him on the street.

A short walk south. The doorman saw him coming, moved to intercept.

"Hey, where do you think you're going?"

Tony feigned bewilderment. "Is this the Carlton Arms?"

"Yeah. So what?"

"I've got these flowers for a Mr. Gigante."

Thinly veiled suspicion flickered in the doorman's eyes. "You don't look like no FTD."

Tony took a chance and said, "I'm new."

"It figures. Yeah, we got Gigante. Go on up."

"Well, that's the problem. Someone at the shop forgot to put his number on the card."

"And you forgot to ask. Sweet Jesus." Muttering, the doorman pulled a photocopied roster from a pocket of his overcoat and ran his finger down the list of names. "Gigante's in 6E."

His voice was heavy with contempt. "That's up on six, you follow?"

"Thanks."

He felt the doorman watching as he pushed through the revolving door and crossed the lobby toward the elevators. Tony waited with a redhead wearing fur, self-conscious with the flowers in his hand, the pistol in his pocket. When the car arrived, he let her enter first. She pushed the button for eight; Tony hit six.

The woman eyed Tony like a hungry cat on the short ride to his floor. She winked at him as Tony edged around her, her brittle laughter severed by the closing of the elevator's door.

He moved along a pastel corridor with deep, soft carpeting. Gigante's door was halfway down on Tony's left. He noticed the peephole, held the plastic flowers up to conceal his face, and jabbed the doorbell.

On the inside, bolts were thrown. The door swung open, and Gigante stood before him in a knee-length bathrobe.

"What is it?"

In the flesh, he seemed less amiable than his photograph, more capable of violence.

"Flowers for Gigante."

"Who they from?"

"I don't know, sir."

"I'll take 'em." Digging into the pockets of his robe, he came up empty on the tip and made a sour face. "Hang on a sec."

Gigante left the door wide open as he moved toward the bar. Without a heartbeat's hesitation, Tony drew the pistol from his pocket, stepped inside, and pushed the door shut with his heel. Returning from the bar with currency in hand, Gigante froze, his eyes riveted by Tony's .38. The man's expression passed from puzzlement to rage.

"What is this shit? Some kinda joke?"

"No joke."

"Carletti send you here? Hey, man, we're friends, you know? Whatever's on his mind, I know that we can work it out."

Without responding, Tony put the flowers down and used both hands to steady the revolver. Something told him he could not afford to miss. Not this time.

"Was it Lopez? Jesus, you can tell me, kid. I know how

these things work, you understand? I'll double what he's payin'
you, an' I'll throw in a one-way to Miami."

"I don't know any Lopez," Tony told him.

"What the hell . . . is this some kinda fuckin' stickup? If it
is, I'll tell you right up front you don't know who you're fuckin'
with. You're bitin' off a world of hurt, my man."

"An Khom."

"Say what?"

"An Khom," Tony repeated. "Your son in Vietnam. The
one who lives. He sends his love."

Gigante paled beneath his sunlamp tan. "What kinda crazy
deal is this?"

In answer, Tony cocked the hammer on his .38. The weapon
could be fired without the hammer drawn, but in the single-
action mode, less pressure on the trigger was required, insuring
better accuracy.

"Hey, wait a second, man!" His prey was sweating now, the
trifling money in his hand forgotten in the panic of the moment.
"Name your price. Just *name* it."

Tony was trembling with contempt and anger when a naked
woman stepped across the threshold from the bedroom. She was
tall and lovely and a little drunk, tawny hair spilling over her
shoulders.

"Come on, Ernie, this is no fun anymore. I—"

She froze, staring first at the gun, then at Tony, and finally
back to Gigante. Her lips kept working, but no sound emerged.

"Carla, get the hell out of here!"

"Ernie—"

"Get out!"

Tony shifted his eyes toward the woman for a second. Time
enough for Gigante to pivot and break for the bar.

Tony fired. Saw a bottle explode as Gigante began to crawl
over the bar, belly-down in the whiskey and the glass.

Tony fired as his target reached under the bar for a weapon
concealed there.

He fired. Caught Gigante low in the side, dark blood staining
his bathrobe.

He fired. Gigante twisted to face him, one hand raised as if it
could fend off a bullet.

He fired. Through the open palm, into the face it concealed, as Gigante slid backward.

He fired once more and Gigante was gone.

Tony broke the revolver, ejecting spent cartridges, quickly reloading. His final six rounds. In the doorway the woman was working her way toward a scream that would bring down the house. Tony pointed the gun at her face, and she clapped both hands over her mouth.

Tony took out the snapshot and turned toward the woman. Recoiling, she moved backward and jumped as the wall stopped her short. Tony held out the photograph. She trembled and stared at him.

"Take it."

Reluctantly, Carla obeyed.

"This is for the police. Say it."

"For the police," she repeated.

"Get dressed."

On his way to the door, Tony thought that she probably would not remain with the corpse. She might not even call the police, but he no longer cared.

Tony's business in Chicago was finished. One target remained. If he managed to get out of town, if his unknown enemies did not pursue him, his mission would soon be completed.

Stepping out of 6E, gently closing the door, Tony Kieu felt invincible. Nothing could stop him. Fate was guiding him, leading him on.

Toward his father.

Toward home.

31

INDIANAPOLIS

Ben Hackett listened to the distant ringing of the telephone, half hoping Patterson would not be in. He was embarrassed by the foul-up in Chicago, but he owed the man a warning at the very least.

"Hello?"

"Ben Hackett, here."

"I recognize your voice."

The agent cleared his throat. "There was a problem in Chicago, I'm afraid."

"You missed him." It was not a question.

"We were counting on a bit more time, an opportunity to get a fix on his position."

"But?"

"There's been another homicide. It fits the profile all around. He left the snapshot with a witness. Didn't touch her by the way. We're calling it a positive."

"So, it's official."

Hackett winced. "Our boy was in and out so fast, the neighbors barely had a chance to punch up nine one one. Chicago PD never had a prayer, of course. We can't blame them."

"Who can we blame?"

Hackett forged ahead. "According to the evidence, our subject had at least one handgun, and he took it with him when he left. He isn't ditching weapons anymore."

"He isn't finished, yet."

"Well, that's why I'm calling. Based on contacts in the past, we think he may be headed your way."

"There's a news flash."

"We assume he's found himself another set of wheels. Chicago's auto theft rate being what it is, he might be driving anything."

"What *do* you have?"

"We've got a pretty fair description, gleaned from several witnesses."

Hackett did not need to scan the printout from Chicago. "He's a white male, roughly six feet tall, around one hundred and eighty pounds, dark hair, eighteen to twenty years of age."

"That's half the young men in the country."

Hackett had been sitting on his bomb, and now he let it go. "We also have a name."

No need to mention Le Chuan Duc, or his embarrassing attempt to bag the killer in Chicago. Duc had lost three men—one dead, two wounded—in the Forty-eighth Street fracas. In the end, Duc had been forced to swallow his humiliation and approach Chicago's SAC with hat in hand. Ben Hackett did not care about the mobster's source of information, just so long as it was accurate.

"I'm listening," Patterson said.

"Our boy's been traveling as Tony Kieu."

Patterson's silence was eloquent. Hackett could picture the guy, making all the connections and searching for options, arriving at one inescapable truth.

And once having arrived, there was nothing to say.

"You should be on your guard from now on." Then, without much conviction: "There's always a chance he may leave you alone."

"Is there?"

"Of course we'll be doing whatever we can from this end."

"Thanks for calling."

Hackett hung up.

Tony Kieu.

It was always a jolt to the ego when favorite theories went lame, but Hackett had been correct, in a manner of speaking. The murders were the result of a brooding vendetta with roots in the Vietnam war. His mistake had been searching for motives in profit and politics. This was a blood feud, the sins of the father returning to haunt him.

Hackett had no idea where the others fit in. They were strangers to Patterson, nothing on file to connect them with him or his enemies. Some had been shipped into Nam after Patterson left, badly wounded, for stateside. If Patterson's woman—Lin Kieu—was the final connection, then it was beyond Hackett's grasp. He would never be certain.

For now, all that mattered was stopping a killer before he could carve one more notch in his belt. And for that, human bait was required.

Hackett hated this end of the business, the gambling with innocent lives. Given options, he would have extracted the Pattersons, planted a "husband-wife" team in their place with sharpshooters supporting. Let Tony Kieu show himself, make the first move, and then blow him away.

But their suspect had photographs. He could identify Patterson, even allowing for age, and a decoy might spook him. If they drove their man underground, God only knew where he might crop up next. What he might have in mind.

He could still pull the woman and child or suggest that they find other lodgings, but it was Patterson's duty to care for his family. Hackett had a killer to capture, by fair means or foul.

Tony Kieu might be stalking them now; there had been ample time since the hit in Chicago, provided the bastard had wheels. He was batting a thousand so far, picking off each new target in turn without leaving a trace—until now.

The description was thin, true enough, but a small town like Calvary made the job easier. Patterson would be their Judas goat, leading his son to the slaughter. It was a lousy hand to play, but it was all he had, and Ben Hackett was grasping at straws.

"Our boy's been traveling as Tony Kieu."

Ben Hackett's words had carried all the impact of a dropkick to the family jewels.

Bewildered, Patterson allowed himself to play "What If?" Supposing he had not been ordered north, had not been wounded and evacuated—What might life be like today? Would Lin have shared her secret with him? Would he have possessed the strength, the courage, to accept responsibility and claim their child?

Had there been clues along the way to Lin's condition? Should he have interpreted some phrase, some gesture, differently? How could he not have known or at least suspected she was carrying his son?

It was a futile exercise in self-abuse, and he eventually gave it up. The facts were simple. Lin had chosen not to burden him, perhaps believing that there might be some mistake. He had been ordered into battle, wounded, and evacuated, all without an inkling that a part of himself was being left behind.

At last he understood the photograph of Lin, the tattered *Ho Kau* page without a father's name. He had been put on notice, but he had been too blind to recognize the signs. . . .

Jan found him seated at the dining table, staring at his hands.

"Was that the telephone just now?"

"Yes."

"What is it? Anthony?"

He saw confusion in her eyes and wondered if he had the strength to drive another spike of doubt and anguish through her heart.

"Sit down," he said. "We need to talk."

32

FORREST COUNTY, INDIANA

Tony Kieu awoke to birdsong at the break of day. The sleeping bag had kept him warm, but it could not prevent the stiffness in his back and legs that came from sleeping in a fetal curl. He was immediately conscious of an urgent pressure on his bladder, telling him to move.

He stood beside the car and urinated. The morning air was crisp and cold, but spring was clearly on its way. No frost had formed upon the Chevy's windows overnight, and Tony had been forced to use the heater only once.

In the thirty-seven hours since Gigante's murder, he had traveled some 230 miles. His exit from Chicago had been trouble-free, although he checked the rearview mirror constantly, even after crossing into Indiana. South on Highway 65 from Gary, and then east on 30, skirting Merillville and Valparaiso. East of Plymouth, Tony intersected Highway 31, an asphalt ribbon that divides the state in half, and started driving south. Each mile recorded on the Chevrolet's odometer increased his feeling of anticipation, kept him looking forward to the final confrontation with his father.

South of Perrysburg he passed a sporting goods emporium,

its windows darkened in the hour prior to midnight, and he doubled back. The door and plate glass windows facing the highway were protected by a folding metal grill, but few precautions had been taken in the rear. An ancient, rusty burglar alarm was mounted on the wall outside, and Tony ripped its wiring loose before he used his knife to snap the back door's simple lock.

Inside he found a flashlight. He emptied out the register first thing, then snapped a slender chain that held the long guns in their racks. With minimal experience to draw on, Tony did his shopping on the basis of appearances, selecting guns that seemed to meet his needs. He choose a twelve-gauge Remington 870 and placed it on the counter, moving on until he stood before the paramilitary pieces. Tony recognized the AR-15 semiautomatic rifles, reminiscent of the weapons carried by Americans in Vietnam, and shied away from them accordingly. Instead, he chose a Heckler and Koch assault rifle, also chambered in .223 caliber, and laid it out beside the shotgun.

A nerve-racking twenty-minute search supplied him with a hundred rounds of ammunition for each weapon, plus another box of fifty for the Taurus .38. To this he added extra rifle magazines and hunter's camouflage fatigues, a sleeping bag and poncho, backpack and canteens. The Chevy held it all once he had dropped the backseat flat, and Tony used a stolen tarp to hide his arsenal from prying eyes.

He drove another twenty miles that night to gain some distance from his crime, past towns with names such as Mexico, Peru, Miami, Denver. North of Kokomo he found a narrow side road overhung with trees and parked to spend the night. He opened out the sleeping bag and slept in back beside his weapons, one hand resting on the loaded .38 revolver.

In the morning Tony had breakfast at a roadside diner, driving aimlessly from there until he found a quiet, wooded area in which to practice with his guns. For targets, he selected several rusty cans picked up along the road.

His recent acquisitions came without instructions, but he persevered. The Remington was relatively simple, a standard pump with five-shot magazine below the barrel. Tony loaded up, experimented with the safety, raised the weapon to his shoulder—and was jarred off-balance by the unexpected recoil. While he did not drop the gun, he did not hit his target either. He worked through one whole box of shells before he felt comfortable with the shotgun, finally laying it aside to practice with the rifle.

Loading of the H & K required removal of the magazine for starters, and he wasted several moments wrestling with the piece before he found the catch. The magazine's internal spring was stiff and new, but Tony loaded twenty cartridges and replaced the clip securely. The safety switch was clearly marked and easily released, but chambering a round was something else. After several anxious moments, Tony found the loading lever, drew it back, and smiled in satisfaction as the first round chambered perfectly.

The rifle had less kick than he expected, and he used up only half a dozen rounds before he started hitting targets with a fair consistency. He was not ready for a trophy shoot, but with a man-size target, Tony was convinced that he could hold his own. When he had emptied the magazine, he took his time reloading, moving on to load the other two before he packed his guns away. The rifle now had eighty rounds, the shotgun seventy-five, the Taurus fifty-six.

His road map told him he was ninety miles from Forrest County. If he pushed it, he could be there in an hour and a half, but Tony took his time, exerting iron control, refusing to be hurried. There was no point in arriving prior to nightfall.

He made the relatively short two-hour trip last five, drove miles out of his way, and entered Forrest County from the east instead of the north. With darkness falling, Tony cruised the quiet streets of Calvary and spent a half hour seeking Galesburg Road. At last an old man lounging on a bench outside the courthouse pointed Tony west on Main Street with the sage advice that Main and Galesburg were the same road. The name changed when it crossed the city limits.

Once he got his bearings, Tony had no problem finding Patterson's house. His pulse was hammering against his temples as he passed the mailbox labeled PATTERSON. Doubling back, he passed the box and driveway once again, rewarded this time with a glimpse of rooftop, lighted windows in the night.

Two hundred yards beyond his father's house, he found a dark abandoned summer home and pulled into the driveway, parking in the shadow of a trailing willow tree. He spent a moment waiting for his pulse and respiration to approximate their normal rate, then tucked the pistol in his belt and struck off through the trees.

He had no trouble navigating in the darkness. Within a hundred yards he knew they had no watchdog worthy of the name. He moved around the house, a shadow in the night, aware of every forest sound. He smelled the evergreens and the sassafrases, heard rodents scuttle through the undergrowth. When he was confident no surprises awaited him, he moved in closer. Standing on his tiptoes, peering through a kitchen window, Tony saw his father for the first time.

A sudden chill crept over him. He felt light-headed and closed his eyes until his equilibrium returned.

It had been no illusion. Seated at the dining table was the man responsible for giving life to Tony Kieu. The years had changed him somewhat, adding lines around the eyes, the barest trace of gray around his temples, but there could be no mistake.

Across from Patterson, absorbing every word his father said, was the woman who had filled his mother's place. Fair-haired, attractive, vaguely sad.

Between them, facing toward the window, sat a boy of five or six with golden hair. Their eyes met briefly and he felt his stomach twist, then remembered that no one looking from a lighted room could see him in the outer shadows.

Angry tears were streaming down his cheeks as Tony drew the .38 and aimed it toward the window. He could kill them all from where he stood—his father last of all, permitting him just time enough to see his world destroyed. As Tony Kieu had seen his world, his life, destroyed. His finger tightened on the trigger, but his arm was trembling. He braced the weapon with his free hand, steadied it.

He stopped himself before the hammer fell.

It was too merciful. Too easy. Bullets from the darkness smashing through a window would not satisfy his need for retribution. Patterson must suffer first, and not for just a heartbeat. He must feel the pain of losing one he loved—the son he cherished.

Slowly he lowered the revolver, slipped it back inside his belt, the barrel cold against his flesh. Tomorrow would be soon enough.

In the morning Tony drove back to the empty summer cabin, parked the Chevy in back, and picked his way through trees. Concealed by thorny undergrowth, he sat and waited opposite his father's driveway. He would wait all day and night, if necessary, for the opportunity that would inevitably come his way.

Just prior to nine o'clock, a sporty station wagon labored up the gravel drive, his father's wife behind the wheel. She looked in both directions, saw no traffic either way, and turned the car toward town. Her son—his father's son—in the front seat beside her. Tony caught a fleeting glimpse of him.

It would be so easy now for him to cross the street and take his father by surprise. A knock upon the door, a bullet in the groin when Patterson responded, leaving him alive and capable of understanding who had found him, why his life was being rooted out, destroyed like some obnoxious weed.

Too soon.

Too easy.

Running, Tony reached his car within a minute's time, afraid that he might lose the woman. It was a short drive into town, and Tony stood on the Chevette's accelerator, drifting on the last, tight curve before the road ran straight and level into Calvary. He saw her station wagon in the distance, signal flashing for a left-hand turn before it disappeared.

He counted off the side streets, hesitating at each intersection, suddenly uncertain of the point where she had turned. He nearly panicked, then he picked her car out two blocks down on Jefferson. He made the turn and cruised by slowly, studying the preschool building and surrounding yard. He doubled back and parked across the street, a block beyond the school. When she emerged, alone, his pulse began to race again, and Tony knew that he had found the answer.

When she was gone, he made a circuit of the block, examining the school from every side.

He parked a short block from the preschool, on its blind side near a busy flower shop. On foot he made a window-shopping tour of the town, aware that he was being foolish, yet exhilarated by the risk. Before returning to his vigil, Tony stopped in at a small cafe adjacent to a suite of legal offices. The smiling, dark-eyed waitress served his burger-in-a-basket while the cook kept up a steady patter from behind the grill, and Tony found it all delicious.

He was waiting when the children came outside for recess, laughing, shouting back and forth. A single girl, no more than Tony's age, had been assigned to watch the troop of thirty-odd potential accidents and keep them out of trouble. He was pleased that she remained close by the building.

Examining his young half brother, Tony felt a sudden pang of sympathy. This child had not selected Patterson to be his father; he was not responsible for crimes committed years before his birth. He *was* the key to justice though.

As Tony watched, Jerod missed a ball and scrambled after it, in the direction of the fence. They were no more than twenty feet apart, and this time when their eyes met, Tony knew the boy saw him and evaluated him as only children can appraise adults.

He flicked a glance in the direction of the "teacher," found her momentarily distracted. Tony raised an open hand and smiled. The ball, forgotten for an instant, kissed the waist-high chain-link fence.

"Hello, I'm Tony."

Cautiously he approached the fence. "Hi. I'm Jerod."

"Sure, I know that."

Curiosity took over. "How? I don't know you."

"I know your father." In the background Tony saw the teacher separating two small wrestlers. "We're old friends."

"You don't look old."

"Your father sent me here to pick you up."

Suspicion flickered in the sky-blue eyes. "Why not my mom?"

"She's having trouble with her car. Your father's working on it, but he wants you home."

"I'm not supposed to leave before my mother comes."

"She can't come to get you if her car won't work."

Behind him, someone called out, "Jerod, throw the *ball*!"

Glancing across his shoulder toward a red-haired, pudgy child, Jerod scooped the ball up, pivoted, returned it with an easy toss.

"I'd have to ask the teacher," he said.

"We don't have time."

A sudden squalling came from the swings, and Tony saw the playground supervisor rushing to assist a girl who sprawled on hands and knees.

"I'm supposed to ask."

"No time."

Impulsively, Tony leaned across the fence and scooped the boy up, hands beneath his armpits, swinging him around and clutching Jerod tight against his chest. He used his body as a shield to hide his burden from the yard attendant if she chanced to notice him. The wounded toddler's angry squeals reverberated in his ears as he retreated toward the waiting car.

He was surprised that Jerod made no protest, offered no resistance when they reached the vehicle. The boy climbed in and took his seat without a word, appearing not to notice as the door was locked behind him. Only after Tony slid behind the wheel and they were under way did Jerod speak.

"Who are you, really?"

Tony felt the tight knot in his chest beginning to unravel as he answered, "I'm your brother."

33

They were sitting down to peanut butter sandwiches and macaroni salad when the telephone rang. Jan picked up the phone and passed it over when the caller asked for Anthony.

"Hello?"

"Anthony Patterson?"

The voice reminded him of the anonymous salesmen who always seemed to call in clusters, selling everything from carpeting to cemetery plots. But there was something different about this one.

A sudden chill shot through him, and his knuckles whitened on the telephone receiver. Fighting to control his voice, he said, "What do you want?"

Patiently the voice came back, "I have your son."

"Who are you?" Even as he asked, Patterson knew the answer.

The caller spoke slowly, reasonably: "He is six years old. His name is Jerod, and his hair is blond. His eyes are blue, and he has lost a tooth in front. This morning he is wearing blue jeans and a green sweater. Do I have your attention now?"

"You do."

"I wish to give you back your son, but you must give me something in return."

"I'm listening."

"I will return your son to you. *You* must come to get him. No one else."

"Agreed."

"Do not call the police. Your son might suffer injury."

"I understand."

He felt Jan watching him intently, trying hopelessly to follow the one-sided conversation.

"Do you know the covered bridge on Highway 47?"

"Yes."

"Two miles beyond, the road divides."

"I've been there."

"In one hour, take the northern fork until you reach the cemetery."

"Chamber Hill."

"You know it. Good. From there, on foot. There is a church, no longer used. I will be waiting for you there. Remember, no police."

"I'll be alone. Don't start without me, Tony."

Patterson was gratified to hear the sharp intake of breath, confirming what he knew already. Such a petty victory, but it was all he had.

He hung up on the angry dial tone, feeling sudden dread, as if he might have murdered Jerod with his stupid, smug reply. Beside him Jan was on her feet, the fingers of one hand like talons on his biceps.

"That was him? Where is he, Anthony? What does he want?"

"He's here, in Calvary. He's taken Jerod, and he wants to trade."

The color left Jan's face. "Trade what?" she asked, when she had found her voice again.

"For me. I'd say we got a bargain."

"No." She shook her head emphatically. "I don't believe this. Jerod's at school." She was already dialing as he turned away, but trembling fingers muffed it, and she had to start again. He heard her weeping softly as she waited for the secretary at the school to answer.

In the basement, Patterson took down the steamer trunk and set it on his workbench. Stripping off his shirt, he heard Jan's voice.

"What do you mean, you're looking for him? Is he there or not? *Goddamn it, find my son!*"

The old fatigues were snug, but they would do. He tried the jungle boots and was relieved to find them fairly comfortable. He had his webbing on, was making an adjustment to the pistol belt, when he became aware of her watching from the stairs.

Jan looked disheveled, winded, like a runner at the finish line. There was an unfamiliar desperation in her eyes.

"Your fault," she said. Her voice was flat and lifeless.

"Yes."

He saw no point in arguing. She had him dead to rights.

"*Your* bastard, trying to destroy *my* son."

"Our son." It came out as a whisper, barely audible.

"He may be dead because of you!"

"Not yet." He was assembling the M-16.

"Where did you get that, Anthony? What do you think you're doing?"

"Going after Jerod." As he spoke, he fed a magazine into the automatic rifle, started filling up the empty pouches on his belt.

"But the police—"

"Will get him killed, for damn sure. I've been told that at the first sign of a badge, he dies. It may be bluff, but I won't take the chance."

He took out some hand grenades, four of the standard-issue fragmentation model used in Vietnam. He clipped them to his harness, raised his eyes to find Jan staring at him.

"All this . . . how long?"

"Before we started dating."

Angry tears were brimming in her eyes. "I don't know you at all."

He stepped around her, shouldering his rifle as he climbed the wooden steps. Upstairs, he took the service pistol from its closet hiding place and slipped it inside the holster on his hip.

"I'm coming with you." Jan trailed him to the porch. "I want to see him."

"No. You'll see him when I bring him home."

"I'll follow you, if you won't take me. I know where you're going."

Hesitating, Patterson turned back to face her.

"Chamber Hill," she told him, sounding like a child unable to maintain a secret. "The old cemetery."

"Too dangerous," he told her, meaning it. "He's got Jerod already. I won't risk you, too."

"It's not your choice to make."

"Yes, it is. You'd be slowing me down, Jan. You'd be in my way."

"You can't stop me."

"Like hell."

Without a second thought he raised the Volvo's hood, reached underneath, and ripped a handful of the cables from its distributor.

"Goddamn you!"

He was moving toward the Blazer when he heard the front door slam. He thought about returning to the house and ripping out the phones, but let it go. If she was rational enough to hate him, she would recognize the risks involved in calling the police. He had to trust her.

He was running out of time.

One hour, with a quarter of it gone already, and a twenty-minute drive ahead of him. If he was late for any reason, Jerod might be forced to pay the price.

He deliberately cut off the dark train of thought, focused in on the game of survival. A soldier in doubt was a soldier defeated before the first shot had been fired. If you didn't believe in yourself, you had no one.

Never mind that the years might have padded reaction time, slowed down the reflexes. Search and destroy was like sex; once you mastered the basics, you never forgot them as long as you lived.

He had tried to forget over time—had believed he was winning—but all of that changed with a phone call. He might have been fresh from the jungle the way he felt now, primed to kill at the first opportunity. That was the hell of it, how fast the instinct came back.

He was more than just *ready* to kill. He was *eager*. It felt like old times.

34

Ben Hackett entered Calvary at twelve-fifteen and asked directions at a small gas station on the edge of town. Ten minutes later he was cruising Galesburg Road and watching for the rustic mailbox labeled PATTERSON.

This trip was strictly off the record. He was working on a hunch, without enough foundation to convince his SAC that any action might be necessary. Tony Kieu was not an official federal fugitive—except, perhaps, from Immigration—and there seemed no likelihood of warrants being handed down. It was a local show according to the book, and Hackett had been warned to keep his distance. Chafing at the order, Hackett had taken a few sick days.

He found the driveway, parked his Dodge. A frantic-looking woman met him at the door before he had a chance to knock.

"Mrs. Patterson? Ben Hackett, Federal Bureau of Investigation."

"Oh, thank God you've come. We still have time to catch him."

He had to stop her several times as bits and pieces of her story tumbled over one another. With each delay, each interruption, she became more agitated. By the time she finished, Jan was weeping openly.

"What time did you receive the call?"

"Between eleven-thirty and eleven forty-five."

"And your husband left . . . ?"

"Around noon."

"You haven't called the sheriff's office?"

"No." She shook her head emphatically. "I was afraid."

The federal agent checked his watch. It was approaching showtime.

"If you'll tell me where he went—"

"I'll *show* you."

"Ma'am—"

Her eyes were flashing, and he knew that he would never pry the information out of her in time.

"All right, get in the car."

He should have his head examined, Hackett thought. It would be bad enough attempting to explain why he had circumvented orders from his SAC. And now, with a civilian involved, he did not even want to think about the consequences of a fumble.

Despite the risks involved, Ben Hackett felt the first, small stirrings of the old excitement that preceded a manhunt. It was something he could never quite describe to anybody else; a rush beyond adrenaline, akin to sex.

No time to contemplate your options when your ass was on the line and any delay could see you killed. The ones who optioned out were those who lost their nerve. Ben Hackett had been hanging tough for over twenty years, and if they burned him over this . . . well, he would have to find another line of work.

The Bureau wasn't everything.

"Which way?"

Without a heartbeat's hesitation she said, "North."

The church was very old. It smelled of rot and creeping things that had come searching for a place to bear their young, a place to die. The windows were boarded over, but the planks had fallen down in places admitting erratic, slanting beams of dusty sunshine.

It was perfect.

Standing at the pulpit, Tony Kieu surveyed the empty pews and peeling walls. Above him bats had roosted in the rafters of the high cathedral ceiling, and their droppings painted abstract patterns on the floor. They and the boy were his silent congregation.

"You're not my brother," Jerod said, his small voice amplified by the emptiness of the place. "I don't have a brother."

"Half brother, then."

"What's that?"

"It means that we have different mothers."

The boy digested that while Tony scrutinized the ladder leading to the belfry. He had picked the church without a concrete plan in mind, but the discovery of ancient bell ropes, coiled beneath the pulpit like a sleeping snake, had given him an inspiration.

"Why different mothers?"

Tony shrugged. "You'll have to ask your father that."

"You want to hurt him, don't you?"

"No." *I want to kill him.*

"If you knew him better, maybe you'd be friends."

"There isn't any time."

He checked his watch and found that it was true. The outside preparations were complete, but there was still so much to do.

"Take off your clothes."

"Are you a child arrester?"

"What?"

"You know, like on the TV news. The child arresters take your clothes away and touch you where they shouldn't."

"No. We're going to play a game, that's all."

"What kind of game?"

"Like hide-and-seek."

"Who's 'it'?"

"Your father."

"Will you kill him when he comes?"

Tony said, "We'll see."

Patterson parked the Blazer in the shade and left his keys in the ignition. Behind him, Chamber Hill was overgrown with grass and weeds, its graves untended, monuments forgotten.

Residents of southern Forrest County had been buried there

until the First World War, when Chamber Hill had reached capacity. The nearby Ebenezer Baptist Church had carried on another twenty years beyond the armistice before it's congregation petered out. As a church, exempt from taxes, it had owed no debts and left no heirs. The state had once considered reclamation of the land, but it was too remote, and after years of often silly, sometimes rancorous debate, the plan was scrapped. Old Ebenezer stood abandoned in the forest north of Calvary, forgotten save by certain local boys who considered it their secret place. Patterson remembered that it had once been his secret place.

A narrow, gravel road had once connected Ebenezer Baptist with the outside world, but it had seen no traffic in a generation, and the forest had reclaimed it. No better than a footpath now, the former road was passable, but he avoided it, keeping to the trees. If Tony wanted him to use the road, it stood to reason that the boy must have a motive. Booby traps or snares, a simple ambush, Patterson did not intend to buy the package sight unseen. He would approach the killing ground obliquely, and if Tony Kieu was waiting for him on the road, he just might have an opportunity to take the killer by surprise.

It is extremely difficult to move with stealth upon a floor of fallen limbs and brittle leaves. He took his time, placed each step perfectly, remembering to test the ground before his full weight settled. It was a cool day, but he found himself perspiring freely, further mottling the camo paint that he had smeared across his cheeks and forehead, on his neck and hands. He kept the gravel road in sight, but he saw nothing of his enemy.

When he was halfway to the church, he found the mantrap. Dirty twine was stretched across his path between two trees at ankle height. Its termini on either side were hidden by the undergrowth, and Patterson was not concerned with learning where it led. The string might be attached to a grenade, a catapult device, a deadfall—but it did not matter, as long as it was not disturbed.

He knelt before the flimsy piece of twine and studied it up close. He scanned the trees to either side, made certain that no backup apparatus had been set to take his head off if he caught the first line of defense. When he was satisfied, he straightened up and stepped carefully across the trip line.

Discovery of one snare meant he had to check for others, every step of the way. He found no more, but it had slowed him down; his watch revealed that he was seven minutes late when he saw old Ebenezer through the trees.

The church seemed little different from the way it had looked when he was twelve. The walls might be a bit more weathered, there were more shingles missing, but he was surprised to find the structure still intact. Somehow, he had imagined that it must have fallen years ago. Today he discovered that it had been waiting for him.

For his sons.

The open ground would be a problem. Twenty yards of dirt and gravel lay before him, sprouting weeds and grass, but not enough to hide a man. If Tony Kieu was waiting for him in the church or in the trees on either side, he would present a perfect target when he broke from cover.

He took a breath and held it, counting down. The M-16 was set for automatic fire, and if he held the trigger down, its magazine would empty in two seconds flat. Forget about the movies where some dogface with a tommy gun could fire all day without reloading. Patterson would have two seconds, maximum, to mark his target, zero in, and hose him down.

He broke from cover, weaving as he ran. At any instant he expected numbing pain between his shoulder blades, the impact of a lethal round from nowhere that would pitch him forward. His muscles clenched in preparation for the blow, as if he might become impervious to bullets through sheer force of will.

Patterson was startled when he reached Old Ebenezer unopposed. His heart was hammering against his rib cage, and his lungs were seared with fire. An easy twenty yards, and he was panting like the point man in a marathon. Sweat stung his eyes, but he could not spare time to wipe them as he scanned the treeline.

Since Tony had not sniped him from the trees, he must be waiting in the church. A frag grenade would clear the way and work some changes on Old Ebenezer in the process, but he could not take the risk with Jerod's whereabouts unknown.

The only way to do it was decisively and swiftly. If he hesitated, thought it through, his nerve might fail him. If he did not do it *now*—

The double doors had once been boarded over, but the plank had recently been pried away and tossed aside. The doorknob had been broken off by vandals years before, and there was no resistance when he hit the left-hand panel with a bootheel, followed through, his M-16 prepared to answer any challenge. He hit the floor behind the nearest pew, expecting hostile fire, astounded that the doors had not been booby-trapped.

Apparently, it was intended that he make his way inside. Whatever Tony's plan might be, the church was crucial to his overall design.

He risked a glance around the corner of the pew . . . and froze.

Above the pulpit, twisting slowly on a twelve-foot length of bell rope, Jerod's body was suspended by the heels.

"Stay here."

"I said I would."

He did not trust the woman yet, but had no choice once he had parked his Dodge behind her husband's Blazer in the shadow of the rural cemetery. She had pointed out the narrow, weedy track that led to an abandoned church. If there was any action to be found, it would be going down *out there*, and Hackett had not driven all this way to miss the main event.

He broke the snubby Smith and Wesson .38 and checked its load. Six rounds would not go far if Patterson and Tony Kieu were playing war games in the woods, but it was all he had.

Hackett had not traveled fifty feet before he knew his suit and shoes were ruined, caked with mud and snagged or torn in countless places.

Following the narrow road would probably have saved him time, but it could also get him killed. He was a sitting target on the road, and while he cherished no illusion of his ability to penetrate the woods with stealth, at least the trees would offer cover if he did come under fire.

A swarm of midges danced in front of Hackett and he waved them off, his eyes narrowed as they hummed around his face. Concentrating on his footing, he tried to keep quiet. The hand that held his .38 was slippery with sweat, and Hackett paused at frequent intervals to wipe his palm against his polyester slacks.

Ahead of him came a sudden crashing in the underbrush. He

roze, his weapon braced with both hands in the classic Bureau
tance. The sounds then faded rapidly, and Hackett relaxed. A
ingle, fleeting glimpse had shown him his adversary was a
vhite-tailed deer.

He moved onward, scarcely felt the trip line as he snagged it,
ore it free. It might have been another root or vine, except that
uddenly the bushes were erupting on his left, an object rushing
oward him, whistling through the air.

Ben Hackett spun around to face his enemy, his pistol rising,
and the sapling lashed across his chest. A spear of sharpened
hickory ripped through his diaphragm and pierced his liver,
odging tight between two lumbar vertebrae. The impact drove
him to his knees.

Reflexively, he squeezed the trigger on his Smith and Wesson,
then again, the wasted bullets gouging bark from nearby trees.
His shirt and slacks were slick with blood, and he could feel it
seeping down into his shorts. He raised one hand to grasp the
wooden lance and try to pull it free, but roaring waves of pain
swept over him, obliterating thought and robbing him of the
strength to scream.

You blew it, Hackett thought disgustedly as his life seeped
away. *You screwed up royally*.

Jan heard the shots and bolted from the car without a second
thought. She hesitated at the entrance to the gravel driveway,
suddenly remembering her promise to the federal agent.

No matter. In her heart she knew a mother's place was with
her child, and she could not sit here idly while her son was being
held hostage in a war zone. Anthony and Hackett might know
best about the killing side of things, but Jan's maternal instincts
made her think in terms of living.

She could not imagine life without her child. If Jerod suffered harm Jan knew that it would break her spirit, ruin everything that she had worked and hoped for from the first time she
had welcomed Anthony into her bed.

And if their son was spared? What then? Could she forget
that Anthony himself had brought this waking nightmare down
upon their heads? Could she forgive him for her pain and anguish? Could she ever quite forgive *herself* for hating him?

Jan knew that she would quickly lose her way if she got off

the road. The shots had come from somewhere to her right
beyond the point where she had watched Ben Hackett disappear
She would have to stake her hopes on simply getting to th
church as quickly as she could. Though she had never seen th
church, Anthony had spoken of the childhood games he used t
play there and had pointed out its general location on a Sunda
drive years before.

After the two quick shots, there had been no more firing i
the woods. She hoped that Anthony or Hackett had surprise
the killer and cut him down on sight. It startled Jan to fin
herself wishing death upon a stranger so vehemently, but Ton
Kieu was trying to destroy her world.

Beyond the nearest trees, Jan caught a glimpse of weathere
shingles, something that might once have been a cross. Th
steeple! She was almost there.

With grim determination, Jan began to run.

It took a moment for his heart to find its rhythm once h
recognized the grisly joke, and Patterson allowed himself t
breathe again. The tiny "corpse," suspended by its ankles from
the bell rope, was a dummy, cunningly constructed with Jerod's
clothes, stuffed with autumn leaves. There were in fact no feet
no hands, no head, but in the semidarkness of the church his firs
impression—as intended—had caused shock.

With recognition came a surge of hope. If Jerod was no
hanging here, he might still be alive. His flesh was crawling, and
he made a rapid circuit of the empty church, examining the
shadowed corners, peering beneath the dusty pulpit, scouring the
long-dead pastor's tiny office in the rear. The building was
deserted, save for bats and flying squirrels that scuttled out of
sight when he approached.

"Patterson!"

He froze. The call had come from the yard. At once he knew
that Tony Kieu had suckered him, permitted him to penetrate the
church and find the effigy of Jerod dangling above the altar. It
was psy-war, down and dirty. Just like Nam.

He moved along the center aisle, past empty pews, his
footsteps echoing among the rafters overhead. The double doors
were open as he had left them, offering a view of open ground,
the trees beyond, not a living soul in sight.

"We're waiting, Patterson!"

Not "I," but "we."

He shifted to the left, expanding his horizon, and beheld two figures, standing one behind the other on the scraggly lawn outside. Jerod was dressed in underwear and socks, hands bound behind his back, a cloth gag in his mouth, a noose or leash of rope around his neck.

The boy who held that leash was six feet tall, athletic-looking, with a fair complexion that belied his Asian heritage. He had his mother's straight, dark hair, but there was little of her in his features.

"Won't you join us, Father?" Tony Kieu taunted.

Sunlight lanced Patterson's eyes as he emerged from the darkened sanctuary, but he kept them focused on his enemy, unblinking. Tony had a rifle, possibly an automatic. He was carrying it casually, muzzle pointed toward the ground, aware that Patterson was not about to fire while Jerod stood between them.

"Let's cut the song and dance," Patterson said. "You wanted me. I'm here. Release the boy."

"When I am ready, I will release him."

"What is it that you want to hear?"

"Your dying breath."

"I never knew that your mother was—"

"You didn't *want* to know."

"For Christ's sake, I was nearly D.O.A. I didn't know my name for nearly three weeks after Tet. When I came out from under, I was in a body cast in Tokyo."

"Your health is better now."

"If she had told me, given any sign at all—"

"You would have married her? Invited her to join your fine white family in America?"

"I would've tried, damn right."

"Forgive me if I doubt you, Father. I'm afraid it has become a habit through the years."

He tried another tack. "The boy has no part in this. Why don't you let him go?"

"I have enjoyed his company. It pleases me to have a brother."

"Kill me, if you have to, but for God's sake, leave the boy alone."

"For God's sake, Father? What has God to do with me? With any of us?"

Two pistol shots reverberated in the forest. Immediately Tony snapped his rifle up, the muzzle boring into Jerod's spine until the boy arched his back and whimpered through his gag.

"I warned you! I told you no police."

"I came alone, for Christ's sake! I don't know who's out there, any more than you do. Jesus, it could be hunters, some clown trying out the piece he got for Christmas."

"I should kill the boy right now."

"And then what?" As he spoke, Patterson swung the M-1 around to cover Tony Kieu. "He's all you've got, kid. When he goes, you go."

Defiantly, the young man stood erect, threw back his shoulders . . . but he kept the muzzle of his weapon pressing into Jerod's back.

"There are worse things, Father, than to die."

Patterson calculated odds and angles, wondering if he could switch to semiautomatic fire and raise his weapon, make the shot in time. If he could make the shot at all.

It would be Tony's head or nothing, instant death to freeze his finger on the trigger, stop him cold.

He was about to swallow caution and make the move when sudden movement in the corner of his eye distracted him. He pivoted, prepared to shout a warning—fire upon the new arrival if it came to that, for Jerod's sake—when he was frozen by the sight of Jan emerging from a narrow opening between the trees.

"Go back!" he bellowed, knowing as he spoke that it was too damned late to save the game.

Jan recognized the standoff in a heartbeat, but her eyes were fixed on Jerod and she shrieked his name. The tiny hostage took one look at her and bolted, covering perhaps ten feet before his tether stopped him short and dumped him on his backside. Tony Kieu crouched as he tried to cover all at once, inevitably swinging back toward Patterson.

Their guns exploded together in a thunderclap.

The H & K was braced against his hip as Tony squeezed off in rapid-fire, no time to aim with any precision. Curiously, at the crucial instant, Tony felt removed from the cacophony of sound,

he smell and recoil of his weapon. In his mind's eye he could
ee himself, the bright brass cartridges that spun away from him
nd glittered in the sunlight.

Sixty feet away his father was returning fire, the M-16 on
automatic, spewing bullets with a sound like canvas ripping.
Tony shifted, ducking, weaving, firing all the while. He felt
invincible.

The sudden, numbing pain of impact staggered him and very
nearly brought him down. He felt hot blood between his shirt
and skin, but he kept on firing, doggedly resisting gravity.
Downrange, his target spun and toppled, dropped his weapon in
the weeds.

Exultant, Tony snapped the rifle to his shoulder, grimacing
with pain. He sighted down the barrel of the H & K, his finger
almost loving on the trigger as he squeezed—and heard the
hammer fall against an empty chamber.

Cursing, he wrestled with the empty magazine. It jammed,
and now he saw his father struggling to rise, recovering his
M-16, the bloodstain murky crimson on his camo tunic. Tony
dropped the useless rifle, sobbing furiously as he turned and
staggered toward the trees.

If Patterson would only follow him, he had a chance. If he
could lead his father to the place where he had stashed the
shotgun and his extra ammunition.

If he made it that far without collapsing in his tracks . . .

He reached the treeline, blundered through the thorny underbrush to hide in the woods. His plan had gone disastrously awry,
but there was still a chance for him to salvage something.

Patterson jettisoned the empty magazine and slammed a fresh
one into the receiver, jammed his thumb against the bolt stop
lever, chambering another cartridge. Underneath his arm the
blood was seeping out where Tony's round had burned across his
ribs. Another inch or two and he would have been finished,
drowning in the fluid from a punctured lung.

Before he found his balance, Jan had Jerod's hands untied,
his gag removed, and she was crushing him against her chest.
Her face was dusty, but the tears etched clean tracks down her
cheeks. Her eyes came into focus as he struggled to his feet and
struck off toward the treeline, following a trail of blood.

"Where are you going?"

"To finish it."

"It's finished, Anthony. Let the sheriff find him."

"No."

She was arrested by a sudden thought. "Where's Hackett?"

Hackett? "I don't know. Jan, get the hell away from here."

He heard her calling after him, but Patterson could not afford to waver now. He had a job to do, for her sake and for Jerod's.

He had wounded Tony Kieu. The tumbling projectiles of the M-16 were specially designed for maximum effect in flesh targets, chewing up internal organs, ricocheting off bones. A decent hit should theoretically have dropped his target on the spot, but Tony had been dodging, weaving. He was lucky to have hit the boy at all.

The thought produced a sudden stab of guilt, competing with the severe pain in his side. It was a bitter fortune that allowed him to draw comfort from the thought that he had very nearly killed his son.

Inside the trees the trail of blood was difficult to follow, but he navigated with the aid of broken ferns and flattened shrubbery. Tony Kieu had been traveling full speed, with no apparent interest in concealment. That would make it easier, unless . . .

He suddenly ran out of trail, emerging from the trees into a clearing, fixed by sunlight like an actor's place at center stage. He hesitated, felt the movement to his left before he saw it, recognizing death before it showed a face.

He was diving back for cover when the shotgun roared. Pellets laced his flank with fire, the impact punching him completely through an awkward somersault. He landed on his back among the ferns, a second blast ripping through the vines and creepers inches from his face.

The M-16 was gone. He could not hope to find it now without emerging from his meager sanctuary. As the sniper fired again, demolishing the cover to his right, he got his bearings, tried to judge the intervening distance. His life depended on perception, the ability to function under fire.

He worked a pair of frag grenades loose from his belt, one in each hand, bringing them up to his chest. The lethal eggs weighed only sixteen ounces each, but they felt like anvils, threatening to crush the air out of his lungs and stop his heart.

He pulled the pins, first one, and then the other, holding down the safety spoons with fingers that felt numb and lifeless. When the sound of rustling vegetation reached his ears, he pitched them backward, overhead, and rolled away to burrow facedown in the drift of leaves.

Another shotgun blast ripped through the bushes, dragon's breath against his spine. Then the clearing rocked with sudden thunder, fireballs sprouting on the floor of the forest and shrapnel buzzing like a swarm of angry hornets through the air.

He came erect, the .45 in hand, his wounded leg like taffy as he braced himself against a tree trunk. He could hear a sobbing, thrashing, in the foliage twenty paces ahead.

Tony Kieu came for him through the drifting smoke, his hunter's camouflage in bloody tatters, wild-eyed in pain and fury. He had lost the shotgun somewhere, but he held a wicked-looking knife, his fingers partly stripped of skin, the knuckles showing white, like ivory.

"Father!"

Headlong through the undergrowth across the clearing he came, gathering momentum. Patterson unloaded with the .45 and kept on squeezing until the slide locked open on an empty chamber.

Before him, the lifeless body of his firstborn son was seeping blood into the thirsty earth.

Behind him, on the far side of the forest, lay the remnants of his life, if only he could salvage something.

He dropped the empty pistol where he stood and turned away. With halting, painful steps, he started back along a deer trail through the trees.

ABOUT THE AUTHOR

Michael Newton was born in Bakersfield, California, and has worked at various trades and professions including schoolteacher, security guard (for country-music artist Merle Haggard), and professional writer. Since 1977 he has produced 69 books, most of them novels in the action-adventure genre. He has been a fulltime author for the past two years.

At present, Newton lives with his wife in a log cabin in Nashville, Indiana. He is at work on a new novel for Bantam Books.

WIN
A CAR A MONTH
With Bantam's Grand Slam Sweepstakes

GRAND PRIZE
TWO BRAND NEW "HIS & HERS" CHEVROLETS

A Sporty New Camaro
And
An Elegant Caprice
And
$10,000 IN CASH!
PLUS ...

EVERY MONTH
Throughout 1988
A NEW CHANCE TO WIN A BRAND NEW CHEVROLET!

CAMARO

THE *Heartbeat* OF AMERICA
TODAY'S CHEVROLET

CAPRICE

Special Offer
Buy a Bantam Book
for only 50¢.

Now you can have Bantam's catalog filled with hundreds of titles plus take advantage of our unique and exciting bonus book offer. A special offer which gives you the opportunity to purchase a Bantam book for only 50¢. Here's how!

By ordering any five books at the regular price per order, you can also choose any other single book listed (up to a $5.95 value) for just 50¢. Some restrictions do apply, but for further details why not send for Bantam's catalog of titles today!

Just send us your name and address and we will send you a catalog!

RELAX!
SIT DOWN
and Catch Up On Your Reading!

☐	24172	**NATHANIEL** by John Saul	$3.95
☐	23336	**GOD PROJECT** by John Saul	$3.95
☐	27148	**LINES AND SHADOWS** by Joseph Wambaugh	$4.95
☐	27386	**THE DELTA STAR** by Joseph Wambaugh	$4.95
☐	27259	**GLITTER DOME** by Joseph Wambaugh	$4.95
☐	24646	**THE LITTLE DRUMMER GIRL** by John Le Carré	$4.50
☐	26705	**SUSPECTS** by William J. Cavnitz	$4.50
☐	26733	**VENDETTA** by Steve Shagan	$4.50
☐	26657	**THE UNWANTED** by John Saul	$4.50
☐	26658	**A GRAND PASSION** by Mary Mackey	$4.50
☐	26572	**110 SHANGHAI ROAD** by Monica Highland	$4.50
☐	26499	**LAST OF THE BREED** by Louis L'Amour	$4.50
☐	27430	**SECRETS OF HARRY BRIGHT** by Joseph Wambaugh	$4.95